THE LAST ROSE OF SUMMER

THE LAST ROSE OF SUMMER

A NOVEL
BY MONTE SCHULZ

FANTAGRAPHICS BOOKS | SEATTLE, WA

Fantagraphics Books, 7563 Lake City Way NE, Seattle, Washington 98115 | Editor: Gary Groth. Graphic Designer: Adam Grano. Associate Publisher: Eric Reynolds. Publishers: Gary Groth and Kim Thompson. Interior graphics by Jenny Catchings, Eric Reynolds, Nicole Starczak, and Geets Vincent. Additional editorial assistance by Kristy Valenti. | *The Last Rose of Summer* is copyright © 2010 Monte Schulz. This edition copyright © 2010 Fantagraphics Books. All rights reserved. Permission to reproduce material must be obtained from the author or the publisher. | To receive a free full-color catalog of comics, graphic novels, prose novels, and other related material, call 1-800-657-1100, or visit www.fantagraphics.com | Distributed in the U.S. by W.W. Norton and Company, Inc. (1-212-354-5000), Distributed in Canada by the Canadian Manda Group (1-416-516-0911), Distributed in the United Kingdom by Turnaround Distribution (108-829-3009) | First Fantagraphics Books Edition: November 2010 | ISBN: 978-1-60699-401-6 | Printed in China

For the Halverson sisters: Ruth, Judy and Joyce,
And Dorothy, all those lovely summers ago

Do not let the will play gardener to your soul

Unless you are sure

It is wiser than your soul's nature

— Edgar Lee Masters

EAST TEXAS

1929

MAY

THE HOUSE IN BELLEMONT had a broad sunporch whose middle staircase faced due west, keeping those sitting out in the wicker chairs warm late into the day. Five wooden steps led up from the wide dirt street, inviting people to stop and share a glass of lemonade or iced tea. Conversation was entertainment in Bellemont. Maude Hennesey had a small circle of ladies who passed three afternoons a week on her porch, playing hearts and whist and discussing those who were absent. Though the wind blew dust up and down College Street, Maude kept the windows open day and night, circulating the air indoors behind storm screens and allowing sidewalk conversations to be overheard from most any room.

Marie Hennesey and her two children were given Harry's old bedroom on the west end of the house, where a pretty chinaberry tree beside the window frame provided a cooling shade and barely disturbed their view of the backyard and the grassy fields behind the Jessup's house next door. Expressed in the room assignment was an understanding of impermanence. Harry was gone on a business venture to the city where he'd taken a hotel room for this season and the next. When he had earned enough to return, he would find his family another home of their own. Somewhere far from East Texas. Until then, Marie and the children were guests of her mother-in-law.

"I expect you'll need all the drawers," said Maude, studying the old walnut chiffonier she had been using for those clothes she hadn't worn in several seasons. "I just don't know where my things'll go. This house is so small."

She looked at her daughter-in-law, as if hoping somehow Marie might volunteer to manage the children's clothes and her own wardrobe from the old steamer trunk. Laying Cissie's worn-out copy of *The Emerald City of Oz* on the bed, Marie avoided Maude's gaze and walked to the window. What could she say? It wasn't her fault the house wasn't bigger, and they weren't taking Maude's bedroom, anyhow. This one was barely larger than Marie's old sewing room on Cedar Street. If she and the children could make do in such a tiny space, Marie felt Maude ought not to complain. Besides, this had all been Harry's idea. If Maude was unhappy, perhaps she should write her son a letter and tell him so. As it was, Marie and Harry had fought about this more than a month, for all the good it had done. He'd brought this to her out of the blue one evening after supper in early spring. The children were upstairs in bed and Harry had gone out onto the porch to smoke a cigar. When Marie joined him after washing the dishes, she asked, *"Did you speak with Eustace yet?"*

"Concerning what?"

"The yard."

"What about the yard?"

"Hiring Eugene to take care of it for us. Eustace assured me Eugene would do it for five dollars a week. I thought that was more than reasonable for the amount of work we need done."

"We still can't afford it. Anyhow, fixing the yard up isn't important anymore."

"I don't follow you. Crabgrass is eating our garden to pieces, the fence needs mending, the lawn has to be re-seeded. You promised we'd have it done for summer."

"We'll be selling the house, dear. We can't afford to live here any longer. There's not enough work out there to keep us in this house. If I sell it, we can take the money, maybe eat for another year or so, keep the children in clean clothes and away from public charity. We've got to move, though. I'm sorry."

"Move where?"

"Down to East Texas. At least between whiles. Just you and the children, actually. I telephoned Mother yesterday from the hotel. You'll stay with her in Bellemont until I can improve my situation with Transfer & Storage, maybe save up some money this summer, then find us a nice place of our own again."

"I'm not so sure I want to move," Marie told him, shocked almost to tears by

his news. "This is our home. We've always lived here. The children grew up in this house. How can we possibly sell it?"

"We need the money," said Harry. "That's all there is to it. We can't go on, otherwise. We either sell the house or let the bank come and take it from us. Jack Ramsey's got a buyer coming out from Urbana on Monday to have a look."

"Why didn't you tell me this sooner?"

"Frankly, I didn't know until this last trip. I thought that maybe if I re-organized myself, finagled a few more clients and made some rapid advances, that I'd finish high enough to keep us pointed up." He shook his head. "I'd really hoped to do something in a big way, darling, but honestly, it was no good. I almost had to take a billposting job just to buy groceries last week."

"Who else knows?" Marie asked, quietly. The humiliation of having to leave Illinois seemed almost unbearable. How could she possibly explain this to her relatives?

"Nobody, except Mother."

"The children won't understand, you know. They'll ask why we're leaving Grandpa and Grandma and Aunt Emeline and all the rest of the family, and I'll be forced to tell them a lie."

Harry's voice became strident, intransigent, which told Marie that he, too, felt humiliated. "Then don't. Tell them the truth. We're not royalty. I'm sure they've figured that much out for themselves by now."

"Harry?"

"Yes?"

"Do you still love us?"

Outdoors now behind Maude's house, ten-year-old Cissie had discovered the long fields of bluebonnets under white oaks and dogwood and was halfway over the fence marking the property line, her little brother in tow. The sky was becoming gray in the late afternoon, clouds entering the landscape from the southeast. A wind swept the fields and stirred up dust in those places where the Jessup's livestock had cropped the rye grass down to the soil.

Maude remarked, "What sort of arrangements did Harry make for you and the children?"

"Pardon me?"

"Five dollars a week would be fair and helpful."

"Well, I've always believed in pulling my own weight. I'm sure Harry would tell you that I have no fear of work. I thought I'd find a position downtown." Marie said, her eyes fixed on the children crossing the fields of clover and wildflowers toward the grazing horses. Henry, dressed in denim overalls, fell in the wild grass and Cissie picked him up and brushed him off, then hurried on into the wind. Their young hearts were as wild as her own. "Just a few hours a day."

"Won't many people hire someone for part of a day's work. Can you do anything useful?"

Marie felt like throwing her clothes down and walking out. She had no desire to feel subservient in this household. The Pendergast women never kowtowed to anyone and she wouldn't be the one to start. She was much too modern. Why on earth hadn't Harry warned her that his mother would be so obstinate in receiving family into her home? Now this was a fine start they'd gotten off to. What was next? Boxing ears?

"I can sew," Marie replied, trying to sound confident against Maude's withering assault, though this was all so terribly unsettling. Why couldn't she just go outdoors and work in her garden? "My mother taught me when I was a little girl. She worked four years as a seamstress in Milwaukee before marrying my father."

Maude opened the top drawer of the walnut chiffonier and emptied its contents onto the bed. "Most folks here can sew. Not much need to hire out for something practically everyone knows how to do themselves."

Keeping her voice as pleasant as possible, Marie replied, "Well, I run a typewriter, too. Fifty-five words a minute. And I've run a cash register. I plan to go downtown tomorrow and see what I can find. Five dollars a week will be no trouble at all. You needn't worry."

Marie turned her attention once again to her children outdoors. Seven-year-old Henry stopped a dozen yards or so from the horses, regarding the animals with curiosity and awe. Her little brother watching from a dozen yards off, Cissie tiptoed up to the sorrel and placed a palm on its flank. The horse ignored her. She motioned Henry closer, but he shook his head. The cautious member of the family, Henry slowly circled the horse at a safe distance. He'd been afraid of the pony at the county fair last summer until Harry plopped him on the animal's back.

"What about the children?" Maude gathered up the pile of clothes from the chiffonier drawers and dumped them into the basket she'd brought with her. "I hope you're not expecting me to watch them every day while you're gone. My babysitting days ended when Harry and Rachel grew up. Every other Monday and Friday my ladies club meets at Trudy's until four. Tuesdays and Thursdays, the club ladies come over here at three sharp and we entertain until five. After that, there's supper to fix. I've simply got no time for children. I'm sorry."

"Mrs. Hennesey," Marie said plainly, "I don't expect you to look after my children. They're not your responsibility. I know that. We're guests in your house, and we appreciate your hospitality. I intend to find employment here in Bellemont as soon as I can. Once I have my hours settled, I'll make my own arrangements for the children. They won't be any burden to either you or Rachel. I promise." So mad now she could spit nails, Marie wondered if she could ever forgive Harry for subjecting her to this indignity.

Maude Hennesey replaced the top drawer and picked up the two empty ones. "Don't misunderstand me, dear. You're family, so we're more than glad to have you here." She slid the drawers back into the old chiffonier and took up the laundry basket. "Rachel comes home at half past five. We like to eat by six. If there's anything you need for yourself or the children, just let me know. It's been ages since I've had young ones in the house, but I don't doubt we'll manage."

She walked out of the room, closing the door behind her. Feeling utterly defeated, Marie sat on the iron bed, her gaze returned toward the window, thankful that conversation with Maude was over and done with. Harry had warned her that his mother might be gruff and difficult at first, but being a man, he'd understated the threat. Nothing Maude had said or done since Marie and the children had stepped off the evening train had made them feel the least bit welcome. But Marie refused to blame her mother-in-law. After all, this was her home they were invading, her peace of mind the children would disrupt.

Presumably, Harry had gone over all of this with his mother long before and she had agreed to take them in. Truth was, so much would be new for all of them, adjustments would need to be made, tempers controlled. Farrington on the Mississippi was behind them now, the house on Cedar Street taken by strangers, the home where her children had been born reconciled to memory. Though leaving still made Marie sick of soul, her anger at Harry was at least beginning to diminish, day by day. Recriminations were wasteful now. Poor Harry had his own fears, which Marie understood much better than Harry thought she did. *Life bestows bounty and burden upon each of us,* Granny Chamberlain had lectured, *it's how we receive it that sets us apart from our neighbors.*

Both children had climbed the fence on the boundary of the pasture and were running out into the grassy fields in the distance. While she watched, Cissie's white dress, fluttering brightly against the gray landscape, dwindled as she and Henry ran far into the northwest. Dust clouds kicked up in the yard. Marie got up off the bed and went outdoors.

Maude was hanging linen on the line below the back porch that billowed wildly as the wind gusted. The street out front was empty. Thunderheads moved on the horizon to the south. *Rain before seven, clear by eleven.* Marie walked down the short path between the Hennesey house and the fence bordering the pasture and entered the open field through the Jessup's gate next door. Stepping carefully to avoid soiling her shoes, Marie walked out across the scrub grass in the direction her children had taken. She loved being in the country, feeling the grass beneath her feet. Not Harry. His idea of a lawn would be to cement it over. The country was not in his blood. Little wonder he had left. Back at the house, Maude was calling for her. The wind caught her words up, swept them away. Marie pretended not to hear them at all.

She neared the sorrel by the fence line on the north. Henry was out of sight, but Cissie's white dress reflected enough light to remain visible through the tall oaks. They were both laughing, a pair of squealing voices echoing across the spring fields of rye grass and bluebonnets. Henry had slowed his stride so his older sister could catch up. Freedom was meant to be shared. Slowing her own pace, Marie smiled because when she was a little girl, freedom had belonged only to her male cousins. Trust, responsibility, and a shiny new Ford automobile to test it with. Drive up to Chicago to see some shows. Spend every hard-earned dollar chasing around after girls whose mothers didn't care what barn their daughters spent the night in. Never had Marie owned a car, never had her chair at the supper table sat empty for a night, never had she slept beyond the echo of her mother's voice: a perpetual child until she married Harry.

Folding her dress, Marie climbed through the fence. *Go east, go west, go north. Any direction is right. Wherever you're headed, it'll get you there. Just don't stop to answer questions.* Advice to her cousins, courtesy of her father. Why not for her? How long did he think she'd be sitting at his table? Until the Lord returned? Well, he was wrong.

Behind her, Maude's house and the Jessup's shrunk back into the pinewoods that marked the town limits of Bellemont. Ahead, the sky looked as big as the whole world.

Cissie had stopped chasing her brother. Now she was dancing slowly in a circle, her skirt held by fingertips away from her body, singing aloud. Henry had gone on another fifty yards or so, arms flailing wildly in fatigue. His voice carried on the wind above his sister's, "Ya, ya, ya, ya, ya!" A chant of his own creation. A boy-child's song of joy.

Walking closer now, Marie realized Cissie's song was one Harry had taught the children the night before he put them on the train to Bellemont.

"The monkey married the baboon's sister. Gave her a ring and then he kissed her. Kissed her so hard he raised a blister ... "

Cissie wore a wondrous smile as she sang loud enough for her brother to hear. Henry, hurrying in circles round and round, raising his own dust storm amid the wildflowers, screeched in laughter, and ran faster still.

On the horizon, great black thunderheads flared lightning in the southern sky, but Marie did not hurry her children to safety, not while Cissie still sang and Henry ran. Instead, Marie took off her shoes and danced lightly barefoot in the soft grass, danced a two-step to a little girl's song in the rhythm of her children's footsteps.

"The monkey married the baboon's sister. Gave her a ring and then he kissed her. Kissed her so hard he raised a blister. She set up a yell."

— 2 —

Rachel Hennesey put down the spring fabrics copy of *Vogue*, danced over to the radio console, dialed up the volume, then took another peek out the window. Sitting at the piano with Cissie on her lap, Marie listened to rain drumming on the roof. She found it comforting, somehow. It was raining so hard the street had become almost invisible from indoors. Mud swamped the sidewalk out front. Roof gutters drained like Niagara Falls. Since sundown, the thunderstorm had dumped three inches of rain onto Bellemont and the surrounding countryside. Summer resorts on the Gulf Coast were already flooding.

Rachel came away from the window, bother on her face. Stopping by the piano, she said, "He knows I can't stand to be kept waiting. How long could it take to hire a room at the aerodrome?"

Marie offered a hopeful smile. "I'm sure he'll be here any minute now." She thought Rachel, at twenty-six-years-old, was perhaps the most attractive young woman she knew, sure to have her choice of a proper beau. She was nearly as tall as Harry with high cheekbones, the prettiest green eyes Marie had ever seen, and lovely blonde hair bobbed in the most up-to-the-minute fashion. Secretly, Marie was envious because she knew Harry wished her own look were more modern. She knew he was unhappy with her these days, but how would changing her hair change his heart?

Rachel said, "He does it to be contrary."

"Oh?"

"No fellow wants a girl to believe he can't find something better to do on a Saturday night than take her out dancing. They want us to think we're no better than third or fourth choice. I don't know why we put up with it."

Marie ran her fingers lightly over the keys, trying a short scale. With the radio console playing jazz from a Birmingham ballroom, she knew it was pointless to attempt anything else. Apparently the piano had gathered dust since Rachel brought the Crosley set into the house. Now only professional entertainment was worthy of her attention, and Maude was too busy to play much herself. The front parlor was the biggest room in the house with space enough for a piano and side chairs, a lovely old horsehair sofa by the fireplace, three tapestry Morris chairs, and several side-tables and shaded lamps. Marie thought it was adorable. Perhaps when she had a house of her own again, she'd borrow an idea or two.

"Of course, I don't mean to suggest we ought to do away with their entire species," said Rachel. "I'm sure I wouldn't want to inherit the digging of ditches and such. And they do remember special occasions every so often with lovely gifts."

"That they do."

"Let me guess: Harry sends flowers."

"Yes, he does."

"Carnations?"

Marie blushed. "You know your brother too well."

"Well, fact is, he's always been too cheap to send roses. Every birthday I had between six and sixteen, he'd buy a bouquet of white carnations and have them delivered. He didn't fancy having anyone see him carrying sissy flowers down the street."

"He sends me red ones."

"Oh, he does, does he? Well, that's a surprise!"

"White carnations are pretty, too, though."

"I prefer roses," Rachel replied, fingering her string of beads. "Any color'll do." A car rumbled past out front, splashing water against the steps. Rachel hurried over to the window again for a look. "I'll give him five more minutes."

"It's still ten minutes lacking the hour," said Marie, amused by Rachel's impatience. "He'd be early." In her own girlhood, she'd known more than one boy who made her wait for a dance. She had always fought the tears and tried to be cheerful, believing no boy enjoys sobbishness on a date.

"That's not the issue." Rachel stood at the windowsill and parted the curtains with the back of her hand. "A boy ought to show more enthusiasm for his date. Sidney Carlyle was always early. Mother had to entertain him for at least half an hour before I came down to leave. They'd play three or four hands of gin rummy for pretzel sticks and Sidney'd usually let her win."

"Why did you stop seeing him?" Marie asked, as she helped Cissie fit her fingers to a D chord.

"He smelled like chicken feathers."

"I beg your pardon?" Both Marie and Cissie giggled.

"His clothes, hat, shoes. Everything he wore smelled like smelly old chicken feathers. Even Mother noticed after a while."

Maude stuck her head into the room. "The boy worked at a chicken farm, dear. What did you expect?"

Rachel laughed. "He might've washed a little more diligently, wouldn't you say? Was that asking too much? My own clothes were beginning to smell."

"That was your fault for sitting too close."

"Mother!"

"Well, it's God's own truth."

"Nonetheless," said Rachel, turning her attention back to Marie, "there are some things a girl cannot be expected to endure."

"He was the nicest boy you ever stepped out with," offered Maude. "In my opinion, of course."

"Of course."

"And he had sweet eyes."

"And he was a Baptist," Rachel added with a smirk.

"The closer to God we are, the more beautiful we grow."

"He smoked cigars, did you know that?"

"So did your father, dear," Maude replied. "You can't hang a man on what he smokes. What he does on a Saturday night isn't half as important as what he does on Sunday."

"He got himself juiced every Saturday night down in the cellar at Frankie's Café, is what he did. And every Sunday morning following, he'd sleep it off in the back pew by the open window. I doubt he heard word one of Whitaker's old sermons in the month we saw each other.

He was nothing but a plain stinking drunk, Baptist or no."

"Nevertheless, in God's eyes … "

"God isn't blind, Mother! For heaven sakes!"

Rachel let go of the curtains and went over to the front door. As she opened it, a gust of rain blew inside over the threshold and onto the carpet.

"Would you mind closing that door!" Maude shouted, coming out from the kitchen. Rachel stepped out onto the porch, pulling the door closed behind her. Marie leaned forward from the piano so that she could see out to the front steps where Rachel was standing now, scouring the street for signs of her suitor. She wondered what position Harry would've taken in this dispute between his mother and sister. He despised these sorts of petty disagreements with which he believed women were obsessed. Half the time, he thought Marie's concerns were silly when she knew they weren't. He could be strict in his thinking, not a flattering habit in Marie's opinion. She often wondered how they managed to get along.

"Even if that boy's got to get here by rowboat," said Maude, taking a look outside for herself, "he'll be here, mark my words. I don't know why she lets herself get so worked up. It's plain as the day is long that the boy's crazy about her."

"Maybe he got stuck in the mud," Cissie said. "It looks awful deep out there." Then she thumped a note on the piano.

"I expect he'll be here any minute. Never known him to be late."

"What's he like?" asked Marie, curious of her mother-in-law's opinion. She took hold of Cissie's right hand and positioned it to play a C chord on the piano.

"Well, he's Catholic," replied Maude, and walked back to the kitchen, closing the door.

Cissie gently played her chord according to Marie's design. A motor horn honked and a car pulled up out front, and Marie heard Rachel's voice above the wind. The headlights went dark and a car door slammed shut. Marie shifted Cissie off her lap, and stood up. The door opened to a draft and Rachel came inside again, her date in tow.

"Good grief, is it pouring out there," she said, shaking her head.

Water droplets beaded up in her hair. She went immediately to the bathroom and closed the door.

CW remained on the threshold, trying his best not to drip any water on the floor. He was a tall fine-looking young man with dark brown hair, soft blue eyes, and a strong patrician face. Marie had no difficulty seeing why Rachel was so taken with him. He spoke to her with a distinctly elegant Southern drawl. "Well, it's rather wet out tonight."

Marie nodded. "So I've noticed."

He smiled. "My hired Ford leaks a bit, too."

"Oh?"

"Needs a new winter top." CW moved forward a bit farther into the room, taking care to avoid the throw rug. "I ought to get it replaced, I suppose."

"Yes."

"Haven't had the time." He grinned as he took his hat off, brushed the rim across his coat sleeve, and hung it on the hallstand. His dark hair was trimmed razor-sharp and slicked with oil. "I've been busy as a beaver this season, flying all over the place."

Marie raised an eyebrow. "Even tonight?"

"No, ma'am, I'm not crazy."

"Do you fly in an aerial circus?" Her Cousin Bonnie actually flew an airplane out in California, an undertaking Marie much admired even though Harry always thought her foolish.

CW laughed. "Not on your life! Aeronautics is much too serious an enterprise to be wasted doing loop-de-loops over somebody's barn. That's called a nut sundae in this business. Actually, I have a contract taxiing businessmen all over the South, picking them up in one town, setting them down in another, making certain they make their appointments on time. It's the newest thing. Have you heard of Jake Mollendick?"

She shook her head, woefully ignorant about flying. "I don't believe so."

"Well, he's considered by many to be the founder of our modern commercial aviation. Why, just last year when I traveled to his Swallow factory at Wichita to buy my airplane, I was shown a future vision of the very heavens filled with commerce, argosies of magic sails, pilots of the purple twilight dropping down with costly bales."

"Oh my."

"Stirring, isn't it?" CW grinned. "Well, I'm absolutely convinced this new aviation game is the future."

"I'm sure it is." Marie offered her hand. "By the way, I'm Rachel's sister-in-law. Marie Hennesey." She smiled sweetly, and blushed. He was fine-looking, indeed.

"Of course you are," CW replied with a mock-seriousness. "And I'm very pleased to make your acquaintance. CW McCall, professional birdman, at your service."

CW took off his raincoat, folded it once, and hung it on the hallstand below his felt hat. He was wearing a smart gray metropolitan suit underneath. "Flying's much more reliable than train service. Quicker, too."

"I don't doubt that."

"Have you ever flown in an airplane?"

"No, I can't say that I have."

CW smiled. "Why not?"

"I suppose I've just never had the opportunity. I'm no coward."

"Then you're not afraid of it, like most people?"

"Are most people afraid of flying?" she asked, coyly.

He nodded. "I believe so. Why, I read recently that more than seventy percent of businessmen would use the air if they had the opportunity, but their wives won't allow it. The very idea frightens them. Jake Mollendick believes we need to teach air-mindedness if we hope to see real growth in this industry."

"Well, I wouldn't be at all afraid." Which was true. Harry hated flying because he had a fear of heights, but Marie had climbed trees on the slightest dare when she was a girl and never minded looking down. She always had more heart for risk than Harry did, except for a deathly fear of drowning in deep water which she did not understand because she loved riding in canoes.

"Would you like to take a flight one day?"

"Certainly." The very idea of it filled her tummy with butterflies.

"Then we'll do it. I promise. One day soon."

"Good."

Rachel came out of the bathroom. She'd powdered her face for the third time since supper. Marie noticed that Rachel's lipstick had also received attention. Cissie slid off the piano bench and went to the window, drawing back the curtain for a peek out into the rainy dark.

"Well, nighty-night, Mother," said Rachel, leaning around the doorframe to the kitchen. "Don't bother waiting up." She winked at Marie. "We'll be back late."

Maude's voice followed from inside the kitchen. "You be careful driving out there."

"Of course we will. I'm sure CW's just as capable on the road as he is in the air."

CW got up from the window seat. He pretended to look puzzled. "Where're we going, darling?"

"To the dance, silly," said Rachel. She offered her cheek to CW for a kiss, which made Marie blush. Harry rarely kissed her in public. He called it embarrassing and un-Christian. "Did your little head fill up with rainwater on the way over here? Goodnight, Mother!"

Marie watched Cissie draw swirls and curlicues in the condensation on the windowpane. Her art mimicked the rhythmic drumming of rainwater on the porch roof just beyond the glass.

"Let's go," said Rachel, urging CW toward the door. "I do not wish to be the last to arrive."

"You won't," said CW. "The roof fell in half an hour ago. Whole floor's under a foot of water. The dance got canceled. Everybody's gone home."

Rachel's face blanched. "You're lying. I ought to slap your face."

"You can go see it for yourself, if you like. A great big hole right there in the middle of the auditorium, like a Bertha shell dropped on it. Thank goodness it didn't cave in a couple hours later. People might've been killed."

Rachel sat down next to Marie on the piano bench, disappointment filling her eyes. "Why didn't somebody tell me earlier before I bothered myself dressing up for nothing?"

CW shrugged. "Nobody knew until it happened. Roof just caved right in. One moment it was fine, the next — KABOOM!"

Maude came out of the kitchen, a dishtowel in her hands. She walked over to the radio and clicked it off. "If you're not listening to that noise, would you please do me the courtesy of leaving it off." She pretended to despise the radio, except for her favorite show: H.J. Seidenfaden Funeral Home in Kansas City, Missouri, with organist Harold Turner, whose Sunday morning program featured mostly religious music. "You know, I've been saying for years that old hall ought to've been torn down. Everybody knew the roof was rotting away. Anybody who tells you they're surprised is just plain lying."

"I think it was done deliberately to ruin my evening," Rachel said, removing her shawl and laying it on the piano top. "There are so few joys in my life and dancing is one of them. Now what am I supposed to do, go fishing?"

Cissie swiveled her head away from the window. "Momma, I see fish swimming in the street. Lots of them."

CW said, "Well then, what do you say we go out and catch a couple of them?" He turned to Marie. "Have you ever fished in the road before?"

She shook her head with a smile. "I can't say that I have. Is it safe?"

"It's crazy," offered Rachel, staring hard at CW. "Why do you want to get all wet? Those are your good dancing clothes. And what about me? I didn't dress up to play in the rain."

"Only a fool'd pass up a chance to do some road fishing," replied CW. He winked at Cissie. "Besides, these trousers need to go to the cleaners, anyhow. Might as well get my money's worth."

"Don't expect to come traipsing back in here later on," said Maude. "I have no desire to scrub these floors again this week."

A thunderclap rolled across the fields, rattling the windows. A lightning strike followed somewhere off to the south. Henry came running out from the back bedroom, eyes wide as saucers. "I saw it, Momma! I saw it!"

"Saw what?" Marie took her son into her arms for a welcome hug. He felt warm and slithery.

"Lightning! I saw lightning!"

"And you want to take these children outside," Rachel said to CW, "to splash about in the road? Your brain must've been struck by lightning on the way over here tonight."

"Oh, it's not dangerous at all. Lightning doesn't strike in the road. It's trees and houses that attract it. Have you ever seen someone knocked dead in the middle of the road by lightning?"

"With my luck," said Rachel, "I'd be the first."

The rain increased to a thunderous downpour, beating furiously against the windowpanes, creating a minor waterfall off the porch overhang. Marie released her little boy to have a look outdoors. He was terrified by stormy weather and she knew he'd cuddle up beside her in bed tonight, but she wouldn't mind at all. Maybe Cissie would join them and they'd all nestle together.

"I've never had such a collection of fools under my roof before," said Maude, peeking out the window over the top of Cissie's head. "It's storming out there, and you want to go play in the street? Don't expect me to come looking for you when you get yourselves swept away into the river."

Rachel laughed. "Mother, that's more than half a mile from here."

CW said, "In the flood of '27, Uncle Edmund's plantation was thirty miles from the delta levee at Cabin Teele when the crevasse broke open to the Mississippi. The next day his gallery was ten feet underwater and there was a cow carcass and a family of sharecroppers on his roof. My own daddy took a boat across seventy-five miles of flood from Vicksburg to Monroe and never once saw dry ground."

"Well, I don't think I've ever seen more than a few inches of water in our streets," said Rachel. "It wouldn't be sensible to live here otherwise. Only an idiot builds in a flood plain."

Maude shot back, "Don't fool yourself, young lady. We've had floods here before. Terrible ones."

"And when was that, exactly?" Rachel asked, a mocking skepticism drawn on her face.

"Well, I'd guess the last one would've been when I was your age," her mother answered, "on a night just like this one. The river rose up like a fox and stole our cows, the chickens, your father's old hound dog, and swept them clear down into the Gulf. It wasn't until morning that we saw they were gone."

"Were y'all drunk?" asked Rachel, heading for the closet. She drew out her raincoat. "I think if they were my chickens, I'd have at least been out there waving good-bye as they were floating off. That'd be the decent thing to do."

Maude turned on her heels and walked back into the kitchen. Then, loud enough for everyone to hear, she said, "*Folly is a joy to him who has no sense.* Proverbs 15: 21," and closed the door.

Pretending to have been deaf to that dispute, Marie pulled Henry onto her lap and mussed his hair. She said to Rachel, "Maybe we ought to stay indoors."

The downpour had abated slightly, but Marie worried the worst was yet to come. She hated storms, too, ever since she was a little girl and her favorite calf drowned in a ditch.

"No, let's go out," Rachel replied. "I can't abide Mother quoting the Bible. Besides, if I can't go dancing, I don't care what we do. Maybe the fish'll appreciate how I look."

"Now you're talking," said CW. He gave Rachel a sweet kiss on her cheek, then pulled his raincoat on and grabbed his hat off the hallstand. Rachel put on her own coat, then took up an umbrella and looked at Marie who was still occupied with Henry in her lap. CW opened the front door and went out. A moment later, he came around to the window in front of Cissie and rapped his knuckles on the glass. Giving Marie a grin, he disappeared again into the dark.

"Aren't you coming?" Rachel asked, waiting at the door. "I'm sure the children want to."

Marie frowned. "I'm not sure it's safe out of doors in this storm. Those floods your mother was talking about — "

"Absolute nonsense," said Rachel. "She's just telling you that to keep you inside with her. Floods like she's talking about would've floated this whole sorry town away, but we're still here, aren't we?"

"I suppose so." Actually, she did want to go out and play in the rain. Why not? Harry wasn't here to fight with over it, not that she required his permission to enjoy herself.

Rachel opened the door. "Get your coats on and come on out. Have some fun for a change." She went out onto the porch, closing the door behind her. Marie leaned over the window for a look outdoors. CW was down in the Ford, fiddling with the headlamps. Rachel stood on the bottom step of the porch laughing, rain dripping off her head. It looked like fun.

"Can we go out?" Cissie asked. "Please?"

"Yeah, Momma, can we?" Henry chimed in. "We won't get drowned or nothing, we promise."

Both tugged at Marie's blouse. How far was the river? Half a mile? Could it really flood so close? Who was right? Whose part should she take? Maude remained in the kitchen, rummaging in the cupboards. She'd dispensed her opinion and now busied herself with rearranging the pots and pans and other assorted utensils, long piling up beneath the countertops. Marie understood quite clearly the wisdom in avoiding conflict within the household, particularly when it involved choosing sides in strife between Rachel and Maude. The radio was a good example. On evenings when they were both home, Rachel cranked the volume up as loud as it would go so she might hear her radio shows in any room of the house. Despising modern music, Maude repeatedly dialed it down in favor of accompanying herself on the piano now and then to the first four bars of "Beautiful Dreamer." Each time she quit the piano, Rachel would sweep back into the room and dial back up the volume which would send Maude back to the piano again, *Beautiful Dreamer, wake unto me. Starlight and dew drops are waiting for thee.* This contest continued sometimes until bedtime, a war of dissonance night after night that drove everyone in the house crazy. Not that Marie ever complained. What would Harry say? Never injure hospitality with disputations.

Henry tugged on Marie's skirt. "Can we, Momma? Can we go out with Aunt Rachel?"

She relented for the children's sake. "Go get your raincoats and boots."

With a cheer, they dashed for the bedroom. Marie got up off the piano bench and went to the closet for her own coat and a pair of umbrellas. Maybe she could keep them dry.

Maude's voice came from the kitchen. "Bring the children back inside through the kitchen when they're done. I'll have some towels warming."

Marie put on her coat, then answered, "Thank you."

"No sense in the little ones catching pneumonia just because Rachel's dance got canceled. Keep an eye on my daughter and that Catholic boy if you can. There'll be another thunderhead following right on the tail of the last one."

"I will," replied Marie. "Thank you."

The children came running out of the bedroom, smiles wide on their faces, raincoats flopping behind. Marie opened the door and ushered them onto the porch where a damp breeze gusted across the threshold.

"Isn't Grandma coming?" asked Cissie. Henry ran down to the bottom of the steps out into the falling rain. He arched his neck backward and stuck out his tongue.

"Grandma's busy," said Marie, fastening the buttons on her coat. Up the street a hundred yards or so where the road ended, the muddy earth was indistinguishable from cloud-blackened fields. Hardly a tree was visible in the rainy dark.

Rachel giggled. Leaning headfirst into CW's automobile, her skirt and bare legs were exposed to the rainfall. CW gave her a sloppy kiss. Marie recalled a time when Harry was still that bold.

"When do we fish?" Cissie asked, tugging on her mother's coat.

"I don't know, honey," Marie replied, having no idea what was planned for them. "Soon."

Henry stepped off the porch and straight into a pothole, drowning his left boot with a splash. Rachel slid backward out of the automobile, then leaned in to give CW one last kiss after which he reached across the passenger seat to pull the door shut. Rachel stepped away and looked up at Marie. She giggled. "Isn't he adorable? He'd make love to me in a hurricane if I'd allow it. I think I may have myself a couple of children, after all."

CW started the engine. Exhaust vapor billowed out into the cold, wet air. Both feet in the mud now, Henry leaned out and touched the front fender.

"You be careful, honey," Rachel said. "Don't get yourself run over now."

"Henry!" Marie shouted. "Get away from the car!"

"Aren't we goin' fishin'?" he asked, trying to free his one foot from the muddy pothole. He wriggled it violently back and forth.

CW put the automobile into gear and rolled away from the house. Henry's boot came free with a sucking noise.

"Where's he going, Momma?" asked Cissie, letting go of her mother's coat. CW swung his automobile out into muddy College Street, honked once, then drove off toward downtown.

"He'll be back," said Rachel, a smile on her face. She sat down on the bottom step and covered up her legs with the edge of the raincoat. "Come on down. Sit right here beside me so we're close to the street."

Henry sat on the far end of the steps away from Rachel, leaving room for his sister and mother. Cissie made her way carefully down the wet stairs and slid in next to Rachel. Marie could still hear the automobile in the next block. A shiver ran up her back and she folded her arms close to keep warm. The rain had lightened to a soft steady drizzle in the yellow porchlight.

"Aren't we gonna fish?" asked Henry.

"We're going to play 'Galveston'," said Rachel, wearing the grin of the cat that ate the canary. "Make sure your coats are all buttoned up tight."

"I don't understand," said Marie, opening her own umbrella. Her children sat huddled up tight six steps below, big smiles of anticipation on their faces. Did they know something she didn't? Harry wasn't much for surprises, and neither was she. What sort of game was this?

"Nothing to understand," said Rachel. "All you have to do is come on down here and have a seat with the rest of us."

A wet gust swirled the slow drizzle in under the porch, dampening Marie's face. She blinked her eyes clear and went down to the bottom step where she had a look in the direction of downtown. Mud blanketed the road that extended ten blocks into the dark cover of billowing shade trees. Then, beginning as just a dot of light in the rainy distance, a car came on toward her.

"You best sit now," said Rachel. "He's coming back."

CW's automobile made a whooshing noise in mud and water and trailed a fantail twice the size of the car. He came on fast.

"Sit down!" Rachel said, urgency in her voice.

Cissie pulled Henry close under the umbrella. "He's coming!"

The headlights illuminated the rain in the road ahead of CW's automobile. His horn honked twice. A hand waved from the driver's window.

"Cover your faces!" shouted Rachel.

"Momma!" Henry cried, tugging at the hem of Marie's raincoat.

Rachel shrieked, "GALVESTON!" as CW's automobile roared past the porch, splashing a great wave of muddy water over all four seated there on the bottom step. Safe beneath the thoroughly drenched umbrella, the children squealed with laughter. Marie was soaked, head to foot, as she hadn't gotten her umbrella up over her face in time. Water dripped from her head and mud stung in her eyes. Good grief! She felt like a fool, but everyone else was up now, shaking off, laughing more loudly. CW's automobile made a U-turn, and headed back again toward downtown.

"Galveston!" yelled Henry as CW drove by. "Galveston!"

Maude shouted from the window, "Rachel, for goodness sakes, what did I tell you last year? Have you lost your mind?"

Rachel called back over her shoulder, "Good grief, Mother! It's just a game!"

"Tell that to your Uncle Palmer the next time he visits!"

"Mother, please! You're spoiling the children's fun!"

"Just you wait! The Lord remembers those who grieve not for the deprived."

The window slammed shut.

As the water dripped from her brow, Marie asked Rachel, "What did she mean by that?"

Rachel laughed. "Oh, Mother's so dramatic. She thinks our playing out here is a disservice to Uncle Palmer's sister-in-law and her poor family who were swept away with their house on Bath Street and drowned in the Gulf during the great Galveston hurricane. Of course it was a frightful tragedy and all that, but to think this game's got anything to do with that horrid disaster is plainly ridiculous."

Marie used the back of her hand to wipe her eyes. Cissie stood three steps up, patting her face dry while trying to stop giggling.

Rachel waved to CW. His automobile disappeared again into the trees down on the next block with a last burst of the motor horn echoing across the rainy night.

Rachel looked up at Marie, muddy water dripping off her nose. "We've been playing 'Galveston' since the first automobiles came to Bellemont. It's the only thing to do around here when it rains."

"Why do you do it at all?" Marie asked, trying not to sound critical, though getting splashed by a passing automobile was not her idea of a rainy evening's entertainment. They'd tricked her into playing this game, but maybe it wasn't the most awful thing in the world.

Rachel wiped her own nose. "Excitement's hard to come by in this town, and anything's more enjoyable than listening to Mother singing 'Beautiful Dreamer' and quoting the Bible."

Feeling a slight chill, Marie folded her coat back over her knees and watched her children, both soaked and giggling.

"Besides," Rachel added, "CW loves driving by here and showing off. He'd race past all night if I'd allow it."

"It seems a little silly to me," said Marie, still blinking water from her eyes. She smiled and felt foolish for getting mad at first.

"Of course," Rachel admitted with a giggle, "but isn't it fun?"

Henry stood a few feet out in the muddy road, sunk up to his shins, peering in the direction of downtown. Cissie had an arm curled around the railing, watching her brother. Both wore enormous grins. That alone gave Marie sufficient reason for staying outdoors.

"He's coming back!" Henry shouted. The children went into hysterics, laughing and disengaging themselves from the mud, lunging for the bottom step of the porch, sitting down and covering up.

"He'll really let us have it this time," said Rachel. "Second pass is always the best."

Marie scrambled for her umbrella. She felt like an idiot. "I don't think I'm — "

"Just cover yourself up and tuck your head in tight," Rachel rolled her head in close to her chest, "like this. You'll be fine. Honest to Abraham."

"He's coming!" shrieked Henry. "He's coming!"

The swoosh of rapid tires in mud and water came out of the north again, engine droning behind. Rain fell harder now in the road. To the south, lightning lit up the sky as CW's automobile roared toward the house. Marie ducked her head and covered up.

"GAL-VES-TON!" screamed Rachel and Henry and Cissie in unison as the automobile flashed by, closer than before, sending up a wave of muddy water that splashed high up onto the porch, engulfing the four spectators on the bottom step. An instant afterward, a thunderclap bellowed overhead in the blackened sky. The reverberation rattled windows up and down the street as CW's automobile ran off into the dark.

When the echo of the thunderclap cleared, both children were screaming. A genuine cloudburst followed, rain falling so hard Marie lost sight of the cottonwoods across the road. Cissie and Henry leaped up off the bottom step. Rachel hurried from the porch into the road, appearing disoriented by the thunder. Henry and Cissie, arms wrapped tightly about each other, climbed up onto the next step. Maude was on the top step calling to them as lightning flashed again to the south. CW's automobile came past, headlights blinking on and off. Rachel shouted at him to stop, but thunder roared once more in the sky and she returned to the cover of the porch. By now, Cissie and Henry were up on the top step with Maude, huddling together inside her arms. Seeing that her children were safe, Marie waited for Rachel, then hurried up the stairs herself.

Rain cascaded down, transforming the road out front into a glistening lake.

"I told you it was foolish," Maude said to Rachel, as her daughter reached the top of the stairs, "but no, you had to go out and be a show-off to these little children."

"Not now, Mother."

"You could've been struck by lightning," said Maude. "Or worse."

Rachel laughed as she dripped water from every part of her body. "Mother, what could possibly be worse than getting hit by lightning?"

"Never you mind. Just stay on the path you're heading and see what happens. And don't say I didn't tell you so."

"Where's CW gone?" asked Henry. "Is he comin' back?"

Wind swirled the rain about, driving it under the porch overhang. Shaking a bit, Marie brought her coat sleeve up to dry off her face. Cissie huddled close to her brother.

"I expect so, dear," said Rachel, though the look on her face indicated she wasn't that certain. Lightning flashed bright blue to the southwest. An instant later, a great boom shook the house, rattling the windows so hard the sunshade fell off its holder in Maude's bedroom, knocking her cactus flower off the bottom sill and cracking the glass.

"Good Lord!" cried Maude, grabbing for the porch railing. Cissie started crying. Henry broke free and ran to Marie, wrapping his arms about her waist. Rachel flew to the bottom of the stairs and stared out down the road toward town where CW had gone.

"Get back up here!" Maude shouted to her. "Have you lost your senses?"

"Cissie, over here!" said Marie, trying to ignore the storm in favor of gathering up her children. Harry would be furious if he saw them now. "Come quick!"

Cissie joined Henry in wrapping her arms around their mother's waist. They both hid themselves behind Marie, all three shivering from cold and fright. Maude yelled for Rachel. Her daughter ignored her, venturing instead farther out into the road for a better look.

"Take the children inside for me, will you?" Marie asked Maude, nudging them toward the open door. Lightning was a worry now she'd prefer to dispense with for her children's sake. "Henry, Cissie, go with Grandma! This instant!"

"Aren't you coming?" Cissie asked, stepping indoors with her little brother in tow. Anytime either she or someone else went somewhere, she'd ask that question. On the night Harry had set his family on the train to Bellemont, Cissie put that question to him at least twenty times. Knowing Harry's answer a week beforehand, Marie felt her heart break a little each time Cissie asked.

"I'll wait out here with Auntie Rachel until CW comes back," replied Marie, trying to sound brave though her heart was all aflutter. Why on earth was she such a coward? Harry would've laughed to see her like this. Not that he was any brave soul! At the sight of a rat in the cellar, he'd telephone the exterminator and lock the door.

"*He in the company of a fool …* " said Maude, taking both Cissie and Henry by the hand and leading them to the door.

"I'll be all right," Marie said, and gave her children a little wave as Maude shut the door behind them. Rachel sloshed about in the middle of the road, restless with anxiety. Her hair hung limp and her face was streaked with mud, yet her attention remained focused in the direction CW had driven. Marie assumed he'd return shortly. Each previous run had taken no more than a few minutes. He was overdue now, but not by enough to worry about. Another lightning strike flared in the sky to the east. Four or five seconds later, the thunderclap boomed, though less ferociously than the last. Maybe the storm was passing on.

"He's coming!" shouted Rachel. She waved both her arms wildly, and slid her feet in the mud back and forth. Feeling a little bolder, Marie ventured to the bottom of the porch once more and cupped a hand over her brow to see beyond the rain pouring in her face. A dim pair of headlights glimmered down at the far end of College Street, bouncing as the automobile negotiated the dozens of ruts in the muddy road. Rachel kept waving as she sloshed a path back to the porch. Were it not raining so hard on the roof of Maude's house, the engine noise would've been audible as the headlights neared. Seeing the automobile trailing a large rooster tail of water, Marie climbed back up three steps. She'd gotten wet enough, thank you. Rachel came up onto the porchsteps beside her, still waving. Seconds later, CW roared by, kicking another wave onto the stairs. His Ford went into a sloshing 180-degree spin just at the end of the block, splashing water and mud in a wide half-circle before righting itself and starting back toward the house. He pulled up next to the steps and honked the horn. Rachel ran down to greet him. CW rolled down the passenger window and she leaned inside. He was shouting excitedly. Rachel popped back out of the window and yelled to Marie, "Tell Mother CW says the school's on fire!"

"What?"

"The school's on fire! Lightning set the school on fire! Go tell Mother!"

Marie turned to go inside, but instead the front door opened and Maude stuck her head out. "Trudy's on the phone! There's a fire downtown!"

Rachel yelled, "We know, Mother! CW was just down there! He says the school's on fire! It got hit by lightning! Whole thing's burning up!"

"Well, what did I tell you?"

Rachel leaned back inside the automobile.

"Just like I said," Maude continued, directing her attention now to Marie. "People have no business being out on a night like this. It's dangerous. You can see now how right I was."

Marie nodded, wondering why she hadn't heard any sirens. Bellemont wasn't so big that the fire could be that far away. Maybe the town didn't have a fire engine. But that would be silly.

Maude called down to Rachel, "Was anybody killed?"

Her daughter pulled back out of the automobile. "I can't hear you, Mother!"

"I said, were there were any injuries or deaths?"

Rachel shrugged. "CW says one man got himself burned pretty badly. He doesn't know about anyone else."

CW said something to Rachel. She nodded and yelled back up to Maude, "He says there's a whole lot of people down there trying to put the fire out, but it seems the whole school's a wreck. If anyone's still inside, they're probably dead." Rachel leaned inside the automobile once more to say something to CW. Then she came back out and said, "CW thinks we ought to go down there and have a look for ourselves. He says it's quite a spectacle."

"Not on your life," said Maude, both children peeking out from behind her now. "You tell CW if he wants to go, he's more than welcome, but I won't have my daughter running around in the middle of the night chasing fires."

Rachel opened the door and got in. "Bye, Mother. We're going." She looked up at Marie. "Would you like to come along? We have plenty of room. Chasing fires is the best entertainment there is in Bellemont."

Rain dripped into the front seat dampening the carpet at her feet.

Marie shook her head. "I should probably stay here with the children. I'm sure they're scared to death."

"Mother can watch them for you." Rachel called up to Maude, "Can't you, Mother? If Marie comes with us, you can watch over Cissie and Henry, can't you?" She looked back at Marie. "Sure, she can. They'll be fine. We'll just drive down, have a look-see, and come on back."

The rain had lightened again to a steady drizzle, and the wind faded, suggesting that the storm was moving off across the prairie. Marie looked up at Maude and the children. She wanted to go. It'd been years since she'd gone to a fire. There was always so much excitement. Why shouldn't she go?

Maude called down, "Just you make sure to keep your distance. A building like that's likely to fall on your head when it goes."

"Will you be all right here with Grandma?" Marie asked her children.

"Can't we come, too?" Henry cried. "I want to see the fire."

"Me, too!" said his sister. Marie knew Cissie was old enough, but since Henry wasn't, they'd both have to stay home or she'd never see the end of Henry's tears.

"Not tonight. You go inside and keep Grandma company 'til we get back, all right? You be good now. We won't be long."

"They'll be fine," said Maude. "You watch out for Rachel for me, see that she doesn't drag you into any nonsense."

"I promise," said Marie, retreating to the bottom of the stairs. "Thank you."

She waved once more to her children, and climbed into the back-seat of CW's automobile. The cushion was wet. Rainwater leaked in through the canvas roof along the edges of the back window, dampening the fabric and soaking through clear down to the floorboards.

"Let's go see us a fire!" Rachel whooped and gave CW a lover's kiss right in front of Marie who blushed to see affection expressed so boldly. My goodness! Were they going to make love here and now? Marie tried to hide a smile. Harry thought this generation lacked decency and proportion, but Marie remembered her mother remarking once how Granny Chamberlain believed no good could come of a boy and a girl alone in a buggy after sundown. Indeed, Marie always wished that Harry would kiss her on the porch now and then when people were passing by.

After Rachel finished nibbling at his ear, CW jammed the automobile into gear and stomped on the gas pedal. They drove away from the house toward downtown, which was hardly more than ten blocks walking. Marie had found that out when she'd gone looking for a job the day after arriving in Bellemont. The town had no streetcars or busses or taxicabs. Most people either went about by automobile or on foot. All the roads leading into Bellemont except the main highway were dirt, but College Street downtown from Broad to Sixth was brick, laid in during the War. There were plenty of shade trees and stores and gas stations where one could stop and buy a cold soda pop and sit awhile. Downtown had benches here and there for mothers and older folks. Marie planned to interview at the Cochrane Building and City Hall for typewriting.

"I tell you, it's just burning like crazy," said CW, veering off from the route Marie took to downtown. "Rain's had no effect on it at all. Wait'll you see."

"Good God!" Rachel exclaimed. "First, the auditorium and now the school. It must be the Lord's visitation on us for all our liquor and sex-madness. Dear, is your steering gear on the blink?" she asked, pointing ahead to the right past a darkened Texaco station. "The school's that way."

"No, it isn't."

"Sure, it is!"

"Why, sugar, I ought to know," replied CW, "I was just there not ten minutes ago."

"Well, I ought to know, too. I spent six years in that old building. Now, turn this heap of yours around."

Instead, CW drove faster down a sidestreet, mud flying like sheets off the tires. Marie felt the leak dripping down the back of her coat. It was raining hard, obscuring the windshield. CW had the wipers working, but they weren't helping much.

"Would you please slow down?" she called out from the backseat. "Good grief!" If CW crashed into a pine tree and killed them all, then what? Marie was frightened of auto smash-ups. Harry thought she was silly, but she'd known three people killed in motorcars and was too terrified to drive herself and had no desire to learn.

"Why, dear, don't worry," Rachel said, smiling benignly, "CW's a terrific driver. I doubt he's had an auto accident in his life, isn't that true, darling?"

"Yes, dear, it is!"

"Well, then, it won't do to have one tonight, would it?" Marie said, closing her eyes as CW swerved around a large fallen tree branch in the road. "Please slow down? You're scaring me to death! I'd rather get out and walk than be killed in a smash-up."

Rachel laughed. "Well, of course, dear! Who wouldn't?"

"There she is!" said CW, swinging onto a side road. "What'd I tell you?"

Up ahead, Marie saw flames reaching high into the rainy night above the gutted wreck of a building sitting in a clearing of old pecan trees. Cars and people were scattered all around the structure, and a line of Negro men were passing buckets across the road from a pine-shrouded creek.

"That's the colored school," said Rachel, relief clear in her voice. "Not ours."

CW ran the automobile up close and slipped it between two trees and shut the motor off. Marie sighed in relief.

"See there?" said Rachel, indicating houselights through the pine woods across the river. "That's Shantytown, where the coloreds live. This is their school. Ours is back the way we came, about a quarter-mile east of us. Thank goodness."

She flung the door open and climbed out. CW followed, holding his door for Marie. Smoke trails drifted in and out of the pecan trees, wet black ash swirling about in the wind and rain and clinging to the soggy leaves. Marie could hear the wood crackling as the building frame was consumed beam by beam. If the rain had helped to slow the fire, it hadn't been by much. Only the front of the school whose wall contained a porch and two windows was completely intact. Nothing from the rear of the structure remained and the east and west walls were in the process of collapsing.

"Good Lord," said Rachel, as she and CW and Marie approached. "There's hardly anything left to save. It's really a shame."

"Why isn't there a fire engine?" Marie asked, seeing nothing but an old-fashioned bucket brigade in the clearing. One night when she was a little girl, she'd watched Uncle Boyd's barn burn down, and she'd cried and had fire nightmares for years afterward. It had horrified her.

CW shrugged. "Maybe it broke down."

"That's absurd," Rachel replied, taking care not to step in the mud. "Why, I saw Percy driving it through downtown only last Saturday afternoon and it was running just fine."

"How old is this school?" Marie asked, feeling tears welling up in her eyes.

Rachel shrugged. "Older than Moses. Daddy had classes here when he was Henry's age. The Negroes took it over when the new school went up."

Walking closer, Marie saw that the bucket brigade consisted exclusively of Negroes in a long line furiously heaving water on those sections of the school least affected by the blaze. None spoke, laboring instead with urgency, catching one bucket and sending it on, catching the next, hardly spilling a drop on the muddy earth. They were not all men, either. Boys, too, carted buckets up from the creek fifty yards off in the dark and passed them on. Mothers and daughters used wet rags to slap down sparks floating out from the center of the fire. Nobody from white Bellemont carried either a bucket or a wet rag. Three police cars were parked in a stand of pines sixty yards back from the fire. Half a dozen patrolmen sat on the hoods of those cars, watching and socializing in the fire shadows. More than a hundred people had come out from Bellemont to spectate. Conversation buzzed like the drizzling rain.

"One would think," said Rachel, "that all this rain would just drown the fire right out."

"It's burning inside the wood," CW replied, "cooking the oil they used to treat the beams with, like a grease fire on your stove. You have to suffocate it."

"That's why our new school was built in brick. I doubt it can burn at all. Look there, honey," Rachel said, directing Marie's attention to the north side of the school where those Negro women not flailing away at sparks held dozens of small children close, huddled against the cold and the storm. "Those poor children," she said, shaking her head. "They ought to be home in bed. Seeing this'll just bring them nightmares, if not pneumonia. Mother would have a fit."

CW strolled closer to the fire for a better look, hand-in-hand with Rachel. Marie's own face and hands ached from the dampness that had soaked clean to the bone. The sight of small children waiting in the rainy dark for the schoolhouse to collapse pierced her heart. What if it had been Henry's school?

"We ought to get some buckets and help out," said CW, letting go of Rachel's hand. He stepped out from under the safety of the cotton-wood back into the downpour. Rachel grabbed his arm. He shook her loose and walked a few feet closer, rainfall drenching him.

"I agree," Marie said, joining CW. She watched the Negroes passing buckets one to another across the darkness. "It's shameful to watch it burn down without raising a hand."

"Then let's not," CW said, striding toward the fire. "I'll be damned if I'm going to stand here like some cold-hearted jellyfish."

"Let's put it out," said Marie, fully determined to fetch a bucket and join the line of Negroes. Furious with the men by the parked cars, she called back to Rachel, "If those men over there are too cowardly to help us, we'll do it ourselves! Maybe seeing us in the bucket brigade'll bring a few of them to their senses."

"You can't help people who won't ask for it," said Rachel, chasing them into the rain. She grabbed CW's arm. "Honey? Please don't!"

CW tried to free himself from Rachel's grip. He yelled at her, "What's wrong with you?"

Rachel shouted back, "Leave them alone, for Christsakes! It's not your concern!" Then she looked Marie in the eye, adding, "Besides, it's too late anyhow. We ought to let it burn to the ground before somebody else gets hurt."

An instant later, heat exploded the glass in the windowpanes on the front wall and the support beams gave way and the north end side of the building toppled over, nearly crushing a group of black men and boys who had been struggling to tear the porchsteps free as salvage. Screams filled the air. The crowd swept back under the trees as millions of blazing sparks flew to heaven. Another beam cracked in half and collapsed into the middle of the charred classroom. Marie watched a great plume of flames explode high into the dark, causing the bucket brigade to pause for a few seconds. Resuming with an increased ferocity moments later, they attacked the flames two and three buckets a shot, understanding that what they saved now would be the foundation for rebuilding. It was a small schoolhouse. Marie decided Uncle Henry's new barn was probably a third bigger. Rachel's brick-and-sandstone school downtown two blocks from the courthouse square was at least twice as wide and long and two stories taller. How did these poor Negro children find room enough to study? Two to a desk? How many grades to one room? How many teachers for the one school? Marie tried to picture her own Cissie and Henry sitting in those desks memorizing the alphabet and arithmetic tables and the story of George Washington who never told a lie.

She saw a Negro woman crying now, wailing somewhere back by the trees where the sparks and flecks of glowing ash were swatted down and extinguished in the greasy mud. The long brigade kept on its rhythm, pass and pour, pass and pour. A child, then another, joined the woman wailing by the pine trees. The back wall collapsed, hurling thousands more sparks skyward. A blast of heat forced the spectators from Bellemont to back up a few steps. Marie shivered with fear and sorrow. She wanted to help, to go join the bucket brigade, but now she felt afraid. She didn't know this town, or these people. What was her place? How was she supposed to behave here? How would she be thought of if she went off to help the Negroes? How would she be treated? And her children? What would Harry say? She was no coward.

While the rain fell harder, Marie reluctantly followed Rachel and CW off under a tall cottonwood back some from the fire where a man wearing a black slicker coat nodded and tipped his sou'wester hat. She started to offer a greeting when rain hissed in the burning timber.

A bitter smoke clouded the darkness.

"It's sure something, ain't it?"

Marie turned to see a husky fellow in muddy denim overalls come out of the rainy dark. The railroad cap he wore was tipped slightly askew. His face looked grimy and swollen.

"Well, hello, Lucius," Rachel said, offering a pleasant smile. "You look soaked to the bone. Did you lose your umbrella?"

"Idabelle swiped it out of my closet at lunchtime."

Rachel laughed. "And you couldn't scare up another? Honey, it's been raining since dusk."

Lucius looked sheepish. "Well, I borrowed this hat from George Blake. It's kept my head dry enough."

"You're a cut-up, dear."

"I know it."

Rachel asked, "Lucius, have you met my sister-in-law?"

"No, ma'am."

"This is Marie," Rachel said, brushing raindrops off her forehead. "She's a Yankee from Illinois."

Smiling, Lucius offered his hand to Marie. "How do you do, ma'am?"

"Just fine, thank you," she replied, her own hand lost in the fellow's immense grip. She noticed a smell of gin on his breath. "I've never been south of St. Louis before."

Lucius laughed. "I expect you'll see a lot here to admire."

Rachel told him, "She's looking for a job downtown. Have you heard of anything? The poor dear's worried about going broke. It seems my brother's resolved to let his wife earn her own keep."

"Sweetheart," CW interjected, jerking his thumb in the direction of the police cars, "are the local cops here putting over a whoopee club?"

Marie watched another squad car roll in under the rainy pines, motor lamps shining.

Rachel frowned. "That's Gene Coulson. Why, I don't believe I've ever seen him out after dark. How peculiar! I'll bet he's just come out here to put the bee on one of the coloreds for starting this fire." She turned to Marie. "Gene takes after his father who was notorious for raking hell all over Shantytown. Mother said once that Tom Coulson was so low he could kiss a mouse without bending his knee."

"Everyone ought to have a hobby," Lucius said, staring off into the woods. Water dripped from his railroad cap. "Trimming niggers is always easier than chasing crooks."

"Now that just tells me piss and swill go together," CW remarked, as the policeman climbed out of his automobile into the drizzling rain. He appeared amiable in the crowd of fellow cops. CW told Rachel, "Maybe we ought to go look into this high-hat mob, dear. What do you say?"

Most of the Negroes had returned to the fire now, working industriously through the smoldering wreck of the schoolhouse, drenching the flames with buckets of water. Marie felt queasy and dispirited. She wanted to go back to Maude's house and sit with the children for a while, perhaps write a letter home, or another to Harry whose letters lately seemed content, though Marie believed he missed his family more than he was willing to confess.

Rachel asked her, "Will you be all right, dear, if CW and I take a little walk? We won't be long."

"Of course." Marie adjusted the angle of her umbrella to the cold raindrops. "I'll just wait here."

"We'll be back straight away, I promise." Rachel took CW by the hand. "Honey, come with me."

They walked off toward the collection of police cars, leaving Marie alone with Lucius. She watched a group of Negroes tear apart a pile of burning timber with pickaxes, stirring through the hot cinders, scattering sparks into the night.

"It's so awful," Marie heard herself remark, and that was truth. She felt ashamed for not having helped with the bucket brigade. Why had she let Rachel talk her out of it?

Lucius held his hat out into the rain to rinse the ash off the rim. "The niggers had a still in the cellar."

"Pardon me?"

"Gallon jugs of kerosene oil and molasses moonshine, parked right down there under the hot stove, likely hidden inside a stack of straw and old sodden boxes or some such. Way that roof blowed off, I'd guess their hootch was better'n ninety-proof. Probably a lightning bolt snaked itself down the chimney, and BOOM! Hello, Jesus! Just like Kehoe done to that Michigan school."

"What will the police say?"

Lucius shrugged. "Not much now, I'd expect. The evidence is all floatin' 'round heaven."

"My goodness."

"Say, honey, you ought to come downtown tomorrow and have a talk with Jimmy Delahaye. He's always looking for help in the restaurant. I'll bet he'll give you a job."

"Do you think so?" She was hopeful. She needed to find work, needed to belong.

"Oh, I'm sure of it. Enid quit last week and we ain't found nobody else to take her place at the register."

Marie smiled. "Why, thank you. I'll do that. I'm sure I'd enjoy being with people much more than typing in an office."

Nauseated from the smell of ash and cinder, she excused herself from Lucius' company and headed back to CW's Ford. She no longer noticed the rain drenching her clothes, chilling her skin. She focused her eyes straight ahead and weaved her way under the dripping pine trees toward the automobiles parked along the muddy lane. Two of the squad cars rolled out onto the road, then rattled off. She noticed a pack of grim-faced men hurrying for another automobile parked near CW's. They piled into a Dodge touring car and roared away into the dark. As Marie reached CW's Ford, she heard her name called from the damp pine grove behind her. She turned to see Rachel and CW rushing through the trees toward her.

"Hurry, dear!" Rachel shouted, excitement drawn on her face. "Get in the car!"

Another automobile farther up the road pulled out into the rain and roared off.

Marie climbed into the rear seat of the Ford and pulled the door closed behind her. CW jumped into the front seat and started the engine after Rachel slid in beside him. As he put the automobile in gear, Rachel turned to Marie. "Something awful's happened."

The river was black and cold and wild in the rainy dark. Tall cottonwoods arched over the swirling water and swayed in the wind. The grassy soil was soaked and muddy, smelling of rot and humid undergrowth. Marie followed Rachel and CW through a wet thicket of buttonbush toward the riverbank where she saw a dozen men or more on the embankment, police and civilians alike, occupied with a grisly discovery in a backwater beneath a grove of willows at the river's edge. The body of a small boy lay drenched in mud, his skull crushed by a violent blow. His name was Boy-Allen.

"He lived just down the street," said Rachel, edging close to the water just upriver from the crowd of men surrounding the body. She clung to CW's arm, oblivious to a drizzling rain. "The poor thing delivered our morning paper."

Marie stood quietly nearby, ill at the sight of the poor child. She secretly hoped his death had been an accident, a pathetic fall perhaps or some other unfortunate circumstance. Isn't guilt over steps not taken preferable to the helplessness of the unknown? Her own tragedy of burying a first born had taken years to subdue. But now she'd overheard the police trading opinions of a deliberate killing, a murder, and felt sick to her stomach.

"It's what we've come to these days," CW suggested, water dripping from his gray felt hat. "Slaughtering our young."

Rachel frowned. "What a horrid thing to say."

"Well, I believe it's true," CW argued, "this moral arrogance of ours notwithstanding. Modern thinking would have us convinced that a new electric Frigidaire in every kitchen will free us of all evils, as if profit and convenience were signposts along the road to heaven. For Godsakes, unless we learn to behave a lot better toward each other, I'd say we're pretty well fixed to be damned, and this sad child is the proof of it."

Heartbroken for Boy-Allen's mother, Marie watched a doctor stride grim-faced out of the rainy gloom with a pair of attendants trailing behind, while one of the policemen waded into muddy backwater up to his knees. Directing several electric lanterns close above him, the doctor knelt low beside the tortured corpse of Boy-Allen and began his examination. Dialogue among the concerned diminished. The river lapped at the reedy shore. In all her life, Marie had never believed that those dark angels who haunt this world have authority over the weak and tender-hearted. Both goodness and evil have consequences. Virtue is chosen, not endowed, while pleas for mercy ring in our ears like the beckoning of old church bells. We hear, or do not, according to our own unceasing struggle with compassion and piety.

The rain persisted almost till morning.

JUNE

BY EARLY SUMMER, Marie had taken a job as cashier at Delahaye's Restaurant in downtown Bellemont. She worked half a day from eight until two in the afternoon, which allowed her to share the expense of boarding at Maude's house on College Street. The children played all about the neighborhood with youngsters their own age and were happy to be out of doors. So far, nobody had been arrested for the ugly murder of Boy-Allen, a circumstance that troubled Marie and many other mothers across town. Detectives traveled from Houston and Dallas to help with the investigation, but left without solving the crime. The newspapers worried Marie with talk of further killings, then quit discussing the story entirely. A month passed and the fear engendered by Boy-Allen's death faded to rumor and gossip. Only mothers kept a suspicious eye on shadows after dark, Marie among them. This disconcerting journey into the South was trying enough, but to have a murder occur practically in her backyard so soon upon arrival was horrifying. At night with the children asleep beside her, Marie was haunted by the blackest thoughts: Henry drowning in the river or trampled under hoof, Cissie tumbling off a roof or disappearing somehow into the twilight like poor Boy-Allen. What parent lacks these fears? Her marriage troubled by her husband's inscrutable behavior, Marie's heart wrapped about her children and refused to let go.

Life went on.

Maude enjoyed the company of her club ladies three afternoons and one evening a week and did her laundry and housekeeping in peace. Rachel went to work at the insurance office and paraded out in the evenings on CW's arm when he was in town, and with friends when he wasn't. Each morning after writing letters, either to Harry or her family back home, Marie walked beneath the elm trees and cottonwoods that led downtown, stopping to exchange pleasantries with the invalid Mr. Gray seated on his shady porch at Third Street, and Dora Bennett, who knew her way around Bellemont and offered Marie fine advice and fresh vegetables from her garden at Church Street. If Marie worked hard and earned her keep, Harry would be proud of her — not that she needed his approval, mind you. She would do her job well and honestly because that was how she had been raised. A husband's opinion had nothing to do with it. Still, she could not deny that effort and ability had always been Harry's constant hall-marks to success, attributes Marie hoped she also possessed — even as she tried to forgive Harry for sending her here. At the cash register she felt calm as a fish, despite the noise of shouting men and banging billiard balls upstairs. The men who frequented Delahaye's were most-ly hard-smoking roughnecks from the mills and oil fields, or those who held no job of any sort and had too much time on their hands. Most were lonely, showing hurt in their eyes while they joked about skirts and bumpy mattresses. Listening to their chatter, Marie guessed life's capriciousness had somehow stolen the lightness from their hearts. Men bear shame differently than women who talk teary, but make themselves agreeable without being scolded. Harry quoted after John D. Rockefeller that if a man believes himself rich and has everything he desires and feels that he needs, then he is really rich, even if he has only ten dollars. Poverty of confidence and hope drags men down-ward, sinks them in despair and bitterness. No good ever comes of it.

Marie sat at the cash register beneath a sign that said: **In God We Trust, All Others Pay Cash.** She counted and numbered receipts as quickly as she could while ringing up customers through the haze of cigar smoke. She was proud of how quick she was. Automobiles rattled past outdoors. Men came and went. In the corner office up-stairs, Jimmy Delahaye was yelling into the telephone, complaining about something or other. Ordinarily, Marie refused to pry into other people's concerns or eavesdrop on conversations that did not directly involve her. Here, she found herself tipping an ear in one direction and then another, trying to learn what she could about her new neighbors. She was awfully curious about this character and that, who was trustworthy or not, whose heart had been broken by whom, who hoped to travel abroad if that oil well ever came in a gusher. More than once she bit her lip before suggesting a solution to some nasty contention because she felt like a guest in town and determined to keep her place until she became more comfortable. She offered opinions only when asked and avoided all manner of disputes. At home, Harry often thought her timid, and there was some truth in that, but Marie also believed the tongue can be an unruly member and not every point of view needs airing in public.

She took a pair of dimes from the man at the counter and dropped them into the till. "Thank you, sir."

"Yes, ma'am," the fellow said, touching the tip of his hat and walking off. Marie reached into the drawer beneath the cash register for a rubberband to bind the receipts. She felt confident today.

Idabelle Collins came out of the kitchen, wiping her hands clean on the white apron she wore. Her red hair was in a net and beads of perspiration dotted her forehead. She was the skinniest woman Marie had ever known, but pretty in a country way. She was the first friend Marie had made in town, and Harry had warned she was a gossip, which made her all the more enjoyable. She was also desperately oversexed, and eyed every fellow that came and went.

"Jimmy wants to see you upstairs before you leave."

"Oh?"

"Now don't get yourself all worked up," Idabelle said, seeing worry rise in Marie's face. She took off her glasses. "He's thinking about offering you another few hours work."

"I'm not sure I ought to take on any more hours than I already have. Did he mention what sort of work it would be?"

Idabelle shook her head. "But a body can't be choosy when the offerings are slim."

"Well, I have my children to consider. They already spend half the day without me. I can't imagine working until suppertime." She was also deathly afraid of the children running all over creation while she was away downtown and Boy-Allen's killer remained at large. Trying to be brave, and actually doing so, was still beyond her capacity.

"Sweetheart, ideals won't put a patch on little Henry's trousers," Idabelle said, her voice rising at the end of her thought. She whistled the same "Yankee Doodle Dandy" she always did whenever she chose to leave her audience hanging, then gave Marie a smile and sat down behind the cash register just as another pair of customers came up, cash in hand. "May I help you gentlemen?"

"Good-bye, Idabelle." Marie smiled. "And thank you very much for the advice." Regardless of the objections she raised, Marie knew she needed the money.

"Of course," Idabelle replied, holding a hand out to the man standing in front of her. "Your bill, please?"

Money was always on the table to be worried over. Not forty-eight hours passed after Marie's arrival before Maude took the opportunity to remark how quickly her sugar had run out. The children loved it on their oatmeal and Maude knew this. Also, though, Rachel poured it in her tea and coffee like an addict and Maude rarely did more than raise an eyebrow. It wasn't at all fair, but Marie refused to complain. Instead, she hustled downtown to the market and bought enough to last all summer. Intrigued by the idea of earning another dollar or two a day, Marie followed the bar to the back of the restaurant and up the rear staircase to Jimmy Delahaye's office where a sign on the door read:

BE BRIEF, WE HAVE OUR LIVING TO MAKE!

The windowless hallway was dark and musty, smelling of tobacco and old wood. Delahaye had several framed photographs hiding cracks in the wallpaper just above the wainscotting, none of which could be appreciated in the dim light. Supposedly the pictures portrayed members of Delahaye's family in an earlier time, although the resemblance was not apparent.

Delahaye's office door was cracked open, so Marie walked up to the threshold and stood patiently outside until he noticed her. Delahaye was busy talking on the telephone. "See, I got myself a delivery problem. Y'all aren't delivering me nothing."

He nodded at Marie and directed her to an old horsehair sofa under the window that overlooked Main Street. Delahaye had a cigar smoldering in an ashtray on his desk and a stack of papers piled beside a plate of day-old lemon cookies baked by Idabelle. His office was cramped and disordered and stuffy with the odor of cigar smoke and Canadian whiskey everyone knew he drank after hours when the building was closed. He was just a year younger than Harry, slender and tall, and wore up-to-the-minute suits and collars and a razor-sharp haircut. According to Idabelle, he was as fine a looking gentleman as there was in the county and had a great lot of sex appeal. Marie agreed that Jimmy Delahaye had a firm jaw and a blue twinkle in his eye that no doubt kept his dance card full on Saturday nights. She didn't mind at all sitting in his office.

"Yes, yes, and then?" Delahaye spoke briskly into the phone. "I tell you, we've got that beaten flat. Yes sir, forty per! … Oh bushwa! A lot he cared for those chuckleheads. They were chasing around like the Rebel cavalry while his sonofabitch brother cleaned up over ten grand in Rooney's cotton mill… No, Perry made that dough square and he wasn't born with any phenomenal intellect, either."

Jimmy Delahaye cupped his hand over the mouthpiece. "I'll be through in a second, honey. You just sit tight."

Marie smiled and pretended not to notice how handsome he was, though she felt like a schoolgirl whenever he smiled at her. Once upon a time, Harry had produced that effect on her, too. There were long-ago afternoons canoeing on Cedar Lake and picnics beneath the river bluff north of Farrington where he strummed the ukulele, rather badly, and brought a smile to her lips that made her feel like a woman when Marie doubted she'd ever lose her girlhood. Remembering made her feel lonely, so she looked out the front window over Main Street where a tattered and sun-faded Confederate flag above the courthouse fluttered in the wind. The children had gone to the river after breakfast with their little friends from down the block. Henry had taken one of Harry's father's old fishing poles with him, swearing to bring back catfish for supper, although he'd never caught one in his life. Harry had never cared much for fishing. On the one occasion he went out with Frenchy and Cousin Alvin to the Mississippi, Harry lost a pole in the current and groused about a pair of shoes ruined in the muck at the river's edge. Frenchy called Harry a milquetoast and got a laugh from the rest of the Pendergasts who knew it to be true and tried in vain to steer Marie into Buddy Theale's embrace instead. No such luck. She'd have nothing to do with a fellow who stuffed birds for a living, and told her cousins to butt out. Were her children not the darlings they turned out to be, perhaps she might admit she'd chosen poorly. But love has its own authority and won't be ignored.

The handsome Jimmy Delahaye spoke again into the phone, "Like I said, this bird knows his way around, all right. What he did was grab a sheet of paper and wrote down a figure so small I had to take out a spyglass to read it. I says to him, 'Listen friend, is this supposed to be funny? Are y'all clowning around here?' So he blows out on me. The next thing I know he's got a lawyer and a date in court. It's a wonder I'm still in business…. How's that?" Delahaye laughed. "Well, bumping him off'd leave me four hundred in arrears. I got obligations, see: room rent, back rent, and a monkey suit to hire for the Fourth. So strike that off the record…. Huh? … I said, *Hoffman*! Try taking the cigar out of your ear. He's the little fellow with a nutcracker face, that squirt in George's speakie who puffed himself up about all the jack he made in Houston after the War." Cupping his hand over the phone again, Delahaye told Marie, "I'll be right along, honey. Have a cookie if you like."

He shoved the plate across the desk and winked. She knew he liked her, but shook her head to the cookies, having sampled one yesterday morning when they were still fresh. Besides, her stomach was too tickled with nerves to eat a thing. She tried to hide a smile. When he offered her more hours, she might agree if he asked her sweetly. Had he kissed any girls this week?

"Well, listen, pal," Delahaye continued, "there's a lot to admire in that combine, but hiring all those niggers of his'd put me in a flat spin, so I got to say no…. Sure, that'd be swell…. Thanks, pal. So long."

Delahaye put down the phone and leaned back in his chair. He said to Marie, "Well, sweetheart, I got a proposition for you."

He grinned and lit a fresh cigar. His flirting eyes gave Marie a pleasant shiver. She felt herself blush.

"A proposition?" Had she heard him correctly? Her throat tightened.

"Yes, ma'am," he said, "a proposition. See, I like you, honey. You work hard. You're on time. You don't steal from me. I like that."

"Well, I can't imagine stealing from anybody." Marie had found a purse once when she was a girl and taken the money and spent it on ice cream cones for her friends. When she'd told her mother about the purse, she was forced to go house to house until she found the owner, then to pay back the money she had stolen out of her own allowance, a lesson she never forgot.

"I know you can't," he smiled. "You're honest as a lamb, and I like that, too."

Gaining her confidence, Marie raised an eyebrow. She didn't intend to be meek. "What do you mean by 'proposition'?"

Just uttering that question came off as fresh to Marie. What on earth had gotten into her?

Delahaye leaned forward across his desk. "Well, you see, honey, I've never had a secretary. Fellows I deal with from Galveston to San Antonio, Texas Rockefeller-sorts, have their own personal secretaries taking dictation and opening boxes, sorting mail. I started thinking, things going so swell lately, maybe I ought to get me one, too."

"I'm sure you'd find a secretary very helpful." Was she flirting now, too? Her knees trembled and she felt a pleasant flush. She was enjoying this. Harry would've been furious, but he could go take a flying leap into a rose bush for all she cared at this moment.

"So what do you say?"

"You'd like to hire me as your secretary?" Harry had once hired a stenographer from Joliet back when he was still working in Farrington, despite Marie's insistence that she was more than capable of doing the job herself. After the girl had dropped a Multigraph machine on her foot, he'd let her out and hadn't bothered interviewing another, nor had he given Marie a chance. She'd felt bitter about it for months afterward, yet never said a word.

"Yes, ma'am, I would." He showed his teeth through a wide smile, and bit down on his cigar. "What do you say?"

"Well, I don't know. I've just learned the register."

Delahaye laughed. "You like ringing up customers, do you? That's sweet."

Marie felt herself blush again. Delahaye had a way of making her feel awkward and girlish. He was so very handsome. My goodness! How many girls had he kissed? Did he want to kiss her, too? What might she do if he tried? Well, she certainly wouldn't run!

"I just meant that learning another job, well, perhaps I wouldn't be any good at it. I've never worked as a secretary for anyone before. I'm not sure I'd know what was required of me."

"Aw, there'd be nothing to it." Delahaye took a couple puffs off the cigar and leaned back in his chair again. "I can train you in a couple days. We'll put Idabelle on the register while you're learning and Lucius behind the counter. If I hide his liquor, he'll do just swell. And if you like, I'll give you a few hours downstairs every week, too, just so you don't feel lonesome for the register. What do you say?"

Before Marie could answer, a tremendous noise thundered from the street below, then the crash of shattering glass in the dining room downstairs.

Delahaye ran to the window. "Good God!"

He rushed out of his office.

Marie hurried to the window and looked out at the wreck of a black delivery truck tipped on its side in the middle of the street and spewing steam into the noon air. Knocked half onto the sidewalk was the mangled heap of a two-tone brown Dodge sedan impaled upside-down on the lower half of the streetlamp in front of Delahaye's restaurant. The driver of the delivery truck hung out the door, blood streaming from a deep gash across his forehead. Marie saw people running down the sidewalk toward the accident. Frightened for the drivers, she hurried downstairs where she found confusion reigning. The upper section of the streetlamp had been sheared off by the careening Dodge and hurled through the plate-glass window, cascading glass throughout the crowded dining room. Dust and smoke clouded the air. The Dodge was smoldering, its lifeless driver hanging through a jagged fracture in the windshield. Lucius Beauchamp yelled for buckets of water. Marie rushed behind the cash register to the end of the counter where Idabelle had just risen from cover, shock drawn on her face. A small cut to the cheek dripped blood onto the front of Idabelle's blouse. Determined to stop the bleeding, Marie went straight into the kitchen to fetch a cloth. She ran water onto it and brought it back out to Idabelle and dabbed the cut clean of blood. Everywhere in the restaurant the smell of gasoline was strong and Marie heard Delahaye outdoors yelling frantically for somebody to call the firehouse.

"Heavens, I feel faint," Idabelle said, sitting on the stool behind the register.

"I think we ought to go outdoors into the fresh air," Marie said, keeping one eye on the smashed automobile and the gasoline leak. She was terrified of the motor exploding. Steam from the punctured radiator issued out from under the dented hood in a swelling hiss. She kept her attention away from the body of the driver. Death's intimate posture, sudden and incontrovertible, gave her a touch of vertigo. She hooked an arm under Idabelle's left shoulder and lifted her to her feet. Men left the dining room through the smashed front window, water buckets in hand.

Marie helped Idabelle around the bar toward the front door, preferring not to cross the threshold of broken glass where more men were gathering with water buckets. Before she reached the door, a great BANG echoed through the restaurant. Her heart skipped a beat and Idabelle fainted, crumpling to the floor.

"Explosion!" someone from outside yelled. "It's blowing up!"

The crowd on the sidewalk beside the front window rolled back like the tide on Lake Michigan as smoke billowed up from under the twisted hood of the Dodge.

A man standing next to Delahaye dropped his bucket and ran out into the street.

Scared half out of her wits, Marie looked at the automobile and saw Delahaye and Lucius Beauchamp swatting at the engine hood with wet towels. Delahaye yelled at the men who had retreated into the street, "GET THE HELL BACK HERE!"

Marie cradled Idabelle's head in her hands, stroking her cheeks, trying her best to bring the woman back to consciousness even as her own legs were shaking. Delahaye saw the two women and tossed his towel aside and hurried over.

"What the hell happened to Ida?"

"She fainted," Marie said, looking up at him. "The noise scared her. She'll be all right."

"Is she hurt?"

"Just her cheek. It's only a small cut." Marie couldn't stop shaking. Was she about to faint, too? Good grief, it seemed as if the world was coming to an end. Where were her children?

"Let's get her out of the building," Delahaye said, grabbing Idabelle and hoisting her up. He yelled out to the men in the street. "Throw some water on the hood, for Christsakes!" As he slung Idabelle over his shoulder, Delahaye muttered, "Goddamn cowards."

A fire engine arrived. As she followed Delahaye out of the building, Marie watched the truck discharge hoses, which were quickly attached to the hydrant two stores down from the restaurant. Idabelle had been taken across the street to recuperate in the shade of the willow trees. A crowd encircled both the smashed front window and the injured truck driver who was still in the cab holding a wet towel as a cold compress to his head wound to stanch the bleeding. Marie heard a siren approaching from across town. She hoped it was an ambulance.

A high afternoon wind twisted the smoke rising from the smashed Dodge into wispy funnels. The crowd had grown to more than a hundred, swelling across the street onto the other sidewalks, the atmosphere almost festive with excitement and danger. Children wandered on the fringe, giggling and hiding, worry and joy on their tiny faces. Still jittery with fear, Marie searched for her own children, hoping if they were about, they would have sense enough to remain at a safe distance. Cissie was born nosy and adventurous, a wearying combination. She'd drag timid Henry along just to be contrary. But the very fact that Marie hadn't seen Cissie sitting atop the fire engine or poking her face into the ruined Dodge meant she was off somewhere else.

Jimmy Delahaye emerged from the gaping hole in the plate-glass window, waving his arms and shouting for everyone to get away from the building. A pair of firemen came down toward him, hurriedly dragging their hose along toward the Dodge. People on the sidewalk began backing up. A second engine, siren wailing, rolled to a stop in the middle of the street a dozen yards or so from the wrecked truck. Three firemen ran a hose from the hydrant on the next corner down the sidewalk and up to the front of Delahaye's. More smoke poured out of the Dodge and again the crowd retreated into the street. An ambulance roared toward the restaurant from uptown. Marie found herself standing only a few feet from the tipped-over truck, just a couple of yards behind the rear bumper where the man she had seen hanging out of the wreck only a few minutes ago was lying flat on his back by the curb. He had suffered an awful laceration to his forehead and another Marie had not seen to his left shoulder. One leg was twisted oddly away from his torso, trouser-leg soaked in blood. His face was gritty and raw as sunburn, his eyes glassy. A trio of men, one of whom Marie took to be a doctor, were speaking to the driver and attending to his agony while awaiting an ambulance. As Marie inched forward, shoved by the crowd at her back, she heard the man moaning over and over, "Mable! Won't somebody please call Mable!"

— 2 —

When Marie returned from downtown, she found Rachel playing the piano alone in the sitting room. All the windows in the house were flung open and a pleasant breeze swept back the curtain lace and chinked the dangling prisms on Maude's glass table lamp. In the mid-afternoon, indoors was cool and smelled of fresh flowers. Marie listened to the casual way Rachel fingered the piano keys in a slow, almost arrhythmic rendering of "Beautiful Dreamer." Marie had thought only radio programs held Rachel's musical interest. Harry had owned his own piano in Farrington and played most evenings when he was not occupied with business or billiards. He performed lovely ballads with the lightest touch on the keys and rarely required sheet music, while his voice was strong and natural. Listening to him play while she did housework upstairs or puttered in the garden warmed Marie's heart. After their first-born's death that awful gray afternoon at Lake Calhoun, Harry sat at the piano every evening for a month, refusing to speak a word while Marie suffered little David's drowning in guilt and silence; for a season, she believed his playing had helped heal them both, but as the years went by she saw that was not so.

Marie slipped into the sitting room by increments, hoping not to disturb Rachel. She leaned against the doorframe and watched Rachel's fingers glide across the keys. She played more softly than did her brother, extracting from the instrument her own distinction. Marie listened until Rachel finished, then remarked, "You play wonderfully."

Rachel frowned, swiveling on the piano bench to face Marie. She was wearing a pale rose frock and she was barefoot. She was still lovely as ever. Little wonder CW had fallen for her. "I despise this instrument. I wish Mother had never persuaded me to take lessons."

"Why do you say that?"

"Because I play like a cow. Nothing ever sounds like I want it to. I feel as though I could do as well banging on the keyboard with my elbows. Harry is much better. He plays like an angel."

Marie smiled. "Yes, he does."

"Did he sell the Bösendorfer?"

"Yes."

"That's a shame. It was a beautiful piano." Rachel got up and walked over to the raised window and nudged the curtain lace open a few inches with the back of her hand and looked out to the street. A brief draft swept into the house, fluttering against her frock and the frilly antimacassars on Maude's walnut side table.

Marie said, "Harry told me it was foolish to choose between a piece of furniture and winter clothes for the children."

"He called the Bösendorfer a piece of furniture?"

"Yes."

"Hmm."

Reluctantly, Marie added, "Well, he really hadn't played all that much recently, so I suppose he didn't feel about it quite like he had when your mother gave it to him."

Actually, the past year or so, she'd noticed that Harry hadn't touched the keys at all. He seemed indifferent to music, or sweet pleasures of any sort. She had no clear idea why, but she supposed it had something to do with what he did while he was away. Her mother once told her that our smiles fade for one even as they bloom for another. Marie hoped that wasn't true with Harry, because she wasn't ready to let go. Everything else aside, for better or worse, she still loved him so much.

Rachel let the curtains close and walked over to the Crosley set, switched it on, then sat down on the couch and relaxed. A sweet ballad from the station in Austin filtered into the room. She said, "I remember the look on Harry's face when he came in and saw it sitting here. I swear we thought he would cry for joy. He'd never responded like that to a gift before. To think he'd sell it as furniture now is almost beyond belief. Mother would have a fit."

"You won't tell her, will you?"

"Heavens, no! She'd disown me and throw us all out into the street. That piano cost her more than … well, I'm sure you have an idea."

"Yes, I suppose I do." Harry, too, spoke often against needless spending. Marie's mother thought him something of a skinflint, but Marie believed he was frugal for his family's benefit.

"Anyhow, I hate playing and wouldn't be sad in the least if Mother sold ours as well."

Marie went to the piano and sat down, running her fingers lightly over the keyboard, though not depressing any of the keys. Dust had gathered in between the black and ivory. She'd take a cloth to it later on. Maude dusted, but not as thoroughly as Marie who learned from her own mother how to spit and polish.

"You'll be coming with us to the circus tonight, won't you?" Rachel asked. "CW'll be here at half past seven to pick us up."

Marie shook her head. "I promised your mother I'd stay home and keep her company. The children'll go, though. It's been two years since they saw the circus. They'll have a wonderful time."

"You shouldn't feel you have to stay home with Mother. She always has hundreds of things to do, besides which her club ladies are coming out this evening, so I doubt she cares one way or the other."

"Well, she asked me to."

"Oh, really? That's queer. I wonder why. Did she say?"

"No, only that she'd appreciate the company." Also, Marie knew it was important to try and please Maude by being friendly and helpful whenever she could.

"I wonder if she's having her change of life again." Rachel laughed, then caught herself.

"I don't mind staying home, actually," Marie said, lying slightly. "I've been to the circus dozens of times. It's lots of fun, but I'm sure there'll be others. I'll go next time."

"Of course you will," Rachel replied, shaking her head. "Mother's got you all knotted up, doesn't she? Why, I'll bet you haven't the faintest notion what you should and shouldn't do."

A scowl on her face, she walked over to the front door and opened it and looked out into the dusty street as a noisy Ford rumbled by. Marie got up from the piano and joined her. Rachel went out onto the porch and took a seat in the wicker settee and fanned her face with her hands. Marie followed and sat in the chair beside her. She told Rachel about the motor accident outside of Delahaye's restaurant.

"My goodness! I'll bet you liquor was involved. When isn't there with a smash-up? Was anybody arrested?"

"I haven't the least idea. It was a horrible mess. I'll probably have nightmares." Hardly anything gave her more fright than auto smash-ups.

"We're supposed to be dry, you know, but I don't doubt we have more drunks here on our streets than anywhere else in Texas. We've probably never been wetter. Mother's club ladies served a pitcher of lemonade last week that was nothing less than alcohol drained from lemon extract frozen in a cake of ice. Trudy refused to admit it, of course, but I've seen bottles of pear extract in her pantry and I know her cats don't imbibe."

Marie laughed. She couldn't imagine Maude drinking liquor on the sly.

Rachel asked, "Has Idabelle offered you a chock beer yet?"

She shook her head. "I've never even heard of such a thing."

"Go on!"

Marie blushed. "Well, I haven't, although I presume it's some new sort of fancy bootleg liquor. Is that right?"

Rachel giggled. "Why dear, you are bucking the times, aren't you?"

"Pardon?" Why hadn't Harry told her these things? She felt like such a fool.

"Well, you ought to know that Lucius and Idabelle drive to Dallas once a month to buy a carload of booze that's nothing more than water, old blackstrap molasses, old yeast, and old cornpone stirred together and left to stew for three weeks. It's sold all over town. They claim it's got a swell kick, although I've never been that thirsty. CW says he's heard of people in New Orleans poisoning themselves with the same cheap liquor. Of course, I'm sure that's just gossip."

Rachel smiled.

As they sat for a few minutes in silence, Marie thought about the man injured in the wreck, that horrid fear in his eyes, his plaintive voice; and the poor fellow in the brown Dodge who hadn't survived. Had the consumption of unlicensed liquor been his end? Marie knew the advantages of temperance went mostly unheeded in a country sopping with rum. Yet she also tended to believe it was the portion and right of every man to walk a crooked path if he so chose. Both virtue and calamity lie in wait. A foundation of optimism is often the only remedy for these trials. Though all our lives are encumbered by tragedy, the courageous heart looks forward and persists.

Rachel sighed. "It's dreadfully hot today, don't you think? I sometimes wonder why I've continued to live here. There must be somewhere else more appealing."

Marie smiled. "There are attachments." Although she'd left Illinois, she wasn't sure how long she'd be able to stay away. Every night she dreamed of the farm and her old cat.

Rachel dismissed the notion with a wave of her hand. "Why live somewhere you despise just because you were born there? That makes no sense whatsoever. Look at Harry. Do you think for a minute he'd come back here? Not on your life! He couldn't stand this one-horse town, absolutely despised it. Mother would deny that, of course, but believe me, it's the truth. Harry couldn't wait to leave. Once Daddy died, that just sealed the bargain. I'm surprised my brother sent you here, truth be told. I don't know what sort of difficulties you were having, and I'm not asking you to tell me, but it must have been quite serious for Harry to make this kind of decision. I know that ordinarily he'd never have considered it. Mother was thrilled, of course, thinking that Harry would be coming back, too. She misses him terribly, though she's never said a word."

"I'm sure that's so." Marie always wondered how Maude felt about this entire arrangement. Harry had made it sound as if she'd be thrilled to see her grandchildren, which may have been so, but that opinion had not yet crossed Maude's lips. Did she really favor Harry above Rachel? Would Maude still favor her son if she knew Harry's sins the way Marie did? Maude had never traveled north, not for the wedding, nor David's funeral. There were always reasons upon reasons, none more convincing than her own desire to stay home to her life here in Bellemont. Harry wrote and cajoled and begged, but Maude remained steadfast; if she was to be a grandmother, the children would have to be placed on her lap. And so it went. *Family*, Aunt Hattie once told Marie, *is a strange concoction.*

A two-door Chevrolet roared past, exhaling a foul cloud of exhaust into the afternoon air, stirring dust and leaves into small whirlwinds.

"She admires CW, I think," said Marie, once the dust had settled and the draft faded.

"Who does?"

"Your mother."

Rachel gave a sarcastic laugh. "Why, I doubt she approves at all! In fact, I'm quite sure she loathes him. I know she hates the very idea of us making love out on her wonderful porch for all the world to see. Not that I care, mind you. If there's anything I've learned to hold onto as my own, it's my relationship with the gentlemen I see. Mother understands that, or at least she's aware of what sort of trouble it causes whenever she even considers interfering."

Rachel got up and strolled to the end of the porch and leaned against one of the posts.

Marie said, "Is it his religion she objects to?"

"Will a cat eat liver?" Rachel replied. "Of course it is, among other things."

"Such as? If you don't mind my asking."

"She thinks he's too big for his Catholic britches, to put it bluntly. She thinks he's got snooty ideas and a fast tongue and no true sense of morals and decency. To tell you the truth, she believes he's a sex fiend."

Marie frowned, shocked at the inference. "She said that?"

"Well, of course not," Rachel said, "she doesn't need to. I know how Mother thinks. CW might just as well be Chinese for all her purposes in discussing his behavior. She has no appreciation whatsoever for anyone or anything that exists outside of this town. She'd feel the same about you, if it weren't for Harry. I'm sure you've figured that much out by now. Having you here only reminds her that Harry isn't. Maybe she even resents you for reminding her, I don't know."

"Well, I — "

Rachel interrupted her. "Look, the fact is, Mother's quite narrow-minded and doesn't seem to mind it a bit." She fanned her face with her hands. "Oh, I don't know why I bother discussing her anyhow. I've trained Mother to leave me alone, and she still makes me so angry sometimes I could just throw myself in front of a truck."

Marie saw a parade of dusty children and animals spilling out of the cottonwood grove across the street, her daughter Cissie at the head of the pack leading a gray swaybacked pony by a short rope.

"Well, look at this!" she said to Rachel, and burst out laughing.

"Isn't he beautiful?" Cissie remarked proudly, tying the pony to the backyard gate. The other children milled about the sidewalk: Henry beside blonde Lili Jessup from next door; a scrawny youngster with thick eyeglasses named Abel Kritt who lived down the street and had hold of a cocker spaniel by a cloth leash; and two tiny Negro girls, Eva and Caroline, barefoot and dusty in floral flour-sack dresses, daughters of the handyman Maude hired to repair the storm gutters after the last rain. Cissie told her mother, "His name's Mr. Slopey and he's a race horse."

"Is that so?" Marie studied the old swayback, its mangy tail, ugly and hopeless, precisely the sort of animal her daughter would rescue and fall in love with. Cissie was always bringing animals home. A stray dog, a basket of kittens, a chicken, a bullfrog, a wounded robin, all recipients of Cissie's unconditional compassion. Cissie loved animals of all kinds. In Farrington, she'd belonged to 4-H and had entries at the October Fair. Last year, her lamb Twinkle won third prize. Her attachment to it was so dear that Twinkle was allowed to live out her natural years in the Pendergast back pasture, safe from the carving knife. Marie smiled, her sweet lovely daughter, Florence Nightingale to the animal kingdom.

"We found him by the river and he followed us home," Cissie explained. "He was awful lonely. Isn't that right, Lili?"

The Jessup girl nodded while Caroline and Eva fooled with each other's dark braids. Little towheaded Abel Kritt let a black bug scurry out of his hand as Marie turned her attention to Henry who was trying to hide behind the old pony, his overalls muddy and wet, water dripping still from his cowlick. "Henry Albert Hennesey! What on earth?"

He cracked a sheepish grin. "I been swimming, Momma."

"He fell in the river," Cissie corrected, "chasing after a silly little catfish. I warned him to stay on the riverbank, but he disobeyed me. He ought to've drowned. That'd taught him a lesson, don't you think?"

"Cissie!" Her daughter found sympathy to be a trying task, choosing instead to pick on her little brother at every turn. Marie scolded her constantly, but saw scant improvement. Perhaps she took after her father.

"Well, he never does a thing I tell him. He's awful!"

"It was polliwogs I was collecting, Momma," said Henry, chiming in on his own behalf. "And whales! Bigger'n our whole house!"

"And alligators, too?" Cissie asked, snidely. "Big awful green ones who swim 'round looking for stupid little boys?"

"That's how come I swum like a frog," Henry explained. "I went underwater and kicked out and swam — "

"Like a rock," Cissie interrupted, fingering her braids. "That's how he swam, as usual. If it wasn't for a pine log he bumped into and our friend Julius swimming out in his good clothes to save him, Henry'd be a goner." She snarled at her little brother, "Not that we'd miss him all that much, the little scamp. I told Henry the next time he disobeys a direct order from me, I'll leave him for the wolves."

"Oh, Cissie." Marie shook her head, exasperated with her daughter. What she needed was a good spanking. Where was Harry? At least in those mournful years after David's drowning, he'd taught the children to swim, thank goodness. Now Cissie streaked through the water like a fish, while Henry, despite his sister's critical eye, did a very passable dog paddle. The thought of her children playing at the river made her terribly nervous, but she also knew they just couldn't be kept away. Thanks to Harry, if worst came to worst, they'd have a fighting chance. Nothing in life was safe, yet it had to be lived, not withstanding. Perhaps she ought to learn a simple dog paddle herself, if only for another gray and blustery afternoon.

Lili Jessup reached under the fence to pick up her little gray kitten. Henry swatted a pair of flies off the swayback's rump. Little Abel sat down on the curb to wipe off his eyeglasses. Caroline and Eva traded flower petals from the white aster bouquets they had picked in the woods.

Cissie asked, "We can keep him, can't we, Momma? He won't be a bother. You promised I could have my own horse."

Rachel spoke from the porch railing, "Mother'll flip her wig."

"We won't tell her," Cissie suggested. "We'll hide Mr. Slopey behind the barn and feed him after dark when Grandma goes to bed. She won't suspect a thing, I promise."

"A kind-hearted fraud, huh?" Rachel laughed. "Well, I expect we'll have to talk that over later, dear."

"It'll be up to your grandma, honey," Marie said, reasonably sure Maude would be sympathetic. She seemed to adore animals more than people. "We're guests here, remember."

"But we will keep him, won't we?" Cissie pleaded. "Oh, he's the sweetest horse I ever met. And he can do the swellest tricks."

"I don't doubt that for an instant."

"There's Julius now," Rachel said, directing Marie's attention down the street where the tall black man emerged from the cottonwood grove, his work clothes damp as Henry's, his boots caked with mud. Following him out of the woods was a small Negro boy in overalls carrying a fishing pole and a brown sack. Eva and Caroline hurried off down the dusty sidewalk, squealing with delight. Julius Reeves greeted them by hoisting both up onto his husky shoulders.

Rachel waved and called out to him. "Hello, Julius!"

Marie gave a pleasant wave, too. She'd known too few colored folks in her life and believed in kindness as a bridge between the races. Besides, Julius Reeves was the most congenial fellow she'd met in Bellemont, clear testimony to the pure idiocy of prejudice.

"Momma, Julius risked his life to save Henry," Cissie told her. "He was so brave. We were absolutely certain they'd both be swept away. I called for Lili to come and bring help, but she and Abel were too busy trying to capture Mr. Slopey who just slipped his rope and wandered off by his ownself. I guess he didn't want to go swimming with us." Cissie broke off a chunk of carrot she'd just pulled out of her pocket and guided it into Mr. Slopey's mouth. The swayback greedily devoured the carrot and sought another. "He's very spirited."

"I'm sure he is."

"See, that's how come I left Henry by himself, Momma," Cissie explained, "'cause I had to help Lili and Abel find Mr. Slopey. Only when I told Henry to stay away from the water, he disobeyed me. I told you, Momma, he oughtn't to be allowed out of the yard. He's entirely too young."

"Am not!" Henry yelled.

"Are so!"

"Children!" Marie glared at them both, embarrassed by their behavior. "Please!"

As Julius Reeves arrived in front of the house, he let his little girls slip back onto the sidewalk to play with their flower bouquets. Then he smiled at Rachel and Marie and tipped his hat. "Afternoon, Mrs. Hennesey. Afternoon to you, too, Miss Hennesey."

"I wasn't scared, Momma," Henry insisted, coming over and standing next to the black man. "I swam all by myself and held onto the log 'til I saw Julius coming for me. Then we both swum out of that old river together, him steerin' and me kickin'. Isn't that right, Julius?"

The black man smiled down on him. "Yessir, Mister Henry."

"Ain't no reason to drown on a sunny day, is there?" Henry asked, smiling up at the handyman. Nothing ever seemed to douse that grin. He was the happiest child Marie had ever known. Cousin Emeline argued that a sweet disposition follows a boy raised on sweets, and fed him cookies at every turn, but Marie believed her little Henry was just born happy.

"No, sir, there ain't."

"I'm sorry you had to get your clothes all wet," Marie said to Julius, "but thank you very much for rescuing my son."

"He's a fine boy," Julius replied, with a friendly smile.

"When he's not causing a stir," Cissie snapped.

"Don't take much for boys to get themselves into trouble," Julius said. "No, ma'am. Got one of my own right here. Willie, say afternoon to these nice ladies."

The boy lowered his eyes, sheepishly. "Afternoon, ma'ams."

"Hello, Willie," Marie said. "I'm very pleased to know you."

Cissie added, "Momma, Julius calls Eva and Caroline his 'rays of sunshine', don't you, Julius?"

The handyman nodded. "Yes, ma'am. I expect I do."

Marie watched a flight of yakking crows sail low over the summer trees, eastward across the blue sky toward the river. Abel and Henry ran out into the empty street to give chase. Abel chucked a stone that barely reached the switchgrass. Willie let his fishing pole dip until it dragged in the dust. Then he followed Henry and Abel to the blackberry thicket across the street.

Rachel came around to the front steps, descending to the sidewalk. "I've always thought those were the two prettiest names I ever heard — Eva and Caroline."

Julius nodded. "Thank you, ma'am."

"You're so lucky to have girls in the family. I've always believed that boys are troublemakers," Rachel added, sitting down on the bottom step and smoothing out her skirt. She made a sunshade for her eyes with the back of her hand. "Avoiding them at all costs should be the female aim in life. Not that it's possible, of course. Soon enough they grow up to be men and our entire sex humiliates itself falling all over them. Isn't that right, Julius? Why, I'll bet you had women worrying you to pieces when you came back from France."

"No, ma'am," the handyman replied, clearly embarrassed by Rachel's question. "That ain't exactly so."

"Oh, I'm sure you're just being modest." replied Rachel. She turned to Marie in time to take the breeze flush in her face. "He's our town's grandest hero of the war, you know."

"Is that so?" Marie asked, cheerfully. She admired his manners and dignity. Why couldn't more men be civil and glad?

The handyman shook his head, pearl beads of sweat gleaming on his skin in the noon glare. "Naw, that ain't so at all."

"Oh, of course you are," Rachel persisted. "Everybody knows it, too. You're just being modest again." She told Marie, "He hasn't an ounce of boastfulness, unlike some of the men around here."

Marie said, "Well, I'm sure everybody's very proud of him."

Julius looked down at his boots as his daughters hid behind him. "Ain't nobody more hero'n another once the shooting starts. Just plenty scared folks praying they gonna get home again. It ain't much to be proud of."

"Well, have it your own way. Modesty's silence deprives truth's consecration," said Rachel. "I'm sure if anyone from Bellemont had shot sixteen Germans and rescued a dozen or more American doughboys all by himself, we'd have another holiday here to celebrate." She turned to Cissie with the swayback, and Lili Jessup who sat up on the fence now chewing on a long stem of dried grass in her mouth. "Wouldn't you kids like that? A grand parade with lots of flowers and horses?"

"Could I be in it with Mr. Slopey?" Cissie asked, her eyes wide and blue.

"Of course," Rachel replied, giving Marie a wink. "Why not? He's family now, isn't he?"

Cissie threw an arm around her pony's neck and gave him a hug, saying, "Did you hear that, Mr. Slopey? You're family. So why'd you try to run away, Mr. Slopey? Didn't you know we love you?"

"That fishin' man was awful mean to him," little Henry said, back from across the street where Abel and Willie were poking long sticks into the blackberry thicket. Henry stroked the pony's mane. "I think he hurt Mr. Slopey's feelings."

"Which man was that?" Marie asked, somewhat nervously. Two mothers on Finch Street steadfastly refused to let their children out of doors unattended until the fiend who murdured Boy-Allen was apprehended. Marie wasn't terrified like some, but she had her worries. Who knew where the killer lurked? "Where was he?"

"By the river where we found Mr. Slopey under the cedar trees," Cissie answered. "He said that Mr. Slopey was ugly and that the only race he'd win was to the glue factory, so Lili got mad and called him a dirty liar, and that's when the man said Mr. Slopey wasn't going to be a champion of nothing except to the dog that ate him for supper."

Marie gasped, "Good gracious! What an awful thing to say!"

"Yes, ma'am," Cissie confirmed. "I think it made Mr. Slopey feel bad, and that's why he ran off like he did."

"Well, I'm sure he's feeling better now," said Marie, glad that her daughter had so much love in her heart. "After all, it's what's inside that counts, isn't it? And I'll bet he's a fine horse."

"I'll show him at the fair one day," Cissie said, "and he'll win a blue ribbon."

"That man said Mr. Slopey'd fit in better at the circus," Henry said, "with the three-headed turkeys."

"Did you hear any of this, Julius?" Rachel asked. "What they're talking about?"

"No, ma'am. I didn't see nobody but these three when I come back from fishing with my boy."

"It was earlier," Cissie corrected, "before Henry went in the water, and farther up the river where there was sand and rocks to sit on. I even dipped in myself, after removing my shoes, of course. It was awful pretty. And there were the loveliest birds singing, Momma. You ought've heard them. We were all having a good time until we met that horrible man. When I told him about Mr. Slopey likely winning a blue ribbon at the fair this year, he said I was a crazy person who ought to be locked away in the bughouse."

"Well, I can't imagine who'd say something like that to a child," Rachel remarked, fanning away a fly. "You don't think it was somebody from away, do you Julius?"

"Oh, those vagrants that fish by the river don't live 'round here. They just camp down there and get orn'ry when they can't catch nothing. I seen 'em all the time. I expect most of 'em are hopped up on liquor."

Marie asked, "Near Shantytown, you mean?" She hoped there weren't vagrants within shouting distance. Good grief! She'd be afraid to let the children out of the house.

Julius told her, "This side of the river, too, close enough I been telling my own youngsters to watch out so's they don't go too near 'em."

"Well, somebody ought to be notified of the danger, in any case," Rachel said. "It's our civic duty to keep the community safe for children, especially after that horrible tragedy with Boy-Allen. Wasn't he killed near there? Perhaps the police ought to be called out to investigate that fellow. Who's to say he's not the one we're looking for? If I had a child of my own, I don't know that I could cope these days. There seem to be cutthroats and ne'er-do-wells behind every bush in the country now." She turned again to Marie with a frown. "Wait until Mother hears about it. She'll certainly give somebody at City Hall a piece of her mind. She thinks the police've been dragging their heels about looking for suspects. I'm sure she'll find this whole mess absolutely disgraceful."

It was hot in the road and flies buzzed as smells of decay and manure traded about on the summer breeze. The old cat two doors down lolled its head out into the sunlight just under the dooryard foundation, dreaming in the afternoon heat.

Julius said, "Well, I expect I better get back on the job." He looked down at Henry who was patiently holding the rope Lili Jessup had wrapped around Mr. Slopey's neck. "You be careful now, Mister

Henry, next time you decide to go swimming in the river. Won't do nobody no good chasing you down into the Gulf, you hear?"

Henry nodded.

"We're going to the circus tonight," Cissie told Julius. "Soon as the sun goes down."

The handyman smiled. "So I hear."

"Eating cotton candy on the Ferris wheel is just about my favorite thing to do in the whole world," Cissie said. "I love the circus! Won't you come along with us? We'd have an awfully good time together." She looked at her mother. "Can't Julius and Eva and Caroline and Willie come with us to the circus tonight? I'm sure CW has plenty of room. I could ride in the rumble seat. I wouldn't mind. I'm sure it'll be warm out tonight."

Before Marie could reply, the black man said, "I appreciate the invitation, but family's got us occupied elsewhere this evening. You know how it is."

"Oh, I suppose so," Cissie replied, disappointed. "Family always comes first. That's what Momma tells me whenever we have to go out to Uncle Henry's for Sunday dinner. His mean old dogs try to bite me whenever I pet them. I never have a good time there. I hate my cousins. They're always awful to us, but Momma says it's important we go."

"It's not that bad," Marie explained to Julius. "I guess they just don't get along particularly well." Cissie didn't care for her relatives at all, but Marie always felt she picked it up from her father who hated the farm and refused to keep his opinion quiet, even around the children.

"They throw corncobs at me," Henry announced, a deep frown on his face. "I got a black eye once."

"And they make fun of us for living in town," Cissie added, "as if playing in manure every day makes them so wonderful. Just thinking about it makes me mad."

"No wonder Harry kept y'all in town," Rachel laughed. "He just despises getting dirty."

"I expect we'll be going along now," Julius said. "It was nice to see you again, ma'am."

"Thank you," Marie replied. "Have a pleasant evening."

"Children." His tiny daughters rose from the sidewalk where they'd been playing patty cake and brushed each other off. Julius smiled up at Rachel. "Good-day, Miss Hennesey."

"Good-bye, Julius," said Rachel.

"Bye-bye!" the children shouted.

After Julius had crossed the street to fetch his little boy, Marie said to Rachel, "What a nice fellow."

"Yes, he is."

Rachel stared toward the falling sun on the dusty horizon. Lili Jessup climbed the fence and ran to the barn to prepare a stall for the swayback while Cissie took her brother by the hand and called for little Abel to join them in the corral. Wind drove Rachel back indoors, but Marie decided to stay out a little longer, noting flora and fauna in the brush across the street for the letters she would write to relatives in Farrington. Few members of the Pendergast family understood why she'd moved away. Prying into each other's lives was not casual to her family. Life in Farrington passed quickly enough without disrupting its harmony with impolitic inquiries and sly accusations. Though her mother despised Harry for selling the house on Cedar Street and stealing her grandchildren away, her father had wished her godspeed, given her a kiss, and squeezed her hand. By memory's grace, her home in the Pendergast heart was assured, however distant from Illinois she and her children were committed to travel.

— 3 —

At twilight, crickets chirruped in the shadows between houses while restless dogs wandered the half-empty streets and backyards, barking distractedly at hidden enemies. On the north end of town, bursting Roman candles brightened the purple evening horizon.

"That's the circus, Momma!" Cissie announced, looking out one of the sitting room windows of Maude Hennesey's house. "That's the circus!"

"I can see, dear," Marie replied, gathering up the tablecloth after supper. The smell of fried pork chops, steamed greens, and hot gooseberry pie remained in the air. They'd had a fine supper and Marie had helped cook half of it, which made her feel useful and happy for once. When she was a girl, her mother had told her that no man who tasted her cooking would leave her side. Now and then, as Harry's business trips became longer and more frequent, Marie wondered if she'd lost her touch in the kitchen. But what did baking have to do with love?

"Won't you come, too?" Cissie pleaded. For emphasis, she tugged on her mother's sleeve and sagged toward her. "I want you to come along with us."

"You know I have to stay here, honey. I promised your grandma I'd help her out tonight."

Rachel walked out from the kitchen after finishing washing dishes. She switched off the radio, then crossed to the window and gazed with Cissie toward the north where another round of skyrockets lit the sky. "When CW gets here," she said, "we'll light the sparklers and wave them from his automobile as we drive across town. Everybody'll come out to watch."

"I want my own," Henry called from the piano bench, flipping a buffalo nickel off the back of his left hand into the air and letting it fall to the carpet. He checked to see which side landed face up, then fetched it off the floor. Harry taught him that, and pitching pennies, which Marie had not found the least bit amusing. Gambling was a sin of sloth and avarice, and Harry knew it.

"They'll be so pretty," Cissie said. "People might follow us to the circus just to get their own."

"They might at that," Marie said, hoping her children wouldn't burn their fingers. She had warned Cissie to be careful and hoped her daughter listened for a change.

Rachel added, "We won't let them, though. It'll be our special trick."

"Can Mr. Slopey come along, too? He'd love to visit the circus."

"Of course not," Rachel said. "Mr. Slopey has to stay here and keep the chickens company. They get awful lonely in the evening when we go away."

"They do?" Henry asked. "How come?"

"I don't know," Rachel replied, looking to Marie for an answer. "I guess they just do. You'll have to ask them yourself."

"May we go outside, Momma?" Cissie asked, already halfway to the living room door.

"Yes, let's all do that," Rachel agreed. "It's too stuffy in here."

Marie agreed and they all went onto the porch where a breeze washed the sweet perfume of nightblooming jasmine across the evening air. Marie listened happily to the voices of children running throughout the neighborhood, merriment and enthusiasm rising for a visit to the circus in the summer dark. Fear of Boy-Allen's mysterious killer was mostly ignored by children who preferred to chase a thousand amusements out of doors rather than hide away in their bedrooms from barely imaginable notions of kidnapping and murder. Maude rattled pans in the kitchen as she straightened things up after supper. Automobile lights flickered in the trees down the street.

"Are you sure we can't persuade you to come with us?" Rachel asked Marie. "I don't see any reason at all for you to stay home and entertain Mother. It's not as if she requires company, you know. I doubt she'd even notice you were gone."

"Yes, yes, yes!" Cissie pleaded, jerking once more on Marie's sleeve. "Pleeeeaaassse, come!"

Henry flipped the coin off his thumb out into the road, and dashed down the steps after it. Marie shook her head with a smile. "Besides, I have all sorts of letters to write home. If I don't hold up my end of the correspondence, they'll forget me. Maude and I may play a two-handed game of hearts until her club ladies arrive."

Rachel laughed. "Mother cheats, you know. She's hoping to win enough money to buy a new stove."

Maude's angry voice broke in upon them from the kitchen. "That's a bald-faced lie!"

Rachel called back at her, "Oh, you do so, Mother. Why, everyone in town knows it."

Maude came to the open window, her face just visible behind the screen, wearing a scowl. "I've never cheated in my life and anyone who says I have is a liar and a thief."

"A thief?" Rachel asked, puzzlement drawn on her face. "Why, I don't get you." She winked at Marie.

"You just stop telling fibs about me," Maude said, striking the screen with the flat of her palm. "I won't stand for my own daughter defaming me in the middle of the street."

"A guilty conscience is the deceiver's own purgatory," Rachel remarked. "I just thought Marie ought to be warned if she chooses to stay home with you instead of driving out to the circus with the rest of us."

Marie moved off down the steps after Henry who had wandered out into the dark street. She looked for automobiles, afraid of seeing her children run down by one. Jinny Branson had been struck by a Ford and killed just outside her gate not three blocks from the house on Cedar Street. Rosemary Branson's wailing had sounded like the ambulance siren across the trees. That memory always gave Marie a case of the shakes.

"She can go if she chooses," Maude replied. "I have plenty to do on my own."

"Why, there," Rachel said to Marie. "You've just heard it for yourself. You're free to come with us if you like. Mother has released you from any obligation you might have felt." She raised her voice, "Isn't that right, Mother?"

"I believe I've just said so."

Henry was on his knees, raking the dirt with his fingers in search of the coin he'd somehow lost in the road. Dust blew into his eyes, and he covered them with one arm and searched like a blind man with the other. Cissie stood in the porch shadows poking her index fingers into her cheeks while staring north toward the fairgrounds where another skyrocket had just burst orange on the black sky.

Marie told Rachel, "Well, I've already made up my mind to stay." She snatched Henry out of the dirt by the crook of his arm and swatted the dirt off his rump. She looked back up at Cissie whose fingers were jammed deeper still into the hollow of her cheeks. Marie frowned. "Honey, what on earth are you doing?"

Cissie let her hands fall away. "Making dimples, Momma. Lili taught me how."

A noisy automobile barreled in their direction. The motor horn honked and the driver stood up in the seat and gave a grand stage salute. Cissie shrieked with excitement as she and Henry returned CW's wave. Passing the house, CW brought the car around in a wide circle and rolled curbward to a stop and shut the engine off. He bounced out of his Ford like an acrobat and bowed to his audience. Both children cheered.

"Why do you show off like that?" Rachel called out, feigning anger. "You know I'm not impressed."

"He's a daredevil!" Cissie shouted, bounding down off the porch. "The bravest in the world!"

"Then somebody ought to get him a stick and a tall hat," Rachel groused. "I think he's a silly old show-off, and I won't set foot off this property unless he promises to quit fooling around."

CW strode to the porch railing. "Aw, you don't mean that, honey. I know you don't." He pursed his lips for a kiss. Rachel had told Marie when they first met that CW was a splendid kisser, which had made her blush. Now she was almost used to these overbold displays. Once upon a time, Harry had made the Pendergasts blush when he called on her after dark. It was pure jealousy on Emeline's part to suggest his manners were lacking when the truth was she longed for a fellow of her own to nibble on.

"Believe your ears," Rachel replied, turning her back to him. "I do so mean it. If you've got your heart set on going to the circus with me, I guess you'd better swear an oath this instant or I'll just go inside and spend the evening with Mother. She's not well enough to come out tonight with the rest of us." Rachel dropped her voice. "She's been suffering a deal from indigestion, you know."

"Really?"

"That's a lie!" came Maude's voice from the window. "Why, I'm fit as a fiddle! I've just got too much to do, that's all. The Lord's got me coming and going tonight. My club ladies will be here in an hour to play cards, and then I've a letter to write to Mrs. Reece in Killeen and another to Enid Todd in Stephenville."

"Oh, my heavens!" Rachel gasped, "That'd be the limit! Why, I couldn't bear it! I'm sure I'd faint dead away from the excitement of it all!"

Ignoring her daughter's sarcasm, Maude continued, "And then I have laundry to take in and a shimmy to sew for Clara Conklin."

"Oh, heart flutters!" said Rachel, and laughed out loud.

CW knelt down in front of Henry. "I saw some boys just your age walking back from the circus, and do you know what they were eating?"

"Cotton candy?" Henry asked, his eyes widening.

"Yessiree. A whole bale of it."

"Wow!"

"Don't tease the child, dear," said Rachel. "You're in enough trouble as it is."

"As God is my witness," CW said, crossing his chest. "I — "

"Are there many people downtown?" Marie interrupted, as a breeze scattered dust and leaves across the steps. She loved company and having lots of people about.

"Not any longer, but did you know there was a motor accident on Main Street this afternoon?" CW asked. "A Dodge sedan was smashed to smithereens by a truck. One man died and another was seriously injured. Bennie told me it was quite a sight."

"Of course we know," Rachel said. "Our own Marie was at the Delahaye building during lunch hour. She's already told us all about it."

"You were there?" CW asked, astonishment in his voice. "Great Scott! How did it all happen?"

"I was upstairs speaking with Mr. Delahaye," Marie said, keeping her voice low as possible to spare the children the awful details. "We heard a terrific collision from down below and went to the window. A truck and an automobile had struck each other and the automobile flipped over onto its back and caught fire. It was just horrible."

CW said, "I would imagine so! Did you see either of the victims?"

"Only the man driving the truck. He was out in the street. The other died inside his automobile before it caught fire." Marie still felt a shiver when she pictured his eyes.

"They ought to arrest someone," Rachel said, "and if it were up to me, I'd start with Newton Devlin, who is without a doubt the biggest horse's ass we've ever had sitting in the mayor's office. I don't know how many complaints he's received about people automobiling like that on Main Street and he's ignored every last one of them."

"You should write a letter," Maude remarked from behind the window screen.

Rachel walked down the length of the porch and looked in toward the kitchen. "Mother, I just said that hasn't done any good. I seriously doubt the man can even read. He ought to be lynched."

"A letter well-composed persuades when passions rise and reason fades."

Henry tugged on Marie's dress. "Let's go, Momma!" he whined. "I want to go to the circus!"

Marie freed his hand. "Patience, please!"

CW leaned into the backseat of the Ford and drew out a sparkler, which he lit with a wooden match. It flared to life with a smoky burst of blue and orange sparks that caught everyone's attention. Waving the sparkler above his head, he announced, "All aboard who's coming aboard!"

Both children shrieked with delight and leaped into the backseat. Marie looked up into the dome of the night sky where millions of silver stars were visible overhead, light from heaven.

"I've decided I'll have a sparkler of my own," Rachel said, climbing into the Ford. CW gave her a soft kiss on the cheek, closed her door, and hurried around to the driver's side and got in and started the engine. Then he reached under his seat, drew out three more sparklers, lit all three and passed them to his passengers, one by one.

"It's a go!" he shouted, tipped his cap to Marie, and slipped the Ford into gear.

"Bye-bye!" Marie called, as the Ford rolled away. "Have a good time!"

A dancing rainbow of sparks flickered and glowed in the dark as they headed off, Cissie and Henry twirling the sparklers above their heads. Their laughter echoed in the twilight and the Ford was swallowed up by the shadows. A last long wailing of the Ford's horn carried backward to Marie before the street was quiet and dark once again.

Maude finished preparing a batch of hard sugar gingerbread cakes for the quick oven, and came into the front room where Marie knelt before the small bookcase, studying her choices beyond *The Sunny Side of Life*, *Pep*, *Church Socials and Entertainments*, a collection of *Ford Smiles* and Dr. Eliot's Five Foot Shelf of the Harvard Classics that Harry had mailed from Illinois last Christmas.

Setting the silver coffee-service down on the card table, Maude said, "I never seem to find the time to read. It's very distressing. My husband was quite the reader, although you'd never have known it by first impression. He presented himself as uneducated and plain. He said it gave him an advantage over more sophisticated men who would be disposed toward underestimating him, which many of his competitors did." Maude sat down on the sofa across from Marie and folded her hands in her lap. "Yet I've never known a more clever, intelligent man as long as I've lived."

"Harry says reading makes a well-informed and gentlemanly salesman. I'm sure he learned that from his father."

Maude smiled. "Jonas believed in bending the twig when it's young. Now, of course, Rachel won't read anything besides those addle-brained *Photoplay* magazines at Hooker's drugstore, but Harry was forever running downtown to the library, utterly convinced that all the books he hadn't yet looked over were about to disappear from the shelves. Unlike most of the boys he knew at school, Harry refused to allow his horizon to be limited by foolishness. Jonas considered him a rare child. He was very proud of his son."

"Cissie adores books, too," Marie remarked, "thanks to her father who's guided her footsteps since she was little, although I must say Cousin Emeline and myself are avid readers, as well. In fact, my family has always believed in the value of education. Granny Ruth went to college in Wisconsin and taught Latin and mathematics before she married my grandfather. And my mother wrote poetry when she was a girl and had each of us recite one canto from 'Hiawatha' after Thanksgiving dinner as a matter of tradition."

"Now, you see, that's precisely the point I was trying to put across to Rachel last night," Maude explained, as a motorcar rumbled by outdoors. "This snarling youth nowadays have too little appreciation for tradition and standards. All they care about is having a good time. For heaven sakes, can you imagine my daughter or any of her fast-stepping friends joining us around the fireplace to hear our opinions on anything modern? Scarcely! Yet we're accused of sobbishness when we describe the heartscald of seeing our children coming home on the milk train at six o'clock in the morning, sick from liquor and sin. I believe this willingness of theirs to ridicule our ideals and counsel will lead us all to the break-up of the family unless this younger generation recognizes its fault and changes its habits. And I mean sooner than later."

The curtains flapped lazily behind the storm screens, drawing a cool draft into the front room. Marie wondered what her own children were doing that moment at the circus, if they were enjoying themselves and were safe out in the dark of the fairgrounds where Emmett J. Laswell's Traveling Circus Giganticus had raised its tents. Until Boy-Allen's killer was caught, a threat persisted, and Marie couldn't help but worry. Who could be safe? Maybe she'd made a mistake in not going with them. What sort of mother leaves her children outdoors after dark? Of course, they were with Rachel and CW, but how responsible were those two? Rachel had no children of her own and wouldn't likely have one at all, except by accident. Listening to her talk about men, Marie suspected it might only be a matter of time before she got herself in trouble. CW seemed quite mature and responsible, but he also let Rachel push him around, not a good sign for a fellow just starting off with a girl as willful as her. Were the circus not on the other end of town, Marie might just have jumped up and hurried over there that minute. After all, what was more important than her children's well-being?

The doorbell rang and a flurry of voices issued from the front porch.

Maude looked at the clock on the fireplace mantle. "Are you sure you won't join us?"

Marie smiled and shook her head. "No, thank you. I have reading and letters to catch up on while the children are out. But I appreciate your asking. Thank you."

She was pleased, indeed. This was the first time Maude had invited Marie to join her club ladies. Were they becoming friends at last? She doubted it, yet stranger things had happened, and Reverend Whitehead always preached the theme of the lamb lying down with the lion. Perhaps anything was possible in this age.

Maude stood. "Will you look in on my gingerbread cakes every so often? Trudy refuses to touch one if it's overdone and that old stove is utterly unreliable. I believe next month I may actually buy a new one, after all."

"Certainly."

The doorbell rang again amid a tittering of laughter. As Maude went to answer it, Marie located a volume of Longfellow and made herself comfortable in the plum tapestry Morris chair in Maude's sewing room away from the card game. While she re-read "Hiawatha," voices excited and agitated carried to her across the house.

"You needn't shuffle more than once!"

"I'll shuffle as often as I please, thank you!"

"What a rotten hand! Just rotten to the core!"

"I do believe I may win this round!"

"Emmy, I'll thank you to keep your eyes to yourself!"

"Cheaters never prosper, Maude!"

"Well, I'll have you know, the prosperous have no need for cheating! Here, take this!"

"Oh, bother!"

"My, oh, my! Luck has deserted this poor old girl tonight! Heavens!"

"If you hand me one more heart, Trudy, I'll slit your throat!"

"Beatrice!"

"I win again!"

"Why Maude, you're nothing but a wicked old witch! I doubt I'll ever play this game again. Trudy, you shuffle this time. I do not trust our hostess! She's much too sly!"

Laughter echoed through the house.

When the hour had passed, Maude came into the room and invited Marie to have a cup of tea and a gingerbread cake with the club ladies.

The cards had been put away and doilies arranged on the mahogany tea table, cups in each place setting, one extra for Marie. The house felt lively.

"That Trudy is such a cheat," said Beatrice, winking at Emily. "I cannot win if she is included in the game. It is utterly hopeless."

Marie sat down on one of Maude's tufted oak side chairs. The club ladies were the most pleasant women Marie had met in town, although they seemed to have little use for anyone outside their little circle and gossiped shamelessly about everyone in the county. Yet people in Bellemont treated them with a peculiar deference explained by rumors about each having gold buried in her back garden and a controlling interest in the bank.

"Don't believe a word that woman says," Trudy replied, with a scowl. "Beatrice is nothing but a sore loser. Always has been. Why, I remember back in school — "

"Don't you dare bring Bobby Watson into this conversation!" Beatrice cried. "You've sullied both his reputation and my own for more years than I can count with that silly story of yours, not a word of which is true!"

"Story? Why, you old — "

Beatrice covered her ears with both hands and shouted, "I am not listening!"

"Of course you're not!" Trudy cried, "You're as deaf as an old shoe! Everybody in town knows it. Bobby Watson knew it before the rest of us, which is why he stepped out with Mary Pearson under the Harvest Moon and you stayed home with your momma and baked a dozen pounds of sweetcake that nobody ever ate and — "

"I'm going home," Beatrice announced, and got up from the table. "That woman is crazy as a March Hare and tells vicious lies all over town."

As she reached for her shawl, Maude came into the room carrying a tray of tea and gingerbread cakes. "Beatrice!"

The woman at the door stopped and turned around, tears brimming at her eyes. "I will not stay and be insulted by you people on my only night out! Maude, it isn't fair."

"Fair's got nothing to do with it, dear," Maude said, her voice calm but a touch louder than normal. "I spent most of this afternoon preparing these cakes and I'll be — " she shot a quick glance across at Marie " — disappointed, if you don't stay and try them. Let bygones be bygones, I always say. Shall we? Ladies?"

"Well … " Beatrice took her hand off her shawl. "As long as you've gone to the effort, I might forgive her just this once." She walked back to the tea table, pausing to cast a cold eye upon Trudy before seating herself on her side chair.

"Emmy?"

"Honey and lemon, please." She reached forward and snatched a cake off the tray and placed it on her plate. Maude handed her the honey jar from which she poured a couple of drops into her tea, then took a lemon slice and put it next to the tea cup. "Thank you, Maude."

"You're welcome. Marie?"

"Honey, please."

When Maude finished her tour of the table, she returned to the kitchen, leaving Marie with the club ladies. No further words were spoken regarding either game conduct or rules or past indiscretions, and once Maude returned all were laughing together over a word of blue humor overheard downtown.

"Emily Haskins, you devil," said Trudy. "How dare you repeat that in public!"

"Why, this isn't public, it's Maude's house. Isn't that right, Maude?"

"I've heard worse," she replied, grinning wryly, "when Jonas was alive."

Beatrice asked, "Then you agree that it is possible for a man to perform that, uh, feat?"

Before Maude could respond, laughter erupted once again.

"Ladies! We have a guest present!"

"Oh, I'm sure she's heard worse, too, haven't you, dear?" Trudy asked Marie. "Northerners haven't as well-developed a sensibility for the silliness of gentility and manners as we do. Your people aren't nearly so stuck on petty proprieties, are they, dear?"

Marie had no idea at all how to respond to Trudy's suggestion. Did she mean that among Northerners politeness had less value than in the

South? If so, then the woman was wrong and ought to be corrected. Basic manners and civility were certainly not determined by the boundaries of the Mason-Dixon line. Yet, on the other hand, if Trudy meant that perhaps the North did not adhere to outdated customs and etiquettes, well, Marie had no quarrel with that. She told them, "I grew up with four older brothers and thin bedroom walls and uncles who drank corn whiskey on the porch outside my window at night when we children were supposed to be asleep, so I've long understood how men tell stories."

She smiled.

To that Beatrice added, "They are crude creatures, aren't they?"

And everybody laughed again.

By half-past ten, the club ladies had gone and Maude returned to her laundry at the rear of the house. The wind had grown stronger, banging the Jessup's storm-shutters next door. Marie peeked anxiously out through the curtains and saw the stars had disappeared behind a layer of black clouds drifting east toward Louisiana. She heard Maude open the back door and go out. A few minutes later she came back in with a basket load of laundry. Marie got up and went to help her with the sorting.

"It'll rain by midnight," Maude remarked, folding linen. "I hope those fools don't keep the circus open much longer. It wouldn't do to have the children caught in a storm."

"I'm sure Rachel has an eye on the weather," Marie said, picking out her children's clothing to sort and fold. "I trust CW, too. I'm sure he'll keep them out of trouble. He seems to be a reasonable young man, don't you agree?"

"He's a character," Maude said, emptying the basket and setting it beside the linen cabinet. "Driving around like a fool's advertisement. I sometimes wonder if he's got half the sense God gave a groundhog."

"Rachel is quite taken with him, isn't she?" She loved telling Marie when they were alone how she and CW made love here and there, and how they were too modern to worry about who was watching. Marie always pretended to be shocked, when in truth she was a bit envious. Marie couldn't imagine Harry interested in making love out of doors. He hated the very thought of dust on his trouser cuffs.

Maude frowned. "She's afraid to death of men, always has been. That fear distorts her judgment, makes her choose the wrong fellows to run with. I doubt Rachel really knows how she feels about this one. The fact that he's a fancy-pants from New Orleans with a sack of money to throw around gives her cause to believe Cupid's sitting on her shoulder. Piffle!"

Maude picked up the laundry basket and carried it into her bedroom. Marie went out onto the back porch. A bedroom lamp was lit at the Jessup's, which meant Lili's father was home from the oil fields, sixty miles away. To the north, Marie could just make out the lights of Laswell's circus. She wished she had been able to go with her children, see that they ate something besides cotton candy and ice cream, and didn't get into trouble. Harry would've gone. He adored playing with the children, taking them to the zoo or a movie matinee. He often complained that she had no interest in silly things, but he rarely invited her out anymore, so how could he know? There's a child's heart in each of us.

Finished with her laundry, Maude came out onto the porch. She stood by the railing facing south. "Perhaps it won't rain tonight, after all. There's much too much wind. Those clouds'll pass on by midnight and we'll have a beautiful sunrise, mark my words."

"I hope so," Marie said, as she studied the black sky, noting how the air held a dry grassy smell not at all like that which presaged summer rain. She thought of Illinois and her apple tree in the dooryard. Who would tend to it now that she was gone?

Maude added, "Watch for heat lightning tonight when you're in bed. You'll see it to the south and east. It won't bring showers, though. I've lived here my whole life and I can feel the sky on my skin and know which way it'll turn. I've never been wrong." When a gust ruffled Maude's apron, she held it down with both hands and put her back to the wind as she stared out into the dark. "Dear, your children will have to know that this is not Illinois, that there are considerations one must pay service to."

"Pardon me?"

"The colored children from Shantytown." Maude's eyes were steely and gray, her expression firm. "I do not say this to disturb you, nor as an apology for those of us who have always lived here. What is in our hearts has been there since birth and we have not denied our inheritance. It is a fact and, though not all of us embrace it, we nevertheless accept what is, and will likely remain, part of our lives here. As much as possible, we stay on our side of the river, and they stay on theirs. This is the accommodation we've arrived at, and everyone understands it. Will you explain this to your children, or would you rather I did so?"

Her heart pounding, Marie gazed out into the dark, not quite certain how to respond. During supper, Cissie had recounted her adventure at the river, the excitement of it still evident in her voice. Henry, too, had been taken by the events and rattled on about flailing in the current and the strong Negro hand that had rescued him. In the years they had been married, Harry regaled Marie with thousands of stories of growing up in Texas, the people he had known, those he had cared for, those he had despised. Race had only now and then been part of those tales, even by inference. Nor had the issue arisen in Marie's imagination about his life in Bellemont. Prior to the moment she and the children disembarked from the train in Bellemont, she had never set foot in the South. Her grandfather had fought with Burnside in the War Between the States, but that was a distant memory now, a forgotten conflict. Yet nobody who read the newspapers was entirely ignorant about the South. The Ku Klux Klan had infiltrated Indiana only a few years back. Cousins Frenchy and Alvin mentioned fishing near colored people along the Mississippi every so often, saying they had come upriver by barge and caught fish to feed their children because it was preferable to buying in town where they might not be welcomed. She never heard anybody else in Farrington express that sentiment aloud. It would have been considered vulgar and ill-mannered to do so, beneath one's dignity and demeaning to all. In church, she was taught that all people, regardless of the color of their skin, were an expression of divine inspiration, and that one's standing before God had nothing to do with race. If it was true that fortune lent its grace more broadly upon white people than dark, that was more a result of worldly constructions than whispers from on high. Implied was the notion that Negroes suffered misfortune derived from a coincidence of birth and that here on earth their station was muddled by inconsiderate and evil people like D.C. Stephenson whose fears overwhelmed the grace God had planted in their hearts at the beginning of time. Only when hurt and suffering and wrongdoing went out of the world would the Negro's stature rise. Yet those lurid and ghastly tales of rape and lynchings in the Deep South that Marie occasionally read about in the newspapers made her debate what she had learned. How long was it necessary for the Negro to wait upon his white neighbor's education of the heart? She was not shocked the night the colored school had burned down in the rain outside Shantytown, not taken aback by the indifference shown the Negro bucket brigade by the white citizenry of Bellemont, nor insulted by Rachel's offhanded remark about not offering help to those who refuse to ask for it. That night, Marie understood how many state lines she had crossed by train, how far south she had traveled with her children. Indeed, the colored man who rescued Henry in the current likely taught the children a better lesson than most people in Bellemont would ever know. Whose side of the river, after all, was more blessed?

In her calmest voice, she told Maude, "I've never told them whom to play with and whom to avoid. Neither has Harry. My own mother raised me to believe the heart sees truths our eyes deny." Marie stared off down the street. "But I am not such a Pollyanna as to think everyone feels the same way. I know this isn't Illinois. Yes, indeed I'll speak to the children this evening before bedtime."

"Thank you," said Maude. "Well, I have to take a bath. Good night, dear."

"Good night."

Somewhat depressed now, Marie turned down the beds in her room and went outdoors where the dizzying fragrance of honeysuckle from the Jessup's fence blossomed with the rising humidity and made her drowsy. To the north, a distant glow of electric colors gradually dimmed and winked out as the circus closed down for the evening.

Marie herself felt deflated at not having gone. Once when she was a girl, a wagon circus had stopped for the night a mile outside of Farrington and put up a campfire performance for the local children who'd collected to see the elephants and clowns and fire-breathing giants. Marie had come down Willitson Road from the farm with her cousins Emeline and Violet and hid together in a stand of willows where they could spy on the circus animals and spangled acrobats without being seen. Huddled in the shadows, Marie saw a pretty girl perhaps younger than herself with crow-black eyes flung to the stars by a pair of strongmen only to somersault safely back to earth. She watched a tiny fellow in a golden suit stand upright in the mouth of a man-eating lion and sing, "Nearer my God to Thee." Terrified of freaks and wild animals, Violet ran home after that. Emeline lasted just long enough to see a silky blonde mermaid emerge from a briny tub to puff rose blossoms off her fingertips for the gathering audience. Marie preferred to stay behind, hoping she might be caught, perhaps even kidnapped, and stolen away to a foreign land somewhere where a kindhearted gypsy would teach her the Arabian belly-dance and how to stand on her head atop the great death-defying highwire. Instead, she fell asleep in the bushes and awoke to an empty clearing and had to walk home alone to a severe scolding by her mother who told her that no adventure on this earth compares to that which a woman undertakes by marrying a man she loves and raising children in a home of her own. True enough, but aren't females permitted dreams beyond dishes and bed linen? Time was, Marie frolicked in the summer woods by moonlight. Why not now?

A gentle breeze swirled in the road. Noisy motors droned far away, then went quiet. Marie walked down to the front gate and stared off past the cottonwoods toward downtown. Her feet were restless. She went out onto the sidewalk and strolled along to the end of the fence. Nights like this led her wandering. Harry had no idea. Now and then, he'd go to the cigar store after supper or slip out of bed in the dark and take walks across Cedar Street down into the vine-clogged ravine. His secret little adventures. Yes, she knew all about them. But she had her own, though not at night when the children needed her; rather, during the afternoon when Emeline volunteered to watch the children play in the yard. Then Marie might take the trolley across town, or board the Limited and ride to Danleyville and back, just to see the sights, be a stranger somewhere, observe other lives in other places. She did so want to go.

Not a block and a half away, she saw the shadow cross behind a cottonwood, a shape in the trees. Startled, at first Marie didn't believe she'd seen anything at all. It was a trick of the eye, she thought, a phantom revealed by the wind. She stared at the figure motionless in the dark, afraid to take another step. Then he became a man, and her arms went cold. She stood very still herself. Was she being watched? The longer she stared, the less she believed her eyes. Many times in the woods at night behind the farm, she'd see strange sights and scare herself half to death and need to run home. Then in the daylight there'd be nothing but birds on branches. She guessed this, too, was nothing and began to walk down the sidewalk, one foot after the other. She had the jitters now, and wanted to turn about and go back to the safety of Maude's yard. Instead, plain as day, she called out, "Hello?"

Her voice carried down the street, which startled her. She'd hoped to be discreet. There were people in bed, after all, Maude included. Regardless, she drew no response from her mysterious phantom. Emboldened by her own voice in the summer dark, Marie took another six steps along the sidewalk, still sticking to the fenceline. What if this were the killer of Boy-Allen? Had she considered that? How reckless was she prepared to be? Just being out after dark under these circumstances would have Harry thinking she'd gone off her nut. He would sit her down and ask if she drank liquor like her cousins, to which she'd laugh and make him angry and they wouldn't speak for at least three days.

Marie moved further along the fenceline, and saw the figure dart off into the woods. She heard the brush crackle and the snap of a large branch. Her breath caught in her throat. What on earth had she just seen? Well, by God, she had no intention of going home now. Acting on some impulse she'd never known before in her life, Marie hurried down the sidewalk to a spot just across the street from where that man (of course it was a man, what woman runs away into the woods?)

had escaped into the darkness. If she'd had a whistle, she would have deflated her lungs blowing it. That was Boy-Allen's killer, she was sure. Who else would hide like that, spying on houses from the shadows? Of course, every town had a peeper. At home, it was William Winningham, a pathetic creature whose mother and father had burned up one night in a terrible fire, leaving him destitute and disturbed. For years, he wandered the neighborhoods of Farrington, sneaking into dooryards and peeking through hedges, more pest than threat, until one night when he stumbled into a potato cellar and broke his neck and wound up in a sanitarium where his Uncle Edgar claimed he was much happier.

So why was Marie crossing College Street now and pursuing her phantom through the dark? She had no desire to enter the brush; she wasn't that impulsive. A month ago, she would have turned on her heel and gone back to the house. That was then. Now, she walked quickly to the corner and took Cordelia Road toward the river, guessing that this fellow, whoever he was, would either disappear into the woods, or emerge somewhere on this road, and if he did, then she'd see him. Then Marie slowed, eyes fixated on the trees ahead. Her legs felt jittery and the skin on the back of her neck crawled like a swarm of bugs. She shuddered. A cool breeze wafted across the dark, carrying a scent of cedar and damp grass.

A moment later, perhaps a hundred feet away, someone crossed the road from the underbrush and passed into the alley between the houses fronting College Street, some lit still before bedtime, others dark. The figure passed so quickly and silently, had Marie not been focused directly ahead, had her attention been drawn away in that instant, she might not have noticed.

She called out, "STOP!"

And her voice echoed back across the sultry night, idiotic and misplaced. What was she thinking? If he hadn't known before that she was chasing him, surely now he did. A trash can banged in the alleyway and a dog began barking in a back garden. Marie hurried across the road. A porchlight came on four houses away and she heard a low voice grumbling. She thought about calling to whomever had come out to attend to the dog, but was afraid of drawing the wrong sort of attention to herself. What would she say? There was a strange man running away from her in the dark? She peered into the dirty alleyway lined with plank fences, absolutely black now in the night. Why hadn't she gone back indoors straight off and borrowed one of Rachel's electric lanterns? Harry would tell her that was the smart thing to do. Whenever they had raccoons in the yard, or boys playing pranks in the neighborhood, Harry fetched his flashlight from the closet and went out to have a look. He rarely called from the upper window, and never went out empty-handed. Fine, so he was right about being prepared. Well, fiddle-dee-dee, he wasn't here now, was he? And this was her chase, her problem to solve. What did she intend to do now?

A man she didn't recognize leaned out a wooden gate halfway down the alley. In the lamplight from the porch, he looked puffy and unshaven, and when Marie drew near, she could smell burning tobacco and a hint of beer on the breeze. She stepped back into the shadows, and knew she was being silly but had no thought of revealing herself. Just ahead, her phantom figure darted past a stack of cordwood and a Ford truck near the end of the alley.

The fellow at the gate called out in a crude voice, "Who's there? You goddamned kids get the hell out of here now! I ain't fooling!"

Another dog began barking down the alley and a cat shrieked.

Trapped between exposing herself as a nasty sneak and losing track of her phantom, Marie wasn't sure what to do. It was all so thrilling. What would Maude think? Or her own children? The wooden gate closed and the gruff fellow went back indoors. Marie stepped out of the shadows and tiptoed past his yard. She'd certainly lost her chance to catch the phantom now, but hurried on down to the end of the alley, anyhow. There were more voices somewhere off in the dark in the next block or the one beyond, and she noticed how completely her fear had gone. Something had come over her now in the dark, a strength she hadn't anticipated. Indeed, she felt braver than ever before. Common sense told her now was the time to go back to Maude's house and wait there safely for her children to return. She did not. Instead, Marie came out of the alley onto Hardin Street and went across, and on into the shadows. She felt like a hunter now, stalking her prey, unafraid. The night buzzed about her, music from indoor radios, errant voices from sheltered porches, angry dogs here and there. None of it frightened or dissuaded her. She walked ahead, determined to find her phantom.

The town was a warren in the summer dark. Narrow dirt streets and cluttered alleyways led every which way, and she chose her route with only slight discrimination. She crept past a livery stable and a hog pen and several tin garages where anyone who chose might hide and let her by. Here and there, she peered into the shadows with her sternest gaze. She refused to rush. Twice, Marie imagined footsteps nearby and stood still as a tree until she was sure nobody was there. She followed a dirt road that paralleled College Street where she smelled lilac from a dooryard and imagined the river was near. Beside her now were the thick woods and darkness. If a killer waited in ambush, he could drag her off and dismember her body and nobody would know until daylight — if then. She felt a chill. Fear crept into her toes. Marie was sure Boy-Allen's killer was watching her that very instant, poised to strike. What on earth would she do if he did? Back on the farm when she was a girl, her male cousins were forever scrapping in the dust and wrestling. She held her own with Frenchy and once gave Cousin Bert a shiner when he tried to pitch her into Uncle Henry's watering trough. *It's wrong to worry over anything before it happens.* Cissie's motto, borrowed from Oz. She clenched her fists, drew a deep breath, and moved straight ahead along the road.

Then she was a block from downtown and there were autos on Main Street closeby and nobody had jumped out. If she'd lost her phantom, well, at least he knew she meant business! Marie walked toward Keister's blacksmith shop, eyes focused on the sign over the rear entrance, still in the shadows, but only a dozen yards from a lamplit porch on the corner.

She heard him step out behind her and the hair stood up on the back of her neck, and her heart froze solid. She felt as if she were walking in mud, her legs numb and useless, like in a dream. He was so close, she smelled the tobacco stink off his jacket. Too frightened to turn and face him, too scared to run, she did nothing at all. Not even breathe. Directly behind her now, he seemed omnipresent, swelling up like a beast, occupying all the alley space between fences. Crossing her brain in the instant before he grabbed her shoulder was the thought that she'd never been brave at all in her life, never anything more than reckless and foolish. And now she'd pay a dear price for that failing.

His hand was big and strong. It closed over her shoulder and she felt feeble beneath that grip. She ought to have screamed or kicked out backward like one of Uncle Henry's mules. Instead, she sagged, almost fainting, and found herself held upright as she slumped, expecting a painful, wrenching death.

But nothing hurt at all. Instead, even as he breathed a stink of gin in her ear, she heard a gruff yet pleasant voice say, softly, "Looking for your cat?"

Then Jimmy Delahaye was staring Marie in the face, that wry smile pumping blood back into her limbs.

"I haven't got a cat," she stammered, feebly. "I don't know what I'm doing."

Even to herself that sounded absurd. She must truly have gone out of her mind. Delahaye stared at her like she was crazy, so maybe she was. Harry would think so. She felt like an idiot.

Delahaye asked, "Are you lost? It's awfully dark out here."

She shook her head. "No, I just went this way because it seemed like a shortcut. I guess I should've stayed in bed."

"You got out of bed to take a walk in the middle of the night?"

Now she was confused. Maybe she had lost her head, after all. "No, I was waiting up for the children. Rachel took them to the circus this evening. I stayed home with Maude to help with her club ladies."

"So, you weren't in bed?"

"No." She folded her arms as Delahaye became more visible in the shadows. He had his eye on her, and she wasn't sure how to behave. Not every woman goes out walking in the dark. It just wasn't done. What did he think of her?

"Are you headed anywhere in particular? Nothing's open downtown. It's kind of late to be out and about."

"Well, I was thinking about going home, if truth be told. I'm expecting the children any minute." That sounded silly, and she knew it, but was much too flustered to tell a better fib.

"Would you like me to walk you back? I'll show you a better short-cut, if you prefer."

Trying to sound sane for a moment, Marie replied, "That would be just fine. Thank you very much."

"My pleasure."

Delahaye offered his arm, and Marie took it as if it were the most natural thing in the world, hoping to preserve what shred of dignity she had remaining. He led her out of the alleyway, past the blacksmith shop, then up the old plank sidewalk on Morgan Lane under the dusty willows. A pleasant breeze sighed across the dark and Marie felt herself calm down enough to tell Delahaye about the phantom she'd seen skulking in the brush.

"I have no doubt whatsoever that he was Boy-Allen's killer. Who else would hide in the bushes, peeping on the Jessup's. How he ran from me gave it away."

"Did you see his face?"

"Of course not," Marie said, as if the question were somehow impertinent. "He was far too clever to let himself be seen that clearly. A vile murderer like that would never allow himself to be caught so easily. We'll just all have to be far more vigilant now that we know he's still with us."

When they reached Maude's house again on College Street, Delahaye let Marie in through the front gate, but stayed behind on the sidewalk. In a tone Marie hadn't heard from him before, Delahaye warned, "I think you ought to be more careful yourself. You know, I'd hate to lose my secretary to a lunatic."

He smiled.

Rachel and the children hadn't come home yet, and the house was dark but for a light on in Maude's bedroom. There was no pressing reason for Marie to go indoors just now, so she didn't. The clouds had parted and the air was warm and moist. It made her feel carefree somehow.

"Did you see me tiptoeing down the alley?" Marie asked, keeping her voice low. She realized what a stroke of luck it was that Delahaye had been there.

"I thought you were a cat on the prowl," he told her.

"That's not a bit funny. I nearly ran myself into one of those ashcans."

"If you wanted company, you ought've rang me up. I'd have been over here in a flash."

"So you weren't at the circus?"

"Earlier, for a while. But I had some papers to look over downtown and when I finished, I thought I'd take a walk."

"I guess I'm fortunate that you did." She felt herself blushing. What was it about this man that had such a terrible effect on her? If only Harry knew — not that he was so awfully private with his own wandering eye, as if he imagined she didn't know how women looked at him, and how he looked back.

"Well, I suppose I'd better drag myself to bed," Delahaye said, casting a long gaze off down the street. He sounded weary, or pensive. Marie wasn't sure which.

"I'm grateful," she murmured.

"Don't mention it," Delahaye said, suddenly focusing his eyes directly on Marie. They had the faintest twinkle, she was sure. He tipped his hat. "See you soon."

"I hope so."

And she did, too.

— **4** —

At half past twelve, CW's automobile parked in front of the house. Maude had long since retired, leaving Marie to compose letters by lamplight in the sitting room off the kitchen. She wrote to Harry about the smash-up on Main Street, recounted Henry's accident on the river, and Maude's angry opinion of the Boy-Allen investigation, then asked his advice regarding Delahaye's offer. She told Harry how terribly she missed him and wished he'd come to visit soon. Knowing he, too, must be lonely, she signed it with an extra kiss and a hug. Maybe she lied a little about how she felt, and ought to have been more honest with her feelings, but what good could come out of that? Nor had she any intention of telling him about how handsome she'd found Jimmy Delahaye, nor one word regarding her exciting adventure tonight. Some things these days needed to remain her own. Marie had just begun a note to Emeline regarding Cousin Alvin's peculiar disappearance from the farm when the sounds of giggling and auto-doors slamming drew her attention. She put down her pen and went out onto the front porch where the children were dancing circles in the road and waving Japanese modesty fans about over their heads. CW wore a straw hat ringed with a garland of laurel leaves; Rachel's blouse was draped in boa feathers.

Seeing their mother, the children let out a shriek. "Momma! Momma! We won! We won!"

"Shhh!" Marie came down the porchsteps to the windy street. "Grandma's sleeping."

"But we won!" Cissie cried, only slightly less loudly than before. She held a stuffed lion for her mother to see. "We won a prize for each of us! Well, *we* didn't win, exactly. CW did, throwing balls at wooden ducks, and he was so good that the man there told him we could each have anything we wanted if he would only stop throwing and go home! So I chose Ali Baba here and Henry got a crocodile and Rachel got some unicorn feathers and CW took Caesar's old hat and each of us got to keep one of these beautiful fans! Isn't it wonderful?"

"I rode on the Ferris wheel, Momma," Henry announced, "and I wasn't scared at all!"

"It was a marvelous evening," Rachel said, climbing out of CW's Ford. "We all had a grand time."

"I expect you did," said Marie, smiling as Henry twirled his paper fan about like an airplane diving and arcing back up into the air. "Did everyone get enough to eat?"

"A bellyful," Cissie said, patting her stomach. She stopped twirling. "I'm so full up, I may explode any minute now."

"The children had packs of fun," CW said, coming around from the driver's side of the Ford. He had a ticket in his hatband and his flannel trousers rippled in the wind. "There was so much to do."

"I even touched a monkey, Momma," Henry said, the paper fan flying out of his hand into the dusty street. The wind blew it away from him and he gave chase.

"My gosh!" Marie smiled. "What do you know about that."

"No, he didn't," Cissie corrected. "He gave it a piece of Cracker Jack, even though the sign said not to feed the animals."

"Sure I did! He was awful hungry," Henry explained, snatching up the paper fan again. "He wanted some Cracker Jacks."

"Henry stuck his hand right through the bars. I was sure that monkey'd bite his fingers off."

"Did you do that?" Marie asked, amazed at her son's bravado. Ordinarily, he was afraid of loud dogs and hissing cats. To picture him offering Cracker Jack to a strange monkey, well, Texas apparently had its spell on all of them.

"He wasn't at all mean, Momma," said Henry. "I liked him."

"There were a million things to see," Cissie said. "I could've stayed all night and not seen them all."

"I believe she's telling the truth," agreed Rachel. "Your children ran us ragged trying to keep up. We had to be pitched out so Laswell could close for the night."

"I liked the show under the big top best of all," Cissie said.

"The clowns!" Henry cried. "They were funny!"

Cissie said, "One of them had a flower that shot water into the audience as he rode by on a giant unicycle. Everyone around us got wet and no one was mad. Then a group of baby clowns —"

"Midgets," Rachel corrected with a shudder. "Why, I've never seen so many in my life. They gave me the heebie-jeebies."

"Well, they looked like babies, Momma, I promise they did! And they all ganged up on one big giant clown and hit him with orange clubs and bouquets of exploding flowers and a powder puff the size of a pumpkin until he fell over and pretended to be dead and shushed us all so we wouldn't tell the baby clowns that he wasn't really dead, only fooling so they'd quit picking on him. I've never laughed so hard! And then the trapeze people came out on the high wire! Oh,

Momma! There was a girl my age named Jenny Dodge and she was so beautiful and not a bit scared to be up so high and she crossed the wire without looking down once and she smiled and waved when she got to the other side and everybody clapped and then she went back the other direction, only this time she stood on her head in the middle of the wire and made a somersault and a turn on one toe and then dove off!"

"Into mid-air?" Marie asked, trying her best to sound incredulous. She was so pleased at her daughter's joy, she could scarcely resist giving Cissie a big warm hug.

"Yes, only another one of the trapeze boys also dived off the platform just above her and as she fell toward us, he caught her, and then someone else caught him and all three of them swung back and forth smiling and waving until they got tired and climbed down to the ground where everybody clapped! I was so scared I thought I'd faint, but I didn't, and I decided, Momma, right then that one day I'm going to join the circus and climb the trapeze and be the first in the world to do a triple flip-flop! Isn't that a wonderful plan, Momma? Isn't it?"

"I should say so, dear."

"Me, too!" Cissie agreed. "And you will all be invited to watch me perform."

"And so we shall," said Marie, "but first, you and your brother'll have to get off to sleep. It's hours past your bedtime."

"But Momma! I want to write a letter to Daddy and tell him all about my wonderful circus plan!"

"You can do that tomorrow, dear," Marie replied, already exhausted by her daughter's excitement. "Enough's enough for tonight. Both of you, this very moment, run along to bed!"

"Aww — " Cissie's voice trailed off. Confronted with the hopeless reality of the situation, she grabbed her brother's hand and led him up the porchsteps. She turned to the adults below her. "Thank you for taking us to the circus tonight. We had a wonderful time." She showed a brilliant smile and nudged Henry for the same.

"Thank you," Henry said, looking disconsolate now that his circus evening was finally over.

"You're very welcome," CW replied with a bow. "It was our pleasure."

"Night, kids!" Rachel added. "Sleep tight!"

"I'll be in shortly," Marie said. "Don't wake your grandma."

"May I mix a glass of malted milk to take to bed?" Cissie asked.

"Me, too!" Henry squealed.

Marie sighed. "All right, dear. Now hurry along, both of you."

After the children had gone inside, Marie said, "That was very kind of you both to take them to the circus. They truly enjoyed themselves."

"I'm sure we'd have stayed all night if it had been up to them," Rachel replied. "They were just a pair of little spitfires, on the run from the ticket box to the moment we dragged them out the gate."

"I hadn't been to the circus myself in years," CW said. "I'd forgotten how fabulous it can be."

"And dirty, too," Rachel added. "Those people who work there? Ugghh! I like to died! That Laswell fellow must hire them right out of a cave. I doubt one of them can read or write. And not only are their manners atrocious, but the language they use with one another! I was embarrassed for the children. If it had rained insect powder, there wouldn't have been enough decent folks among us to bury the rest. One would think Mr. Laswell would have better sense than hiring ignorant good-for-nothings like that. Then again, perhaps that's why his vile little circus is no Barnum & Bailey."

"Aw, quit crabbing," CW growled. "You're not being at all fair. Why, it's a swell circus. Sure, those fellows working the midway are a little rough. I won't gripe with you about that. But, gee whiz, there was so much to see and do there, well, for a small wagon circus, I was quite taken."

"And I wonder why Mother is constantly drawing your good taste into question."

CW laughed. "Now, darling, you're just sore because you had a chance to win that beautiful crystal vase and you missed the bull's-eye!"

"Crystal?" Marie exclaimed. She had no idea they offered such prizes. "Oh my!"

"It was certainly not Viennese crystal," said Rachel, "probably just ordinary glass, and the darts that ugly man gave me were bent. No one on earth could've thrown them straight. I was cheated out of my prize."

"Poor sport." He kissed her cheek as two boys rode past on bicycles, one carrying a stuffed dog and the other a half-eaten stick of cotton candy. Wind chased them off into the dark. Hadn't they any thought at all of Boy-Allen's killer and the threat that hid in the woods?

Marie felt a chill and wrapped her arms tightly about herself. It was late, too, and she was growing drowsy. Were the children in bed yet? She'd give them another couple of minutes, then go indoors to be sure.

Slipping an arm about CW's waist, Rachel told him, "Well, you needn't sound so smug. After all, I consider myself at least partially responsible for your winning."

Marie turned to CW. "Did you win many games on the midway?"

"He was the greatest champion of them all this evening." She kissed him softly on the cheek. "My hero! You should have seen him pitch those baseballs. I believe he ought to try out for a professional team!"

"I did all right," CW admitted, blushing visibly even in the dark. He drew her close enough to briefly nibble her neck. "But that colored boy's the one who could really throw. My goodness! What an arm!"

Rachel pulled free of CW's grasp. "Oh, quit talking about him. What's done is done."

He caught her hand, trying to pull her back to him. "Well, dear, it was just plain rotten."

"What are you two talking about?" Marie asked, utterly perplexed by their bickering.

"A Negro boy," said CW, "with a wing like a Springfield rifle. He knocked down every single one of those milk bottles, just popped them off the shelves one after another fair and square like Sergeant Alvin York at a Tennessee turkey shoot, and what did he win? Not a blessed thing."

"No, that's not true at all," Rachel argued. "He was given a prize. Every winner got a prize."

"Yes, an old clothespin," CW said to Marie, "given only to humiliate the boy. To put him in his place. What did that fellow behind us call it? 'A nigger prize!' I was ashamed to witness such disgraceful behavior." He shuddered in disgust.

"I was surprised to see so many of them there tonight. Usually they come in after most of us have left. I know they prefer it that way." Rachel slipped loose of CW's hand and moved off.

"How do you know that?" CW said, following her. "Have you ever asked a colored person?"

"I don't need to," Rachel replied, testy now at being challenged. "It's understood."

"Well, I understand, too," CW said, "but I'm not sure I'd like it if I were one of them. Humiliating and venal, is what it is."

"And you don't have such restrictions in New Orleans?" Rachel inquired, the edge to her voice growing steadily.

"Of course we do! And such proprieties are just as rotten there as they are here. Rotten and despicable! Why we choose to continue inflicting this shame upon ourselves simply mystifies me. It's the social blight of our age." CW tried to catch her, but Rachel strolled away from his reach.

"Oh, snap out of it, can't you!" She turned to Marie. "CW suffers so for the downtrodden and put-upon of society. It's a wonder the Catholics tolerate him."

"Empathy for the unfortunate is considered commendable in most civilized societies," CW said to Marie. "Wouldn't you agree?"

Trying to be neutral yet honest, she replied, "Well, all our lives are diminished by the suffering of others. We learn that in church."

"Did you hear that, dear?" CW turned to Rachel who refused to let him near. "Now, what do you have to say for yourself? What is the Baptist response to human suffering and indignity?"

Rachel steeled her eyes, then said, "We pay the same nickel at the entrance to the Hall of Freaks as you Catholics." She turned to Marie. "Or you Methodists, or the Pentacostals or the Congregationalists, or anyone else for that matter. And then we go inside the tent and stare for as long as we're allowed because the horrid Turtle Boy reminds us that, but for God's sweet grace, the freak's misfortune might just as well be our own. Therefore, my dear, we Baptists are thankful! That is our response. What else could it be?"

— 5 —

Marie lay in bed listening to the wind as it swept across the piney woods blowing storm clouds toward dawn. Nearby, a small electric fan whirred in the dark where her children breathed quietly and slept well, thoroughly exhausted from the thrills and enchantment of a visit to Emmett J. Laswell's Traveling Circus Giganticus. She knew they would dream of spiraling aerialists, sequins, spangles and sawdust, cotton candy, tumbling clowns and cascading fireworks illuminating a purple sky at twilight: a world come and gone in one summer evening. Across the faint light, she watched Henry's eyelids flutter and jump, Cissie's lips form a silent laugh, a squeal of whispered awe. The wind banged the storm-shutters on the rear of the house, tore at the laundry line, and kicked up clouds of dust that dirtied the chinaberry tree and rattled on the siding next door. A thousand miles away from her husband, in a house she barely knew, Marie Hennesey lay on her back and closed her eyes, remembering her girlhood and the dreams she'd herself had late at night after an evening at the circus.

Across what tightrope had she tiptoed in golden slippers to reach this place? What dangers lay before her still? Everyone has fears that toss with sleep and steal into our dreams. Back across the highwire was her home on Cedar Street in Illinois, unreachable now, lost for good. But whose good? This was not her bed, nor her room. Her children were orphaned from familiar surroundings. She slept in sheets that bore no scent of her husband. Where did he sleep now? And by whose scent? *When we have the least reason for getting into trouble,* Cissie learned from the Tin Woodman, *something is sure to go wrong.* The sad fate of Boy-Allen was not her only warning. She had to watch her step, and her children's, too.

Then soon Marie slept, and dreamed of home.

JULY

LATE ON THE MORNING of the Fourth of July, Marie Hennesey stood in the warm sunlight at the bedroom window folding linen. In the kitchen, still wearing a checkered apron from rolling pie crust after breakfast, Maude finished cleaning the pan she'd used to make puff-paste for a blueberry pie and ran a cotton cloth under the faucet while Rachel flitted about the front room, dusting the walnut side tables and bookcases, and listening to a musical radio program from Wichita. A parade in celebration of the Glorious Fourth was scheduled for noon through downtown Bellemont and Maude insisted the house be tidied up beforehand.

"What on earth for, Mother?" Rachel argued loudly enough for Marie to listen in. She didn't seem at all to mind sharing her disputes. "Are you expecting the parade to make a detour through our sitting room?"

"It's how we show respect," Maude answered, quickly polishing the blue porcelain enamel on her new Windsor range. "What the heart conceals, the face reveals."

Marie heard Maude shake out the floor mat by the kitchen door and replace it on the back porch. Henry had been playing in the stalls since sunrise and stomped dirt all over the porch when he came in for breakfast. Marie apologized to Maude for the mess, but secretly she was happy because it meant that Henry wasn't tiptoeing about; instead, he was acting like he did at home, silly and carefree. Maude could stand a little of that herself.

"I assume you won't mind then if I wear my spangled skirt to the parade," Rachel called to her. "It has Uncle Sam written all over it.

CW thinks it's very patriotic."

"My dear," Maude cautioned, "if you walk out of this house in that costume, you may just as well keep walking. I'll disown you and have a yard sale with all your possessions. I may even rent your room to a stranger."

"Oh, Mother!" Rachel laughed. "How thoroughly dramatic! Have you ever thought of traveling to Hollywood for an audition in the squawkies?"

"Never mind about that," Maude replied, picking up a stack of mail-order catalogues Rachel had left on a chair by the rear door. She took them into Rachel's room and put them on the bed. "You just remember what a wonderful country you live in, and show your respect for those who've come before. Our inheritance is their glory."

"Well, hallelujah, then!" Rachel cried. "I'll be sure to wear my Jefferson Davis button to the parade."

Marie heard Cissie laughing around front. Looking out the bedroom window, she saw Lili Jessup run up the sidewalk from next door, her arms loaded with straw. Maude had gone from Rachel's bedroom to her own, closing drawers and fussing about. After folding the last of the bedsheets, Marie slipped them into the bottom drawer of the dresser and walked out to the shadowy sitting room where Rachel lay on the sofa, her arms splayed limp in a pose of utter exhaustion. On the radio, an orchestra played a brisk Paul Whiteman number. A summer breeze fluttered in the curtain lace. Marie sat down at the piano, her favorite place in the room. Her feet were sore and she was weary. The draft clinked at the glass beads hanging from one of Maude's lamps. She told Rachel, "If you're half as tired as I am, I pity you. I can hardly keep on my feet."

"Well, I can't for the life of me imagine why," Rachel replied, her voice languid, almost drowsy. "I doubt there's a rooster anywhere in this town who wakes before you do. CW and I both feel you're suffering some rare affliction."

Marie laughed. "Oh, I enjoy mornings. It's so quiet, and I can get everything done I need to do without worrying about crossing anyone. I find it simplifying somehow." Back home in Illinois, Harry hated waking up early and generally stayed in bed while Marie bathed and dressed. She thought it strange not to wake at sunup, but was loathe to tell him so, knowing he'd likely ask why it was any concern of hers. She always felt it was important for a husband and wife to share the basis for these small incompatibilities with each other, in order to be better understood and get along more easily. Harry had no interest in that, which Marie came to believe was a grave fault in any marriage, hers included.

Maude called out to Rachel from her bedroom. "There, what am I always telling you? You just listen to her, dear! Trudy says that Vivian's been exercising at half past seven each morning to a radio class in pyjama calisthenics, and she was just raised to thirty dollars a week. I don't imagine it would hurt you to rise an hour or two earlier every day."

Rachel dismissed the suggestion with a wave of her hand. "Oh, apple butter! Why, I've no interest at all in eating the early bird's worm, Mother. Besides which, CW hates mornings and has to be routed out of bed himself. If we're to be married, I might just as well accustom myself to his schedule — it's the chief duty of wifehood, remember? Right after dishes and didies."

"If you don't watch yourself, young lady, you won't become anyone's wife."

Rachel leaped up from the sofa and went to the hallway where she shouted, "Don't you dare try and put the bee on me today, Mother! I simply won't allow it!" She came back into the sitting room with a wicked grin on her face. Fanning herself by the window, she said to Marie, "It's horrid in here, isn't it? Since Mother bought that idiotic stove, she's been broiling us out of house and home. I don't believe I can stand it another minute."

"Maybe we need an air conditioner," Marie suggested, patting the perspiration on her own cheeks, "or at least a new electric refrigerator to sit next to. Idabelle says they sell them on time now at Heywood's." She found the heat of East Texas utterly horrid, but the children raised little objection at all. Perhaps a small body is more adaptable to adverse circumstances than a big one.

"Of course they do," Rachel replied, taking out a cigarette from a patch pocket, "but anything I show a fondness for, Mother automatically disregards as utterly unnecessary. Fact is, we'd all better brace up for another unbearable summer, and that isn't bluff."

She crossed to the front door and went out to take her smoke.

Marie rose from the piano bench and followed. She felt antsy, ready to shake out the cobwebs. A warm draft had come up in the past half hour, drying the morning air and chasing dust and leaves from one end of College Street to the other. Marie brushed the hair back off her forehead and strolled around to the side porch where she could look down at Cissie's project under the fig tree: the construction of an authentic three-ring circus in doll-size scale. Naturally, the idea had come to her that night after visiting Laswell's circus. It was all Cissie had talked about for several days until one morning when Julius Reeves passed by the house pushing a wheelbarrow piled high with scraps of canvas and colored string and a fractured old wagon wheel he'd planned to cart away to the dump north of town for a couple of dollars in salvage redemption. Cissie stopped him and requested a thorough examination of the booty he'd collected, explaining that, seeing as how her mother had not permitted her to run away and join Laswell's wagon circus, she'd decided to build one of her own in her grandmother's front yard where anyone could stop by and be entertained for a penny. In a few minutes, Cissie persuaded Julius not only to give her half of what he'd planned to take to the dump that day, but to provide her with further materials until she completed the circus, at which time he'd become part-owner and share in the profits she was certain would exceed the value of any materials he could turn up. A portion of her own profit, she and Lili determined, would go toward daily flowers for Boy-Allen's grave. A handshake had sealed the bargain and, since that afternoon, with the help of Henry, Lili Jessup, and Abel Kritt, a big top was erected with several smaller tents housing the animal exhibits and the Freak Show (old dolls of Lili's beheaded or similarly crippled by Henry) along the midway and other exotic attractions.

"Cissie?" Marie called out, looking for her daughter. She saw Cissie's new brown elk sandals lying atop a small rabbit cage. Her daughter had no less a penchant for trouble than any other child, and she was more clever than most. Harry joked that one day she'd become a criminal genius, but Marie saw little humor in the notion. There was trouble enough in the world.

Henry crawled out of the tiny tent they had built from Julius's canvas. "She ain't in here."

Little Abel stuck his head out, too, his thick glasses cloudy with dust.

"*Isn't* in here," Rachel corrected, studying the layout of the circus grounds where Lili's worn-out dolls lay about in varying states of amputation and paint. Henry and Abel had been experimenting with dark-shaded dyes in order to create a more frightful flavor to their collection of freaks. "I'm afraid that living here in Bellemont has had a deleterious effect on your children's grammar, dear. Sorry."

"Henry, where's your sister?" Marie asked, craning her neck to search the grounds back of the circus and below the porch overhang. Lili's voice, raised in laughter, echoed somewhere nearby.

"She's collectin' wild pigs," Henry announced, getting up, his trousers dusty and worn at the knees from crawling about under the Big Top. "I'm s'posed to build the cages, but I can't find any wire. Do you think Grandma's got some me and Abel could borrow?"

Rachel said, "I think your children have gotten into Mother's medication cabinet."

"That's not at all funny," Marie replied, concerned that it might be true. One afternoon in her own girlhood, she had tried to paint her nails with mercurochrome and Cousin Violet licked the bottle cap and threw up all over them both. "Henry, where's your sister?"

"I told you!" he whined, stamping his foot in the dirt. "She's collectin' wild pigs for the circus!"

Frustrated, Marie called out, "Cissie!"

She heard a spate of giggles nearby, then a muffled reply. *"Over here, Momma!"*

Rachel said, "Why, I believe she's under the house."

"Oh, for goodness sakes!" Marie hurried down off the porch, joining Rachel by the corner of the house where a broken section of lattice revealed an entry to the foundation. This was just what she needed! Good gracious! What would they get into next? Marie leaned down to the black rectangle outlining the entry and called out. "Cissie?"

Her willful daughter's voice came out of the dark, *"Yes, Momma?"*

Marie could hear some shuffling in the dirt closeby. As firmly as possible, she said, "Come out from under there this instant."

"I can't," Cissie's disembodied voice replied. *"I think I'm stuck."*

Lili's distinctive giggle carried to Marie from the shadows. Marie asked, "Is that you, Lili?"

"Yes, ma'am."

"Is Cissie stuck somewhere under there?"

"Yes, ma'am." Lili tried unsuccessfully to muffle another giggle.

Maude's summer jasmine blooming along the lattice breathed a pretty scent as the morning breeze rose and fell. Out in the street, a new black Studebaker rattled past, chalky clouds of dust billowing up in its wake. Next door, the Jessup's collie began barking.

Cissie called out, *"Momma?"*

"Yes, dear."

"You don't need to wait. I'm sure I'll be free before the parade."

Her patience waning, Marie said, "Young lady, I'd prefer you to come out of there now and get cleaned up."

Lili giggled again.

"Where is she?" Rachel inquired, leaning down for a better look. "Can you tell?"

Lili answered, instead. *"We're by the chinaberry tree. I can see Mrs. Hennesey's bedsheets from where we're sitting."*

Rachel frowned. "Why, the girls aren't even by this side of the house."

"Well, for goodness sakes," said Marie, getting to her feet. She hurried around to the sideyard, ducked under the laundry line, and knelt beside an old wicker basket Maude had thrown out when its bottom tore free. She called again, "Cissie?"

"Yes, Momma?"

"Am I close?"

"I can see your shoes," she giggled. *"You're getting dirt all over them."*

"You can touch her foot if you stretch out." Lili appeared at the bottom of the foundation, peeking from the darkness with a smile.

Rachel knelt beside Marie. "It's been years since we've had a man out here to exterminate the rats."

Marie pulled back, astonishment drawn on her face. "Rats?"

"Yes, isn't that awful?" Rachel said, "If I've reminded Mother once, I've reminded her a thousand times. Of course, she's much too old to reform. We're lucky the Public Health Service hasn't come to board up our house. I can hear them at night, gnawing on the floorboards beneath my bed. I expect eventually to fall through and be eaten alive."

Marie frowned. She detested rats. Frenchy used to kill them in traps, then chase her and Emeline around the yard with the mutilated carcasses. "You're joking, of course."

"Ask Mother! She's heard them! Harry, too. He used to tell me they were leprechauns building a ship to sail back to Ireland. Some nights it does sound as though they're sawing and pounding nails."

Marie ducked back to the foundation and called out, "Cissie?"

"Yes, Momma?"

"Where are you stuck?"

"Right here! Can't you see my shoe?"

Marie inched her face forward, pressing her cheek to the dirt and staring sideways into the dark beneath the house. First Lili Jessup in pigtails, then Cissie, became visible in the shadows. Lili was sitting up against one of the wood supports, her arms folded about her knees, while Cissie lay on her side wedged between two other supports. They were no more than four or five feet from Marie, and both wore grins. Marie saw nothing amusing at all in this circumstance.

"Lili?" she asked, trying to remain calm. "Can you push Cissie from behind if I grab her feet and tug?"

"Don't hurt me, Momma," Cissie pleaded. "I'm really stuck."

Henry came up and kneeled in the dirt next to Marie, sticking his face into the dark. "I can help," he suggested.

"You just stay right here," Marie said. "I'd rather not have to call the fire department."

She slipped her arms under the lower wall and reached forward and grabbed Cissie's ankles. "Ready?"

"Yes, ma'am."

Marie pulled, gently at first, then more firmly when she realized how much more force was needed. Under the house, Lili groaned with the effort of shoving Cissie forward. Marie tugged a little harder. Cissie yelled for her to stop.

"My dress is tearing!" she cried. "It's stuck on a nail!"

"We can sew your dress," Marie said.

Another flurry of whispers passed between the girls, then Cissie called out to her mother, "Oh, swell! It's torn already. Go ahead."

Marie gripped her daughter's ankles more firmly, gave a sharp tug, and pulled Cissie clear, ripping the dress clear down the inseam, but freeing her daughter from the support posts and sliding her out from underneath the house. Lili crawled out after her. Both girls were filthy and Cissie's rose plaid gingham hung torn from one shoulder, soiled with grime of all sorts, spider web in her haircurls.

Marie took one look at her daughter, grabbed her by the arm without saying a word, and took her into the house, the screen door slamming behind them. Marie led Cissie to the bathroom and closed the door. "Now get out of that dress this instant and don't squabble!"

"Momma!"

"You heard me," Marie bent down to stick the plug into the bathtub drain. She swiveled both spigots and water began to run into the tub.

"I don't feel like a bath," Cissie protested. "I won't take one."

"Yes, you will. Now get out of that dress, young lady. I won't ask you again."

"But I didn't do anything wrong!"

"I haven't said you did," Marie corrected, testing the temperature of the water with her fingers. Who claimed daughters were neater than sons?

"Then why do I have to take a bath?"

"Because I say so." With Harry gone, both children were constantly testing her patience and she was not at all pleased. If they persisted in doing so, there'd be trouble ahead. She'd had more than her share of agitations this summer already.

Cissie unfastened the buttons of her dress with dirty fingers. "You always side against me. You know you do."

"Sides have nothing to do with it. Just have a look at yourself in the mirror. Good grief! What do you think your father would say?"

"That I'm filthy. Then he'd clench his teeth and ask me what the devil I thought I was doing under the house."

"No smart cracks, young lady."

There was a knock at the door.

"Yes?"

Maude peeked her head in.

"We're taking a bath," Marie said, somewhat embarrassed at her daughter's plight.

"Momma?" Cissie frowned. "My feet stink."

Maude came in, shutting the door behind her. "Grab her ankles."

"Pardon?"

"Go ahead, dear. Do as I say."

"All right." Somewhat confused, Marie bent down and grabbed Cissie by both ankles as Maude slipped her own arms under Cissie's shoulders.

"Now, lift her up over the tub."

"Momma!" Cissie cried.

"Hush!" Maude looked Marie in the eye and nodded for her to begin lifting. Somewhat reluctantly, Marie raised her daughter up to horizontal, and helped Maude maneuver her above the water. "Now, give her a good shake."

Marie frowned. "Pardon me?"

"Honey, do as I say!"

"Momma, help!"

Maude twisted Cissie by the shoulders vigorously back and forth, up and down. Seeing she had no choice, Marie did likewise. Cissie shrieked out loud, but Maude continued until Cissie's clothing fluttered above the water. Cascading filth in the form of dust and web fragments filtered down to the surface of the water. Another few vigorous shakes, and Maude motioned Marie to carry Cissie away from the tub where they set her back on her feet.

"Now, dear," said Maude, "have a look at what you got yourself into crawling around under there. Fleas! The kind that fester in the wounds of dead vermin and make life miserable for everyone in the household once they're brought indoors."

Both Cissie and her mother leaned over the tub. If there were fleas, they resembled dark particles of dust floating on the cloudy water. Maude reached down and pulled the chain on the plug, draining the tub. "We'll refill the bath when you get out of those clothes." She showed Cissie a scowl. "Go on now. Hurry up. Take off your dress. The parade'll start soon enough and I'm sure you'll want to go."

Cissie reluctantly pulled the torn gingham dress over her head and stood humiliated beside the old tub in her white cambric drawers.

Maude looked at Marie. "If we hadn't shaken them off her clothing, we'd have had to burn it. Nothing less would have removed the eggs laid in the time it took her to come indoors, not to mention germs of all sorts, which Beatrice says are our constant associates. She was a nurse once in Houston, you know."

"I had no idea," Marie said, embarrrassed at her own ignorance of pests.

Maude leaned down around the side of the tub and drew out a porcelain pitcher and basin. She filled the pitcher with water from the bath spigot and used it to wash the filthy water, fleas and all, down the drain as the bath emptied. Replacing the plug, she dialed up the hot water and allowed the tub to begin filling once more.

Marie said to Cissie, "Honey, take your drawers off, too. They're filthy."

"Momma?"

"Melissa Jean Hennesey! This instant!"

Cissie began whimpering.

"Listen, dear, it's as much my fault as yours," Maude said, replacing the pitcher and basin. "I ought to have known you children would find a way underneath the house. Rachel and her friends used to play under there every Saturday morning until her father caught a rat the size of a Chihuahua in the rose bushes by the steps. Pestilence is the Lord's opinion of the ignorant. I'll wash these clothes this afternoon."

Maude scooped up Cissie's soiled clothing and left the bathroom.

"I'm sorry, Momma," Cissie said, climbing into the tub. "I was only looking for mice to invite into our circus. If Grandma or Auntie Rachel had told me there were rats under there, I'd never have let Lili persuade me to go."

The water rose to her belly as she sat down in the lukewarm water. "I know, dear," said Marie, grabbing a bar of soap and a washcloth as Cissie dunked her head underwater. "Rats!"

She shuddered and began to lather the soap.

Farrington, Illinois
June 28th, 1929

Dearest Marie,

It is now two months and a day since you've been gone from us. We all miss you so horribly. Granny Chamberlain thinks you're off to St. Paul on holiday and will be back next week. Were it only true! Had your letter when it arrived here not been carried around in the pocket of our forgetful postman's mackintosh, an answer would have reached you sooner. But such is life in the northern farms, and when Mr. Giroux is headfull of buying a house and thinking of his future-intended, you can easily excuse such errors.

Now it is Saturday. My spoiled little bottle-baby has been such a worry this week that I gave a call to Auntie Emma. She came here fast as lightning and seems heaven sent, as always. What would we do without her? I wish you could see what a darling the baby has become since Easter. Roy is already pestering me for another! He fusses when I accuse him of sex-madness, but it sure keeps him hopping! Yesterday I was out to Galesburg to buy a new hat and a pair of gloves, letting the house struggle along without me. Strange to say, Roy and Uncle Boyd managed very well, and I found the kitchen all intact upon my return. It was a perfect day and I enjoyed myself to the limit, though my head was full of plans for a fall garden, and how best to finish my arduous duties today. Tomorrow is Sunday and as yet we have no teacher. Last Sunday we picked up Mr. Vernon H. Cowsert, a Methodist minister from Peoria, and enjoyed the lesson almost as much as if you had been there with us. Who is to teach tomorrow I don't know. Maybe another Methodist minister floating around, in which case it will be all right. I rather hesitate to attempt to teach or even lead a discussion myself. Seems too much like a blind leader of those who see. No, this is not modesty, but a candid recognition of facts as they are.

Bonnie and I went out to Mrs. Milo's to a young ladies missionary society meeting and waited on them. Such appetites! We were all decked out in white aprons and caps. Edith had one the size of a postage stamp. Bonnie nearly cut herself in two trying to put one of Dorothy's aprons on. Everything went off splendidly, especially the pineapple ice. Corrine Frank sang for us and they all left at the seasonable hour of 9:45. Harlow's automobile was in great demand, but too many girls were too much for the engine, and it broke a couple of ball-bearings, corresponding, I suppose, to a heart. It only returned in time to take Dorothy home, together with Edith and Corrine.

You spoke of my library being untouched, but you are wrong. I finished *Middlemarch*, but have been too busy to write anything about it. I am reading Hawthorne's biography evenings, and Shakespeare Sunday afternoons. So you see I am not neglecting my education. I can't afford to do that, for I need it so much. By the way, that was a good joke of yours, though I had not eaten breakfast and my internals were roaring like the little pigs going to market, much to Roy's amusement.

But here I am filling up these pages with the chatter which is becoming natural to me. I wish I had your ability to glorify the commonplace, and mix in a little of the sublime. As it is, I can only keep on in my own way, or be accused of being sentimental. News is scarce.

I love you bushels.

Your loving cousin,

Emeline

— 2 —

By half past eleven, people were wandering about the sidewalks in the direction of downtown or sitting up on shaded verandas along the parade route. Smelling of fresh Barbasol and hair tonic, CW arrived on College Street, four flags of Old Glory fluttering from antennae mounted on the corners of his Ford. Across both the driver's and passenger's doors, he'd draped larger flags, folded and hung like bunting. Idling, the engine dulled to a hornet's hum.

"Why, dear, I believe you could enter the parade and not appear at all out of place. It's absolutely grand!" said Rachel, stepping out of doors behind Marie who walked to the porch-railing.

CW tipped his straw hat. "Thank you, darling." He shut off the motor and bounced out of the automobile. Rachel greeted him at the gate and gave him a kiss much too intimate for a public sidewalk at midday. Soon Marie expected to see them making love with the top down on Main Street. What would Harry say? He used to have that spark of sex in his eye. Maybe Rachel wasn't overbold, after all. Why couldn't everyone be so daring?

Wind blew in the street and rippled the flags on CW's car. It was warm out, tending toward a hot afternoon. Henry dashed down the steps and bounced into the rear seat. "Let's go now!"

"We won't be taking the automobile, dear," Marie said, "even if it is quite spectacular."

"Why, I think we ought to," Rachel argued. "Who says we can't? A parade is for everyone, isn't it? Can't we join? Don't we count in that crowd?"

"But it's much nicer to walk, don't you agree?" Marie suggested, anxious to stretch her legs. "More festive?" She could walk downtown, even if she had to do it alone. Being housebound all morning left her feeling both wan and restless. She needed the society of neighbors to perk up. Apropos of that spirit, Marie had dressed for the parade in a lovely French blue silk flat crepe frock, and felt very up-to-the-minute, even if Harry might not agree it was modern enough.

CW laughed. "Don't forget, dear: Rachel absolutely despises exertion of any sort. Why, she'd take a trolley from her bed to the breakfast table every morning if she could."

Maude came out onto the porch, fastening her Sunday bonnet and squinting into the sunlight. Already, the distant rhythms of a marching band carried across the afternoon air. Children squealed with joy, dancing and waving small flags in the middle of College Street. A dog with a patriotic ribbon tied to its tail ran past in the direction of the children, barking loudly. Motor horns honked constantly.

"Mother, why are you wearing that silly old bonnet?" Rachel

laughed, taking CW's hand. "The parade doesn't lead to church."

"It's no concern of yours what I wear." Maude sniffed as she studied Rachel's skirt a moment or two. "Though I don't see how dressing like a harlot honors the birth of our country."

"Mother, if you're dyspeptic this morning, chew a stick of Beeman's." Rachel laughed again. "I'll have you know this dress is an exact copy of the one Martha Washington wore on the night she visited Thomas Jefferson while his pal George was away at Valley Forge. How can one be more patriotic than that?"

Cissie came out of the dooryard arm-in-arm with Lili Jessup, skipping into the street. Henry and Abel Kritt ran to catch up with them. Marie looked down the sidewalk and saw dozens of people strolling toward downtown. Overhead, the sky was clear and blue, a fine day for a parade. With the children running on ahead, the adults were hoping to find a nice shady place on the lawn of the courthouse square from which to view the grand procession. They walked beneath the dense green canopy of cottonwoods and willows and waved at neighbors drinking tea and lemonade on screened verandas and shaded stairs. Maude called out a greeting at each address and touched her bonnet, which elicited an equally gracious response. Marie exchanged holiday pleasantries with Mr. Gray, whose wheelchair, high on his shady porch, was swathed in Old Glory, and shared a fine recipe for rhubarb pie with Dora Bennett out tending her lovely summer roses, too busy for any old parade. Rachel and CW strolled side by side, nuzzling each other affectionately as they went, teasing with whispered flirtations. Glad to be out and about, Marie watched the children darting in and out of the tall shade trees, playing tag and kick-the-can with a rusty Campbell's Soup tin. Two men dressed in Confederate gray and bearing shiny sabers rode quickly by on horseback, late for parade formation. Closer to the square, Marie passed several women carrying fringed mulberry parasols and American flags and a full-skirted young girl with a trim little figure pushing a wicker baby carriage. All were chatting casually in the shade of the weeping willows as they walked along.

Marie and Maude, Rachel, CW and the children found the courthouse square filled with people wandering about admiring the decorations and waiting for the parade. American flags of all sizes rippled in the breeze, while barking dogs and popping firecrackers echoed across downtown.

"Can we light some firecrackers, Momma?" Henry asked, hopefully. Standing behind him was little Abel, a look of mischief on his face. "Please?"

Marie frowned. "Why, I don't know. Where on earth would you find any?" Harry had taught his son a love of fireworks that Marie found distressing. They scared her half to death.

He gave a shrug. "Maybe there's some lying 'round somewhere. Me and Abel could go lookin', if it's allowed. I guess they ain't too hard to find."

"*Aren't* too hard to find," Rachel corrected, as she gave CW a kiss on the cheek and sent him off across Main Street to Hooker's drugstore. She followed Maude onto the lawn.

Marie turned to Henry's little friend, Abel. "Honey, what does your mother say about playing with firecrackers?"

The quiet towhead adjusted his glasses, and shrugged. "She don't mind if I ain't popping them off in the house."

"Thank you," said Marie, pausing with the children. "Henry, I suppose it would be fine for you and Abel to have a look around, so long as you promise not to set any off without my permission."

"We will," Henry promised. Then he called to Cissie and Lili petting a black Labrador on the lawn next to the sidewalk. "Momma says me and Abel can go find firecrackers!"

"Oh?" Cissie called back from beside the Labrador. "Momma, is that true?"

Marie nodded. "You can go, too, if you keep an eye on your brother and promise not to get into trouble."

"Well, I'm not sure I want to blow up any firecrackers," Cissie confessed, rising to her feet. "They hurt my ears. Besides, Lili and I'd rather go see the horses saddling up."

Henry stamped his foot. "I want to blow up firecrackers!"

Little Abel came up beside him, wiping his glasses off again on the back of his sleeve. His brown moleskin knickers were already dusty and his hands caked with dirt. He and Henry were a pair, all right.

"Oh, go to it, you little ninny," Cissie snapped. "What in the Hades do I care?"

Marie blanched. "Cissie! Would you like to go home right now?"

"No, ma'am."

"Well, then, you'd better change your disposition, young lady. You've been flip since breakfast and I won't have anymore of it, do you hear me?" Her daughter had been trying Marie's patience for days now and this was the limit. She had much too much on her own mind to be sorting out Cissie's nasty behavior on such a pleasant afternoon.

Cissie brushed grass off her skirt. "Yes, ma'am."

"Now, are you going to go with your brother or not?"

She looked at Lili still kneeling on the lawn beside the panting Labrador. "We'd rather see the horses."

"Well, you suit yourselves." Marie turned to Henry. "Honey, you and Abel be careful, all right? And don't forget to be back here before the parade ends. Dinner's at two."

"Yes, Momma."

Marie watched a flock of sparrows sail past as the midday heat swelled and men and women all about downtown fanned themselves briskly with hats and handkerchiefs. There were scores of Shantytown Negroes among the Main Street crowd, as well, young and old alike, waving crisp flags of the Republic and carrying on in the spirit of the hour. Did public events restore God's intended gravity to the world, Marie wondered, that holy equity inspired from Eden? Kindness is easily reciprocated without need of plot or hidden motives. Tolerance instructs the soul and soon the heart warms to it as naturally as love. Seeing grand holiday smiles on so many black faces along Main Street gave Marie herself a delightful shiver of sorts, soft as sleep.

A band struck up a lively John Philip Sousa march as CW cut through the crowd and hurried across the street carrying two strawberry ice cream cones already melting in the heat. Marie saw Rachel and Maude beside the flagpole and worked her way through the vibrant crowd to reach them.

"Now and then," she heard Maude say to Rachel as she approached, "perhaps the less we know, the longer we live."

"Pardon me?" Marie said, hoping to catch the thread of conversation as a flurry of motor horns honked across town. "Did I miss something?"

"Boy-Allen's mom," Rachel replied, as she directed Marie's attention across the street to a slight young woman in a shabby peach housedress and dark scrambled hair, half-hidden in the alleyway between the Electric & Battery Shop and Lippincott's Dry Goods Company. "I was just telling Mother, I believe this is the first I've seen Loretta out of doors since the funeral."

"Perhaps she's been keeping a solitude," Marie remarked, still disturbed by the memory of the little white hearse rolling under the cottonwoods that grim and windy afternoon. To her eye, the woman appeared frightfully woebegone.

Fanning herself with her hands, Rachel added, "Boyd Powell says Loretta telephones downtown every morning at eight o'clock to ask if the killer's been caught yet. It's obvious she's been driven into great extremes. I expect it'll be tough going for her in the future."

"There's your clue," Maude remarked. "Well-being is more than seeming to be well. Do you remember my commenting on how slim and proud she used to be? That was only last summer. Why, I doubt a girl her age has the wherewithal to cope on her own. I blame Fred Stevens equally with Boy-Allen's killer for wrecking that poor girl's outlook. To hear Trudy tell it, Loretta was completely devoted to that man. She fell for him like a ton o' brick and when he chucked her, well, you can see for yourself."

"She does look awfully worn out," Marie agreed, as she watched a cluster of red and blue balloons float sluggishly off into the midday sky from the rooftop of the First State Bank. The clamor of a large marching band drew nearer. A Negro man had been arrested just last week for Boy-Allen's murder, then released the next day when the court at Henderson admitted they'd been holding the same fellow in jail the night Boy-Allen died. Where was the true killer? Had Marie seen him across College Street that night of the circus? It was both frightful and maddening how close she'd come to identifying his face, if that indeed had been him.

Rachel said, "Mother, I'm going to write your life and include all the correct living habits that you and those dirty old snoops of yours like to paw over the rest of us for lacking. It's sure to be one of the biggest volumes in the world."

Maude scowled. "Oh, horsefeathers! Fact is, Trudy says that boy was always full of hop and crying for trouble, and I agree. A lot he cared for Loretta or that poor child. I saw him hiding under his hat at the services and I doubt he shed one tear. Why, I'll lay his heart wasn't even chipped."

"Whose heart?" CW asked, arriving now with the strawberry ice cream cones. A thundering of bass drums caused a great stir in the crowd along the sidewalk. Children shrieked and rushed for the curb. Marie craned her neck, looking for the parade to start. She loved the horses and the drums.

"Thank you, darling." Rachel took her ice cream cone from CW and gave him a kiss on the cheek where perspiration droplets beaded from the heat. "Mother insists that Fred Stevens' making love to one woman after another is the moral equivalent of murder."

"I never said that," Maude protested.

A flurry of torpedoes burst loudly on the sidewalk behind the bandshell, giving Marie a start. She hoped Henry and Abel weren't involved with that.

CW asked, "Who's Fred Stevens?"

Rachel licked her strawberry ice cream, then replied, "Boy-Allen's father and a notorious rake-hell who could pick out any sweet girl he wanted when he was still fit. For ten years he pretended to be a devoted husband, then he quit her cold last September and now most people in town think he's just a fat-headed dub who only married Loretta because he got her caught while out tomcatting one night."

CW laughed. "Well, you can't blame a fellow for trying to make love at sight, can you? It's in our blood. Sure we'd like to duck it, but quite frankly we can't."

"Hmph!" Maude snorted. "I tell you, Fred Stevens had no genuine fondness at all for poor Loretta, and his absence since Boy-Allen's murder has made that plain as day."

"Oh, so he's beaten it, has he?" CW said, licking his own ice cream cone. "Lit out for the territories like Huck Finn?"

"A rolling stone gathers no whiskers," said Rachel, turning to the north end of the block as a great cheer went up. Marie heard a chorus of brass horns and a raucous clash of cymbals. Maude moved forward to get a better view of the street as the Panola Citizens Marching Brass Band came into view. Fourteen men in spit-and-polished blue uniforms, trumpets and flutes and trombones and drums playing for the assembled multitude, each earnest member wearing hats with feathered plumes and tiny flags of the Republic. The crowd cheered loudly as the brass band passed in revue. The Women's Relief Corps followed in flowing white dresses with flower-rimmed parasols and bonnets. Marie recognized Beatrice and Trudy and heard Maude give a cheerful yell as her friends passed by. Behind them came a long marching column of stern-faced war veterans, rifles at shoulder arms. At the front were half a dozen elderly men in long white beards wearing butternut gray and carrying a faded battle flag of the old Confederacy, trailed by a youthful bugler playing "Dixie." While kiddies with flags and horns chased along the curb, many a straw-hatted fellow gave these weary veterans a solemn salute. Marie's own heart contracted as she recalled great Uncle Philander who helped chase Braxton Bragg across Stone's River with the 19th Illinois Infantry, despite losing his left thumb to a Rebel bullet, and survived to march in the regimental colors each Glorious Fourth until he passed away on Hattie's porch after supper one spring evening in 1924.

When a flurry of young maidens wrapped in flags of the Republic tossed garlands of rose petals and daisies in the footsteps of the old soldiers, Rachel remarked, "Isn't this the most disgusting display of garishness and bad taste you've ever witnessed? Surely no Northern town debases itself so thoroughly as do we here in the South."

"Don't be so sure," Marie replied, her attention on the parade. "We're all proud of our heritage, don't you agree?"

"If you say so."

Rachel took out a handkerchief to wipe her mouth as she finished her ice cream. CW cheered as soldiers from the War with Spain followed down Main Street, half a dozen infantrymen with rifles and horns and two saber-clad Rough Riders on horseback recalling

Teddy's First Volunteer Cavalry from the camp at San Antonio whose mounts wore war's grand regalia of pomp and patriotism. Each offered a brisk and dignified salute to Mayor Devlin and Bellemont's city council as he passed the courthouse grandstand and the colorful display of American and Republic of Texas flags hanging there in the midsummer heat.

"We have parades in Illinois," Marie remarked, raising her voice above the thundering drums, "and I don't recall them being much different than this. I always enjoy them, in fact. Don't you?"

"Not since Mother forced me to march down this very street dressed up in a tiger costume that attracted every dog in Texas. I was bitten on the ankle and laughed at from one end of Bellemont to the other. I'd never been so humiliated in all my life."

"Well, you can't blame that on the parade."

"Of course I can," Rachel replied, "and I do, every year at this time. My foot swelled up fat as a pumpkin. I refused to leave the house for a week."

Cissie and Lili had wormed a path through the skirts and dark suits and crossed over to the far side of the street where they waved to Marie and clapped for the sixteen brawny doughboys from Black Jack Pershing's A.E.F. when they came into view. The crowd roared. The brass band played "Over There" and an old Confederate cannon in the empty lot behind Hooker's drugstore boomed a loud salute. Marie recognized one of the doughboys as Wilfred Morrison, who worked the butcher's counter at Metcalf's Market, and another as Maude's dentist, Dr. Carl Holt. Both looked fit and proud in smart overseas caps and uniforms. She wondered how many of their classmates hadn't returned from France. Tears spoiled the face-paint of more than one on Main Street this sunny afternoon. Pride and sorrow wrestled with the past. *Memorials may warm the heart now and then,* Granny Mae once told her, *but the terrible quiet of an empty chair abides forever.*

CW came up beside Marie just as a hired brewery truck transporting a dozen or more Uncle Sams arrived on Main Street playing the fiddle and singing an enthusiastic chorus of "The Yellow Rose of Texas." He said, "Rachel's not telling you that silly tiger costume story of hers now, is she?"

"You hush your mouth, mister know-it-all," Rachel snapped back. "Dignity's forfeiture abides not reason nor calendar. All Mother cared about was participating in the parade without actually having to set foot in the street herself. I ought to've had her arrested for scurrility."

CW's response was drowned out by a particularly boisterous section of marching tuba players leading a procession of fraternal orders in triumphant precision, then a men's glee club, a barbershop quartet in old-fashioned handlebar moustaches, fifteen foot-racers in tights, and Bellemont's volunteer fire brigade.

"Well, your personal suffering notwithstanding," Marie said, angling to see past a portly woman holding a large fringed parasol, "I think it's a grand parade."

— 3 —

The kitchen screen door banged shut as Henry rushed dusty-faced out onto the back porch. Down the sidewalk, little Abel Kritt was called home to dinner by his mother. Having changed out of her glad garments into a more practical gingham, Marie busied herself about the kitchen while Maude set the dining room table. Potatoes hot and mealy simmered on the stovetop; fishcakes sizzled in a pan beside them. Though Rachel had argued all morning for lettuce sandwiches and iced tea, Maude insisted on a warm meal for the children who would have happily settled on Grape-Nuts with cream or a dish of Beech-Nut orange drops. After rinsing water glasses in the sink, Marie put on a pair of mitts and took Maude's blueberry pie out of the oven. She had to concede this new range was a fine improvement over the old one; both the firebox and reservoir were larger and the whole range could be cleaned with a soft cloth. She had already written about it in a letter to her mother whose own cook stove was just about worn out.

"You're a marvel," Rachel said to Marie, as she came into the kitchen from the sitting room. "Do you know that, dear?"

Marie smiled. "I'm not sure what you mean."

"Oh, this divine urge with which you attend to us, your dizzy relations." Rachel giggled. "You've helped us get out of our rut by removing the ruts. I don't know how we ever managed before."

"There's no need to idealize her," Maude called out from the dining room. "It ought to be enough to say Marie's a credit to her family, and leave it at that."

Rachel sniffed over the hot fishcakes. "Why, I don't idealize her at all, though she must have the patience of a flea-tamer to spend all day with you, Mother." She winked at Marie. "Daddy always said you can choose your friends, but you can't choose your relatives."

The telephone rang.

Rachel shot off into the hallway where Marie heard her shout, "Don't touch the phone, Mother! It's for me!"

"How do you know that?" Maude asked. "I'm expecting a call from Trudy."

"Mother, please!" Rachel caught the telephone midway through the second ring. "Hello?"

Marie gently placed a red-checkered cloth over the steaming blueberry pie. She made it a point never to answer the phone here herself unless asked to do so.

"Oh, how are you, dear?" she heard Rachel speak into the telephone.

"Who is it?" Maude asked, impatiently. "If it's Trudy, I won't — "

Rachel snapped back, "Mother, would you please sit down before you burst a blood vessel! It's not for you! It's Sophie and she has news from Robert in Port Arthur. Now go on! Shoo!"

"Piffle!" Maude walked back into the dining room.

Marie returned to the stove. Of course she was pleased by Rachel's flattery. *Let another praise you, and not your own mouth,* Aunt Hattie always said, though Emeline was often boastful, and Violet, too, when she was alive. Marie was proud enough to see that she had made herself useful this summer, that she and her children had been no heartscald for Maude or Rachel in a trying circumstance. She imagined Harry would be pleased, regardless of their difficulties. He had told her that it was always harder to make others believe better of you than you believe of yourself. From fear and apprehension she wept one night after packing, but that was all. Afterward, a mother's sacred responsibility gave her strength enough to endure until she saw the miles and miles of pretty bluebonnets from her sleeper car window; then she knew they would survive, and whatever duties were required of her in that household she could perform without reticence or complaint.

Marie heard Cissie yelling at Henry outdoors. She put down the spatula and went to the back door. The children had returned to work on the circus. Cissie proclaimed herself ringmaster and began delegating tasks to her brother and Lili Jessup in hopes of completing construction on her Big Top and midway by the end of the week. Several children they had met at the parade donated the use of worn-out stuffed animals and a box full of paper dolls Cissie intended as spectators under the tent.

Stepping onto the back porch, Marie saw Henry in tears by the Jessup's fence. Lili knelt beside him in the dirt, scratching her old gray cat.

Cissie stood in front of Henry, shouting in his ear. "You are utterly hopeless! I told Momma she ought to have left you under that bridge where she and Daddy found you!"

"Don't say that!" Henry cried.

"I will say it because it's true. Momma told me you were no better'n a silly little groundhog crawling in the mud underneath that dirty old bridge. She and Daddy just felt sorry for you, that's all."

"Liar!"

"Groundhog!"

Marie shouted from the porch railing. "CISSIE!"

Her daughter turned toward the house. "Yes, Momma?"

"Stop telling stories about your brother!"

"I ain't born from a groundhog, am I, Momma?" Henry asked, tears carving thin rivulets through the dirt on his cheeks.

Marie frowned. "Of course not. Your sister's just teasing."

"He ought to know the truth, Momma," Cissie insisted. "Why, I'm sure he's old enough to put up with the shame."

"You hush, young lady," Marie warned, "before I trade you and that smart mouth of yours to Mr. Laswell's circus."

"Oh, would you, please? I have no doubt I'd enjoy myself much more in a cage full of wild animals than I do living with this little urchin. Send me away this instant, Momma! Please!"

"Don't tempt me, darling," Marie replied, watching a pair of motorcars roll by, packed with young people fit out for the doings scheduled in the Bellemont pavilion at twilight. "Now unless you'd like to stay indoors for the rest of the day, stop tormenting your brother. I mean it!"

With that last warning, Marie went back inside where Maude was opening the windows to admit a draft in the warm afternoon. "That too-clever daughter of mine is turning into a little gangster," said Marie, attending once more to the stove. "I've half a mind to send her to bed after dinner." Next time she wrote to Harry, she intended to ask that he put a word or two of caution for Cissie in a future letter of his own. She believed that was the least he could do for being away so long.

"Truth be told, she takes after her father," Maude remarked with a smile. "When Harry was her age, he was so full of vinegar, he made us wild. He was flip and careless, and I didn't think Jonas or myself could ever bear it, yet we all made out, and Harry grew into a fine man, which told me plenty about the heart of a child."

"Then you don't think there's much to worry over with Cissie? You can see she's been quite a caution."

"I expect you'll both pull through just fine," Maude replied, disappearing into the pantry. "I have no great concern."

Rachel hung up the telephone and came back into the kitchen, wearing a smirk. "Sophie says Robert's been running around with a doll named Grace who traveled to Japan last year. It seems she owns a fortune in stocks and can buy whatever she pleases. Robert says her aim is to retire soon and spend the rest of her life knocking about the world, going where the jazz is the thickest! Isn't that remarkable? He says she's just got that certain air about her."

"Is she decent?" Maude asked, taking the potatoes off the stove.

Rachel frowned. "Oh, I'm sure she smokes cigarettes, Mother, and drinks gin with her eggs in the morning and hasn't been to church since Harding died. Good grief! According to Sophie, Grace gave Robert a man-sized hickey when they went out sailing one afternoon in the Gulf. Do you suppose that makes her cheap?" She grabbed a dishtowel and wiped off a puddle of water on the countertop.

"Don't snipe, dear," Maude answered. "I just believe it's easy for a girl to get in wrong these days, all the more so if she's rich and spoiled." She turned to address Marie. "It's always dreadful when a defect of character alters the course of a human life."

"Yes, it is."

Rachel rolled her eyes. "Mother, who said she was spoiled? I just told you she's been investing in the market for all it's worth and earning a king's ransom doing so! Playing the high and the low these days is no dip in the river, you know."

Maude stuck a fork lightly into the potatoes. "All the same, Robert's Miss So-and-So ought to be careful whom she decides to run with. Breaches of moral law don't exist for men. Beatrice says Helen told her that Rose Foster went to a nudist colony last year in the company of three oil barons from Dallas. Imagine that, if you will! Well, Helen claimed Rose was the picture of death during the Easter Egg Hunt at Hunziger's farm, and I couldn't disagree, though I refused to say anything as raw as that."

Rachel laughed. "Oh, of course not. You're much too polite, Mother. You'd never say anything against a neighbor, would you?"

Rinsing the fork, Maude told Marie, "I've never held for low insinuations. I believe it's bad manners."

Rachel cracked a mischievous grin. "Still, dear, wasn't it you who told Roland Butler he ought to take care picking a right girl because a bad one's like a viper swollen with poison?"

"Honey, I merely suggested to him that bringing a young lady back from Matamoros might prove to be a difficult proposition, that's all. Marriage is serious stuff, I told him. Why collect fresh fish for all the old cats to feast on?"

"Yet he and Yolanda are getting on gloriously, aren't they? That good-for-nothing Roland — that waster, as y'all used to call him — seems as if he's been married since the first day he shaved. He wasn't ruined at all. In fact, he's well thought of now and making good, and most of us agree he's got Yolanda to thank for that."

Maude sniffed. "Well, that may be so, but Trudy tells me Roland's people still don't think much of her."

"Oh, for crying out loud, Mother, that's ridiculous! Where'd she get that hooey?"

"Why, I believe Lois confessed it over tea last month."

Rachel laughed out loud. "Well, then, Trudy's landed the real lowdown, hasn't she? You people just burn me up! Why won't you concede that — "

The doorbell rang.

Rachel threw down her dishtowel and dashed off to the front room.

"I think the fishcakes are done," Marie said, removing the skillet from the stove. Maude made room on the counter next to the pan of potatoes.

"Perhaps you could fetch a bottle of milk from the ice-box, dear," Maude said.

"Certainly," Marie replied, heading into the pantry.

"Could you bring more sugar, as well? We'll need to refill the bowl. Rachel practically emptied it onto her corn flakes this morning. I'm surprised her teeth haven't rotted away."

The pantry was cool and dark and Marie had to switch on a light to find the sack of sugar on the middle shelf. Emeline once left hers on a bottom shelf and woke one morning to find it swarmed with ants. *Draw a line with chalk across the threshold and along the baseboards*, Aunt Hattie suggested to them both, *and no ant will cross it.*

Marie came out of the pantry just as Rachel walked in carrying a bouquet of red roses.

"Isn't this frightfully romantic?" she announced, smiling broadly. "Why, I do believe CW McCall is today the finest gentlemen in the great state of Texas. That is, if I'm allowed to utter such flattery in the presence of ladies less fortunate than myself."

"Of course you are, dear," CW said, entering the kitchen behind her, straw hat in hand. "It's a holiday."

"They're beautiful," Marie said, admiring Rachel's flowers. She turned to CW, "Where in heaven's name did you find them?"

"Why, I don't know," he replied, feigning ignorance. "One moment, my hands were empty, and the next I had this wonderful bouquet to give to my sweet patootie lamb. Didn't I, dear?"

Rachel kissed him square on the lips. "I had no idea men were capable of such displays of affection." She turned to Marie. "Isn't he a surprise?"

"You're a lucky girl," said Marie, smiling. "I'm sure if it weren't for Harry I'd be quite jealous."

"Oh, luck's got nothing whatsoever to do with romance," Rachel said, dancing through the hall to the front room where she stroked the piano keys lightly with one finger. "A girl knows when she's special. Even if she just can't see it in her vanity mirror, every man on the street'll let her know when she walks by. It's God's apology to Eve for His temper that horrid morning in Eden."

"Trust a woman to remember," CW remarked. He leaned over to smell the fishcakes and smiled. "My oh my!"

"Only by love doth the heart reveal its most innocent desire," Rachel called out. "Our Heavenly Father ought not to have intruded upon Eve's privacy. You'd think He'd have better manners than that."

"I'd be careful what I say, young lady," Maude scolded, as she walked back into the kitchen. "It's been more than a month since you've attended Sunday service. The Lord's neither deaf nor blind, and His memory is — "

"I know, Mother," Rachel interrupted. "Greater than all Creation."

"Well, that's a fact."

"Honest to goodness, Mother. Why do you ever have anything to do with me at all?" Rachel giggled, then sniffed her red rose bouquet. "I must make you awfully bitter."

Maude went into the pantry and came out with a bowl of carrots. "I've learned not to remember your faults, dear." She smiled at Marie.

"That seems sensible," CW remarked. "I wonder if I'll develop the same patience."

"Well, it's certainly not too late to pull out, otherwise," Maude added, rinsing the carrots under the faucet.

"I resent that, Mother," Rachel said. "Why, I've received gifts from men and been admired at one time or another on nearly every single day of the year. A gentleman told me once that he found me even more charming on Sunday mornings than on Saturday nights."

"Who might that have been?" Maude asked, doubt etched in her expression. "Herbert?"

"Who's Herbert?" CW asked. "A former flame? A schoolyard sweetheart?"

"A most suitable beau," Rachel answered, "provided that I were struck on the head by a boulder and rendered insensible for the rest of my life."

"He's addled?" CW asked.

"Blissfully ignorant of life's drama and grandeur."

"The town idiot," Maude corrected. "Why his people allow him to wander the streets alone is beyond me. I've often held that Herbert's entire line must be afflicted, each to his own dark angel. Truth be told, I wouldn't be at all surprised if the solution to Boy-Allen's mystery were to be found with that seedy lot."

"That's cruel, Mother," Rachel argued. "Herbert's no Edison, but he's a decent enough boy who has a perfect right to walk on public streets. If he is the laughingstock of the community, why, we ought to have more laughingstocks in Bellemont. Herbert has a good heart. You should know that as well as anyone, Mother."

"The fact that the boy can perform simple tasks is no excuse to allow him out and about at all hours."

"Mother, he helped you out of the mud and carried those packages of yours half a mile in the rain!"

"And I offered to pay him for his trouble, if you'll recall."

"Mother!" Rachel cried. "For goodness sakes. Herbert doesn't know the difference between a dollar and a dog bone. You might've invited him indoors, at least until it stopped raining. Would that have been so great an imposition? Honestly now?"

"We've had this discussion before, young lady," Maude replied, her voice becoming testy. "I won't allow you to draw me into any further argument concerning my behavior towards that boy. I acknowledged his good deed and offered a more than generous compensation when, in truth, I'd found the entire incident quite embarrassing. In hindsight, I'd have been better served to leave those packages where they fell. Beatrice and the other club ladies thought I'd lost my mind."

Rachel burst out laughing. "Why, Mother, how ever could they tell?"

A motor horn blared just outside.

Rachel went to the front door for a look. Marie heard her shout, "My God! That idiot ran the child over! Somebody call a doctor!"

Rachel went out, CW directly behind her.

Marie rushed onto the back porch and down around to the front where she saw a green Franklin cabriolet stalled at the curb and a pudgy fellow climbing out from behind the wheel, waving his derby hat.

When Rachel screamed Henry's name, Marie felt a chill sweep over her and she felt faint for half an instant. Then little Henry crawled on his hands and knees from underneath the front bumper of the automobile, dirt and oil covering him head to toe. Cissie ran out of the yard from beneath the fig tree and grabbed Henry by the wrist, jerking him away from the motorcar. The man yelled at her, "Goddamn kids! Are you crazy? Christ Almighty! Why, I ought to — "

Rachel rushed straight out the gate to the man, and slapped him. "How dare you speak to a child like that!"

Stunned, he took a step backward, staring at Rachel with amazement, his cheek crimson from her blow.

"How dare you!" she shrieked.

Scared silly, Marie ran up the sidewalk to Henry who was crying, hugged tightly by Cissie, his grimy face streaked with tears. Kneeling beside the children, she found one of Henry's elbows was skinned raw, his new trousers torn at the knee, but he was not seriously injured. Marie felt her own legs. She realized she was crying and hadn't even known it. Cissie was weeping, too, and Lili had raced to the fence carrying an armful of headless dolls, her eyes wide as saucers. Harry had warned her about letting Henry run in the street, as if that was at all necessary. She knew about autos and children, thank you very much, dear!

"Oh, honey, you're all right. You're just fine." She hugged Henry close and tried not to let him see her tears. Her hands were shaking. She looked up at the driver. "What on earth happened? Didn't you see him?"

By now, Rachel stood nose to nose with the driver of the green automobile, rage flush on her face. She shouted, "Are you insane? Why, we ought to have you arrested this very instant!"

"Aw, you're nuts, lady! That youngster run right out in front of my new motor. I damned near broke my ankle stomping on the brake. Y'all ought to be the ones apologizing to me."

"Good grief," Marie shouted up at him, her tears abating. "You almost killed my son!"

Rachel became furious. "Shut your mouth, mister crazy man, or I'll slap you silly!"

The man backed up another step. "You hit me again, darling, and I'll see you in court."

"You'll be lucky to get there!" CW shouted, arriving onto the sidewalk just behind Rachel, his fists clenched. "I'll gladly finish this right now! What do you say?"

"You stay right there," the man warned weakly.

Maude came out onto the porch, still wearing her apron. As frightened as she was angry, Marie huddled with her children, trying both to console Henry and discover what exactly had happened. All he had done so far was mumble about one of Lili Jessup's dolls running away from the circus. Rachel moved toward the man who immediately backed up against the Franklin, his eyes flicking back and forth from Rachel to CW and Maude.

The man drew a handkerchief from his vest pocket and used it to wipe the sweat from his brow as Maude said to him, "I'd appreciate an explanation, sir."

He blew his nose into the handkerchief. "Ain't nothing to explain, ma'am. That youngster there run under my car and almost got himself killed."

"The man's insane, Mother," Rachel asserted. "First he nearly ran little Henry down like a dog, then he had the fat nerve to curse the poor child, scaring him half to death. I'm sure we have grounds to have him thrown in jail. Mother, go put a call into Sheriff Lloyd before this lunatic tries to escape. I know he'd be properly furious."

"You ought to get married, honey," the man shot back at Rachel. "Learn yourself some manners."

"Maybe I'll teach you something myself," CW said, bluffing forward.

"I refuse to converse with a raving maniac," Rachel added, turning her back. "Mother?"

Wind riffled Maude's apron and fanned more dust into the yard. "I suppose we ought to put a call into the sheriff," she said. "Raising voices just turns sense into nonsense."

"I've heard my share of nonsense, all right," the man said, sliding back behind the wheel of the green Franklin. "You're all nuts."

Maude turned to Marie and asked, "How is the child, dear? Is he injured?"

Still shaking with fear and relief, Marie looked at Henry and wiped a patch of axle grease off his forehead with her fingers, then gave him a warm hug to reassure him that he'd survived to enter the three-legged sack race at the fairgrounds later on that afternoon. "He's just fine. Aren't you, dear?" She hugged him again as he whimpered. "We'll put a little Unguentine on his scrapes and he'll be good as gold. He wasn't hurt badly. Just frightened."

"That's good."

Angry now, too, Marie added, "I just think everyone drives too fast on this street. It scares me half to death. It's not safe to walk the children."

"I'll go put in the call myself," Rachel said, gleefully. "Nobody should be allowed to drive like that."

"Aw, let's just forget it," the man said, pulling the door closed. "I ain't got time to talk with your cops. I got appointments in Wichita tomorrow. I wasted enough of the day in this damned town as it is. If the kiddie's not hurt, I say let bygones be bygones. I got no more beef about it, so long as my auto's not damaged."

He cranked the engine over and started it up.

"Mother, don't let this reptile drive off like that," Rachel protested. "He's a criminal. He ought to at least be forced to spend the night in jail." As the black exhaust cloud rose, she covered her mouth with the back of her hand and turned her head away.

"Come on indoors, honey," Marie said, helping Henry to his feet. "Let's get you patched up."

"Well, I suppose there's no further issue to take so long as Henry's fine and this man's willing to forgive and forget," Maude remarked, glancing at Marie once more. Then she lowered her voice and spoke directly to the man in the Franklin. "Children remain near and dear to our hearts here in Bellemont. Their health and well-being concerns us greatly. You'd be strongly advised to consider that the next time you hurry down one of our streets. The speed limit here is ten miles an hour and not all our citizenry are as disposed toward reason and sensibility as myself. Good day, sir."

Then Maude reversed herself and walked back up the stairs into the house.

"Good riddance, you old windbag," the man mumbled, sliding the car into gear. As the motorcar rolled forward, Rachel darted up and gave a kick to the rear fender.

"Hey!" the man shouted, leaning out the window. "Cut that out!"

— 4 —

Half-a-mile east of town, past P&B's cotton mill near the pinewoods along old Langston Road, lay the Panola fairgrounds in a grassy meadow of white oaks and shady cottonwoods. By late afternoon, when Marie arrived with Maude from College Street, hundreds of people already crowded long picnic tables and chow lines half-hidden in cook smoke under the leafy trees. Rachel and CW had driven over with the children at four o'clock, hoping to enter a few of the field contests. There were mud pits for tug-of-war teams dug out near the rodeo corrals, and chalklines cut and drawn for sprints and sack races and hammer throws. Cissie had won a sack race on Field Day at Brookfield School in Farrington the week Harry came home to sell the house on Cedar Street. She skinned a knee and her elbow and still won a blue ribbon. Today, she intended to win another. Likewise, Henry hoped to enter the three-legged race with little Abel, if he arrived in time. Telephoning

Mrs. Kritt's house on Ninth Street after dinner, Marie was told that little Abel had gone off outdoors somewhere and hadn't yet come back, despite his favorite apple dumplings waiting on the table. Marie carried this worry with her to the fairgrounds.

Under the shade of a broad oak, she watched anxiously as Cissie stepped into a shabby gunny sack for the race she planned to win. Other children with equally worn gunny sacks lined up beside her, yelling and bragging of past triumphs. Rachel nervously lit a cigarette. CW clapped loudly. Maude fanned herself with a handkerchief. A skinny fellow in a striped shirt whom Marie remembered from Hooker's drugstore raised a pistol at the starting line.

"ON YOUR MARKS!"

Children in the crowd leaped and squealed.

"GET SET!"

Marie stood up, her heart fluttering with excitement. She nearly fainted whenever her children competed.

"GO!"

At the crack of the pistol, twenty-three valiant young sack racers were off. Dust flew violently along the track. Straight away, six children went down all together in a hilarious collision. The crowd of adults roared. Marie saw Cissie lunging forward among the lead pack, her pigtails flopping in the air. She shouted, "GO, HONEY! GO!"

A freckled-face boy stumbled and fell. A dark-haired boy tumbled to earth just beyond him. The leaders resembled Mexican jumping beans. Marie heard herself laughing and was surprised. Was she so excited for her daughter to win? Beside her, Rachel stamped out a smoldering Chesterfield and shouted encouragement while CW called for more speed. Half the pack was lost now in the dusty track, given over to defeat and laughter, rolling about hysterically like big June bugs. Cissie chugged forward, nearing the goal. A last boy collapsed as a pair of towheaded twins fell through the tape side by side at the finish line, a tie for the victory, Cissie just behind in third. The race was over. Everybody gave a big cheer for the contestants. Parents hurried to their children. Marie and Rachel and CW reached Cissie in time to help her struggle to her feet where she'd fallen just past the chalk.

"I lost, Momma!" Cissie moaned, as she rolled over in the grass, grimy sweat on her face. "I lost!" She kicked at the gunny sack to free herself.

"Oh, you did fine, honey! Just fine!"

A handsome man in a blue worsted suit and felt hat hurried to congratulate the two winners, all smiles and innocent bravado. The umpire, too, hustled toward them, blue ribbons in hand.

"Oh, don't get sore, dear," Rachel said, lifting Cissie out of her torn gunny sack. "It's just rotten luck. You did awfully well."

Marie brushed the dust off Cissie's shoulders. "You were wonderful, darling! Absolutely wonderful! Your father'll be very proud. You won a ribbon!" She gave her daughter a kiss.

"It was the race of the century!" CW enthused.

"Aw, phooey," Cissie grumbled, giving the dusty old gunny sack another kick. "Let's never talk about it again."

Rebuffing the umpire's attempt to give her a white ribbon, Cissie shot off in a huff toward the rodeo corral. Knowing her daughter's temperament, Marie let her go. Harry, too, hated to lose; whether ping-pong or billiards, it made no matter. When he lost, she had learned to avoid him for at least an hour or so. Only that and a warm cup of Horlick's malted milk soothed his bitterness.

"The poor dear," Rachel remarked, watching Cissie disappear into the great crowd. "I had no idea she'd be so cut up about losing a silly race. It's not as if there were scads of dough on the line."

"That's because you're no competitor," CW replied, biting the end off a five-cent cigar he'd had in his vest pocket. "When that fellow from Plaquemine beat me nine up last month at Springhaven, I was so sunk, I nearly threw my new Spalding clubs into the river."

"How childish," Rachel scolded. She turned to Marie. "Don't you agree that's silly?"

Marie smiled. "Well, my Uncle Boyd always says we ought to hope for the best, be prepared for the worst, and bear resolutely whatever happens. I can't imagine quitting something I enjoy just because I haven't done particularly well one day."

CW lit his cigar. "Oh, I haven't quit. On the contrary, I just learned

Bobby Jones' overlapping grip, so I'm all geared up for another whirl next week with that same fellow. I've even placed a bet for a thousand berries, just to prove I'm no dub." He blew a smoke ring into the air. "I tell you, I can't lose." He darted forward to kiss Rachel on the ear.

"Oh, I can't bear it any longer," Rachel snapped, dodging a second kiss. She shook her head in disgust. "CW's skull's so big he'd tell the devil how to stoke a furnace." She took Marie by the arm. "Dear, let's go have some fried oysters. I'm really done in. CW can shift for himself."

"Aw, cut it out," CW laughed, lurching forward to take Rachel's arm. "You know I don't give a hang about anything but romance, don't you, darling?" He gave her a kiss on the cheek.

"Don't overplay your hand, dear," Rachel warned, squirming away, "if you have any desire to make love to me today. I have too much fondness for wealth and charm in a husband-to-be, qualities I've somehow yet to find in you."

"Now, darling — "

"And another thing — "

The midsummer heat lingered, slowing the pace of celebrants to a drifting passage from one entertainment to another. Cissie had gone off to see the rodeo ponies with Lili Jessup; Henry won a pair of nickel balloons at the penny pitch and popped them both straight away. Marie located Maude at the pie booth, chatting with Emily Haskins and sipping lemonade from a porcelain cup. She bought a lemonade for herself, and went off with Maude and Rachel who led CW about from contest to contest, pitting his skill against Bellemont's finest in games of strength and skill, praising his courage in competitions of all sorts. Somehow Marie felt reassured in the summer crowds, confident that she and the children were growing comfortable here and discovering true affections in those they met. If only Harry would come down to see them. She smiled, watching Rachel with CW. They were both happily afflicted with sex-madness. Once long ago, she and Harry had been, too, and though she had feared being inadequate to the task of womanhood, neither had her husband bounded out of bed in disgust. She watched Rachel now with CW and saw two young people with most of their lives ahead of them, and discovered she was secretly envious, for once she, too, had felt playful and joyous on a summer holiday. Where had it all gone?

"You must admit he's game for most everything," Marie suggested to Maude as CW removed his coat and joined a crowd of young men at the Test of Strength pole. "I admire his pluck."

"Pluck's got nothing to do with it," Maude sniffed. "Rachel's never content until she's proven to every other bachelor in this town that her choice in rejecting each one of them was correct. I feel sorry for the poor boy. If he's not willing to stand up to her, she'll have him driven to his own grave by sundown."

Marie watched Rachel hold CW's coat while he struggled to raise the sledgehammer. She kissed him for luck, then stood back as her beau swung down hard, launching the weight only halfway up the pole. CW laughed at the feeble result and took his coat back from Rachel who looked somewhat disappointed. They kissed again, more passionately than Marie's mother might have approved of, and walked off arm-in-arm in the direction of the shooting gallery.

"Love encourages him, I think, as it does us all, wouldn't you agree?"

"Rachel doesn't know the first thing about love," Maude said. "She flirts and curtsies for men she hardly knows, and when they're granted an audience with her, she treats them like children begging for candy. Never in her life has she offered herself with sincerity to a boy whose affections are genuine. If she were truly to fall in love, as a young woman ought to, I doubt she could bear the burden. She'd be petulant and scared. She'd cling to the poor fellow like a cat caught upside down in a tree and frighten him half out of his wits. In any case, it's not love Rachel wants at all. The responsibility would terrify her."

"Well, my mother always warned me that love's obligations can poison the heart against itself. She told me, 'To be true to another, we should first be true to ourselves, accept how we feel about the one we love and treat him always as we would have him treat us.' I've always regarded that as wise advice."

"Oh, I doubt Rachel sees herself as obligated to anyone but herself. When she's in love, it's Rachel around whom the world revolves, every affection directed naturally to her, every little kindness. I can't recall the last time she sent one of her gentlemen a gift of any sort, nor if she's ever written her affections to someone in a letter. Pure unconcealed selfishness guides her every action, and I'd be surprised to hear her gentlemen argue otherwise."

"And yet CW seems to be quite taken with her, wouldn't you agree?"

"I imagine he's infatuated beyond hope. Half the time he acts like a lovesick schoolboy," Maude replied, reaching into her bag for a handkerchief. "Mark my words, though, one day he'll come to his senses and that'll be the last we'll see of him." She blew her nose, then put the handkerchief away. "It's foolish for them to step out with each other, anyhow. For the life of me, I don't know what Rachel was thinking. After all, she knew he was Catholic."

At dusk, skyrockets showered the sky above the fairgrounds with color and noise. The crack of explosions echoed overhead as splintered rainbows arced across the evening, while children squealed with delight and adults wandered about in the dark and the voice of the figure-caller for a plain quadrille echoed from the pavilion: *Honor your partner … corners the same … head couples right and left through … promenade across … promenade back … change your ladies now!* A faint wind brushed across the meadow, bending stalks of dry grass and tossing in Marie's hair, carrying, too, a scent of summer she had forgotten since Farrington. A smell of fresh grass and wildflowers were loose in the warm summer night. As she watched Rachel and CW take the children to the chow line for barbecued hotdogs and potato salad under the boom and glare of bursting fireworks, Marie wondered where Harry was this night, if perhaps he might be thinking of her. Did he miss her, as she still missed him? She knew Harry was no saint. Her heart did not permit her that foolishness. No man has eyes only for the woman he marries. Every so often, rumor and dark intuitions troubled her dreams and gave her worry. Now and then, she grew angry and jealous and had ugly thoughts that shocked her in the dark. Marie had read once in a magazine that infidelity arises out of some unnamed hollowness in the heart of the unfaithful. She had also overheard her own mother say that a man who strays even once has a lump of coal in his chest where his heart ought to be — something Marie did not believe was necessarily true, at least not when applied to her Harry. His heart was good. Not perfect, but kind and decent. When he was home, his eyes never strayed from hers. The trust they shared between them was complete, even when love's passion dimmed. What he did while away, she did not know, nor did she care to know: moral sins, imagined or confirmed, mortally wound a jealous heart. As often as she could, Marie tried to believe in the good a man brings to a woman when he arrives on her porchstep, flowers in hand. Her mother thought her foolish and naïve. She hadn't cared for Harry from the day they met at the Lake of the Isles. She cared for him even less when Marie told her about the selling of the house on Cedar Street and the proposed move to Bellemont. Her fury astounded everyone. She urged Marie to return to the farm and swear never to see Harry again. She begged for the sake of the children, for Marie's sake, and the entire Pendergast family. Marie walked quietly out of her mother's house to the barn where she asked Cousin Frenchy to drive her back into Farrington so that she could begin packing that very afternoon. At the rail depot, the morning Harry sent them to Bellemont, Marie tried her best to say something kind to Harry, words to make this separation pleasant and fair. She refused to cry and so she did not, even when he whispered a last affection in her ear as the train whistle sounded. Her own anger abated by apprehension and sorrow, she squeezed his hand softly and closed her eyes and kissed his cheek and allowed her arms to fall around his waist to let him know he was loved and would be missed as much by his wife as by his children. As hopeless as it often seemed these days, Marie understood that love had come into her world by this man's yearning heart. Somehow, in her compassionate moments, Marie still believed she was meant to care for him her entire life, excusing his weaknesses, tolerating his vanities, encouraging her own love for him to grow daily, despite the distance. Was it cowardly to love simply for well-being? Perhaps, but Marie saw no dignity in loneliness for pride's sake.

The skyrockets flared brightly again on the purple summer sky, raining color down across the stars and disappearing near the evening horizon. A series of booming echoes followed and the crowds roared with delight while Marie wandered out across the grass, letting it brush against her skirt as she walked. She paused long enough to see a string of fire balloons ignited and set aloft by the Ladies Auxiliary, glowing orbs ascending slowly, slowly into the night sky, rising, drifting above the fairgrounds like sparkling fairies come to earth for a midsummer celebration. As the fire balloons disappeared high and faraway into the starry dark, Marie, alone now, beyond earshot of her children, strolled off under the leafy cottonwoods. The dance orchestra struck up a song back at the gaily decorated pavilion, and laughter swept out into the dark. A breeze brushed the dry tips of grass and washed across Marie's face, a pleasantly warm breeze, scent of sweet wildflowers and honey. Her girlhood was long behind her; nevertheless she felt young this evening, younger than she had in years, wayward while alone, yet not lonely. If Harry rode a train all night to see her, she would welcome him back into her arms gladly, whisper old affections in his ear, greet him with a kiss and a tear. He was her husband, and she wanted to love him dearly. Yet if he did not come back to Bellemont at summer's end, did not return to her and the children by harvest, still she would go on confident that life had not forsaken her. Therefore, as she strolled about in the summer grass, love's oldest music played in Marie's ear, a sweet sentimental melody of quiet confidence and private longing, a lingering song of hope and desire, fear and comfort, that rang in her heart all these years. Listening to this music, Marie was reminded why she had allowed Harold Louis Hennesey to take her hand in the cool darkness and lead her out behind Uncle Harlow's barn and steal a tender kiss under the autumn moon. In her life, love meant this to Marie: a belief in beauty and tenderness and the everlasting good that comes from a gentle smile.

"There you are, dear!" Rachel cried, seeing Marie walk in under the electric lights outside the grand pavilion. "Mother was afraid you'd wandered off into the woods and become lost. We were just discussing a search party."

Marie felt herself blush. "I hadn't realized how late it was. I'm sorry." Had she been gone so long? She had enjoyed her freedom. It wasn't often she managed to rediscover it.

"Oh, it isn't late at all," Rachel enthused. "Why, I haven't even danced yet and my card is full."

CW held up a glass of fruit punch. His eyes looked weary, his straw hat tipped slightly askew. "Would you like me to get you something to drink? Rachel's been sending me back and forth to the punch bowl all evening just so I won't notice the recruiting for her dance card."

"Oh, I have not," Rachel argued. "I'm not that kind. In fact, I've turned down many more offers than I've accepted." She turned to Marie. "CW's quite the jealous sort, you know. If I'd known six months ago, I doubt I'd have encouraged his attentions."

"Is that so?" Marie laughed.

"Wait 'til I marry you, darling," CW said, leaning over to give Rachel a kiss, "then you'll really see the mess you're in."

The evening wind was rising now, scattering flecks of dried grass. Marie looked up at the grand old dance pavilion, constructed like a wooden carousel with a shingled cupola on top and a balustraded gallery with broad white staircases at the four cardinal points of the compass. Banners and Independence Day flags and pennants flapped wildly along the rooftop overhead. Wherever she looked, people crowded the gallery railing. Marie felt festive and lively herself.

"Where are my children?" she asked, brushing a strand of hair off her face. "I hope we haven't lost them." Given half a chance, Cissie would be on a train to Timbuktu. Somehow the joyful atmosphere of the fairgrounds had beaten back her worries over Boy-Allen's killer, but that didn't mean she'd entirely forgotten.

"Well, your lovely daughter's been eating sugar cookies hand over fist with Lili Jessup by the punch bowl," Rachel replied, taking CW's glass for a sip. "I thought she'd be full as a tick from the hotdogs and chunks of cream pie she ate for supper, but apparently I was wrong. And last I saw, poor little Henry was sleeping in Mother's lap at the Ladies Auxiliary. I expect they're both ready to go home soon."

Indoors, the orchestra began playing "Waltz Me Around Again, Willie" to a great ovation.

"Let's go inside," Marie suggested, when the wind gusted once more. "Shall we? I hear the decorations are wonderful." And she desperately wanted to see the dancers and hear the music, be with people now, gay and laughing.

"Now that's a swell idea," CW agreed, taking Rachel by the arm and hugging her tightly to his side. "I'm in just the mood to tickle the floor. Darling, do you hear what the band's playing? Why, that's our theme song."

"Isn't CW a fine boy?" Rachel remarked, as they walked through the grass toward the east staircase. "And he dances like Vernon Castle."

"Before his smash-up, of course," CW corrected, a gleam in his eye.

"I have no doubt he can waltz with a glass of water on his head," Marie remarked playfully. Just ahead of her, the wide stairs were draped in bunting and gleaming with new white paint. She could scarcely wait to go inside. Was Jimmy Delahaye here tonight? She felt breathless and bold once again. Perhaps she would dance if asked. Harry might not approve, but he wasn't here, was he? And it had been years since he'd waltzed with her. Despite everything else, she had a right to smile, didn't she?

"Now, promise you'll keep that under your hat, won't you?" CW told Marie. "I wouldn't want the other girls to cut in on my sweet. Doesn't she look radiant tonight?"

"Of course she does. You'd better keep your eye on her. There are wolves all around here tonight. I think both of you ought to watch out."

Rachel giggled. "That hideous Amy Keene and her gang of thieves already gave CW the once-over by the punch bowl just to stir me up, though he's much too swell for the chewing-gum set."

"And, boy, were you sore!" CW observed, reaching the bottom steps under a tall glowing lamp pole. "I thought you were about to clean up on her."

"Oh, I was not," Rachel snorted. She turned to Marie. "He's utterly wrong, you know. I was just queening my public, that's all. Why, I'm perfectly harmless this evening."

"Like a black widow spider!" CW laughed, as he marched them both up the staircase through the gallery crowds into the noisy pavilion.

On a humid evening long ago, a gentle silver light shone upon the dark waters of Lake Minnetonka where seventeen-year-old Marie Alice Pendergast stood by the dock station at Excelsior watching the summer moon rise over Big Island Park. Tickets to the steamer "Minneapolis" were ten cents apiece for the trip across to the amusement park and back again, and Harry Hennesey purchased two while Marie listened to the careening rollerskaters in the rink above the promenade and the shrill ferry boat whistles out on the lake. Crowds of tourists from the Hotel La Paul mingled about the docks, men in strawboaters smoking fat cigars, women chattering together like birds in a thicket. Marie had already enjoyed the forty-minute ride from downtown St. Paul on the electric railway through the swampy woods of Deephaven and Purgatory and Vine Hill, with those pretty cottages on the inlets, and distant ferries ablaze with electric lights. Harry had given cheerfully casual handwaves to people along the tracks and comforted a teary-eyed child with a jam-stained blouse by sharing his sack of lemon candies. He looked so brash and handsome in his new navy-blue serge suit, Marie found herself smiling from St. Paul to Excelsior Station.

Aboard the "Minneapolis," Harry performed a clever coin trick for a family of tourists from North Dakota and declared lovely Marie Pendergast his inspiration. She blushed and felt her shy young heart pierced with joy. This season already, Emeline had boys call on her all the way from town, riding to the Chamberlain farm on horseback with a fistful of daisies and chocolate drops that Aunt Hattie ate after she'd sent the boys away. All spring and summer, Violet snuck out after dark to kiss Orson McCardell under the old apple tree on Falls Road. But until Harry had come into her life by the boat docks at the Lake of the Isles, Marie had no boy to swoon over, no dreamy thoughts of tender reassurance at bedtime. That left-out feeling evaporated with Harry's quick and confident smile, the pluck in his step, the innocent flutter of his eyelids as he handed her a bouquet of red carnations and kissed her blushing cheek.

At Big Island Park, Marie persuaded Harry to break from the flossy crowd on the Main Walk to stroll under the trellised pergola where light from the great Electric Tower splintered and dimmed, and dance music from the casino bandshell serenaded the wooded dark. As they walked about, Harry directed her gaze across the lake waters to the distant lamplit façade of Lucian Swift's summer home, Katahdin, and the elegant grounds of Frank Peavey's Highcroft at Breezy Point. He described the history of the northern woods and the clever Indians who camped and hunted along the shores of the big water, then guided Marie to a bench at Point Charming where he held her hand and expressed his genuine affection for the girl she was and the woman he declared she'd one day become. Fretful of uttering a silly word, or acting too proper, Marie sat quietly by his side, trembling like a dove, one hand warmly entwined with his, the other grasping the red carnations close to her breast as she prayed he saw her strength, a serene and considered devotion to one who would care for her and keep her forever close at heart.

Amber light from dozens of Japanese lanterns flickered high in the rafters of the Bellemont pavilion above all the people Marie Hennesey knew in town, knotted on the crowded dance floor or beside the busy punch bowl, drinks and cookies in hand. The orchestra from Shreveport played leisurely. Across the buffed pine floor, Idabelle Collins did a shuffling Fox Trot with a newsdealer from downtown named Clinton Morrison whose teeth bore the unfortunate stains of tobacco smoke. Behind them, Lucius Beauchamp shamblefooted with Verna Grieg from the beauty salon on South Main. Near the bandstand, Rachel and CW danced cheek to cheek, exquisitely in love. Marie sighed. Henry had gone home for the evening with Maude, while Cissie and Lili went back with Mildred Jessup who told Marie she was licked from carving up chickens all afternoon for the barbecue and thought she might have a touch of ptomaine. Alone now in a gay crowd of Civic Garden Club ladies by the south exit, Marie sat in a cane chair by the wall and tapped her toe to the jazzy rhythm of the orchestra. If only …

"Would you care to dance, honey?"

Looking up, Marie found Jimmy Delahaye beside her, dressed like a gentleman in a tux with a white boutonniere on his peaked lapel. He smelled of Wildroot hair tonic, a hint of gin on his breath. His jaw was firm, his bearing confident. Truth be told, Marie thought him the handsomest man at the pavilion. Her heart fluttered.

"That is," Delahaye added, a twinkle in his eye, "if you're still spry enough."

"Why, Mr. Delahaye, how nice to see you," Marie stammered, her throat tightening. Was he serious? Should she? "You know, I haven't danced in years. I'm sure I'd be quite an awful partner."

"Nonsense," he replied, smoothing his hair. "I'd be honored."

She bit her lip. "Are you sure? I wouldn't want to trip you up." Perhaps she couldn't dance a step any longer. Perhaps she ought not to try. What would Harry think if he found out? Did she even care? No, not tonight she didn't.

He arched an eyebrow, then offered a firm hand. "Please?"

"Well, if you insist." She blushed like a schoolgirl as she rose to her feet, knees trembling. She was excited. "You are my boss, after all."

"Yes, ma'am."

On Delahaye's arm, Marie waded hesitantly into the sea of dancers, her feet unsure of the new steps. Timid and embarrassed, she glided into motion with her handsome partner. He felt strong and certain, and in his arms, her own confidence grew. Overhead, the paper lanterns glowed like yellow moons above the revolving dancers. Jimmy Delahaye's hands were firm and warm, his eyes alight, perspiration visible on his brow and upper lip as he slid easily from step to step, maneuvering them away from the band to where the light was dimmer, the din of the pavilion crowd less pronounced. Her anxiety increased, even as desire bloomed within. Delahaye drew her closer to his chest and she felt her heart warm, too.

"Honey, you step like an angel," he said to Marie, as he led her about the floor. His breath was hot, but not unpleasant.

"Thank you," she replied, feeling intoxicated by the orchestra. She adored music. On Cedar Street she played the Victrola while cleaning house and sang aloud to herself in the attic. Emeline took piano lessons when she was a girl and Violet played the organ at church on Sundays. Both made a joyful sound, yet just as often Marie felt blue when the music was the loveliest, a strange and subtle discomfort inexpressible as a butterfly tickling her heart.

"I have to confess that I paid Frank Merritt ten dollars to keep his band playing as long as I stay on my feet tonight," Delahaye told Marie, guiding her back toward the crowded middle of the pavilion where a hundred dancers blotted out the pine floor. She loved dancing with him. She loved his firm grasp, how his hand felt on her lower back, how they seemed to glide in step together here and there about the floor. It had been years since she and Harry had gone dancing. Marie supposed it no longer interested him, business concerns flooded his life now, but whenever a waltz or a Fox Trot played on the radio set, she thought about those wonderful ballrooms he used to take her to, all the music and dancing they'd enjoyed together.

She told him, "Idabelle says you caught cold yesterday. Are you sure you ought to be here at all?" She peeked up, offering a coy smile. Could he see how she enjoyed his touch?

He danced Marie about in a gentle arc. "Tell the truth, I've been slugging quinine since breakfast to work it off."

Marie smiled. "Is that wise?"

"Idabelle doesn't think so," Delahaye replied with dusky eyes, his speech almost languid. Marie liked it, though, almost as if he were murmuring to her alone in the dark. "When I showed her the bottle this morning, she laughed so hard I thought she'd lose a filling."

Across the floor, CW and Rachel abruptly quit dancing as the orchestra began a waltz. Rachel walked ahead of him without looking back so Marie guessed they had taken a disagreement over another triviality and were heading out of doors to quarrel again. A pack of young men in black waistcoats rushed gleefully through the pavilion and out the south exit. Where were they going?

Changing his step for the waltz, Delahaye spoke softly in Marie's ear, "Honey, I've been busting to dance with you all evening."

His breath tickled, and she blushed. "You're teasing, aren't you?"

"No, ma'am," Delahaye replied with a smile. "Smartest thing I did all year was hiring you to the restaurant."

Marie's heart skipped as they traversed the crowded dance floor. She felt crazy and fluttery. Her knees wobbled as she danced. Her breath felt short, her eyes watered, and she was smiling widely and knew it. When had she last felt this flush with Harry? "Well, I have to tell you I'm very grateful. Everyone's been terribly decent to me since I began." That wasn't at all what she wanted to say, but it was what came out. Now she was a bashful schoolgirl again, afraid to look that charming boy in the eye and say she liked him.

"Lucius and Idabelle adore you."

"Oh, they've both been ever so sweet," Marie said, locating Lucius with Verna Grieg across the pavilion at the punch bowl, then Idabelle and Clinton Morrison waltzing with a crowd of older dancers in the lantern shadows. Everyone seemed so congenial together. Why was she alone so nervous? "I realize my half-a-day's have been inconvenient to all of you."

"Don't give it another thought," Delahaye said, his thick voice growing huskier. "You know it's your brains I'm paying for, not your hours at the desk."

A fellow in a checked coat with a wide-brimmed straw hat came up and tapped Delahaye on the shoulder. "Cut in on the pretty lady?"

Delahaye shot him a fierce glare. "On your way, Bob."

"Sorry."

As the fellow slunk off to try his luck elsewhere, Delahaye drew Marie close enough to his chest that she could feel his breathing and the heat off his skin. "I refuse to share you tonight. Do you mind?"

She smiled. "Not at all."

Marie glanced away just as Delahaye leaned his face near and whispered beside her ear, "You have lovely hair, honey." He drew a deep breath through his nose. "Smells like what my sister Edith used to wear, gardenia or some such."

"Lilac," Marie corrected, feeling herself close to swooning. He'd aroused her unawares and she was shocked to discover how she felt. Yet she remained close in his arms, not relaxed but comfortable, and far too happy to pull away. Where was her heart tending? Too often Harry had made love to her when she felt cold and tired; too often he was unwilling to give her desire a chance to rise and meet his own. When had she last felt so feminine as she did tonight?

Delahaye hovered closer still. "Harry's a damned lucky fellow. It's not easy working close to you."

Marie felt his gin breath on her bare neck as he spoke and thought he was about to kiss her and imagined that if he did, she'd likely faint and cause a scene, so she began humming the orchestra melody as if it were the most natural thing in the world to do just then. She dared not look Delahaye in the eye, because she felt feverish with desire and desperate to be kissed.

"Go with me to a picture, won't you?" Delahaye asked, gently squeezing her hand. "Maybe one night this week?"

When she felt his lips brush her forehead, she raised her chin ever so slightly as her own lips quivered. She looked into his eyes, saw them gleam. Woozy and confused, she sighed. "Oh, I don't — "

"Look, I'm not trying to get fresh with you, honey," Delahaye said, offering a boyish smile. "You know, I just thought you might like to get out of the house some evening, go downtown with me and shoot the moon. Where's the harm in that? We'd have a good time, and it wouldn't cost you a bull nickel."

Marie had no idea what to say. Why had she agreed to this dance? What did she think she was doing now? Did she want to kiss him or not? She was terrified by the pounding of her own heart. What should she say? "Well, the children have been such a share lately," she offered, meekly. "I'm afraid Maude hasn't had a moment to herself this entire month, so you see I swore an oath yesterday we'd stay out of her hair all week long." Now that she'd thoroughly humiliated herself, she peeked up at him to see the same disarming smile. She believed he was staring straight into her heart. She felt both panicked and flushed with sexual passion. She had no idea where she was any longer.

"Then we'll make it some other time, all right?" Delahaye suggested, his blue eyes glistening in lantern light as he danced her in a slow circle. She was too frightened to speak. Did he think she was lonely this evening, so wanting of a man's touch, his whispered affections, his kiss? Was she so obvious? How humiliating that would be! Was it true? And did Jimmy Delahaye imagine that Harry, gone off alone to the city, had gone, too, from Marie's heart? Surely not. She realized now that she ought to offer a word or two to Delahaye, something clever or wise to express clearly both her appreciation for his sweet affection and her faith in Harry's return. That failing, Marie was quite certain she would need to walk away from the pavilion very soon now and lie down beside her children in the small bedroom by the chinaberry tree where she knew she belonged. *Oh, Harry! Where are you?*

Honeymoon couples in rented canoes stirred the moonlit waters off Big Island Park where Marie and Harry strolled the lakeshore, trading glances across the summer dark. Loons cried in the marshes. Inland, a gala crowd swarmed the rollercoaster and the noisy shooting galleries. Marie hoped desperately to dance with Harry at the casino. One spring night, Violet had run away to a tea dance at the La Salle Hotel and done the two-step with a suave young Jewish dramatist from New York who lent a sympathetic ear to romantic yearnings. When she'd told her story in Marie's bedroom after dinner the next day, Emeline had refused to acknowledge that embrace of courtship belovéd of choreography and rhythm, but Marie had understood very well: the heart seeks proportion in all things; unobserved, love has less gravity, while blesséd touch rekindles the divine order.

Late that evening, she and Harry crossed the tree-shaded lawns of Big Island Park toward the bright casino, stopping briefly for orange soda and popcorn at a refreshment booth where they watched the lighted rollercoaster rasp and rattle up the steep track, high into the night sky, packed with screeching young riders. Marie hummed a dance melody for Harry as music from the bandshell beckoned, and hinted her desire by shameless flirtation. She needn't have begged, after all. Finishing his soda pop, Harry took Marie by the hand and led her through the wild crowd to the casino pavilion, sweeping past the potted palms and the orchestra in the bandshell and out onto the dance floor, his hand hardly pressing her fingers as he brought her to the center of the pavilion under the crystal chandelier and into harmony with the other dancers whirling about the floor to a brisk Viennese waltz Marie had never heard before but whose beautiful melody she could hum even now.

What dreams come true? Dance after dance late into that summer night, hardly a whisper passed between them: Harry too proud for words, Marie hushed by a secret peace deep in her heart. By midnight, the lights had dimmed and the other dancers had either departed Big Island Park by steamboat or retired to the damp lawns to be intimate while she and Harry remained in the center of the dance floor, close in each other's arms, even as the orchestra quit playing for the evening and the musicians packed up and left. All Marie could hear was distant laughter from beyond the casino and the soft scraping of Harry's shoes on the polished wood floor. Alone in the ballroom as the ceiling lights winked out one by one, Harry

Hennesey whispered ardent affections in her ear, words she'd expected to hear, words she hadn't, promises he'd keep, ones he would not. Aboard the last ferry boat crossing Lake Minnetonka for Excelsior and St. Paul that night, Marie Alice Pendergast made a promise to herself as well, a promise to which she would swear to hold true wherever she went with his name, a vow of fidelity and trust to keep her own heart honest, her affections pure, so long as thoughts of that summer night at Big Island Park reminded her of precious romance first discovered.

Marie stood on the pavilion's south gallery facing into a pleasantly cool breeze. Delahaye had developed a stitch in his rib and tugged at his linen collar with a complaint about the heat indoors, so they'd quit the dance floor and went out together. Rachel and CW hadn't returned from their squabble and Marie supposed they'd already left the Panola fairgrounds for home. Many other dancers had also wandered off the floor as a draft passing in and out of the pavilion tussled with the Japanese lanterns and the strings of electric lights. Marie could see people down in the shadowy meadow. Somewhere nearby, a gaggle of young teens shared a joke, voices tittering laughter on the breeze. She felt a sudden shiver as Delahaye stepped close beside her. A gust stirred in her hair and her dress fluttered. She held the skirt down with the back of one hand and brushed the hair out of her eyes with the other.

Delahaye remarked, "Lucius came to work today smelling like a distillery. He's probably been in with the gents most of the evening. I'll bet you Verna's gone home with Archie Pollard. He doesn't have much gumption, but he's straight as a rule. Spends every Sunday reading the Bible, which never has made him a big hit with the ladies. Verna thinks Lucius needs a good jacking-up and she knows Archie won't try to make love to her."

"I imagine I ought to be getting home, too," Marie told him, as she considered the hour. How late could she be out? What was expected of her in this place, a married woman residing with her mother-in-law? "I'd guess it's awfully late, and I wouldn't care to be locked out. I'm still a guest in Maude's house." Sunday morning, she'd sing hymns between Maude and Rachel in the fourth row of pews, raising her voice in song to the Lord in appreciation of all the joy in her life. Harry had a good strong voice himself. That was something she'd noticed straightaway.

Delahaye said, "Did you know Lucius used to give Harry a hell of a razzing when they were in school? Sometimes he laid it on pretty thick, too, but Harry wouldn't get bitter. He told everyone Lucius was all right, except for that one bug. Harry was an awfully good sport. I suppose he always knew that Lucius was all beef and no brains, and that he'd wind up a mediocrity. Of course, some of the boys around here thought Harry Hennesey was swell-headed because he wouldn't go out and raise a lot of Cain like the rest of us, though I can see now that was just a misapprehension on our part. Truth is, a fellow of his type had to get out of here to make good."

"Don't feel that way about it," Marie said, staring off into the evening wind. Her stomach fluttered, her knees still trembled. What if Delahaye took her hand now? What if he kissed her? "Why, it's such a foolish thing to say. After all, Harry's father had just passed away, and you know they were very close. I remember Harry suffered quite a deal over his decision not to return to Texas. He's always spoken fondly of his life here and the friends he grew up with."

"Oh, cut it out, honey," Delahaye chuckled, as he took a cigar out of his vest pocket and bit off the end. When he smiled at Marie, his eyes sparkled in the lantern light. She believed he was the handsomest fellow in town. "Harry's never been full of sentimental prune juice. He knew there's something doing all the time in the city, and he worked like a nigger to get there. I admire him for that. I don't know that I could make the grade where he's gone. I'm probably too thick in the head. Even if he overplays his hand one day, I'll lay you he won't come back here. And why the hell should he? Any fellow that's ever grown up in this town's wanted to strike it off his record, get himself elsewhere someday. Of course, that's hard to do because usually no place else wants him. He can't fit in. He's stuck being a simple fish from a bum little town. But not Harry Hennesey. He knows his own mind, and he'll never come back. Not in this life. You can't make a steamroller out of a racing car."

"Well, I believe he's still very strong for all of you," Marie persisted, knowing as she spoke that if Delahaye chose to kiss her, she might let him. If he took her hand, she'd wrap her fingers in his and lean close so he could smell her perfume.

Delahaye lit the cigar. "Don't bet your teeth against it."

Marie watched him exhale a ragged smoke ring into the breeze. She felt excited and lonely together. She wished Delahaye would lead her off somewhere into the dark to kiss her under the cottonwood trees, yet she also wished she were home writing letters or lying in bed with her children. Why had Harry left her here like this? Why didn't he love her like he had so many years ago? What was so wrong with how she'd loved him all these years?

Somewhere in the dark meadow, beyond sight of the gallery, a sudden peal of laughter fluttered across the night, a girl's voice carrying uninhibited joy, a summer giddiness. *When Marie was young, she and Violet and Emeline would sneak out after midnight in the summer months to play in the deep pinewoods surrounding the farm whose branches were filled with songbirds and noisy squirrels. Just across the creekbed, up a short rise and behind a dense thicket, Violet had discovered a hidden meadow, a secret clearing of clover and wildflowers shrouded in pine branches where wild cats hunted and three pretty young fairies slid off their nightshirts and slippers to dance together naked hand-in-hand in a perfect circle, swearing oaths to romance and beauty and eternal sisterhood. Binding tiaras of snapdragons and daisies into each other's hair like ancient wreaths of laurel, their bare skin nearly translucent under the silver moon, they would share stories and private confidences until dawn shone faintly in the treetops. Then all three girls would dress hurriedly and race back through the dry creek and the thick dark woods, across the wheat fields that led home again before sunrise. Their special game was a confidence Marie never in her life shared with anyone else — not her family, not Harry. Nor did the other girls ever speak of it once the game was over and they'd each grown up. In fact, poisoned by a hidden spider in an old sugar bowl, Violet took their secret to her grave in the summer of 1916. Emeline never mentioned it, either — even alone with Marie up in her uncle's attic on the morning of Emeline's wedding to Roy Gallup. So many summer nights spent in that pretty meadow, a perfect secret preserved forever like perfume on parchment, a childhood trust never broken.*

Marie gazed out across the dark meadow where the summer grass bent low in the warm evening wind and wondered how much of that sweet fairy-child still dwelled in her heart. Did she yet hold adventure and romance in such esteem? Was there somewhere in her life a gold heart-locket waiting to be opened, its lovely inscription still to be read? A quick breeze swirled up dust into her face, causing her eyes to water. Suddenly she felt as though she ought to take off alone, run again in the long grass, remove her shoes and feel the earth between her toes, listen to the wind blow in the trees across the fields nearby, listen for songbirds and the low rustling of wild cats in the thicket, laughter of fairies at play under the summer moon.

"How about taking a walk?" Delahaye asked, gently resting a hand on her shoulder.

Marie felt her heart leap. She trembled and her mouth went dry. What should she do? Was it wrong to let herself behave like this? Could she be forgiven for longing to be a girl once more in the summer dark? Why was love so fleeting and mean? Incredibly, she told him, "Yes, I'd like to."

They went down from the pavilion for a stroll in the grass under the cottonwood trees. They crossed into the shadows where the breeze rustled through the branches above. Marie had never felt so anxious in the company of a man. Had many people seen them go? Once Morris Farwell had taken her on a buggy ride by moonlight out past Mitchener's duck pond. When she saw him tie off the reins, she knew he intended to kiss her and became so nervous she started laughing, which led him to take her home unkissed. But she wouldn't laugh tonight. She was sure of that.

Delahaye didn't speak for the longest while. He smoked his cigar and guided Marie with a hand gently on her lower back. Her head swam and she felt almost feverish. They walked for about five minutes farther into the dark under the cottonwood trees, then stopped and listened to the breeze crossing the evening air. Harry was a thousand miles away tonight, Marie thought, as she felt Delahaye put his arms on her shoulders to draw her close. The breeze ruffled her skirt. She smelled the tobacco on his breath when he brought his face to hers and he was smiling. She kissed him.

Just once.

A schoolgirl's kiss, brief yet not entirely chaste.

Then she hid her face. He kissed her forehead and held her close to his chest and murmured something she couldn't hear and they stood together for a long while letting the evening breeze wash over them across the dark. Marie felt both relief and shame. She did not say a word. Why had she done this? A man who was not her husband, not Harry, had kissed her and she'd kissed him back with scant hesitation and had not run off afterward. Neither had she extended any further affection to him, but merely allowed herself into his arms. What would become of her now? Had one kiss led her astray? She wondered why her wandering heart felt so anxious and alive. She might stand here in the dark all night and watch young lovers hurry by toward a distant rendezvous and know something about their urgency she'd forgotten until a few moments ago. Why had she waited so long to remember? When would she wander off into the dark again? Would Harry go with her? Perhaps she'd invite him, but only once more. And if Jimmy Delahaye called? She might answer again.

Soon enough it grew late and Marie found herself feeling thoroughly self-conscious and missing her children and told Delahaye she ought to go.

"Well, let me drop you at home, honey," he offered, as she stepped away from him.

"Oh, that's not necessary," Marie replied. Her passion subdued by the hour, now she felt sad and weary, ready for sleep. It had been a long and fitful day, and she was glad it was over. "It's not far and I know my way."

"Say, I hope you don't feel I was doing Harry dirty by trying to drag you off to a picture show."

Marie shook her head, embarrassed by her own timidity and her foolish flirtations. What on earth had gotten into her? "Of course not."

"Honey, let me run you home." Delahaye flicked his cigar off into the dirt. "Please? I don't care for the idea of you out alone so late by yourself. I'll bet Harry wouldn't either. Nobody knows what the hell happened to Boy-Allen, whether it was a nigger or some maniac, but until we do, well, you never know what can happen, do you? I say, there's no sense guessing."

Marie smiled. "Well, all right. It's sweet of you to offer. Thank you."

— 5 —

Near midnight, Delahaye let Marie off by the curb at Maude's house and motored away alone into the dark. It was quiet now, the street empty, only crickets audible in the summer night. Marie opened the small gate to Maude's backyard. A breeze fluttered through the wash that hung on the line, items Rachel had forgotten to bring indoors. Bits of dry grass skittered across the ground at her feet. She could hear Mr. Slopey shuffling inside his stall. The Jessup's collie began barking as Marie ducked under the linen she would have to re-wash tomorrow for Maude and went to the back steps where she removed her shoes, lifted the latch on the screen door, and stepped quietly up into the kitchen. Indoors, the air was humid and still. Marie loosened the top two buttons on her blouse and went to the sink, guided by moonlight that reflected off the glass cupboards and rows of Mason jars along the wall beside the pantry. Sometime since dinner, Maude had baked sweetcakes and gingerbread; their warm and spicy scent filled the small kitchen, reminding Marie how long she had been absent that evening. She ran the cold water and slipped her hands under the faucet, letting them soak nearly to a chill. After drying them on a cotton towel beside the sink, a turn in the hallway past the kitchen brought Marie to her bedroom where she saw a note beside the door. She picked it up and brought it back to the kitchen and switched on the light above the sink. The note read:

> Mrs. Kritt tells us that Abel had been lost in the woods but is safe at home now, though he doesn't seem to be himself just yet. They intend to see a doctor tomorrow. She thanks us for our concern.

This gave Marie a peculiar feeling which sent her quickly to the bedroom. Easing the door open, she peeked in and looked at her children as they lay there together in the bed beneath the open window, arm-in-arm, cuddling like tired kittens. Henry's soft breath feathered his sister's hair; Cissie dreamt, her eyelids stirring. Marie wondered what happened to little Abel, and what his poor mother must be feeling just now. All she prayed for each night was that her children be safe and happy. Too often in the modern world that simple desire seemed elusive. How would we ever survive if our children were not able to be safe at play? And who was that phantom haunting this town? That dark angel? If only she'd caught a glimpse of his face that night.

Gently, Marie closed the door and tiptoed ahead to the front parlor where she decided to read for a while until sleep called her to bed. Although she had danced all evening and walked more than three miles since dinner that afternoon, Marie felt more woozy than fatigued. She also felt strangely nervous, anxious somehow. Why had she gone off under the cottonwoods with Jimmy Delahaye? She'd kissed him and felt shameless and thought she might do it again if the opportunity were right. Or maybe not. Was it awful, what she had just done? Why had she done it? What had come over her? Rainbows of skyrockets and Japanese lanterns and elegant dancers swirled maddeningly in her head as she went to sit by the window where Maude had left an oil lamp burning on a stand against the night. There, cooled by the evening draft of nightblooming jasmine, Marie heard voices murmuring just a few yards away.

"A gentleman wouldn't hold such an opinion," came Rachel's petulant voice. "You only say that to injure me. Innocence offends the guilty heart. Why else would you persist with such petty viciousness?"

"Don't be childish, darling," CW drawled, his voice slurred with liquor.

Looking through the lace, Marie saw CW braced against the post, Rachel only a foot or so away. She saw CW kiss her, then slide away. Were they having a lover's tiff?

"If you use that word with me again this evening, I swear I will slap your smug little face. I will not be insulted on my own front porch."

A match flared in the dark. Moments later, cigarette smoke wafted in at the curtain lace. Rachel's voice followed, "Besides that, it's just not fair. Not fair at all."

"Oh, now I'm the villain, am I? That's a hoot!"

"I have no idea what you mean by that remark," said Rachel, flicking the burnt match into the rose bushes. "Why, I've defended your character on more occasions than I could possibly count, and to whose benefit? Certainly not my own. You have no idea how often I've had to explain your intentions away as innocent flirtations in order to preserve my reputation among my other admirers."

"Why, that's just it, isn't it? You're ashamed of me!"

"Of course I'm not!" Rachel folded her arms and put her back to CW.

"Why, you most certainly are!" CW cried, his voice barely under control. "You're so afraid your reputation is becoming soiled by being seen in my company. That's why you were reluctant to dance with me tonight. That's why we left early and followed that filthy alley most of the way back here afterward. It was fine to be escorted by me to the pavilion with your mother along beside you, but the moment she left, you became terrified that somebody might conclude you'd stepped out with me in earnest, and we both know what sort of gossip that would incur, don't we?"

"If you choose to speak without any consideration as to my feelings," Rachel replied, "then I'd rather not discuss this any longer. I've never heard such rudeness."

Rachel faced the street and blew smoke from the cigarette into the night air. Hooking her little finger about the bottom of the lace, Marie nudged it aside for a better view. She was curious to know how these two fought, because it revealed how firmly their hearts were, or were not, bound to one another's. CW held a small silver flask in his right hand, unscrewing the cap slowly with his left. Both he and Rachel were staring into the road.

Across the room, Marie heard Rachel's radio set playing with the volume wound low, filtering Gershwin's jazz into the dark from some distant station on the Gulf Coast. CW took a drink from the flask, then spoke flatly. "Rachel, dear, I want to say something to you that is terrifically important, and I want you to listen very carefully. This has gone quite deep with me, do you understand?" He glanced across at her. "You see, I believe there are Negroes who enjoy more consideration in the vilest parishes of Louisiana than I've ever received in this household." He sipped from his flask. "Do you deny that?"

Marie was shocked, scarcely able to believe her ears.

Without raising her own voice in the slightest, Rachel replied, "That is the most disgusting thing I have ever heard, and a filthy lie as well. If you don't apologize this instant, I'll never forgive you."

"Darling, you know I'm no milquetoast, and I've no intention of getting down on my knees when I've never been treated as anything more than a stuffed coat in your mother's house."

"Then you can go climb a rose bush for all I care."

"Sweetheart, she despises me for reasons of religious conviction, a prejudice I find inexcusable for any true Christian man or woman. Were it not for the promise of our engagement, I'd hardly be able to tolerate her slurs. I'm surprised she hasn't accused me of murdering Boy-Allen as part of some ritualistic Catholic conspiracy."

She turned to face him. "What an ugly thing to say! Only your — "

"Rachel, I love you dearly, but love has its limits, shame being one of them. I'd never thought of myself as pious or reverential when conversation turned to religion. Spirituality, I was raised to believe, deferred to privacy and personal belief. No one has the right to judge another on matters of faith. I certainly would never have asked you to quote chapter and verse in defense of your own interpretation of the Lord's desire. Therefore, it's not fair for you to insist on my doing so, either for your benefit or your mother's. And, in any case, I won't."

Marie watched CW tip back his flask once more, then replace it in his jacket pocket. She was astonished at what she just heard, yet she couldn't entirely argue against all of it, either. Bellemont's religion was not her own, the witnessing of their faith foreign to her understanding of scripture. No God who preferred hellfire to the mercy of a tender heart would hear her prayers in the dark, nor those of her children. What part of Bellemont's piety involved love?

An automobile rolled past slowly, the driver's window open, a hand waving a lighted cigar out in the draft. CW walked down to the bottom step and stared off up the street.

Rachel said, "So that's how it is? You don't love me, do you? Perhaps you'd prefer not to visit here any more. Perhaps you'd rather have nothing more to do with me." Her cigarette had burned down to the butt, so she flicked it into the honeysuckle. "You see, I only ask because if you have no further interest in pursuing this courtship, I'd rather know tonight. Mother has invited several of her club ladies over to a tea tomorrow afternoon and I promised her we'd attend so that you might regale them with stories of New Orleans at Mardi Gras. They've never had the opportunity of attending and Mother assures me they're all quite intrigued to hear about it."

Indoors, the latest radio melody ended and for a few brief moments the house became silent. Marie shifted her position on the chair, terrified she'd be caught spying. Ordinarily, she detested eavesdropping, but tonight she found the urge irresistible, if only for catching this glimpse into her sister-in-law's heart of hearts. A fresh ballad issued from the radio, a soft melody composed for lovers dancing late into the night. Marie wondered what made Rachel and CW feel the need to be so brutal. Was this how she and Harry sounded? Had the children heard them through the walls in the dark? She hoped not, but knew it was likely. How stupid and cruel.

His eyes locked on Rachel, CW said, "Darling, I believe we ought to marry as soon as possible."

A gust of wind blew through the wisteria, rippling in the curtains by Marie who, for the second time, was stunned by CW.

Rachel replied, "Pardon me?"

"Well, you know yourself the longer we delay, the greater pressure your mother brings to bear upon the differences between us, those meaningless incompatibilities that most people use as excuses to remain apart. I'd rather not have that happen to us. I love you, and I believe we ought to marry. No later than summer's end."

"That's impossible," Rachel said, decending to the next porch step. "Even if Mother approved, which she wouldn't, I don't favor in the least the idea of a wedding thrown together with so little thought given to its arrangement."

"Well, I've spent considerable time thinking about it," CW said. "In fact, I've hardly had anything else on my mind since I arrived here this morning."

"A man's notion of time is quite different from a woman's," said Rachel, "especially in terms of planning for occasions of importance such as this. A wedding is worth a lifetime of consideration. I wouldn't dream of ruining mine through rash behavior."

"And you think that marrying me this summer would be rash?"

"I don't expect you to understand," she replied. "A man's heart is simply not conditioned for such sensitivies. Don't be dismayed. It's not your fault."

CW laughed and drew his flask out for another sip. He tilted his head back and drank, then laughed once again, his voice echoing out into the road. Marie sat back, afraid she'd be seen as her sister-in-law glanced toward the house. She felt badly now for both of them, and wished she had the courage to intercede, even warn them of the heart-break they were instigating for no good purpose.

"Shhhh!" Rachel hissed at CW. "You'll wake Mother!"

He waved the flask at her, then wandered down to the bottom of the stairs. "My goodness! Wouldn't that be a crime! Maude Hennesey, the grand dame of Bellemont Baptists, awakened in the dead of night by a drunk Catholic proposing marriage to her lovely daughter! What would people say!"

"That you've become very ugly in the past half hour, so much so I can hardly believe I ever surrendered my heart to you. I must have been insane."

"Love's wondrous intoxication leads us all to the brink of lunacy. Come down here and share in my delirium!"

He held a hand out to her with a crazy smile. When Rachel failed to budge from the porch, CW removed his straw hat and tried bending down on one knee to offer his hand again. Instead, he lost his balance and toppled over into the dirt. "Nerts!"

"For heaven sakes, you *are* drunk!"

Marie stifled a giggle of her own. He did look very funny.

Prone in the dust, CW grinned up at her. "Blissfully spifflicated by your beauty, my little sunshine!"

"Don't insult me."

"Let's marry tonight! We'll fly to Baton Rouge. Simon Beauregard's father is a justice of the peace there. He'll perform a civil ceremony for us free of charge. We can cable your mother from the aerodrome and tell her the good news. Have you ever been to Cuba? I'll fly us there for our honeymoon tomorrow evening. Dining in Havana! Wouldn't that be romantic? What do you say?"

"I'm going off to bed now. I expect you ought to as well. I'll write you a letter tomorrow and try my very best to forgive your ugly behavior this evening."

CW struggled unsuccessfully to get back on his feet. Balancing precariously on hands and knees, he cried, "Aw, sweetheart! Don't be like that! I love you!"

"Then please say goodnight."

Hearing Rachel's hand on the doorknob snapped Marie to her senses, aware that she was about to be caught. She rose from her chair at the window and tiptoed quickly to the rear of the house. As the front door opened, Marie grabbed her shoes off the laundry stool and darted out onto the back porch and down the steps. Outdoors, she heard CW's plaintive voice still calling to Rachel as the front door closed with a muffled thud. Marie tiptoed up the steps, and shut the rear door behind her. She heard Rachel cross the house and enter her own bedroom on the west side. A yellow glow from Rachel's handpainted Japanese vanity lamp shone briefly onto the chickencoop, then extinguished.

Marie slipped her shoes on and eased down the steps into the yard where the hard corners of fenceline, shed and water trough, appeared clearer now in the pale moonlight than when she had arrived home earlier. A pair of brown bats chased above College Street. Marie watched until they'd gone, then crossed to the gate, craning her neck for a look around front. CW was seated behind the wheel of his Ford, smoking a cigarette and tapping the dashboard with his other fist. The engine was rattling loudly, exhaust billowing up like coal dust from the rear, ruin on his face.

The Jessup's collie bounded around a corner from their backyard and leaped up against the fence beside Marie, panting with excitement. Marie opened Maude's gate and went out onto the sidewalk. CW saw her and flashed his headlamps once. A chill came over Marie as she closed the gate and headed up the sidewalk. She hoped nobody was watching from indoors. She felt sneaky and bold. What would Rachel think if she saw her? Who was the bigger flirt tonight?

CW stumbled out of the Ford, but left the door hanging open.

As Marie approached the automobile, CW dropped the lighted cigarette into the road at his feet, stamped it cold, then tipped his hat to her. "Good evening, ma'am."

"Hello," she said, brightly, hoping she was doing the right thing. Would Rachel say she was butting in where she didn't belong? Probably, but Rachel was also too proud to admit when she was wrong.

"Out for a constitutional?"

Marie lowered her voice. "I suppose it's rather late for that, wouldn't you agree?"

"Yes, it is. How are you?"

"Very well, and yourself?"

CW leaned toward the bumper of the Ford to catch his balance. "Actually, I'm lit to the eyebrows."

Marie smiled. "I can see that." Though she didn't entirely approve of liquor, she found CW's condition amusing tonight. Rachel could be such a share, perhaps CW needed a drink now and then to be pleasant. Often Harry's behavior led to her thinking about wine tonics. Maybe one day soon she'd consider a glass of something to make her dizzy for an hour or two. Marie saw no great moral wrong there.

"Your company's always a pleasure, of course." He bowed, striking his forehead on the car roof. Marie barely stifled a laugh. He looked very funny.

"Oh my!" CW rubbed his head. "I am squiffy, aren't I?"

Marie giggled. "Yes, I'm afraid you are. Perhaps you ought to go to bed."

"*If thou wilt ease thine heart of love and all its smart, then sleep, dear, sleep,*" CW recited aloud.

The Jessup's collie jumped against the gate next door and began barking at something across the road. Marie looked down the empty street, then stole another furtive glance at Maude's window. A tea kettle whistling at dawn would rouse her with little trouble. A peculiar shiver ran up Marie's spine. CW forced a smile and tried once more to stand upright without aid of his automobile.

"Rachel's gone to bed," said Marie, unsure of what else to contribute. "I suppose she'd have a fit if she knew you were still here. I'm sorry." Marie couldn't mend her own wounded heart tonight, much less his. Truth was, she hated hearing them fight with such bitterness. It seemed so utterly wasteful and pointless. Too many nights she and Harry had gone to bed with cold shoulders and what good had come out of it? Did they kiss more often afterward? She knew better than that.

"Oh, don't be. We've had our glittering evening out, and now she thinks I'm a skunk. It's all a mess. I was just preparing to depart."

"You don't intend to fly back to New Orleans tonight in this condition, I hope."

An expression of incredulity crossed CW's face. "Why not? It's a birdman's evening. No clouds. A beautiful moon to guide me home. Once the take-off is dispensed with, there's really very little danger to be had. Other than landing, of course."

Marie smiled. "Of course." She thought CW overbold, and liquor made him worse. She worried for him. "You will be safe, won't you? I'm sure Rachel would be worried sick to have you fly off like this."

CW swayed outward, then staggered back against the automobile. He burped softly, and chuckled. "Did you know she and I intend to marry later this summer?"

"No, I hadn't heard," Marie replied, wondering what Maude would think if she heard that. "How nice!"

CW leaned forward, supporting himself on the driver's door. In a low voice, he said, "Her mother may not be attending, however."

"Oh?"

CW shook his head vigorously. "No. You see, rumor has it the Pope himself intends to perform the ceremony, in which case any Baptist in attendance would burst spontaneously into flames!"

His laughter echoed into the dark.

Down the street now, a motorcar's lamps shone in the pitch-dark shadows beneath the tall cottonwoods. The automobile came quick as lightning, engine roaring, dust and exhaust trailing like a black tornado. Top down, all heads and arms from driver to rumble seat, singing and shouts rising above the engine noise as it drew nearer. Instinctively, Marie backed up close to the sidewalk, having little desire to be run down like a dog in the road. Since Henry's frightening incident this afternoon, Marie was doubly concerned about the children's safety out here. CW, on the other hand, seemed to wander away from his own automobile toward the middle of College Street, drifting like a boat cut loose from its mooring. A block away now and closing, the oncoming motor let loose with its horn, loud and long. Marie called to CW, but her voice was drowned out by the steady honking. He stood at military attention now, near the center of the road, one arm at his side, the other pressed to his brow, locked in a sober salute. Headlamps illuminated his tan suit as the automobile drew closer. Scared silly now, Marie shouted for CW to give way, but he remained resolute in his determination to greet this company of late-night revelers up close. The driver laid on his horn less than fifty yards off, zooming toward the Jessup's where he flashed the headlamps once more. CW's gaze remained stern, unwavering, his salute firm. The motor roared forward, past the Jessup's, toward CW, caught now in the glare of the lamps, lit like a monument statue, fully aglow — when Marie saw a strong dark hand reach over his shoulder from behind and jerk him out of the way of the speeding automobile, pulling him down into the dirt as the motorcar raced by, horn wailing, voices hurling vulgar epithets to CW's stupidity, disappearing on ahead into the dark, the horn echoes tailing off with the headlamps at the town limits.

"Oh my goodness!" Frightened to death, Marie rushed forward to see if CW had been injured.

As she did, a window flew open on the side of the house, and Maude's voice issued forth. "Good gracious sakes alive! What's all that racket! Who's out there? Is that you, Rachel?"

Her words carried across the street. Knowing Maude would not be able to see around the blooming honeysuckle and wisteria, Marie crept beside the running boards of CW's motorcar and remained quiet. By now, CW had risen from the dirt and slid back behind the wheel of the Ford, dust covering his jacket, clouding his hair. His straw hat lay crushed in the street. CW ran a hand over his forehead, smoothing his hair back, then reached over and pulled the driver's door closed with a bang. He seemed to have survived. Thank goodness for that!

Maude called out, "Rachel?"

CW leaned across the passenger seat toward the open window. He said, "Good night, Mrs. Hennesey."

Then he straightened up, looked at Marie. He dropped his voice. "Give my regards to Rachel. Please let her know I'm still nuts about her."

Putting his motorcar in gear, CW drove slowly away from the curb and headed off down the dark street.

As the Ford puttered away into the dark, Marie walked out of the road, back onto the sidewalk, just out of Maude's sight. She heard Maude say, somewhat testily, "Rachel, we'll discuss this in the morning."

Then the window slammed shut.

Straight away, Marie looked for the fellow who had tugged CW from traffic, and discovered him in the shadows by the east corner of the house, her attention drawn to the scraping of his shoes on the sidewalk. "Julius!" she whispered.

"Yes, ma'am."

Dressed in work-soiled overalls and a flat brown cap, he was nearly invisible.

"How nice to see you," she remarked, noticing the wheelbarrow parked behind him under the fig tree Cissie had adopted as the site of her grand circus. It was filled with more of the same sorts of scraps from the junkyard Julius had been bringing since Cissie conceived her summer project. She added, "Thank you for saving CW's life. I thought for sure he would be run down by those hooligans. I doubt he appreciated the danger he was in."

Who had been scared worse, she or CW?

"A body needs to keep moving."

"Pardon?"

Julius smiled. "Just somethin' my granny told me when I was a young-ster. 'Don't never stop movin'.' When she was one hundred and four years old, she'd be walking along the river by moonlight, callin' after them catfish to give themselves up so's there'd be breakfast come morn-ing for all her grandchildren. She never quit taking them walks of hers, died on her feet coming out of the hen house one afternoon, chicken in one hand, hatchet in the other. Bless her sweet heart. She passed on with the love of Jesus-walkin'-on-the-water plain on her face."

Marie wandered another few steps up the sidewalk away from the front porch. Nearer to Julius, she saw some of the scraps he brought for Cissie's circus: an old wire bird cage, six balls of binding string, a cracked apple crate, cotton balls, dried corncobs, chicken feathers, a wagon wheel, and a mildewy collection of old coffee cups whose place in the grand scheme only Cissie knew. Still in the wheelbarrow were a pair of Mason jars filled with cloudy dark water and peculiar drifting shapes like frogs in formaldehyde or an ancient wizard's shelved homun-culi that Marie was unable to discern in the pale moonlight. In any case, she assumed they were intended for Henry and Abel's House of Frights.

A train whistle shrieked across the darkness from somewhere be-yond the river, most likely a freight headed for the Gulf. Both Ma-rie and Julius looked in that direction, although the tracks were more than two miles east of Bellemont and visible only from that side of the woods. Marie could hear the train whistle howl again across the distance. She stood perfectly quiet with her arms folded and listened while Julius stepped back into the shadows, emptying his wheelbarrow of the Mason jars.

"Thank you," Marie said, finally. "Cissie's in love with her circus."

"It's nothing but a joy for children to play at making a game out of something they love."

"Well, it's very generous of you, to say the least." She let her eyes roam across that part of the circus already completed: part of the Big Top rendered by gunny sacks and old canvas, a trapeze erected in thread and fishnet, the revolving Ferris wheel constructed out of an old bicycle wheel, booths along the midway cut out of old coffee tins turned upside down, lion cages made of cheese graters. "I'm afraid to say that Cissie has an extravagant imagination. I'm not sure where she gets it from, perhaps her father. Harry's always had a fanciful outlook."

She smiled, remembering all the evenings her husband had spent reading to Cissie and Henry from *Grimm's Fairy Tales*, crossing his heart and swearing every word was fact.

Julius told her, "In all God's creation, nothing got more magic wrapped up in it than a sweet child's heart. Sees things we can't. Hears 'em, too. Ain't our fault neither, that's just how it is."

Marie studied Cissie's circus rising from the weeds beneath the fig tree like the most natural thing in the world. Julius set the last of the Mason jars side by side next to the half-finished tent and backed the wheelbarrow out of the weeds.

Marie asked, "Do you think the children will complete this by the end of summer?" She desperately wished some dreams this summer might yet come true. In each of our hearts reside wishes for joy and contentment above all else.

Julius put his cap back on, then smiled and shook his head. "Circus ain't never done, Mrs. Hennesey, never finished. Can't be. Got too much hidden up in it to see one time around. Got to come back again, buy another ticket, have another look-see. Circus always got something you never seen before, always something new. Ask your children if that ain't the truth. No, ma'am, circus ain't never done. That's why it's still here."

Then, whistling a tune Marie didn't know, the black man steered the old wheelbarrow about and rolled it off into the summer night.

AUGUST

THREE MILES EAST OF BELLEMONT, a late afternoon breeze blew in the summer grass surrounding the old Rickenbacker Aerodrome. The warm blue skies of late August were cloudless on the prairie horizon. Marie stood anxiously beside the open hangar, watching CW push his De Havilland "Gipsy Moth" out of the shadows while Rachel smoked a cigarette nearby and Cissie and Henry played tag a hundred yards off in the middle of the dirt runway. Marie had dressed in a thin wool sweater and a pair of tweed knickers that CW had suggested she wear for her first flight. Although she felt silly, everyone assured Marie her attire was entirely appropriate for the occasion.

"To my eye, she looks just like Harriet Quimby on her way across the English Channel," CW enthused, shoving the airplane into the sunlight. "Isn't this a marvelous day for flying? We're darned fortunate."

"I'm awfully glad to hear that," Marie said, smiling nervously. "I've been worried the clouds would come in and spoil everything." All morning she'd had butterflies in her stomach from the thought of going up in the airplane. But she was terribly excited and absolutely certain she wanted to fly. She had read somewhere that this world was just a big vaudeville stage with some of us sitting in boxes, some in the gallery, and more people on stage than know it. Well, she'd been spectating longer than she wanted to, and now she, too, wanted her turn on stage, even if it weren't entirely safe. Dear God, she hoped the plane wouldn't crash! What would the children do?

"Oh, there's nothing to worry about at all."

"Why, just last night you assured us that modern aviation is a science," Rachel remarked, exhaling smoke into the air. "You said flying about the clouds has nothing whatsoever to do with luck. Well, I ought to have known you couldn't be trusted to tell the truth for fifteen minutes. It seems Mother was right, after all."

CW stopped. Sunlight glinted off the silver fuselage of the "Gipsy Moth" forcing Marie to shade her eyes. He smiled. "My dear, what I meant to say was that flying is an awfully serious enterprise. Up there, a simple puff of air under the wings is all that separates life from death. Yet, when properly applied, an aviator's skill will overcome the most precarious conditions."

"Is that true?" Marie asked. "You know, this makes me awfully nervous."

Rachel laughed. "Of course it isn't! Don't be ridiculous! Why, even Lindy carried a rabbit's foot to Paris with him."

"I doubt that," CW replied, taking a pre-flight walk around the De Havilland. "Colonel Lindbergh would never have attempted that historic flight if he hadn't been confident of success. I met him, you know."

"You did?" Marie asked, suitably impressed. She only agreed to go up after Rachel assured her that CW had the reputation for being one of the very best pilots in Louisiana. "When?"

"He's lying, of course," Rachel interjected. "CW's never met anyone of note in his entire life."

CW held his own smile, while continuing his walk-around. "Actually, it was in '25 at the Carterville aviation field in Illinois where he was performing with Vera Dunlap's Flying Circus. We met in the hangar after the show. I remember Colonel Lindbergh being a very pleasant fellow. Quite personable, in fact, and a true enthusiast. He told me he'd rather fly than eat."

"I've been to Carterville, once when I was a little girl," said Marie, strolling over to the biplane, touching one of the wing struts. Was it sturdy enough? It looked awfully frail. What if it broke mid-flight? The thought of tumbling out of the clouds put a terrible fright in her heart. "It was in autumn and our entire family visited a pumpkin festival in a Lutheran auditorium. I'd never been on a train before, so the trip down from Farrington was very exciting."

"Did you meet 'Lucky Lindy' there, too?" Rachel asked, finishing with her cigarette. She dropped the butt in the dirt at her feet and stamped it cold.

"No," replied Marie, feeling her stomach do flip-flops. "I've never met anyone of note in my entire life." She smiled timidly at Rachel. "Except you and CW, of course."

CW climbed into the rear seat cockpit and disappeared below the lip of the fuselage. Out on the narrow runway, Cissie and Henry danced in a circle, kicking up dust. Marie called to them and they stopped dancing. Cissie waved and Marie called again and the children raced back from the runway.

"I swear I won't fall out, Momma," Cissie pleaded, reaching her mother ten steps in front of her little brother. She tugged on Marie's skirt. "Please? I want to fly!"

"I believe we've already discussed this." She had no intention of letting the children take a flight. Harry would throw a fit, not that she cared all that much any longer. She had the children with her, after all, while he was off galavanting about the country. The responsibility for their safety and well-being was hers now and she was doing just fine. She didn't need him at all — unless the plane fell out of the sky. She wondered if he'd make it down for her funeral.

Cissie threw her arms around her mother and hugged her tightly. "But it just isn't fair! I've never flown in an airplane before!"

"Neither have I," Marie replied, welcoming Henry into her arms. Could he tell she was frightened? She hoped not. There was no reason for them to know how nervous she was. "Nor has your brother."

"I don't want to fly, Momma," Henry said, freeing himself. "It's too scary!"

"Why, you stinky little coward!" Cissie cried, pinching Henry's ear. "You just told me you wanted to ride in CW's lap! You're nothing but a yellow-bellied coward!" She chased him a few feet away, then came back to Marie. "Couldn't I ride in your lap, Momma?"

"Absolutely not," Marie said. "The subject is closed. Now, go over and wait by the hangar until your Aunt Rachel says it's safe."

"Are you gonna fly now, Momma?" Henry asked, creeping near his sister. The breeze ruffled his hair, kicking dust onto his dirty trousers. Henry's laundry was twice his sister's.

"Pretty soon," Marie replied, as CW finished fueling the De Havilland. The aerodrome's sole mechanic, a skinny young fellow Rachel referred to as "Benny Beeswax," trotted out of a shed next to the hangar and handed CW a sheet of paper to sign, a fresh invoice for Red Crown aviation gasoline. Then the mechanic walked off and CW waved for Marie to come back over to the airplane. He reached into the front seat and took out a leather aviator's cap and a pair of goggles. "Here you are," he said, handing them to Marie. "You'll need a jacket, too." He leaned back into the seat and drew out a fleece-lined leather jacket.

"Will it be cold?" She felt her knees weaken. Why on earth had she agreed to this? Had she completely lost her mind? Good grief!

CW grinned. "Well, we'll be flying nearly eighty miles an hour, and perhaps reach an altitude of a thousand feet! Gosh, yes, I should think you'll be glad to have it on."

Taking the jacket from CW, Marie said, "It just seems so funny to dress for winter in August." She laughed nervously. "I'm afraid I'll suffer heatstroke before we leave the ground."

Rachel walked over and helped Marie fit the jacket over her sweater. "You'll be glad to have this once you're airborne. Believe you me, it's cold as the North Pole up there."

"I thought you said you haven't flown with CW."

"Well, I haven't," Rachel replied, stepping back for a look at Marie, attired now for flight. "But his hands always feel like icicles when he arrives from Shreveport."

"Oh, that's not so," CW said, giving a wave to the mechanic. "She's just teasing. In fact, I always wear gloves, so the cold doesn't bother me at all."

"Will I need gloves, as well?" Marie asked. "I already feel like an Eskimo." What would Harry think if he saw her now? Or Jimmy Delahaye? She knew he thought her to be shy and perhaps a bit mousy. Would this change his estimation of her? Had he ever kissed a girl who'd flown in an airplane?

"No, I don't believe so. If you keep your hands in the jacket, you'll be fine."

Marie watched the children wander inside the old hangar, fading into its shadowy interior. Then the mechanic's shed opened and "Benny Beeswax" trotted over to the airplane.

"Well, here we go!" CW announced, and took Marie's hand. "Are you ready?"

She nodded while her stomach churned and she searched once for Cissie and Henry and saw them standing near the hangar's entrance, barely visible in the brown light. Trembling now, she said to Rachel, "Will you watch the children for me?"

Rachel laughed. "You've already asked me nine times since we left home, dear. Are you sure you want to go? Nobody would blame you for changing your mind. I'd planned to quit work early today, anyhow, so don't feel obligated to risk your life on my behalf."

"Well, yes," said Marie, placing a hand on the fuselage beside her forward seat. "I might be a little afraid, but I'm no coward. I'm ready to fly." She smiled bravely and tried not to faint.

"That-a-girl," cheered CW, taking her free hand and helping her up. Marie stepped over into the seat and slid down into place. It was cramped, but not as tight as she'd imagined it would be. She positioned her legs so that neither was touching the joystick, then leaned back so that she could see Rachel and CW. Her stomach all aflutter, Marie attempted enthusiasm. "Let's go!"

While Rachel walked off toward the hangar, CW took his own seat, fastened his goggles and gave "Benny Beeswax" a brief wave. A light breeze swirled across the field, gently fanning up little whirlwinds of dust on the runway. She heard CW call out, "Fuel on! Mags on! Clear prop!" A moment later, "Benny Beeswax" stood on his toes and gave the propeller a hard tug and the motor roared to life. A cloud of blue smoke puffed from the engine and the entire fuselage vibrated. Marie looked back again to the hangar and saw the children huddled next to Rachel. She waved just as the De Havilland lurched forward and began rolling out toward the runway, bouncing across the rough ground. Every few yards, the engine rattled and sputtered. CW guided the airplane briskly along the edge of the dusty field where the summer grass provided a boundary and the sun angled in Marie's eyes and the heat from the engine caused her to feel faintly claustrophobic.

As they taxied toward a dense stand of pecan trees, CW called to her from behind, "Do you see the stick and rudder pedals?"

Marie swiveled her head to reply. She was almost too scared to look. "Yes, they're at my feet."

"That's right. Well, you'll be able to see me operating them from where you are. They'll look like they're moving all by themselves, but they're not. Just be sure you don't touch them. We wouldn't want to have any confusion as to who's actually flying the plane, would we?"

Marie shook her head. She had no intention of touching anything on the airplane except the part she was sitting on. By now, they were several hundred yards from the hangar, out in the middle of the fields, exposed to the dusty breeze and the afternoon sun. At the end of the runway, the De Havilland spun about abruptly, facing back toward the hangar and the mechanic's shack. Just off Marie's shoulder, an old tractor sat in the tall grass, its iron wheels and rusted rear carriage half-swallowed up by a thick bramble of wild blackberries. She worried it might be the last thing she ever saw on this earth.

"Are you ready?" CW shouted above the rumble of the motor. He laughed as Marie nodded. She was quite nervous now, frightened half out of her wits, in fact. Was this all a disastrous mistake? Harry had once taken an airplane on a short flight across Indiana the summer Henry was born and had passed through a black thunderstorm just south of Muncie. Harry told Marie the plane was battered about so violently even the pilot had gotten sick. What would he think now, his silly timid wife about to go aloft? Maybe she wasn't timid, after all. In fact, maybe Harry didn't know his wife as well as he thought he did. CW shouted for her to keep an eye on the altimeter in front of her once they became airborne. Then the engine roared louder and the "Gipsy Moth" rattled forward down the runway. It was bumpy, yet felt as though the airplane were skipping along the ground as they raced forward. She craned her neck briefly for a glance back at the hangar where her children and Rachel stood cheering.

And then the De Havilland left the ground.

Beneath the airplane, the prairie horizon fell farther and farther away and the sky above it expanded like the interior of a great blue circus tent, raised higher and higher as the airplane gained altitude. She watched the arrow rise on the altimeter and airspeed gauges, and noticed the pedals shifting position slightly and the joystick tilting left as CW brought the airplane about in a long slow circle, returning for a pass above the aerodrome. Then her stomach dropped as the "Gipsy Moth" fell into a lazy dive toward the old hangar. Now only a couple hundred feet above the fields, CW slowed the engine speed and the din lessened and Marie heard him shouting for her to wave and she swiveled her head in time to see the tiny figures of Cissie and Henry racing across the runway as CW brought the airplane on a direct line between the hangar and the runway. He tilted each wing once up and down as they roared over the heads of the children and flew toward the pecan trees, then high up into the blue sky and over the pinewoods north of town. It was exhilarating. In Cissie's favorite daydream, a young wingéd monkey named Clarissa, blown out of the Land of Oz by a great gust of wind, lived in the attic of the house at 119 Cedar Street. In exchange for a plate of lemon cakes and a cup of ginger tea, she promised to teach Cissie how to fly. Whenever Cissie closed her eyes and whispered the secret command of the Winkies, she'd rise above the farmlands of Illinois, up above the clouds, and fly with Clarissa until her mother's voice called her to earth again. Not until CW banked the "Gipsy Moth" over the river toward Bellemont did Marie truly appreciate her daughter's fantasy of flight.

The De Havilland was noisier than she expected, smoky, too, and the fuselage shook and creaked whenever CW wrenched it into a half-loop. Once she even thought the struts were about to break off, flinging them both to the earth in a crumpled mess. Yet, despite an eighty-mile-an-hour wind in her face, and the persistent engine roar in her ears, she felt thrilled. They swept over the mudflats and pine trees and those small gray shacks of Shantytown near the river, sailing smoothly five hundred feet off the ground following the railroad tracks, then over the squat depot itself toward downtown Bellemont. Marie located the green lawn on the town square where she and the children had watched the Independence Day parade, and the white steeple of the First Baptist Church of Bellemont, and the red brick library where Cissie borrowed her Oz books, and the Bijou picture house and Bellemont Normal School and the business district downtown where dozens and dozens of tiny people strolled about the concrete sidewalks she followed every day from Delahaye's Restaurant downtown to Maude's small white house on College Street with the narrow backyard and the white linen on the washline and Lili Jessup's pale brown house next door, the grassy oak meadows beyond.

As CW brought the "Gipsy Moth" into a lazy circle, Marie saw Bellemont as she hadn't before, a small community clustered tightly along the banks of a twisty river in the middle of pinewoods and meadows, a plain rectangular settlement parceled into small sections by irregular fencelines and connected to the country beyond by thin dusty roads and a single stretch of railroad tracks. The De Havilland was rising now, higher and higher, a thousand feet above the earth. Marie tried her best to track a flight of redbirds half a mile away, and wondered how the Pendergast fields and the rolling hillocks of York's peacock farm and Miller's dairy would appear from the summer sky. *In the summer fields of Illinois long ago, Marie and her cousins run in the wake of the mowers, playing hider-seeker among the haycocks, chasing butterflies about with lacy straw bonnets, gathering a bed in the fresh mow upon which to lie back and watch the sparrows and starlings in the blue sky overhead. How sad and clumsy people must appear to birds, thinks Marie, how crude and graceless. In those halcyon years before the World War, all she knows of life are the Pendergast farmlands and Farrington's shady sidestreets and a mile of sandy river bluff along the muddy Mississippi. All the beauty in the world, she knows by touch. Basking in the warm haycocks until sundown, musty fragrance of fresh-mown hay in the summer air, the loud echoing voices of her father and uncles and brothers laboring in the fields until dark, supper by lamplight, later a cool breeze at a bedroom window, familiar whispers in the night. Where will her own children find fields of summer hay to play in? Across the wake of whose mowers will they run?*

CW called to Marie, telling her it was time to return to the aerodrome. She nodded, and the "Gipsy Moth" banked smoothly over the pinewoods east of town. Then the engine sputtered. Marie heard CW curse and instantly felt the plane drop. He cursed again and Marie saw a vapor trail of fuel misting off the back of the airplane. She called to CW, "Is there something wrong?"

He looked back at her in obvious distress. "The gas line's busted!"

"Oh?" She knew nothing about motors of any sort.

Then the engine quit completely and the wings dipped. CW leaned forward, yelling at the plane and Marie became utterly convinced she was about to die. She was a fool for taking a chance like this. The children were going to watch her fall out of the sky and crash before their eyes. She must've lost her mind to go up in the air like this. The biplane swooped into a slow but steep dive to Marie's left and she was so terrified all she could do was watch the earth spinning toward her. Dear God, she didn't want to die! Would it hurt badly when we crashed? How would Harry react to the news? Is this why she'd come to Texas, to die in a stupid accident? What'll happen to the children?

"We're going to try to land!" CW shouted to Marie. "I'm bringing us around in a circle. Hold on!"

Good grief, she was petrified with fear. The plane rolled into a tight left turn that almost tossed her out of the seat. Without the roar of the engine, she could hear the rush of wind and seemed to become light-headed as they swooped down over the cold river beside Shantytown. Trees grew larger and the grassy fields around the aerodrome flattened out wider than ever. She had always imagined airplane wrecks to be loud, but somehow there was no noise at all anymore and now she saw the end coming quickly. This was it, after all. Her life was finished in a silly airplane ride.

"Hold on! We're going in!"

Then Marie saw the runway and watched CW fighting to line up with it. As the biplane descended, the hangar came into focus once more. Marie saw her children hurrying across the runway from the safety of the hangar and the airplane seemed to float down over the flying field, gently crossing the pecan trees and the old tractor in the blackberry bramble, closer and closer to earth, down, down down, then … alighting finally on the dusty runway with a fierce bump that jolted her head. The Gipsy Moth bounced once, twice, three times, lurching left and right, CW yelling loudly, fighting to keep it from flipping over, and then the airplane rolled to a stop, and everything was still. Marie let out her breath. Was she actually alive? She could scarcely believe her eyes. They were on the ground and all in one piece.

"Well, I guess we made it," CW announced, his attempted glee at having brought them in safely sounding more like abject relief. "I haven't the vaguest idea what happened to the gas line, but that sure was exciting, wasn't it?"

Unable to speak, Marie squeezed her hands tightly together so they'd quit trembling.

"Thank goodness you got back safely!" Rachel said, hurrying up to the plane as CW helped Marie climb down out of the cockpit. Waves of heat swelled off the motor. She shaded her eyes to the sun's glare. "I was absolutely certain he'd do something idiotic like flipping the airplane upside-down and tossing you out."

CW took off his goggles and shaded his own eyes to the afternoon light. "Why, I'd never pull a stunt of that sort with anyone on board. I'm no show-off."

"Of course you are," Rachel insisted while giving Marie a brief hug. "Welcome back, dear."

"Why, thank you," Marie replied, still so frightened she could scarcely speak. Nor had she any intention of telling the children what had just occured. "I can hardly believe I did it. CW was wonderful. I've never had so much fun!"

"Good for you!" Rachel kissed her on the cheek. "Now, for the children's sake, I'd advise you never to fly again. It's much too dangerous."

Marie removed the goggles and aviator's cap and the leather jacket and replaced all three items into the forward cockpit. She waved to her children who had been kept back from the biplane by Rachel. Her legs felt a wobbly, but somehow she had survived and now had a terrific story to write home about. She grinned like crazy, imagining Emeline's astonishment over her flight. She could hardly wait to tell her all about it. "Why, it was the most marvelous experience I've ever had!"

"Oh, you're just dizzy," Rachel remarked. "You'll be fine again in an hour or so, I'm sure."

"Oh, Momma!" Cissie shouted, rushing forward ahead of Henry and giving her mother a big hug at the waist. "You really flew! I'm so proud of you!"

— 2 —

Maude was standing by the porchsteps, gabbing with the old postman when they arrived home. CW swung the Ford around in a U-turn and parked at the curb where Cissie was constructing her summer circus beneath the fig tree. Marie saw that Maude still wore her sewing thimble on one hand and had the remnant of a scarf tucked into the front pocket of her dotted blue percale apron dress. She'd been sewing for her club ladies since dawn. Her eyes sagged and she looked fatigued. Cissie ran around back to the stables to look in on Mr. Slopey, Henry trotting dutifully after her. After greeting Maude, CW followed Rachel indoors, while Marie remained out in the sunlight where the heat was just beginning to abate and the afternoon air was lightly redolent of jasmine and dusty roses. She was still feeling terrifically giddy over her flight, and proud, too, for doing something she never imagined she'd have the nerve. Were Harry only here to have witnessed it, perhaps he'd see her in a different light. Would that make a difference between them? She could only hope somehow to change the direction his heart was tending, and if that wasn't possible, then she'd show him that she had a lot more gumption than he guessed and that one day soon he'd have to recognize that, for both their sakes. Too little sympathy already plagued them.

Maude thanked the postman for his delivery and watched as he went off. She remarked to Marie, "That's the sweetest man in this town. A saint, if I had the vote to cast. Clarence has been delivering my mail since Harry was in knickers and never has anything but a good word to say. He's outlived three of his own children and both his sisters and it looks as if he'll bury his wife before autumn. Yet he doesn't let on that life hasn't always treated him well and decently."

"Perhaps resilience ought to be counted a virtue," said Marie, passing through the gate, and closing it behind her. *"Has not man a hard service upon earth?"* she quoted, her father's favorite epigram from the Bible. He held little more sacred than constancy.

"Well, if any man were a latter-day Job, it would be that one," Maude replied, watching the old postman fade into the shady cottonwoods down the street. "I do believe we've forgotten how grace delivers the futility of sorrow from our hearts."

Clucking her tongue as she did when lost in thought, Maude removed the remnant of the scarf from her dress and followed Marie indoors.

Rachel already had the radio tuned to a dance orchestra playing jazz from a ballroom in Baton Rouge. Marie watched her waltz about the front room through amber slants of sunlight that penetrated Maude's lace curtains, while CW sat on the piano bench with his back to the keyboard and tapped rhythm on his kneecaps. Swirling about like a child ballerina, her spirits clearly brightened by the music, Rachel danced close to CW, rustled her fingers in his hair as she pirouetted past, kissing his ear and cheek before dancing off again. Marie wondered if Rachel imagined that love would always be like this.

> *I love him in the springtime,*
> *And I love him in the fall.*
> *But last night on the back porch,*
> *I loved him most of all.*

After straightening up another of Henry's messes in the bedroom, Marie went out through the back door intending to bring in the laundry. Seeing it had already been taken off the washline, she looked for the children in the stables and in the chickencoop, then walked around to the front of the house where she found Cissie helping Julius Reeves remove a lazy Susan and an old Victorian table lamp with a beaded fringe shade from a kitbag in his overloaded wheelbarrow. Abel Kritt and Henry sat side by side in a splint chair under the fig tree, Abel cradling one of Rachel's hens like a football, a stray white cat pawing a twig at his feet. Little Abel had gone missing for the better part of a day after the Fourth of July and refused to tell anyone where he had been, though his clothes had been caked with dried mud and he had lost his eyeglasses and had suffered nasty scratches and one of his fingers was bruised and swollen. His frantic mother had put him to bed for a week and brought a doctor to look him over, and a policeman from downtown, too, but not much seemed to have come of it. Mrs. Kritt plainly refused to discuss the trouble and closed her door to prying neighbors, several of whom claimed she went about teary-eyed and angry and talked to herself after dark when the bedroom window was open to the night air. There were dark rumors, naturally, and Boy-Allen's name popped up in conversation along with Abel Kritt's. If there was any consensus at all, it was that something ugly was occuring in Bellemont's shadows and the end of it was not yet in sight. Still, life went on, and soon enough little Abel and Henry were back playing together, apparently cheerful as ever, unmindful of the torment Abel's brief disappearance had caused among those who cared for him, and those who feared for their own children all about town.

Still buoyant from her flight, Marie walked over to the fig tree. In the wheelbarrow was a toy wooden horse head sticking out of a small box. When Cissie noticed her mother, she jumped up. "It's a flying-jinny, Momma! Isn't that wonderful? Our very own flying-jinny!"

Julius looked up at Marie and touched the bill of his old railroad cap. "Afternoon, Mrs. Hennesey. We're buildin' us a fine circus here."

Marie smiled, pleased to see her children occupied with the business of having fun. "You're constructing a merry-go-round?"

"A flying-jinny, Momma," Cissie corrected. "That's what they call them down here. Julius made it out of all these scraps." She got up and went to the wheelbarrow and took out the box full of discarded toys from another era, labeled *Humpty-Dumpty-Circus*.

"Oh my goodness!" Delighted, Marie bent over the box and found more horses of various colors and poses, a pair of giraffes and a donkey, a camel, a lion, a trio of trapeze aerialists, several painted clowns and a mustachioed ringmaster dressed in a red coat and black top-hat. Under everything were toy stools, pedestals, a ladder, a colored ball and a piece of white cloth stitched with red garlands. Marie looked over at Julius who was busy fastening the lamp to the lazy Susan. "Santa Claus brought me one of these for Christmas one year when I was a little girl. Wherever did you dig this up?"

"There's all sorts of places where things other folks don't want no more been collecting," said Julius, tapping another hole in the lazy Susan. "It's just a case of knowing where to put a hole in the dirt." He pulled a screwdriver from his overalls and drove a screw through the base of the lamp, connecting it to the lazy Susan.

"Why, when Julius gets done putting our flying-jinny together, Momma," Cissie enthused, separating the wooden horses from the rest of her miniature circus menagerie, "I guess we'll have just about the best circus in the whole country, won't we?"

Marie smiled. "I expect you will at that." When Emeline saw Marie's Humpty-Dumpty circus, she was so jealous, she refused to come play until after New Year's.

She bent down and brushed her fingers across the beaded fringe of the Victorian table lamp that would serve as canopy to the merry-go-round. Marie's mother still owned a similar lamp and shade with prism glass, which she kept atop an embroidered lambrequin on a table in front of the parlor's east window where morning sunlight drew rainbows on all the walls and ceiling. Marie thought it was the most beautiful object in all the world.

Julius tapped the final hole into the lazy Susan and screwed the lampstand down tight. Then he hitched up his overalls, grabbed the shade, re-attached it to the lamp, and sat back. "All right, Mister Henry. Throw the switch!"

Henry gave the lazy Susan a push and they all watched the little merry-go-round revolve with only a slight tilt.

"Oh, it'll be so beautiful when we put our horses on it!" said Cissie, brushing the beads as they went by.

"I want to ride a tiger!" Henry cried, grabbing one from the box. He placed it on the merry-go-round. It slid off and Abel snatched it for his own with a big grin. The hen hopped free, scaring the cat. Marie heard Maude call to her from the front of the house.

"Excuse me," she said, getting up.

She walked back around to the front steps where Maude waited in the late sunlight, a letter in hand.

"I think I must be slowly losing my mind," she said, handing the letter to Marie. "This came with the rest of the mail today, dear. It's from Illinois."

"Why, thank you."

Maude went back indoors as Marie read the envelope and saw the return address with Auntie Emma's name. Before Marie could tear the envelope open, Cissie came running past the honeysuckle bush shouting, "Wait, Momma! Wait! It's my turn!"

Marie frowned. "Pardon me, dear?"

Cissie stopped beside her at the stairs, one hand shading her eyes to the late sun, the other held palm up. Her pigtails were as dusty as Henry's trousers. "Don't you remember?" she said, brightly. "You promised the next letter I could read first!"

Marie slipped the paper out of the envelope. "How about if we read it together?"

Cissie shook her head. "No, me first this time. You got to read Daddy's on Tuesday. It's my turn today."

"Well, all right." Marie handed the letter to her daughter, and sat down in the middle of the stairs. "I'll just wait here until you finish, but be quick. We'll be eating soon."

A pair of black automobiles droned past, oilworkers heading east to home in Clementville. One of the drivers beeped his horn and a pair of arms thrust out from the back seat of the second car and gave a wave as they passed. The Jessup's collie began barking and Marie heard Lili yell to it from the backyard. Earlier in the day, Lili had claimed to be too busy giving a bath to a scruffy terrier she and Cissie had rescued from an abandoned well to play out at the airfield, and Cissie worried perhaps their friendship was waning, though less than a week had passed since they'd sworn an oath of eternal affection. Back in Farrington, Cissie had constantly formed clubs and tested her members' loyalty with silly challenges: cross Lovett's creek barefoot in December, go an entire day with both shoelaces untied, write an anonymous letter to the mayor telling him that Widow Allyson is secretly married to an Indian. Since Cissie had arrived in Bellemont, only Lili Jessup had yet paid her the compliment of following her about, helping her rescue orphaned animals, being her friend. If Cissie's bossiness led to her losing Lili's friendship, she'd be sorry.

Cissie gasped and dropped the letter. Before Marie could say a word, she raced up the steps and went indoors. As the screen door slammed shut, Marie picked up the letter and quickly read it through.

Farrington, Illinois
July 30th, 1929

Dear Niece,

My, how these months have hurried along! Your mother reminded me just this morning that we've been without you for almost half a year now. Of course, we all miss you so very much. Did you know Josie just celebrated her fifth birthday? It is remarkable how the days pass when one works too hard at living to observe the calendar. I'm getting older yet I rarely notice. Do you suppose that means the Lord will postpone my appointment? These are questions I ponder when your mother and Leora are away and I am left to my thoughts.

Last Friday Auntie Eff had the Ladies Missionary Society out to George's farm and we all went. I had a fine time. Abby's young nephew Milton waited on our tables. You ought to have been there and seen him. He had a cap with a little blue bow and he looked pretty as anything. If his hair had been long he would have looked exactly like a girl. There were over a hundred ladies there. George made out that they were a terrible crowd but he was in a foul temper again. Cousin Francis sang. Doesn't she sing dandy? Milton was quite struck with her. He says he is going to the church where she sings some Sunday so that he can hear her again. He also thinks Mattie McCall is fine. Perhaps he'll call on them both. Grandma, Roy, Emeline, Victor and I went out to Uncle Charlie's Sunday. Milton thinks Hazel is awfully cute as well. That boy is a Gallup, isn't he?

Mattie gave Uncle Charlie a white tie for his birthday and sent a letter with it. Grandma thought you would like to see the letter so I am sending it next week with a postal card. Mr. Williams, Aunt Et's nephew, was here the other day. You know he came on the Glidden tour. He wanted to run off with your table. He says it's worth more than a few dollars and if he sells it, there's quite a lot he can buy. Don't worry. He won't be allowed indoors without a policeman standing by! Grandma is doing fine.

Effie's more worried than ever about your cousin Alvin. No one has the least idea where he's gone off to. He has not written nor did he say where he was going. We are all worried and pray for him daily. Doctor Hartley believes Alvin's t.b. has returned and that his running off is very dangerous. If Alvin wishes to do without his family only the Lord can say how he'll end up. Frenchy claims we ought not to worry. He believes only Alvin knows why he has gone off like this and when he is good and ready he'll come back home again where he belongs. We can only hope this is so.

Now for some terrible news. Yesterday when Lottie and Sam went out to the barn to feed the pets, Cissie's little ball of sunshine Punky was nowhere to be found. They looked high and low for hours and when they discovered him under the steps of Uncle Boyd's workshed it became a tragedy. Punky had died in the night. Effie thinks it was poison but nobody can imagine where the poor cat could have gotten into any so we have a mystery with our sadness. Please let Cissie rest assured that Punky will be missed by all of us and that the children gave him a touching burial. I'm so very sorry about this. I trust Cissie will forgive us. Please write soon. We miss you dearly.

Your Loving,

Auntie Emma

Marie folded the letter in her lap. She sighed. Cissie had worried herself to tears over Punky remaining behind on the farm. She insisted he would be unhappy and might even run off. Despite her protestations, Harry had driven Punky and Cissie together out to the farm and seen to it that Cissie say good-bye to the old cat outside Uncle Henry's barn. Necessity demanded sacrifice, Harry had told her on the road home. Regardless, that night the poor dear cried herself to sleep.

Marie got up and went inside where the sunlight had disappeared and the interior was mostly reflection and shadow. Rachel had stopped dancing and now sat in CW's lap on the piano bench, kissing him so deeply Marie blushed to see them. The radio orchestra played an instrumental arrangement of Rudy Vallee's Fox Trot melody "Betty Co-ed." Rachel gave a brief nod to Marie, directing her toward the back of the house, then returned to kissing. Maude was baking cinnamon cookies when Marie passed by the kitchen. Even before she got to the bedroom, Marie could hear Cissie sobbing.

In the shadow of the chinaberry tree, Cissie lay on her side atop the quilted bedspread, tears running down her cheeks.

"Oh, honey," Marie said, sliding onto the bed beside her, "I'm so sorry. We all loved Punky very much."

"I miss him already, Momma," Cissie sobbed into the pillow. "It hurts so bad."

"I know it does." She stroked Cissie's hair. "He was a very sweet cat. We'll all miss him dearly."

"It was my fault for not bringing him with us," she cried. "I let Punky die."

Marie leaned forward and pulled Cissie into her arms and hugged her tightly. "Oh, honey. No, you didn't. It wasn't anybody's fault. Your cousins loved Punky very much and took the best care of him they knew how. Punky had a wonderful life. He was very happy."

"But he died, Momma! He died, and I wasn't even with him! He must've been awful scared." She began sobbing again. Looking out through the window past the chinaberry tree, Marie saw Lili brushing down her horse. The horse's mane tossed with dust swirling in the small corral. The young girl was struggling to finish her chores before sundown.

Cissie murmured, "Momma, I'll never ever love another cat like Punky."

Marie kissed Cissie's cheek. "Of course you will, honey. One day you'll have another kitty you'll love with all your heart."

"How do you know, Momma?" Cissie moaned. "I never had a cat before Punky. What if I found one who wouldn't love me like Punky did? What would I do?"

Marie laughed. "Oh, baby." She gave Cissie another big hug and a kiss. "How could it not?"

Outdoors, the breeze gusted and the chinaberry tree scratched at the window and dropped more ripe berries into the dusty backyard. After a while, Cissie stopped crying and cuddled beside Marie. "Momma?"

"Yes, dear?"

"Where's Punky now? Is he in heaven?"

Marie smiled. "He's in a very special place, honey, where I'm sure he's very happy."

"Did they bury him by the creek under the Indian tree with the other cats?"

Marie nodded. "Probably beside old Mister Stockingfeet."

"That's such a silly name, Momma," said Cissie, wiping a tear off her cheek. "Do you still miss him?"

"Of course," she replied, softly stroking Cissie's hair. "Mister Stockingfeet was the sweetest kitty I ever owned. I cried just like you when he died. I thought I'd never love anything again as long as I lived, but then I had my children and they taught me how wrong I'd been."

Next door, Lili undid the slip knot she'd fixed to the fencepost and led the horse back across the yard to his stall. A rooster fluttered across the dusty ground and skittered under the Jessup's backstairs. Lili's gray kitten chased a leaf through the gate between the two properties.

"Did Boy-Allen go to heaven, Momma?"

"Of course he did, honey. Heaven's a providing place where sadness and hurt are washed away in God's eternal joy, and nobody feels lost or neglected any longer."

"I'm glad, Momma. I'd feel awfully sad if he wasn't in heaven now."

"Me, too."

Thinking about that for a few moments, Cissie said, "Sometimes I still miss David, Momma." She looked up at her mother, eyes still damp and red with tears. "Did he love me?"

"Very much so," Marie answered, somewhat taken aback. Although her firstborn never drifted far from remembrance, since his death a week after his fifth birthday, rarely had Marie spoken David's name aloud. Nor had Harry. To lose a child so young proved an almost unbearable burden, worsened yet by memory's insistent whisper. Time dulled the ache, but that was all. Moreover, Marie had become convinced the Lord did not allow such wounds to heal in the belief that denying sorrow only forfeits love, since both share a common place in the heart.

A blustery wind is hissing off Lake Calhoun, stirring whitecaps out on the cold water. The afternoon sky is grim and threatens rain, perhaps by evening, but Marie has promised David a picnic, so here they are with a basket of fruit and sandwiches. They are not alone. Sailboats drift across the waves and a fisherman guides his skiff by the shore where other people stroll the walkways or relax on park benches and study the clouds. Marie ought to have more company for her excursion today, but Cissie is napping at home with Aunt Ruth while Harry is over to St. Paul on business. Little David doesn't seem to mind at all. He scurries about the grass like a bug, tumbling and laughing, showing off for his mother, having a grand visit to the lake. Marie enjoys a pear and a cheese sandwich, and watches the sailboats flutter like kites on the steel-gray water. The fisherman brings his flatbottom boat to shore, then gets out, anchoring his skiff on the grass with a rock tied to a rope. He hurries off through the trees. When David heads over to the boat, Marie warns him to stay clear of the lapping water. He nods, and kneels to study the knotted rope. Wary of his intentions, Marie rises from the picnic blanket to go fetch him back from the shoreline. As she stands, a terrific gust of wind billows under the blanket, upsetting the picnic basket. Startled by the sight of her napkins and Dixie cups blowing away toward the cycle path, she takes her eye off David. The blanket ripples under the wind as Marie quickly grabs what she can reach. Glancing back toward the water, she sees the fisherman's skiff has come free of its anchor and is drifting out into the lake, her five-year-old David perched at the bow. Marie screams. She runs to the sandy embankment at the water's edge and calls to him as the windblown current carries David's skiff farther from shore. Marie jumps into the water and sinks up to her waist. She shouts frantically for her little boy to come back. Horrified, she watches David climb up onto the bow, and plunge overboard into the pitching waves. He cannot swim. Neither can she. A brave fellow from the shore dives into the lake, but David has already disappeared. Hysterical with fear, Marie splashes toward the skiff, loses her balance, and goes under. By the time strong arms carry her out of the lake, she knows her little boy has been lost, and the suffocating grief lays her unconscious.

Cissie said, "I was just a baby when David died, wasn't I, Momma?"

"Yes, you were," replied Marie, giving Cissie another kiss on her ear while hugging her tightly, "but he'll always be your brother, just as Henry is. We lost him a good while ago, honey, but he's stayed in our hearts all the same, hasn't he?" How strange that Marie could no longer recall David's voice, yet his soapy after-bath scent persisted whenever she remembered him in her arms. What persists for eternity, if not a mother's devotion to her child?

"Yes, Momma," Cissie agreed. She folded her fingers into Marie's and squeezed gently. "That's why I still pray for him every night before I go to sleep."

"So do I, honey."

"David knows we still love him, doesn't he, Momma? Even in heaven?"

"Of course he does," Marie said, watching now as Lili crossed her yard to the backstairs and went indoors, her small gray kitten trailing just behind. "That's why God brought him there, so he'll always be loved, no matter what. His being in heaven teaches us how precious life is, honey. Every single day of it. That's why we'll never forget our dear little David."

"Or Punky," Cissie added, wiping away another tear.

Marie smiled, "That's right. We'll always remember Punky, too."

Then she gave her sweet daughter another kiss and cuddled with her in the small bed beneath the back window until evening's shadows crept out from the pretty chinaberry tree and Maude called them both to supper.

— 3 —

Over Maude's objections, Rachel tuned the radio set to an NBC orchestra broadcast from Kansas City's Meuhlebach Hotel while they ate. Arguing that music aids digestion, she had set the volume so every note could be clearly heard in the dining room. CW didn't seem to mind, but it drove everyone else crazy. Marie knew Harry would've taken the radio and tossed it out a window, nor was she herself exactly pleased to have it playing during supper, but Rachel was obstinate. Between servings of vegetable soup and the veal Maude cooked to resemble pork chops, Rachel fidgeted with her fork and spoon, tapping rhythm to "The Sheik of Araby" and singing along with the broadcast.

I'm the sheik of Araby
Your love belongs to me.
At night when you're asleep,
Into your tent I'll creep.

The children giggled when her spoon struck the side of the table too hard and flew off onto the carpet. Maude slapped her own hand down beside her plate. "Rachel!"

"Yes, Mother?" Rachel bent down to retrieve the spoon.

"You're behaving like a wild animal. I'm asking you to stop it this instant. It's spoiling my appetite."

"I resent that, Mother," replied Rachel, putting the spoon back onto her plate. "It's an ugly thought. Why, I suppose next you'll be telling me to sleep out in the stalls."

"Don't give me cause," Maude threatened, her eyes steeled to the occasion. "You're acting more childish than these two little ones. I won't stand for it."

"Why, you've just proven Darwin's theory, Mother." Rachel giggled like a clown. "I've evolved from a wild animal to a child in less time than it took Eve to swallow the apple. Somebody ought to wire John Scopes."

"Laugh at the dinner table and you'll cry before bed," Maude scolded. "I'm warning you, young lady."

"Young lady? I thought I was a child. Please make up your mind, Mother. You're confusing me now."

"Rachel!"

In one swift stroke of her left hand, Rachel knocked the bowl of potatoes off the table. It landed upside down on the rug beside Marie's chair. "There, Mother," she said. "Now, that's childish!"

"My heavens!" Maude cried, rising from her chair.

Marie was shocked. Had her sister-in-law gone insane? She told her, "Good grief, dear! You're scaring the children!"

"Darling!" CW leaned forward, clearly shocked. "If you ask me — "

"Well, I didn't ask you!" Rachel seized her glass of water and splashed it between his eyes. "And I refuse to look at your stupid face another instant!"

Then she slid her chair back, got up and ran out of the room.

They all heard the front door slam.

Maude stood at the table. "Why, I believe she's lost her mind."

CW wiped his face with the cloth napkin. Marie looked across the table at the children, both of whom appeared goggle-eyed by the nasty display of adult temperament. She put her finger to her lips just as Cissie began to say something. Henry kept his own eyes down, his fork stuck in a pile of mashed potatoes. The radio played on.

> *While stars are fading in the dawn*
> *Over the desert they'll be gone*
> *His captured bride close by his side*
> *Swift as the wind they will ride.*

CW pushed his chair back. "I suppose I ought to go out and see where she's run off to."

Marie slid her own chair away from the table and picked up the bowl of potatoes, scooping onto Rachel's plate all that had spilled. She felt horribly embarrassed for Maude and the children. What had gotten into Rachel? CW went out the front door. Marie heard him calling for Rachel as Maude came out of the kitchen with a wet rag, angrier than Marie had ever seen her.

"Here, let me do that," Marie offered, taking the rag. "Cissie? Please?"

Her daughter got up and came around the table to help. Henry sat still, intent on finishing his dessert of tapioca pudding that apparently no one else had any interest in.

"I declare I ought to put that nasty mouth of hers out into the street," said Maude, at the window now, her fingers curled inside the curtain for a look outside. Marie scrubbed the rug while Cissie used her fingers to pick up smaller bits of potato. A bright peal of laughter issued from out of doors, Rachel's voice echoing across the early evening dark.

"I don't know what came over her," Marie said, cleaning as best she could. It was an awful mess. What on earth had just happened? "I've never seen her behave that way before."

"You just haven't been here long enough." Maude shook her head in disgust. "If she were destitute even a short while she might learn how to behave. Jonas spoiled Rachel when she was little and now there's nothing to be done with her. Beatrice tells me that practically everyone at Corby & Beauchamp is scared to death of her throwing these sorts of fits. They say she's a holy terror. I presume that's how she's managed to hold onto her job for so long." Maude came away from the window shaking her head. "Even in an insurance office, secretarial is nothing to sniff at, you know. More than thirty girls applied for that position. I'm sure the fact that Rachel was hired proves she's capable of impressing people when she sets her mind to it. What I don't understand is her refusal to accept the notion of courtesy and decent behavior. She ought to realize there are those who will hold it against her one of these days. Nobody is entirely belovéd. Why, even a peacock envies his own reflection."

Marie went out onto the back porch where she heard Rachel and CW busy in conversation. She gently closed the screen door. With a fresh batch of gingerbread cookies in the oven, Maude had gone to draw a rosewater bath for herself, while the children played slapjack across the hall in the back bedroom. Outdoors, the night air was sultry and calm. Moths flapped at the washroom screens. Automobiles rattled by every so often and hordes of youngsters chased about in the next block, their shrill voices echoing adventure and quarrel in the summer dark.

As Marie crossed the yard, she heard Rachel still explaining her outburst at supper. "Well, of course you all were ganging up on me. When don't you? To tell the truth, I've felt persecuted in this house since the day I was born. All for speaking my mind. Am I not entitled to voice my opinions now and then? I tell you, it's just not fair!"

"Now, darling, be reasonable," CW said, kissing Rachel on the cheek. "Say, didn't I let you decide where I'd be escorting you tonight? Ordinarily that would be a fellow's decision, but in the interest of fair play and all, I let you choose, and so we're going to the picture show, aren't we?"

Rachel broke away and wandered over to the fence by the Jessup's corral. CW flipped his straw hat on one finger and strolled after her. The plumbing rattled under the house as hot water ran toward Maude's bathtub. Rachel saw Marie and waved to her, so Marie walked across the backyard to meet up with her and CW beside the Jessup's. She knew Rachel wasn't done fussing yet, although her moods were as changeable as the wind. Harry found his sister impossible to understand and had warned Marie to avoid her as often as possible. That advice seemed silly, and Marie mostly ignored it. More often than not, Rachel was quite endearing. But her behavior tonight had been disgraceful and Marie intended to tell her so. "Hello."

"Is Mother still put out?" Rachel asked, with a grin. "I don't know what came over me. That was such a silly thing to do."

"It was very rude," Marie said, her lips tightened. "I don't see why the children had to witness something like that at the supper table. It's hard enough just getting them to sit down."

Rachel turned her face away, and feigned a shiver in the wind.

Marie refused to indulge her. "Did you hear what I just said? There's no excuse for involving the children in your own drama. It's mean, and you know it."

"I'm sorry, dear," Rachel replied, casually. "I had no idea I'd made such a scene. Were they very upset?"

Marie knew Rachel was trying to soften her up, but she'd have none of it yet. "I'm sure they'll live. That's hardly the point. My dear, you behave sometimes as if you're the only person on earth, and that's very selfish. Why your mother puts up with it is her business, but I'm telling you right now that I won't. It isn't at all fair to the children. They don't understand why you're acting so idiotically, and they shouldn't have to."

"Piffle!" Rachel muttered, shaking her head. She looked away again. "Maybe I'll be run down by a car tonight and solve all your problems."

"Don't be so dramatic, dear," Marie advised, with a frown. "That doesn't help a thing."

Maude opened the back door and set the garbage out on the porch. Indoors, Cissie was shouting at Henry to stay out of the bath. The screen door banged shut as Maude went back inside.

"Do you know, I feel light as a feather tonight," Rachel remarked, gazing up into a black sky of stars. Then she fanned her face with both hands. "Though, it's so warm out I can hardly breath."

"Actually, it seems quite pleasant to me," CW said, leaning against the fence. "If you think this is hot, you ought to try New Orleans in August, dear. Without an evening breeze blowing off the Gulf, humidity from the bayou makes just getting up off a stool seem impossible."

Rachel stamped her foot. "There! What did I just say? I can't utter a syllable without being contradicted. This engagement is becoming utterly hopeless."

"Well, if you're so put-out with me, dear," CW remarked, "perhaps you ought to go back indoors and bake cookies with your mother. I've already been to the picture show eight times this month alone, and I've got several appointments at Lafayette and New Iberia tomorrow."

"You realize, honeypie," Rachel continued, her voice languid as she brushed her hair back with one hand, "this is precisely why Mother has objected so strongly to our seeing each other all summer." Then she leaned over, kissed CW on the lips, tousled his hair, and giggled. Marie glanced off into the dark, not the least bit interested in watching them make love. Why did they have to behave so? What were they trying to prove?

Breaking from Rachel's embrace, CW flipped the straw hat back onto his head. "Why, I'd say pure viciousness informs her opinions, dear. That, and disgust for people different from herself and those silly old hags she plays cards with. Honestly, I feel sorry for her. How do the narrow-minded find the courage to go outdoors every day among their inferiors? It must be fairly intolerable."

"Shhh!" Marie shushed him. "For goodness sakes, the entire neighborhood can hear you!"

The Jessup's collie came to the fence, wagging its tail eagerly, anxious for attention. CW scratched the collie's snout. A light came on in the Jessup's back bedroom.

Quite pleasantly, Rachel asked Marie, "Did you hear CW's offer to buy us tickets for the show at the Bijou tonight? It's a movie with that funny little man. Do you care to come along?"

"Pardon?" Marie was shocked how Rachel's mood could change so quickly.

"We're planning on having a wonderful time."

"Oh, I wouldn't want to spoil your evening out," Marie replied, still feeling a little testy towards her, not sure she wanted to share Rachel's company. She was tempted, though. Truth was, she'd wanted to go to the pictures all summer long, particularly since Jimmy Delahaye had hinted at asking her to one. In fact, she was fairly desperate to get out of the house for a few hours.

"You won't be spoiling a thing, dear," Rachel said, as a faint breeze drifted through the cottonwoods across College Street. "Why, we'd be glad to have you. Unless, of course, you'd rather stay home and help Mother cook potato soup and discuss her club ladies' theories about who murdered Boy-Allen. Last Wednesday, they chose the Pig Woman. Can you feature that? Call the papers!"

"Well, I don't know," Marie answered, checking back toward the window at the chinaberry for signs of the children. She hoped they weren't making a wreck of the bedroom. "Wouldn't CW rather have you to himself? I'm afraid I'd be a nuisance."

When she'd first peeked out through the kitchen window, Rachel and CW had been embracing each other much too recklessly, in Marie's opinion. She didn't consider herself a bluenose, but there were proprieties, weren't there? Had she and Harry ever been that bold in public? Well, maybe that was one of their problems; they hadn't taken any true risks for the sake of love and romance.

Rachel dismissed Marie's suggestion with a wave of her hand. "Oh, he's not sure any longer if he even wants me at all. CW claims he was trapped for years between whores and chastity. Now I suppose he's found love to be equally tiresome. Just you watch; he'll let me talk myself out, then he'll wash us up and fly home alone."

"Why, dear, you know that's just not so," CW countered. "I've asked you to marry me, haven't I? What greater example of my devotion can I offer? In fact, you're the one who's lost her faith in true love! If a fellow can't please every point of this ideal you've worked up, you throw them over. And on it goes. If you're not careful, dear, you'll end up an old maid, sitting with your mother at the supper table, just the two of you kicking about everything under the sun."

Rachel laughed. "Oh, aren't you vile? Why, honeypie, it hadn't occurred to me that marriage was one of the special favors you dole out to the girls you entertain. How ignorant of me! Have there been any children? I should think you'd make a wonderful father."

"You know, darling, you're even more sarcastic than your mother."

"Oh, Mother's not sarcastic at all," Rachel said, poking her leg through the fence. "She literally means every word she says. That way, her insults are never misunderstood. Fact is, I admire her consistency. Rarely am I able to be so honest. I consider that one of my few genuine faults."

Marie watched in utter amazement. She had no idea what to say. Sister-in-law was a difficult relation, especially with Rachel so petulant and spoiled, yet slyly aware of her own faults. She prided herself on possessing a sharp wit that offered little compromise in a contest of wills. Even Maude struggled to retain her authority over Rachel, while freely admitting that her daughter was old enough to pursue her own path, wherever it might lead. So Rachel skipped church on Sundays when she'd been out late with CW the night before, smoked cigarettes outside her mother's window after dark, performed only those household duties that served her own interests, and asserted her independence by threatening at least once a week to pack up and leave town. For her part, Marie refused to choose sides. Nor did she offer to mediate, as it wasn't her nature to presume her opinion had value in such longstanding disputes. Besides, as the summer wore on, she had become tired of the drama. She wanted smiles and joy now, and felt she deserved it.

"Oh, I'm sick to death of quarreling," Rachel said, pushing off from the Jessup's fence. "Aren't you? I say, let's just forget about everything and have a swell date tonight." She turned to Marie. "Shall we?"

Marie nodded, warily. "Agreed."

Atttending a picture show did seem like a wonderful idea. If it helped keep the peace, that was all the more reason to go. Besides, Harry went all the time and rarely invited her along, believing she had no interest in the movies. Trouble was, he always seemed to choose those evenings when Emeline was off somewhere and there wasn't anyone else to watch the children. What could she do? Maybe if Jimmy Delahaye asked her again she'd go. Why not?

"Resolved," CW then announced, placing the straw hat over his heart, "that this old world is fair as heaven when sweet harmony rather than discord rules the day!" He took his pocketwatch out and examined the time. Smiling, he snapped it closed, and took Rachel by the arm. "Well, three hours from now I turn back into a damn pumpkin, so I suggest we go; Little Charlie's awaiting us at the old Bijou."

— 4 —

On summer evenings in Bellemont, people came out onto galleries to sit in wicker rockers and listen to the crickets' soothing tremolo and watch neighbors pass by along the shadowy sidewalks. It was too hot indoors for sleep. On Second Street, eighty-year-old Widow Shoemaker sat propped up in bed by a cracked window with a cold wet towel wrapped about her forehead and played Mah Jongg with her Mexican nurse and the ghosts of her two late husbands. Over on Arbor Lane, where weeping willows draped branches over picket fences and mosquitoes floated in the damp leaves, four gin-soaked oilworkers sent their wives next door for the evening and stacked poker chips on a card table inside a screened-in back porch and played Seven-toed Pete by the light of an old kerosene lamp. In the third house west from the corner of Hyperion Road and Tenth Street, Wilma Domeier sat on a tufted loveseat in her parlor and counted old valentines from grade school and imagined handsome Lewis McGraw ringing her doorbell with a bouquet of fresh pink roses in his hand and crimson passion for her in his heart. While Rachel and CW strolled arm-in-arm on the sidewalk ahead, Marie listened to the children in the next street playing tag and hider-seeker under the black cottonwoods: *Ready or not, you shall be caught!* Littler ones younger than Boy-Allen wandered unattended about the dusty sidewalks, dragging streamers of colored ribbon or naked dolls, or sat forlorn in rusty red wagons waiting impatiently to be tugged along toward a new game in the next block. Dozens of lanterned bicyclists flew past like falling stars, dinging bells street to street, while voices of all ages spoke from every corner veranda and treeshaded stoop.

Downtown Bellemont was bright and lively. Most stores were closed, but adults sat in the booths of late-closing cafés and restaurants or stood about in the parking lots of a dozen gas stations, hoping that lively conversation and a bottle of ice-cold Dr. Pepper might help them forget the evening heat. Cars were parked along the curb in a line to the Bijou where a noisy crowd gathered under the flashing theater marquee.

BIJOU — PHOTO-PLAY HOUSE — MOVING PICTURES

"I tell you, there's no such thing as being late to the picture show," Rachel argued, as they approached the crowd. "Nobody's on stage to be disturbed when people come in after the curtain goes up. It's entirely different."

At the box office, a pretty freckled brunette with a pleasant smile sorted coins and distributed ticket stubs to movie patrons one by one. Behind the glassed-in booth, a lanky youth with a ragged haircut stood waiting. As the line shortened, the girl pointed to the clock inside the box office and smiled for him.

"This used to be a vaudeville theater, you know," Rachel informed Marie, as they neared the ticket window. "All the cleverest acts came here to perform — Harry Lauder, Loie Fuller, Joe Weber, Honey Boy Evans, the Cherry Sisters. Lots of others. It was quite popular. Why, there was even an elephant on stage one evening with a trio of pygmies from darkest Africa."

"I love shows," said Marie, watching the girl exchange coins for tickets. "Farrington had a nice little theater that Harry used to take me to on Saturday nights before Cissie was born. We had W.C. Fields one night, and Irene Franklin and Nora Bayes the next."

"Say, don't you think they ought to put on something more up-to-the-minute?" CW asked, pointing to the marquee overhead where **CHARLIE CHAPLIN in "THE CIRCUS"** was advertised in big block letters. "Why, I saw this in New Orleans two years ago."

"Oh, I doubt that," Rachel snorted. "We feature only the newest photo-plays here in Bellemont. Feel free to look it up at the Chamber of Commerce if you like. It's in our charter."

"Is that true?" Marie asked, studying the playbill. "I wouldn't care to see the same show twice, unless it's John Barrymore. I think he's so handsome." She grinned.

CW stepped forward and paid for the three of them, flirting with the young brunette. "Twenty-five cents a piece! My goodness, that's steep. Why, the last picture I saw only cost me a dime. Is there a reduction for aviators?"

The girl blushed. "Not that I'm aware of, sir."

"Well, there ought to be, don't you agree?"

The girl shrugged, her blush deepening.

"Well, thank you, anyhow," CW said, sticking the ticket into his hatband as he led Rachel and Marie into the theater.

Inside the lobby, an old red velvet carpet was dirty and threadworn, scuffed through to the cement floor in several places, and the gilt ceiling stencils of Turkish arabesques and rose garlands had faded from the accumulated grime of three decades. On every wall, old lobby cards in glass frames reminded visitors of past dancehall nights and vaudeville attractions, while a new one mounted on an easel announced the program for the evening.

Chas. Chaplin
Merna Kennedy & Others
"THE CIRCUS"
&
3rd Episode of
The Serial Sensation
"THE CRIMSON STAIN MYSTERY"

2 SHOWS TONIGHT!!!

The auditorium had already dimmed for the Hearst Metrotone News. Cigarette smoke drifted across the pale blue light from the projection booth high atop the rear of the theater. Down in front and off to one side, a small woman in a print frock played "My Bonnie Lies Over The Ocean" on the piano with her eyes fixed on those black-and-white images that flickered across the silver screen.

"Look there," CW said, leading Rachel and Marie to their seats near the middle of the auditorium, "what've I been telling you?"

Up on the screen, "Metrotone News" featured the Graf Zeppelin's ascent from Friedrichshafen on its flight around the world. After a brief round trip from Germany to Lakehurst and back, Hugo Eckener's great airship would travel east from Germany past Moscow, over Asia toward Tokyo, then across the Pacific to San Francisco and Los Angeles before descending at Lakehurst, thereby completing history's first circumnavigation of the globe by aircraft.

"Six days!" CW remarked, as he sat down. "Incredible! Why, that'll be less time than one needs to steam across the Pacific now. My goodness! The Age of Flight is certainly upon us, wouldn't you agree?"

"Yes, indeed!" Marie said, examining the seats. She hoped they were clean.

"Upon you, perhaps," Rachel sniffed. "I still think it's far too dangerous."

CW kept his eye on the screen. "Oh, that's not at all true. In fact, I'd wager that within a few years anyone who wishes will be able to make the same trip whenever he chooses. Of course, it won't be by airship. No, they're much too slow and ridiculous. Instead, we'll travel by airplane to every corner of the earth. Why, I wouldn't be surprised if one day I fly myself around the world in less time than it takes to sail from New York to London."

"Well, I'd prefer to go by sea," said Rachel. "Besides, it's much more romantic."

"Suit yourself," CW replied, "but soon enough you'll go alone. Why, even your sister-in-law is an experienced aviatrix." He grinned at Marie. "I doubt she'd rather trawl around the globe aboard a silly old steamship, would you, dear?"

Smoothing her skirt as she took the seat beside Rachel, Marie said, "After today, if I were to travel around the world, I suppose I'd like to fly across land and sail between ports. Then I'd enjoy the best of both." Truth be told, after her experience today, she'd rather fly than be on the water any day of the week. Somehow, she no longer feared aviation as she did crossing a cold dark sea.

CW laughed. "That's very diplomatic!"

"Marie's quite clever," Rachel added. "I'm sure that's why my brother married her. He despises quarreling."

Four young men came down the aisle with bags of hot popcorn from Hooker's drugstore and sat down in the front row. When the pianist finished her song, the clattering noise of the projector filled the theater and the Metrotone News finished with a short segment that featured President Hoover offering encouragement to his fellow citizens from the steps of the White House. Then the screen went dark for a couple of minutes while the pianist played "Me and My Shadow" and the projectionist prepared a serial, *The Crimson Mystery*, which didn't really interest Marie much. Although she adored cartoons, in her opinion serials were for children whose attention spans were short enough to ignore the frustration of endings that weren't really endings. Also, whenever there was a chase in a cowboy serial, kids in the theater would begin kicking the seatbacks to mimic the galloping horses. Henry loved cowboy serials, except when a girl got kissed. Then he'd hide behind the seat. Marie found it stuffy in the auditorium of the Bijou, worsened by cigarette smoke and perspiration odor. In the balcony up above and behind her, voices of Negroes from Shantytown murmured to each other across the dark.

When the serial closed with another deadly climax, the screen went black. Rachel groaned as the pianist began playing "Beautiful Dreamer." Leaning toward Marie, she remarked, "If Mother were here, she'd stand up now and lead a sing-a-long."

Just then, a familiar voice spoke from the row behind her, "Well, who's the fresh number?"

Jimmy Delahaye stood with a sack of peanuts in one hand, a bottle of Coca-Cola in the other. He leaned down over Marie's shoulder, grinning. "So, honey, I see somebody's finally dragged you out to the picture show, after all."

Marie felt her heart skip a beat, a thrill she hadn't enjoyed in a while.

"We kidnapped her for the evening," Rachel replied on Marie's behalf. "She's been awful tired lately. Why, I hear you've been working the poor girl half to death."

"It hasn't been that bad," Marie offered, somewhat embarrassed now. She noticed that people were staring. She also knew she was blushing. Jimmy made her knees tremble.

"Well, she should've said something," Delahaye replied, his grin widening. "I'd have been more than happy to drag her out to a picture myself. She knows I'm that way about her."

He winked at Marie and she hid her eyes. Did he really know how she felt? Was it so obvious? She wondered if he intended to try and kiss her when the lights went down. *I must be losing my mind,* she thought.

"Don't tempt her," Rachel giggled. "Without Harry to hold her hand, Marie's been ever so lonely this summer."

"Rachel!"

"Well, it's true, isn't it?" Rachel giggled even more loudly now. "Everybody knows that a married woman has needs that aren't satisfied by housework or typewriting. For Godsakes, dear, even if he is my brother, I believe Harry's been a fool all summer long, and I hope you know it."

"Thank you very much, for telling the world." Marie prayed the movie would begin. Since being turned down on his invitation to a picture show that night of the Fourth, Delahaye had asked Marie more than a few times and on each occasion she had offered a silly alibi. Now Rachel's teasing was humiliating her. Certainly she wanted to go downtown with Delahaye one night. Perhaps she would soon enough. Husband or not, Harry didn't have a rope tied around her ankles, not forevermore.

"Well, I doubt it's been all that bad," said Delahaye, rising to his feet. "She doesn't seem that lonely to me."

"It's a clever ruse," Rachel asserted. "Trust me."

"I think Rachel talks too much," Marie said, glaring at her now. The fun was over. She wanted to watch the movie and not think about how she might behave with Jimmy Delahaye in the dark. Was she panting?

"I'll say she does," CW added, locking an arm around Rachel's shoulder, drawing her near. He kissed her flush on the mouth.

The auditorium went black.

Beside her, Marie saw Rachel rise wordlessly and slip past, moving toward the aisle. CW followed. Now the pianist began playing a soft lilting melody and the shuttering projector light flickered onto the screen as the credits ran. Delahaye climbed over into Marie's row and took Rachel's seat. He murmured, "Leonard says it'll be another month at least before the Bijou gets that Western Electric sound system. And the Vitaphone's not working, neither. I know living up north you're probably used to the talkies." Marie noticed he smelled like gin and witch hazel, yet she didn't mind at all.

Marie told him, "I haven't been to a picture show since last winter. Harry prefers going alone."

Delahaye chuckled. "Where's the fun of sitting in the dark all by yourself? I couldn't stand it. Not if I had a pretty wife at home."

Marie blushed. Had anyone heard him? What if everyone in town thought she flirted with Delahaye? What then? Delahaye took a cigarette out of his shirt pocket. He leaned close to her as he did, brushing his sleeve against her bare arm. She almost leaned back into his shoulder. Instead, she pretended to look where Rachel and CW had gone. She thought she heard them somewhere along the back row to the right of the door. *Up on the silver screen now, a pretty young brunette swings from the trapeze in the Big Top, soaring above the trick riders on horseback and the silly painted clowns.*

"I hate seeing pictures alone," Delahaye whispered, breathing on her cheek. His breath was hot and stale, but not unpleasant. She felt drawn to him.

"But you did come by yourself, didn't you?" Marie murmured, facing forward again. "I mean, you are here alone, aren't you?" Why had she asked him that?

"Not at all," Delahaye replied with a grin. He dipped a hand into the sack of warm peanuts, drew out a fistful, and dropped a couple into the bottle of Coke. "I'm here with you, honey."

Charlie Chaplin, dressed in his familiar costume as "The Tramp," ambled along the midway between the sideshows. Just the sight of his cane and bowler and his funny walk made Marie giggle. *After a pickpocketing dispute, he's chased into a mirror maze by the cops, then into the Big Top where the show is already started. He hides in a magician's cabinet, upsets the act, causing hilarity in the circus audience and ruining the humor of the real clowns who follow. The circus audience boos them and calls to "bring on the funny man!"*

"I saw you walking down the street with Rachel," Delahaye said, offering the sack of peanuts to Marie. Too nervous to eat a bite of anything, she shook her head politely and looked again for her sister-in-law and CW. Now she spotted them in a corner of the auditorium, nuzzling together in the shadows. Sex, sex, sex. Did Maude really know her daughter?

The pianist changed music, a lovely tune now, strains of sadness. *It's mealtime and the aerialist is hungry, but her boss won't let her eat. Meanwhile, he's decided to hire Charlie as a clown.*

Trying to be bold, Marie asked Delahaye, "Are you telling me you followed us in here? It's awfully peculiar. Why on earth would you do that?"

"Well, I thought you dropped something in the lobby, but when I went in, I saw it belonged to someone else. Of course, by then, I'd already bought myself a ticket, so I came on in and sat myself down. You know, I can't keep away from you." He poured a swig of Coke into his mouth. *Back up on the screen, morning has come and Charlie's boiling an egg in a tin can for breakfast. The poor girl still hasn't eaten and Charlie feels sorry for her and shares a piece of bread.*

Rachel's angry voice echoed across the auditorium. She was eye to eye with CW. Others in the back of the theater were watching her. A woman's voice yelled at Rachel to shut up. Rachel shouted a curse back and the pianist began playing more loudly. Somebody behind Marie blew cigar smoke toward the stage. Marie watched Rachel leave the auditorium, CW at her heels.

On the screen, a card read "The Tryout." *The circus owner is talking to Charlie. "Go ahead and be funny." Charlie plays a skit with a pair of clowns and fouls it up. "That's awful." They try something else, an archery joke.*

Now the pianist began playing the William Tell Overture. High in the balcony, the Negro crowd was mostly silent, the faint hot glow of cigarettes burning here and there in the dark. The projector stuttered slightly and the film slipped and blurred.

"Maybe I should go and see about Rachel," said Marie, glancing back up the aisle. Delahaye was leaning over her shoulder now, smelling her hair. She was certain he was about to kiss her and not certain whether she'd kiss him back or not, although she knew if she did, everyone in her family and on her block would think her a fool, and Harry would likely hear about it and probably leave her and the children in Texas forever. Well, maybe he'd take the children.

The rattling projector noise increased and the film smoothed out again. *Charlie disrupts the last tryout act by lathering the ringmaster's face with shaving cream. He's fired. "Get out and stay out!"*

"I'd keep out of her way tonight, if it was up to me," Delahaye replied, folding the empty sack of peanuts into his lap. He shifted his body closer to Marie.

Lucius Beauchamp stopped beside her seat and whispered at Delahaye. "Hey, Jimmy."

"Hey, Lucius! Come on in here!" Delahaye replied, pulling his legs back to make room.

"Excuse me, honey," Lucius whispered, slipping by as Marie folded her own legs inward, allowing him to pass. He stank of liquor and sweat. Idabelle had told her that Lucius brewed corn liquor in his basement and sold it in Longview. He drank all day long, but he was always polite to Marie who assumed liquor anesthetized a broken heart, though Lucius never mentioned a culprit.

The pianist began another sad melody. *Charlie thinks he's seeing his lovely aerialist for the last time. Then, outside the tent, there's trouble with the property men. No back pay. "They've quit." Charlie's hired. He's carrying a stack of plates when a mule chases him in the Big Top. He drops the plates and hides in the magic cabinet of Prof. Bosco - Magician. "Don't touch that button!" Birds, rabbits, geese, everywhere! Thinking Charlie's troubles are part of the show again, the audience roars with laughter. He's a sensation, but he doesn't know it! The ringmaster decides to let Charlie stay on. "Keep him busy and don't let him know he's the hit of the show!"*

Delahaye lit a cigarette and began talking about automobiles with Lucius. Marie decided she really ought to go see after Rachel. Also, she was uncomfortable sitting with Lucius who troubled her when he'd been drinking.

"Pardon me," Marie said, rising to leave. She felt agitated and near feverish from the heat. Or was it even the theater at all? In any case, she needed to get away from Delahaye, if only for a moment or two, so that she might regain her wits and good sense, provided she still had any.

"Don't go, honey," Delahaye said, grabbing her arm. "Picture's not over."

"I have to find Rachel," she replied, easing free of his grasp. "I'll come back." She hurried to the aisle, hoping Rachel and CW hadn't left without her. Delahaye called after her, but Marie walked out of the auditorium.

Except for a youth sweeping the carpet, the theater foyer was empty. One of the doors to the street was propped open and a draft passed throughout. Marie had no idea where Rachel and CW had gone. Across the lobby, a narrow carpeted stairway led up to the second floor balcony. There was a door at the top, half closed. A great roar of laughter issued from the darkness behind it.

"You looking for somebody, ma'am?" the boy with the broom asked. He collected the last of the refuse he'd pushed around into a dustpan.

"Did you see two people leave a few minutes ago?" Marie asked.

"Lady with a temper?"

Marie smiled. "And a tall fellow wearing a blue jacket."

"They beat it," replied the boy, dumping the contents of the dust-pan into a trash can next to one of the theater doors.

"Do you have any idea where they went?" Marie asked, listening to the piano music from the auditorium, cheery now and bright. Perhaps Charlie had won the aerialist's heart, after all.

"Nope."

Marie frowned. Had they fought so harshly she'd been forgotten? She wondered what had set Rachel off, or if they'd simply chosen to rehash their earlier debate. The boy walked off toward the office. Inside the auditorium, the pianist lightly fingered the keys, playing a pretty melody that was followed by a smattering of laughter from the audience. She looked up the stairs. Maybe that's where they'd gone. CW wouldn't have left without telling Marie. He had better manners than that, even if Rachel did not. Were they allowed up-stairs? She decided to go have a look. What sort of trouble might it cause? Harry would suggest she mind her own business, but he wasn't here now, nor was the boy with the broom. Could she be arrested? She went up, anyhow.

At the top of the stairs, she stopped to listen at the door. The audience was laughing in the dark. She slipped inside and closed the door behind her. The heat here on the second floor of the theater was more suffocating than Maude's kitchen at midday. Cigarette smoke hung like gray haze. The walls smelled like fresh calcimine. She edged forward a couple of steps so that she could see the full balcony. The clattering projector sounded louder, too.

The lovely aerialist is pleading with Charlie. "Please don't do this!" It's no use. Charlie foolishly heads for the highwire. "You're on!" Above the upturned faces of the circus crowd, Charlie does a handstand, then a one-handed spin. Another trick. His harness breaks, but he doesn't know it! He dances about until he realizes he's balancing on his own and becomes jittery.

Searching the crowded rows, she didn't see Rachel or CW any-where, but somewhere off to Marie's left, a burly Negro rose from his seat in the back row and climbed over into the narrow aisle. She backed up against the wall again and held her breath. He ambled across the rear of the balcony toward her. The audience laughed loudly. Marie felt him draw close as she lowered her eyes to the floor. Perhaps he'd pass and not notice her. The heat made her feel faint. He stopped a few feet nearby and leaned against the calcimined wall and drew a hip flask from his shirt pocket and took a sip. She saw him staring at her. Flickering light from the old projector danced on the seatbacks in front of Marie. The Negro lit a cigarette and exhaled smoke in her direction. She stifled a cough as her eyes watered. Her stomach felt queasy.

He spoke so closely now she felt his hot breath on her face, but the audience burst out in another roar of laughter, so Marie couldn't hear what he said. A Negro boy and girl seated two rows down in front of Marie leaned toward each other and kissed. The boy slipped his hand inside the girl's blouse. The large Negro mumbled something else she couldn't quite hear above the tittering crowd and slid a step closer, just off her shoulder now. Somebody wearing a porkpie hat down at the bottom row of the balcony lit a cigar and bent forward, propping his elbows on the brass railing.

"Honey, you oughtn't to be up here," the black man's voice murmured in Marie's ear, stink of gin and tobacco on his breath.

"I was looking for someone," she mumbled, as the audience laughed again.

"That's fine," he whispered. "It's just that they could be a misapprehension."

Now she knew how silly her plan had been, how idiotic and senseless. "I'm sorry."

She ran for the small door and rushed down the stairs, across the lobby and out to the sidewalk. She hurried a dozen yards up the street away from the Bijou theater, then stopped, her legs shaking. What in God's name had possessed her to go up into that balcony where she knew perfectly well she was not permitted? She felt both angry and embarrassed. Harry would have called what she'd just done idiotic, and Marie would have had no good counter to that. She remembered her mother lecturing once on curiosity when she was little, explaining that a closet locked is shut for a purpose and if that purpose were hers to know there'd be no need for the lock. She understood, of course, that the Negro hadn't meant to scare her. A woman's fear was both burden and blessing. Running out of the balcony had not humiliated her at all. Curiosity had done that. Probably she ought to have minded her own business and watched the picture show downstairs with her own crowd. Race was not supposed to be her concern. Or was it? She was reminded of what Maude had told her earlier in the summer. *What is in our hearts has been there since birth and we have not denied our inheritance. It is a fact and, though not all of us embrace it, we nevertheless accept what is, and will likely remain, part of our lives here in Bellemont.* Well, Marie also remembered Granny Chamberlain's Sunday dinner admonishment that *"Only a fool inherits the sinner's wisdom."*

It was late and the crowds she had seen downtown earlier had gone home for the night. A cool breeze carried the scent of pine trees and damp grass and the river farther off. The nightblue sky was lit with stars, quiet all about. A green Buick puttered by, an older man behind the wheel. He smiled at her as he passed. She pretended not to have noticed. Where had Rachel and CW gone? Why had they left her alone in the Bijou? Had they expected her to walk home by herself? How could they both be so rude?

Just then, a familiar voice called to her from down the sidewalk. "Darling, what's your hurry?"

Marie turned back toward the Bijou and saw Delahaye strolling toward her, burning cigar in hand. He wore his usual smile and seemed pleased to see her. *Well*, she thought, *at least someone is interested in my company tonight.*

Delahaye said, "I thought you were coming back."

She blushed. "That's right, I did say that, didn't I?" Once again, her heart fluttered felt like a schoolgirl's.

"I got lonely waiting on you when the show was over with and you weren't there." Delahaye gave her a wink as he puffed on his cigar. "They turned the lights out on me."

"Oh, they did not."

"Yes, ma'am. Just lonesome old Jimmy, there in the dark."

"Well, that seems awfully inconsiderate," Marie remarked, barely containing a smile. Suddenly, her evening had taken a turn for the better. "I hope you didn't bump your knee on the way out."

Delahaye laughed as he drew near. "Honey, that's the first nice thing you've ever said to me!"

"Why, that's not true," Marie protested. She felt almost giddy now. "Is it?"

"Cross my heart."

"Well, I'm sorry if it is, but, like most handsome men, you can be very difficult."

Her knees wobbled as she spoke the last of that. Never before in her life had Marie been so bold. She was out on a tightrope now, tiptoing into mid-air. What on earth was she doing?

Delahaye stepped close, looking her in the eyes. His own expression firmed up, his smile fixed and confident. "You make me feel handsome as hell."

Her throat tightening, Marie said, "You don't need any help with that."

"Thank you."

"You're very welcome."

They stood there on the sidewalk in the light evening breeze as a pair of motorcars drove past from downtown. Marie felt crazy and quick, desiring something she hadn't felt in years. A lunatic passion swept through her heart. Everything was racing so suddenly, she had fallen off-balance, lightheaded, confused. The automobiles disappeared and the street became quiet and she didn't notice anyone but Delahaye who asked if she'd care to be escorted home.

"Oh, I don't know," she replied, looking up and down the sidewalk.

"You shouldn't walk home alone."

"I believe you," Marie heard herself say, "but I'm just not sure I'm ready to go home at all. Not yet, anyhow."

Delahaye tossed his burnt cigar into the gutter. He reached out and touched her arm ever so gently. "Well, then, how about we take a walk somewhere?"

Marie needed only a moment to reply. "Yes, let's do that."

The more you fish for what you want, the less chance you have of getting it.
Cissie quoted that line from one of her Oz books to Henry at supper

last week when he was pestering her for a favor. As Marie strolled the dark sidewalks west of downtown with Delahaye, she wondered what she could possibly be fishing for herself. All her life she had craved that intimate heart to share things bleak and bright. Throughout her girlhood, Violet and Emeline heard her confessions and forgave her faults. On Cedar Lake, Harry swore an oath to take her part through any threat. Now, so much had fallen away, she could hardly recall any of her longings fulfilled. Perhaps her dreams had been misguided, her expectations unrealistic. Marie had never thought of herself as impetuous or flighty. Each decision, she believed, was made with great caution and consideration for all possible eventualities. Yet somehow she had been led to this estrangement from husband and blood relatives, so far from all she held dear, those old desires, how could she possibly find her way back again?

They walked several blocks into a part of town Marie didn't know very well, whose houses seemed large and fit with nice yards and trim fences and tall old trees for shade. This, too, was enlightening, because the very fact that she had neglected this neighborhood in what was a very small town, proved to her, once again, how much of her summer had passed housebound with Maude. Now tonight she felt bold somehow, adventurous, eager. Certainly it was late and she needed to get home to look in on the children, then put herself to bed so she'd have enough energy to face tomorrow, whatever puzzles might arise, but couldn't that wait? There still ought to be another hour just for her. Was that so terribly selfish?

"These homes are lovely," Marie remarked, as they strolled down the narrow sidewalk. She adored tall houses. Cedar Street had many of them, her old blue one at 119 as pretty as any.

"They sure are," Delahaye replied.

"I'll bet they're comfortable, too." She loved having a large bedroom and kitchen, and an attic upstairs to store things away. When Harry called them back to Farrington, Marie vowed to find another house with big rooms and private corners, all her own. "I'd be awfully curious to have a peek inside."

"Even if the owners weren't home?"

Marie giggled. "Oh, I don't know that I'd be that brave. I'd hate to be arrested. What would I say to the children?"

"Who's to say you'd get caught?"

"What if I did?"

"What if you didn't?" Delahaye replied, with a sweet endearing smile. "What if you just tiptoed right up to, say, that house there at the end of the block and snuck inside for a look-see? Who'd be worse off for that? You wouldn't steal anything, would you?"

Marie barely suppressed a laugh. "Of course not!"

"Well, there you go. Why not do it? Right now, in fact." He picked up his pace, heading along the sidewalk toward the house in question, a fairly elegant two-story pale green framehouse with a gallery on both floors and thick bougainvillea blooming scarlet on the sides. Marie hurried to keep up. He was joking, wasn't he? She presumed he was, but her heart began pounding with the excitement of it all. Once they drew near to the old house, Delahaye stopped beneath a towering elm. The window shades were drawn shut and the interior was dark, offering not a hint whether anyone was home.

"All right," he said, lowering his voice to a murmur. "Here we are."

"Are you daring me to go in?"

He smiled. "I'm double-daring you."

"What? Nobody's double-dared me since Cousin Emeline thought I was afraid to eat an earthworm." Marie steeled her eyes. "She paid off with her favorite doll, Baby Margaret."

"Gee, I don't have a doll."

"I'd think of something."

"I'm not worried, because I know you won't go in."

"What if the door's locked? I hope you don't expect me to break a window."

"Nobody locks their doors in this town," Delahaye said, stepping out from under the tree. "Go ahead, see for yourself."

Marie stepped out, too. "Maybe I will."

"Maybe you won't."

With that, Marie did something she never in her life would have believed she was capable of doing. She left Delahaye on the sidewalk and strode through the yard gate, then up the wide stairs to the front door and tried the front door latch.

The old oak door swung open to a dark foyer.

Startled to her toes, Marie almost ran off.

Behind her, Delahaye called out, "What did I tell you?"

"Shhh!"

She stared into the unlit entry, listening for approaching footsteps. She leaned inside for a furtive peek. Delahaye joined her on the threshold.

"Not going in?" he asked. "Too scared?"

Like a ghost, she slipped past him onto the carpet runner that led off into the shadows. The house had a curious odor, neither musty nor florid, but quite pleasant, something like lemon blossoms and wood polish, as if the place had just undergone a visit by diligent housecleaners. Delahaye eased the door closed behind her.

"What are you doing?" she whispered, then held her breath to listen once again for the legitimate occupants. She was scared to death, but excited, too, particularly knowing that Harry would never do anything like this himself. Would he even believe where she was right now?

Delahaye lit a match.

When the light flared, Marie saw how near they were standing to the parlor and a curved staircase up to the second floor. The entry hall led off to the back of the house, presumably to a kitchen, and all of this much bigger than Maude's home on College Street. Her heart was racing. She felt wicked and it thrilled her. Suddenly, she wanted to explore the downstairs, room by room. Perhaps nobody was home, and if they were, well, that made it all the more exciting. She'd be quiet as a mouse and nobody would ever know she was here.

The match went out and everything was black once again. Delahaye put his hand on Marie's shoulder and she felt a flush in her cheeks. Whatever trouble she might be getting herself into, at least Jimmy was beside her to share. Somehow Marie found it difficult to believe James B. Delahaye would do anything that might get him tossed into jail. He seemed too self-assured, too clever for that. She admired his confident demeanor, never letting anyone cross him at work, bending people's will to his own needs. If he thought sneaking into someone's home in the middle of the night was a good lark to pursue, why, by all means open the door! Maybe she needed a little of that herself.

"Are you thirsty?" Delahaye whispered in her ear.

"Hmm?"

"There's a liquor cabinet in the kitchen."

"How do you know that?"

"Come with me," he murmured, gently taking Marie's hand and leading her down the darkened hall.

"This is positively insane," she whispered, stepping quietly. What if the owners were home, after all, and came downstairs with a shotgun? Or they telephoned the police and she got arrested? How could she possible explain any of this to Maude or the children, or Harry, for that matter? He'd think she'd lost her mind, and he'd be right.

Once in the kitchen, Delahaye began searching through a cupboard above the ice-box, and whistling!

"Shhh!" Marie hissed at him.

"Found it."

Delahaye switched on the kitchen light.

Marie's nearly fainted from shock. "Are you crazy?"

"No," he said, calmly. "Why?"

"We're going to get caught!" Marie exclaimed, trying to keep her voice down, though Delahaye didn't seem to care about that. "Good grief!"

He shook his head. "No, we're not."

"No? What if the owners are home?"

"Actually," Delahaye opened the mahogany cupboard directly in front of them and took out a bottle of Scotch, "he is."

Marie frowned, utterly confused now. "Pardon me?"

"He's home this very moment and standing right beside you," Delahaye announced in that authoritative voice he used upstairs in the restaurant office, "and he doesn't mind one bit that you're here."

A trick!

And she'd fallen for it. Good heavens, he'd scared her to death. Delahaye laughed and went to another cupboard and found a couple of shotglasses. Marie felt both embarrassed and relieved.

"I grew up in this house," Delahaye said, as he poured them both a drink. "When my folks passed away, I took it over. I guess it's solid enough to see me off, too, when the Lord comes around. Here."

He handed her a shotglass of Scotch, barely wet.

"Oh, I don't think I ought to," she told him, watching the golden whiskey sparkle under the glow of the kitchen lamp. "I really don't drink liquor."

"Just a nip won't hurt."

"Well, it's awfully late, too."

"It'll help you sleep. Believe me."

Marie felt he was daring her again and wasn't certain she was interested this time. Hadn't she already proven her courage just sneaking into the house? Liquor of any sort gave her a headache, though she'd sipped peach brandy at Emeline's on more blue afternoons than she'd care to recall. Besides, what kind of invitation was Delahaye really offering? She'd gone for a walk with him and now she was in his house. Yet part of Marie didn't care in the least, and that's what gave her the greatest worry. She saw herself reeling out of control and could scarcely put a halt to it. She drank the Scotch whiskey in one gulp, and winked as she handed the shotglass back to Delahaye.

He laughed. "I thought you wouldn't."

"Never predict a woman's behavior. We're very mysterious creatures."

Why was she talking like that? What had come over her? Stepping out with a fellow who wasn't Harry, and drinking liquor after dark?

"Would you like to see some of the house?" Delahaye asked, draining his own shotglass. His eyes sagged from the booze, but he spoke clearly. "I've been fixing it up."

In fact, yes, she did want to see his home, if only to gain a better sense of him. Also, she loved comparing how people lived. Back in Farrington, Marie and Emeline used to make a game of getting themselves invited to homes all over town. Aunt Hazel thought it shameful to pry, and told them so one Sunday in front of the entire family. *We are each of us just where we belong,* she lectured, *and it is our duty to try and find our own duty and not to get into the duty of another.* True enough, yet everyone knew Hazel herself smiled at Hiram Johnson when he was married and was first to offer her condolences when poor Eleanor was run over by a haywagon. *Where was the harm,* Emeline argued, *in counting a neighbor's doilies?*

"If we're quick about it," Marie told Delahaye, a yawn coming on. "I really ought to get home, don't you agree?"

"They got you on a curfew over there?"

"Of course not," she replied, somewhat testily. Did he think she was a milquetoast? "It's just sensible, that's all. I keep my own hours." An obvious lie, simply because of the children. Oh, she was becoming more and more confused now over what to say and how to act.

"Come here," Delahaye said, guiding her back toward the hallway. "Let me show you something."

Though still black as pitch, the big house didn't seem as forbidding to Marie now that she wasn't a burglar. Delahaye led her into the front parlor where he switched on a brass table lamp. It was a lovely room of walnut bookcases, a carved mahogany library table, overstuffed sofas and armchairs, an Eastlake parlor organ, lambrequins covering pedestal tables, a tile-and-wood mantel and beveled mirror, paintings and portraits hung on the walls, lace curtains draping the windows to the street. Not the sort of thing she would ordinarily have associated with a man of Jimmy Delahaye's taste and sympathies, given the look of his office downtown.

"Momma's favorite room," Delahaye told her, by way of explanation for the old-fashioned furnishings and appointments. He smiled. "I wasn't allowed in here until I grew up."

"Your mother must've been a smart woman," Marie said, admiring the old burgundy fabric on the organ stool. "I doubt I'd have let you play in here. It's much too wonderful for little boys."

"What if I told you I was well-behaved?"

Marie smiled. "I wouldn't believe it for an instant."

"Well, let me show something," Delahaye said, going to a cabinet beneath the bookcase on far wall. Marie followed as Delahaye popped it open to draw out a gilded birdcage. He set it on a small marble top table. "Listen."

He tipped it over and wound a small brass key like a clock, then put the birdcage upright once again. Within the cage was a tiny yellow mechanical songbird. When Delahaye nudged a small lever on the lower side of the cage, the hand-feathered bird began to sing.

"Oh my goodness!" Marie exclaimed, utterly enchanted. It was one of the most beautiful things she had ever seen. How on earth could a human hand build a bird that sang so exquisitely? "It's so life-like."

"This was her favorite toy." Delahaye was standing now so close to Marie she could smell the Scotch on his warm breath. "It's pretty, huh?"

"Very."

Then he wrapped her hand into his palm, entwining fingers, squeezing gently. "But it doesn't hold a candle to you, darling."

Suddenly, Marie grew faint, her heart pulsing wildly, legs slumping. *Is this why he brought me here? And why I followed?* Delahaye leaned down to kiss her neck and Marie froze. His mouth was hot as he grazed her ear.

"That bird's in a cage just like you are," he murmured awkwardly.

"What a silly thing to say," she argued, barely able to breathe. "I'm not in a cage." *Is that what he thinks of me? A pathetic captive in my own marriage?*

The bird's delicate song began to fray as the clockwork ran down.

"You just deserve better," Delahaye whispered, kissing Marie's cheek.

Never in her life had she been so frightened. A flush bloomed through her body. Her eyes teared. She yearned to lie down. What on earth had persuaded her to sneak into this house tonight?

Delahaye maneuvered them face-to-face and kissed her passionately on the mouth, and she kissed him back. He urged himself against her, entangling her, kissing her shamelessly now, illicitly. Marie offered no resistance. And why should she? Wasn't this why she was here? How cowardly to flee from one's own seduction!

Delahaye tussled his thick fingers into her hair, kissed her cheek, her neck, her ear. Marie breathed his bitter whiskey odor and held him tightly and kissed his chin. How foolish was she to be here like this? Delahaye mumbled a lustful suggestion into her ear and Marie retreated to the sofa where she flopped back against a pair of soft chenille cushions, preparing to shame herself if that's what Jimmy Delahaye desired. He loosened his tie, then shed it along with his coat, and slid onto the sofa to claim her. His gaze was lopsided but solemn, his lips swollen as he moved to straddle her. Marie lay back in a bewildering trance, her soul gaping and lunatic. Her eyelids fluttered, her fingers felt cool and feathery. Astonished by her wilting resolve to be good, she awaited Delahaye's carnal embrace, and, indeed, prayed he'd be swift and irreverent.

And then —

A crash of metal ashcans clattered onto the sidewalk as a motorcar roared out of the driveway next door. Youthful voices yelled out in drunken laughter.

Marie perked her head up.

And, just as suddenly, she became aware of a face hovering over hers that wasn't Harry's, and a duplicitous romance she needed to flee this very instant.

Marie sighed, sobering up.

Delahaye saw it in her eyes as she squirmed beneath him. Flatly, he said, "You need to go home, right?"

She nodded, guilt flooding her with breathtaking grace. "I really ought to."

Delahaye stepped back to let her rise from the sofa. There was a sudden hush between them as Marie stood and collected herself in the golden lamplight. She felt clumsy, fallen, and yearned for fresh air out of doors. How big a mistake this had been, if at all, did not concern her just yet. First she wanted to escape with her dignity.

Delahaye switched off the table lamp, darkening the front of the house, for which Marie was grateful. He followed her to the door where he offered to walk her home. She asked how far Maude's house was, and when he told her, she said, "In that case, thank you, but I guess I'd rather go alone, if that's all right. It's so close, and I'm not at all worried anymore."

Letting her out onto the shadowed gallery, Delahaye gently kissed Marie's cheek as he whispered, "Honey, don't be ashamed of falling for someone other than Harry. There's nothing wrong with it. Show a little faith in yourself."

— 5 —

Arriving at Maude's house in the dark, Marie found Rachel sitting alone on the bottom step of the front porch smoking one of her modern Tarryton Spuds. CW's Ford was gone. Marie looked at the window beside the chinaberry tree and saw her own bedroom was dark, the children likely sound asleep. Rachel spoke from the steps, her voice flat and low. "I must've been insane to involve myself with that man. He's entirely too arrogant and selfish."

"I looked for you two all over," said Marie, still somewhat miffed at being abandoned at the theater, despite her confusing transgression with Delahaye. Since when had Rachel become incapable of seeing past her own nose? "You left without me. I hadn't any idea where you'd gone."

"I tell you, he's mean-spirited and vain."

"And how was I supposed to know you'd left?"

Rachel tapped cigarette ash into the dust below the step. "Why, he's the most disagreeable person I've ever known. Of course, any chance of an engagement is off. I hope I never see him again."

Marie stopped at the trellis of nightblooming jasmine as a bony white cat dashed across the street into the dark brush beyond. Unable yet to know how she felt about her own evening out, Marie told her sister-in-law, "I just think that was very inconsiderate."

"Of course."

Noticing that Rachel had been weeping, Marie relented somewhat. "I thought you two were in love."

Wiping a tear from her cheek, Rachel shook her head. "Oh, I doubt I've ever been in love. I'm not that big a fool. All men want is somebody to show off for. Someone to listen to all their dirty little lies. Why, not one of them even believes in love."

"Did he say why he left?"

"I asked him to," replied Rachel. She puffed once on the cigarette, then exhaled smoke into the dark and drew a deep breath, trying to compose herself. "He's held a low and ugly opinion of us for as long as I've known him. Well, mostly of Mother, but I suppose he finds me guilty by association. Yet I should say it's he who's bigoted and narrow. Why, I've never harbored the slightest resentment toward any Catholic man, woman or child. I'd be ignorant to do so! In fact, I don't believe I know the first thing about the Pope, and don't care to. It's just not my concern, and I've told CW so on several occasions. But that's not enough for him. Not by a long shot. No, he's got to prove that being a Baptist ought to be legal grounds for having oneself institutionalized. Well, it's plain enough for anyone to see that he looks down on us and that just being here causes him the worst manner of suffering. So, I merely suggested that as an act of mercy I hereby relieve him of any obligation to set foot in this stupid town again."

Despite her own disturbingly indiscrete brush with romance, Marie found herself still upset with Rachel whose selfishness was inexcusable. What was she supposed to say, anyhow? CW wasn't her problem. So, all that came out of her mouth was that same white lie she'd begun with. "I walked back here all alone in the dark. Did you expect me to wait there all night?"

Rachel shook her head. "It's just silly to imagine that a man like him actually cares about someone enough to marry her. Mother was here when we returned from downtown, you know. She saw CW drive off and thought he was behaving awfully cruelly to me. Of course, it was impossible for her to fully take my side. In fact, she had the gall to suggest that I ought to keep a keener eye out for the men I choose to see, as if I deliberately ask to be punished like this. Why, it just burns me up! Sometimes I think I should do like Harry, just pack up and drive somewhere far away and forget I ever knew her. Now, that'd teach Mother a lesson, wouldn't it?"

Rachel extinguished the cigarette in the dirt. She stood and brushed off her skirt. "Well, I simply refuse to pretend any longer that he and I share even the slightest compatibility. I suppose I was blinded by the flattery of his attentions. We each have our own silly weaknesses, don't we? Mother assured me a Catholic could no more be content here in Bellemont than a Baptist in Rome. Of course, she's just as insane as he is. Mother doesn't know one iota more about the Catholic Church than CW does about Baptists, but I simply could not tolerate his hatred of Bellemont. We may be small-minded and ridiculous, but there's no deception to it, and nobody cares what he thinks, anyhow. Who says a Negro from Shantytown couldn't have murdered Boy-Allen? That's utterly absurd! I told him to go fly home to Louisiana tonight and forget he ever called on me. If I never see that man again, I'll be happier than I have been all summer long."

Then Rachel went up the stairs and back indoors.

Except for a lamp lit in the back hall, the house was quiet and dark. Sneaking inside, Marie could smell the gingerbread cookies Maude had cooked after supper. An aroma of cinnamon tea and lemon floated in the kitchen hallway and made Marie desperately wish she had stayed home for the evening, played games with the children, and written another letter to Harry explaining the difficult circumstance of being without him. She crept quietly into the bedroom and checked to see that Henry was asleep. Her dear little one had been awake most of the night before suffering troublesome dreams. Cissie had told him a bogeyman lived underneath the house and that unless he swore never to draw in her Oz books again so long as he lived the creature would steal him away after midnight and either sell him to a thieving gypsy or eat him for supper. Tonight, he slept quietly. So did his cantankerous sister. The window facing the pretty chinaberry tree was cracked open an inch admitting a mild draft that cooled the room. Marie changed into her slipover gown and folded her dress and dropped it quietly into the laundry basket. Walking back and forth from downtown had soiled the hemline with dust. She would wash it tomorrow.

Returning to the kitchen for a glass of water, she heard Rachel fidgeting in her own bedroom. How could anyone be so self-centered? She didn't seem to care about anyone's feelings but her own. What did Rachel even know about love? Still, knowing how difficult love can be, Marie tried to feel sorry for her. A romantic separation was always cruel, and the tears Marie had seen on Rachel's face were genuine. Anger only lessened sorrow; it did not relieve it for long. She knew this to be true from years of bitter disputes with Harry, who rarely allowed his own anger to relent. He preferred his constant solitudes and the festering of grudges that made him mean and selfish.

Marie looked out the back porch window. Next door, a light was on inside the Jessup's house, Lili's mother or uncle moving about, restless in the heat. Marie hadn't met Lili's father, Howard Jessup. He labored in the oil fields a hundred miles to the south and rarely came home. Lately, since Mildred's brother Fritz had come from Tallahachee to live with her and Lili, Mildred didn't act as though she missed Howard much at all. Perhaps it was true. Sometimes love evaporates into a sullen nothingness between two people and cannot be retrieved, eventually passing away forever. After enough time has gone by, both forget it had been there at all. But probably Lili hadn't. She would see herself as proof that her father and mother had loved each other once, yet not fully understand why they no longer did. Perhaps children knew more about love than they ought to.

Marie drank her water, rinsed the glass out and put it up in the cupboard, then tiptoed back to the bedroom. Rachel's light had gone off and Marie heard no more sounds behind her door. On her own dresser was an envelope she hadn't noticed before, a letter from Harry to Maude, left for Marie to read. She took it in hand, and went to her old steamer trunk for something else her strange mood compelled her to fetch, a blue cardboard shoebox of postcards and letters and notes from Harry she had saved since that first summer when she was sixteen and Harry Hennesey was "that most intriguing young salesman from Texas" her cousins fawned over and her mother warned her to avoid. Marie brought the old shoebox and Maude's letter from Harry with her into the front room where she could sit under the reading lamp and not disturb anyone while she read. The letter was brief.

Warsaw Hotel

Box 14, 254 Jackson St.

August 2, 1929

Dear Mother,

I am sending along thirty dollars as per our agreement and intend to send another twenty no later than next week. Charles Follette has been gracious enough to defer my debt to next month in exchange for a percentage of my commission on the sales I've managed recently. He is tough yet honest and I believe we've struck a fair bargain. There's been no hardship on my part. I am well and busy. The Kogan deal is still in the making and may materialize. I'm hopeful because I just received a note today from Mr. McDonald saying that unless I pay at least part of the rent by Saturday next he will have to ask for my apartment. Last week he put a tenant into the street for one month's arrears.

I hope you can help Marie for she is making such a grand fight to make a go of her job. You remember I told you that she thinks that you think she is out of her league. Be sure to let her see how you admire her ability and determination. I really believe she has more to her than any of the women her age in Bellemont. She sees lots of things that the rest of us are blind to. I sure take my hat off to her. Please give her and the children all my love and best wishes.

Your faithful son,

Harry

With a peculiar ache in her bosom, Marie slipped the letter back into the envelope and opened the blue shoebox and began sorting through the other envelopes and carefully folded notes. Harry had pursued her like a crazy schoolboy for six years, arriving by train once a month and staying a weekend at the Excelsior Hotel in east Farrington. He would telephone an hour after checking into his room and visit her on the farm before sundown. When she went off to Stout to study Domestic Science, he called on her at the dormitory by six o'clock every third Friday for two years until she graduated and returned to Farrington where his routine at the Excelsior began again. He had a patience her father found perplexing, and a talent for flattery both Violet and Emeline admired. Flowers and clever postcards. Saturday picnics in the shaded meadows about Farrington. Sunday outings after church with her family. Little affections to seal her confidence. Marie knew Harry loved her. He gave her a thousand reasons to trust her heart, and so when he joined them on Easter holiday at Cedar Lake, and floating her away in the canoe like a yellow water-lily to tell her all that was in his own heart that warm April evening, by moonlight she accepted his proposal.

Marie reached into the box and sorted through several envelopes until she came across a section of newspaper clipped out of the Farrington *Herald-Dispatch* by Cousin Emeline fourteen years ago: her wedding announcement, dated June 17th 1915.

Hennesey-Pendergast

One of the first peony weddings of the season was solemnized last evening at 8:30 p.m. in the home of Mr. and Mrs. Louis M. Chamberlain, 540 Pillsbury Avenue, when their niece, Miss Marie Alice Pendergast became the bride of Mr. Harold Louis Hennesey. A color scheme of pink and white predominated and masses of pink and white peonies were artistically arranged throughout the house. Miss Florence Dow of Chicago, friend of the family, sang, "I Gave You a Rose" and "O, Radiant Hour"... The bridegroom and his best man, Mr. Victor Ferguson, son of Mr. and Mrs. Archibald M. Ferguson of St. Paul, entered together and they were followed by Miss Violet Pendergast, first cousin of the bride, who was a bridesmaid ... Miss Emeline Chamberlain, a second cousin of the bride, who was maid of honor, preceded the bride... The Misses Margaret Rutherford and Lucy Leonard, who were classmates of the bride at Stout Institute, Menominee, Wis. were ribbon stretchers. Receiving with the bride and bridegroom were the bride's parents, Mr. and Mrs. Harlow H. Pendergast, Miss Emma Pendergast, aunt of the bride and Mrs. H.P. Pendergast, grandmother of the bride... Mr. Hennesey and his bride left on a motor trip and they will be at home after July 1, at 119 Cedar Street.

Marrying in the shaded flower garden at Emeline's house had been Harry's desire. He despised the farm where Marie's family had expected the wedding ceremony to be held. Emeline agreed that the delicate floral decorations might spoil in the heat and dust and promised Marie to lend her own bedroom to the bridesmaids. More than a hundred people attended and when Harry whispered his love to her as she took his ring, her heart swelled with joy. Afterward, they enjoyed a lovely honeymoon at the Grand Hotel on Mackinac Island, and when they moved into the pretty blue house on Cedar Street, Marie placed some reminder in each room — a glass flower, a Japanese fan, a handtinted postcard, a sweet notion — that by touch or glance might restore some small hint of that wonderful courtship. Whenever Harry traveled away now on one of his business trips, she would choose a memory in the dark and hold it close, praying that Harry loved her still as she knew he had in that summer long ago.

Marie brushed the curtains back with her fingers as a motorcar clattered by toward downtown. Several autos had passed as she walked home from Delahaye's house and she had taken great care to stay deep in the tree shadows, praying not to be seen. That fear was greater now than any she had of Boy-Allen's killer. Flushed with worry and confusion, Marie rummaged deeper in the shoebox, sorting here and there, glancing at envelopes whose contents she hadn't studied in many years, still searching for one item in particular. She paused at a slip of paper that had lost its envelope, a brief note Harry had sent to her a year ago from St. Paul, his first visit to Minnesota since they had passed a sad season in the upstairs of the Fergusons' grand Summit Avenue residence in the summer of 1920. He had composed it on a piece of fine stationery from the Nicollet Hotel and hired a courier to deliver it by sundown directly to the front porch at 119 Cedar Street where he knew she would be sitting at that hour. It read:

Dearest Marie,

I drove out today by the Lake of the Isles. I stopped at the bridge over the channel into Cedar Lake and looked out over the lake. Then I began remembering. In my vision I saw a canoe and a boy and a girl. He was pretty hopeful, in his opinion, when he began a little story — a story as I remember, of his life and his hopes — and ended with a proposal to that girl. He told her he was proposing when she was too young, but he still hoped.

The lake was still there, but each drop of water is a new one. The blades of the grass along the shore are new. Every fish in the lake is new. But the islands are there and the trees are the same ones. The air is different air. But one thing hasn't changed. That man felt he was with the girl he wanted to be with for the rest of his life. And he still feels the same way. Although more than a decade has passed, he knows that as far as he is concerned, he made no mistake. She is still the object of his love, but deeper and broader than it was then.

I remember the wedding, the days that followed, the weeks, months and years. I remember the joys of anticipated and realized children. I remember, with a sweet but heart-tightening memory that still chokes me and brings the tears, the little fellow whom God let us have for a while. His little self lies not a short distance from where I am and where I expect to lie beside him. And there is no terror about it. It is life …

"Marie?"

Rachel stood in the hall wearing her pink nightgown, tears again on her face. Marie dropped the letter back into the box. Rachel's voice had startled her and her hand shook.

Rachel said, "I'm sorry I left you at the picture show. I was upset with CW, but I know that forgetting about you was inexcusable. Please accept my apology." She lowered her eyes, clearly humiliated by the entire episode.

"I forgive you," said Marie, closing the box. What else could she do? Whose sin was greater tonight? She shifted in the chair to face Rachel. "I admit to being angry myself, but I was also concerned for you both. My mother always says that quarreling worries the heart while solving little and leaving scars that heal too slowly. It does pierce me very cruelly to see either of you hurt."

Rachel walked into the room and sat on the piano bench. She wiped a tear off her cheek, then folded her hands into her lap. She looked tired and sad. "Well, I'm afraid one of us is already hurt. I can't explain why, but I was horribly mean to CW tonight. I lost all sense of proportion and just made a grand to-do out of nothing. I must be crazy."

"You poor dear," replied Marie, offering a sympathetic smile. Who hasn't known heartache and sorrow? "Why, I'm sure he'll be feeling just as badly tonight."

"Oh, I'm sure he doesn't care at all. Why should he? I've treated him as rotten as anyone who's ever called on me. I've no idea how he's been able to stand me for this long, except that he's got the patience of a saint. I've had a horrid temper all summer now, yet he's only raised his voice with me once."

"He loves you," said Marie, trying to sound hopeful. "Isn't it obvious?"

"He's from a fine family, did you know that? Very well-to-do, in fact. Catholic, of course, being third generation New Orleans. They own a grand old home near the Vieux Carré. CW himself lives in a garden cottage that used to be a Creole house built by a family of mulattos. His grandfather owned a plantation and his mother's family were merchants from Amsterdam. Isn't that romantic?"

Though entirely unfamiliar with Louisiana history, Marie smiled. "It's very interesting."

"The point is, CW's family has more money than all the wealthiest people in Bellemont taken together. They're invested in business ventures all across the South and are very well thought of in New Orleans society. CW's told me of garden parties his mother's given where the guest list runs into the hundreds, can you imagine?"

"No, I can't. Where would everybody sit?"

Rachel returned a brief smile, but her unhappiness persisted. "Compared to any girl he's known in New Orleans, I'm hopelessly plain."

"Of course you're not."

"Yes, I am, and Mother knows it better than anyone. Our entire family is common as ditchwater, except for Harry, of course, who had the genius to go away and make something of himself. Why CW ever called on me at all is an utter mystery. The fact that it was I who sent him away and not the reverse just proves the point. He had no business engaging himself to a silly Baptist girl who's nothing more than a stupid secretary in an insurance office. Well, the mistake's been corrected now, hasn't it? I doubt I'll ever hear from him again." Rachel slumped against the piano next to the metronome, tears running on her cheeks once more.

"You love him, don't you?" Perhaps it was more than sex-madness between them, after all.

Rachel nodded, blinking tears from her eyes. "You wouldn't understand how."

"Well, then, if it were me, I think I'd wire him a telegram in the morning."

"Pardon?"

"You know, we've all had words with those we love at one time or another, things we ought not to have said, isn't that true? Ordinarily, you seem quite happy together."

Rachel wiped another tear away, a frown on her face. "Why, I'm afraid these were more than words. I deliberately humiliated him, practically associating him with those Negroes he seems to adore so much. I'm sure any wire he received now from me would go straight into the trash. Nor would I blame him. I've done it and I'll have to accept the consequences. That's all there is to be said."

"Well, of course it isn't," Marie argued, impatience with Rachel rising inside her. "You're being foolish now." Why are lovers so foolish? Is pride more dear than true affection?

"I wish I were."

"And feeling sorry for yourself, too. What does your mother always say? Self-pity is a beggar's vanity."

Rachel forced a grin. "Why, if Mother had her way, I'd spend the rest of my life right here with her, an old maid washing clothes and playing hearts every damned evening until the day I die. Besides, with Mother pulling against CW since he and I first met, what chance have I had?"

"Wire him a telegram in the morning. Admit you were wrong. Apologize and ask him if he can't fly back on Saturday."

"Oh, I haven't the nerve," Rachel said, getting up from the piano bench. "I'm afraid he'd say no, in which case I'd probably wish I were dead."

Another automobile drove past outside, its driver hollering out a strange profanity that caught Rachel's attention. She went to the window and pulled the curtain aside. After muttering someone's name Marie hadn't heard before, she let the curtain fall closed, then remarked, "I just believe that CW deserves to court a girl who appreciates his good qualities, perhaps someone of his faith, as well, although did you know he hasn't attended Mass since Easter? Well, it's the truth. If Mother had known that, I'm sure she'd have been much happier with my seeing him."

"Listen to me, please," Marie told Rachel in all earnestness. "If you don't at least make the gesture of conciliation, you'll never forgive yourself. If you truly believe he loves you, allow him another chance to prove it."

Rachel wiped another tear from her cheek with the sleeve of the nightgown. She walked across the room to the front door and opened it and looked out into the road. After a few minutes she closed the door, and turned to Marie. "All right, I'll wire an apology in the morning. I doubt he'll respond, but at least I'll have made the attempt, isn't that so?"

"Yes."

"Are you happy now?"

Marie smiled. "Very."

"Then I'm going to bed," Rachel said, heading for the hallway. At the threshold to the hallway, she paused long enough to say, "Thank you, dear."

Marie nodded. "You're quite welcome."

After Rachel had gone back to her room, Marie reopened the blue box and continued searching for her most treasured memento from that long-ago courtship. In her own girlhood, love and romance had occupied her waking thoughts more completely than she had ever dreamt possible. According to dear Auntie Emma, love was a fever in the blood cured only by a sweetheart's kiss. Marie felt sorry for Rachel. Whose broken heart prevails, unmended by a lover's ardent hand? She wondered, did marriage truly provide rescue or relief from the vicissitudes of romance? Will all worries linger long after those vows are taken?

Near the bottom of the old shoebox, wrapped in a lace handkerchief, a slender blue "book" smaller than her own hand enclosed a typed letter offered to Marie as a gift by Harry on the occasion of her twenty-first birthday. She drew it out, unfolded the lace. On the front cover, lettered in white against the sea-blue paper was written:

To Miss Marie Alice Pendergast
Sept. 17, 1892 ---- Sept. 17, 1913

On several tiny neatly spaced pages, he had composed a typewritten letter of a sort she had hardly expected, even from Harry.

Dear Marie:

Time was when you regarded the age of twenty-one with some apprehension, not unmixed with awe. You could have anticipated nothing more dismal than to have reached that age and be neither married nor engaged. As a matter of fact, though, actual marriage itself would have appeared fully as undesirable.

What sort of girl have you come to be? I am going to do a daring thing. I am going to see if I can guess correctly how a young girl has felt in the four years before the present, drawing a conclusion — perhaps — as to how she views things at this mature age.

Do you know, the words of some of these "popular songs" often surprise me, as much as I dislike the most of them. Somehow men seem to have given expression in some of the songs to thoughts that occur to the most of us.

"When I first met you" — do you remember when that was? I do. It was at Cedar Lake during the summer of 1909, when your Uncle Harlow first got his Stanley steamer, the car that was to revolutionize the automobile business. You had just turned seventeen. Weren't you young then, though? Yet, you had not gotten over talking about the husband you were going to have. We were out riding in the Stanley, you and the rest of the family and I, only a month before our night at Big Island Park. Try as I will, I can't remember what was said, but it was something about your future husband. You suddenly realized there was a 'man' along; he fitted the description — and you looked fixedly ahead while the family laughed. Perhaps I blushed. It didn't take much to make me blush then. Now I am a hardened criminal.

So there you were — seventeen years old. Men? They hadn't entered your horizon in reality, although you read over and over the 'touching' parts in the novels. You could have told 'him' just when to draw you to him and enclose your hand in his. But a real man! Huh! Let Emeline go with 'em, if she wants to. I don't. They're too much bother.

Am I right?

It was in the spring of 1910, when you were still seventeen, but fast nearing eighteen, when Violet went East. Do you remember "our" first party? The machine brought our little patrician in a white sweater to the bridge over the tracks at Lake Poague. From there we went to the Griffith's where you played the Melody in F and I told them what it was. I knew the names of about three pieces in those days and that was one. I know but very few more now. No one could have suspected my deep-laid plot to finally settle on the owner of the pretty black hat.

But, alas, my too-frequent attentions brought out a trait of your nature, peculiar to the age of eighteen. People saw us together one time. Very well. They saw us together again. Still all right. They saw us together a third time. They invited us together at a picnic. Himmel! Do people think he has strings on me? I'll show him. No, thank you, I'm sorry, and you would grab Harlow by the arm and say, "Come on, Unc", smiling a sweet goodnight to me over your shoulder. (Really, though, there is a period of a boy's life when a rebuff is a good thing. It cultivates patience in him.) This was a real, girlish turndown or flyaway — not a turndown in the real sense, but a will-o'-the-wisp sort of attitude that was due to an inward clinging to girlhood freedom — a dislike of even having people say you had a 'sweetheart'.

What kind of a girl were you, then? Now I am on dangerous ground. You wanted the fellows and enjoyed having them come around. Still you objected to being taken for granted and you wanted them only a few times in succession. I learned this from harrowing experience the following winter. One night Roy had asked Emeline to go out with her. I was singing in the parlor and could not see you before it was time to go home. The music over I dashed madly out and got my hat and made for you — who were leaving the Chamberlain drive. I saw you clutch Roy and hurry out the door and if you did not run you did some tall moving, for you were out of sight before I got outside.

Know what I did then? I walked and walked some more. And gradually as I walked my thoughts changed. I would leave you in peace for a month. Still I would be as nice to you as I wanted to be. I could see your reason and the same pessimism that worries Emeline, worried me. I saw a family looking with approving eyes at your 'keeping company' with a deserving young man. And yet I saw with a clearness that was not all a mistake, that to you I was, as any young man so painfully steady would be, an ogre looming upon your girlhood horizon and clouding the sunshine of your youthful imagination.

When I came home that night I had reached my conclusion. I would pay no attention to this. I would be no quitter and in spite of the attitude of rebellion I knew you had, I saw no way to give up to it without also giving way for 'the other fellow'. What mental disturbances impelled you to act that way? Maybe I will get into trouble if I guess. Well, first of all was that objection to being taken for granted and having strings tied to you. You were still very much of a girl — were you not? You preferred to have a fellow around only once in a while and the rest of the time you wanted to be with the family. Then, possibly it was nice to be a little perverse. The folks liked that 'him' too well. You wouldn't fall for it. Then again it was sort of natural, being a girl, to like to prevent 'him' from getting too self-confident. Your time was not to be won so easily.

That was last summer. You turned twenty at the end of it and you started to school at Stout. You have finished a year; you spent another summer; you have turned twenty-one — and without apprehension or awe. Your Granny says, "Marie has improved wonderfully this past year. She has matured. It is very noticeable."

Let this be said: Here is a family of high ideals and love for Christian things. Honor, patriotism, loyalty, reverence, love for home, broadmindedness, willpower, freedom from dissimulation: Will she absorb none of it? Will she be such a snob that she will be called 'stuck up and proud', so that the other girls dislike her? Somehow I think she will be liked because she really won't feel any better than someone else because of anything she has, although she may be better because of something she is.

Listen, girl, this is shallow water, although it may look deep. I refer to things a man and a woman would naturally talk freely about. I speak of the little things that bother and that look big — such things, for instance, as occurred to you when you spoke one night of how a girl would feel to meet the members of her husband's family. I want you to feel free to talk about things like that. I guess I am simply trying to ask you to have confidence in me and not to be afraid to talk naturally for fear I will not understand.

Now what does the age of twenty-one bring to you, who claims so lately to have matured? Do you feel the "soul within you climb to the awful verge of" — something or other that you never felt before? Or do you still feel like a schoolgirl, undecided as to how you are to approach the reality of life and afraid, to some extent, of the seriousness of it?

What shall I wish you first? This — the thing I most desire for you. That you shall retain the lightness of girlhood that will make your laughter wholehearted and free. This will be only done as you realize that life is not so serious as young people sometimes think. That is what people are telling me and I am passing it on to you. Your brightness is your charm, but not your only one. I would not, for the world, in spite of anything I say, have you lose it.

Next — those day dreams. Do they not clothe friends and more than friends with qualities they may or may not possess? I wish — so very earnestly — that the troubles that come to so many will not come to you. And I don't think they will, for they are mostly the result of wickedness and you are going to be good.

Finally, may another year roll around and you be twenty-two, with a capacity for care, but with no increase of care to test your capacity.

Thus Endeth This Book and Letter.

Harry L. Hennesey

Neatly glued to the rear inside jacket was another, smaller blue envelope encasing a business card. On the card, Harry had these words inscribed:

and now, dear
little girl, I wish
with all my heart
you were with me
H.

It hadn't been until after supper that Marie took the opportunity to sneak out to the barn and read Harry's long love letter. Of course, everyone in the family knew she had received it and had badgered her mercilessly about its content. However, none but Violet and Emeline were allowed to read it and their impassioned response had been to warn Marie of the perils a man can bring to a girl's life, and the equally dreadful solitude she would invite by sending him away. By nightfall, perched in the darkened hayloft of Uncle Harlow's barn, she had decided that if one day he would ask her to marry him she would say yes, and since that warm September evening long ago only Harry had owned her heart. Now sixteen years had passed. Did she yet retain that lightness of girlhood against the seriousness of adult life? Were her daydreams yet evidence of qualities she was proud to possess? Would Harry believe her heart to have been good, after all?

Carefully re-packing each of the letters, folding her wedding announcement into an empty envelope with Harry's touching note from the Nicollet Hotel and placing it atop the little blue "book," Marie switched off the reading lamp and went to bed. Lying in the dark an hour later, she wondered how different her life might have been had she not stepped into the birch canoe with Harold Louis Hennesey that evening on Cedar Lake, had not invited him along that bright Sunday with Uncle Harlow in the Stanley Steamer, had not sworn a blood oath with Violet and Emeline when she was thirteen that the first man with whom she fell in love, she would marry. Now Cissie slept quietly. Henry slept quietly. And gradually falling into dreams herself, Marie listened closely but heard nothing above the beating of her own heart.

— 6 —

Shading his eyes against the glare of the noonday sun on the office windows, Jimmy Delahaye shouted into the telephone, "Mistake my eye! Trust me, they'll take to him like Mabel Willebrandt at Texas Guinan's... Oh yeah? Well, that hopheaded union sonofabitch'll settle up quick when I get my hands on him or I'll knock his block off."

In the next room, Marie kept typing notes to the stockroom invoices Delahaye had dumped onto her desk after breakfast and tried not to listen to his conversation. He had been speaking by the telephone to one person or another since she had arrived, hardly paying her any notice at all. She looked up at him every now and then, hoping to catch his eye. What did he think of last night? Had she angered him by fleeing his company? Was he still interested in their little flirtation? She worried he had given up on her and, amazingly enough, she didn't want him to.

"Oh, for Christsakes, Charlie, don't flood the room. I tell you, it's a faked-up charge … No, that was Logan. Who else had the punch to put over a deal like that? … Oh, he did, eh? Well, I'd play innocent, too, if it came to that. He may be bugs on fighting, but snap a dispossess on him and, trust me, he'll come across. He's nothing but a big yellow louse… . Yeah, I'll wait, but do it pronto. I got a business to run here."

Delahaye cupped the receiver into the palm of his hand and leaned across the desk. "Honey?"

Marie stopped typing. "Yes?"

"Do you want to come in here a second?"

She put her work aside and got up. Delahaye's office had an electric fan switched on and the temperature felt several degrees cooler than where she had been sitting. She felt herself perspiring unnaturally and was happy to change rooms.

Delahaye winked at Marie as she took a chair, then spoke back into the phone. "Yeah, I'm still here, but I don't have all day to fiddle around … All right, I'll be in the office another hour or so… Yeah, you tell him that for me… Swell!"

He hung up the phone, grinning. "Well, haven't you been a little church mouse this morning."

"Pardon?" She blushed. He was always teasing her, and she knew how to take it. He was always sweet to her, perhaps too much so, considering everything.

"You ought to make a little noise so I won't think you're slipping in late on me or something."

"You were on the phone," Marie said, smiling coyly as she glanced out the window where a light breeze rippled the state flag on the courthouse across the street. "I didn't want to disturb you."

"Honey, you ought to let me take you to the show next Saturday night. I seen the card this morning. They got Mickey Mouse and Lon

Chaney both. What do you say?"

Marie blushed. So he was still interested? Now what should she do? How much trouble did she want to make for herself? This was all absurd, and getting worse. What should she say? "Well, Maude always has her club ladies over on Saturdays and someone has to be there to watch the children."

"Let one of them do it," said Delahaye, with a laugh. "They love those kiddies of yours."

"Well, I don't know. It's awfully difficult finding time to get away, what with my children's needs, you understand." She had gone too far last night, and she knew it. They had almost made a dreadful mistake which she had no intention of repeating. What if she accepted his invitation to go downtown with him one night soon and see a picture and let him sit close enough that people started talking? Did it really matter? What would Maude think? Or her club ladies? Well, let them all have their gossip, so long as it all appeared silly and innocent. Besides, Harry had been gone long enough. Surely Maude knew that better than anyone.

She offered Delahaye a partial answer. "Would it be all right if I think about it? See if it's possible?"

He smiled and took a cigar out of his desk. "I hope you do, honey."

Next she had to warn him that nothing like last night might ever happen again. "Of course, you understand I can't stay out too awfully late."

"Sure I do," he smiled. "I'll have you home and tucked into bed plenty early."

She blushed. "Thank you."

And, of course, when the time came, Jimmy Delahaye would also have to understand this wasn't to be considered a date, by any means, just a chance for her to go out for the evening. She should also tell him that Harry was coming down by train to see her and the children, perhaps in a few weeks. If that made him jealous, all the better! Emeline once had three boys courting her and always said it was the best time she'd ever had.

"Look here." Delahaye reached down and opened the drawer beside his leg and drew out a stack of checks. After riffling through them once, he handed the checks across the desk to Marie. "Honey, I need you to run these over to the bank for me. I'd have Lucius do it, but he's been on a bender since Tuesday and I don't think he could find his way across the street this morning. Have Edgar deposit them and write up a bill of receipt for you."

"Certainly." She looked at the wall clock behind Delahaye. It read a quarter to noon. She said, "Would it be all right if I brought the receipt back after lunch? I have to go home to feed the children today. Maude's out for the afternoon. I'll be very careful."

"I suppose so," replied Delahaye. He cracked a grin and lit up his cigar. "I like you, honey. You're swell."

"Thank you." He was so handsome. She couldn't help but feel like a girl again. Was that really so terribly wrong?

"Picture show next Saturday night?"

She smiled. "I'll see what I can do."

"Good enough," Delahaye replied, then picked up the telephone and began dialing a number. Pleased with herself for a successful balancing act between flirtation and sanity, Marie walked out of the office.

Downstairs, the restaurant was just beginning to fill for lunch. Idabelle sat at the cash register talking to a short puffy man Marie knew only as Blind Jack. Most of the regular customers were already seated at their favorite booths or tables, and the young waitress Delahaye had hired that week, a thin brunette Rachel's age named Amelia, hurried from a redheaded businessman in a cheap yellow linen suit to a pair of cotton gin supervisors at one of the middle tables near Idabelle, distributing cups of hot coffee and scribbling furiously on her order pad. Smells of vegetable soup and freshly baked chicken pie and cornbread gravy floated out of the kitchen. Conversation hummed. The revolving glass doors opened and more customers poured in. Idabelle called Marie over to the cash register. "Say, sweetie, how'd you like to earn a couple of dollars? Mister Wonderful here wants to take me on a picnic and I can't get away unless you cover for me."

Blind Jack removed his hat and attempted a grin, but his jaw screwed into an odd grimace instead. Hidden under a black felt derby-hat, his forehead looked lopsided and he hadn't shaved in a week or more. "Do a fellow a favor, honey. Idabelle's been giving me the heebie-jeebies all month. If I don't get her in my jalopy this afternoon, I don't know what I'm liable to do!"

"What do you say, sweetie?" Idabelle begged. "Don't it sound like he's got a crush on me?"

Marie nodded. "It certainly does, dear, but Jimmy just gave me these checks to take to the bank for him, and I told the children I'd be home for lunch, and I have to stop at the five-and-ten for Maude. I just don't think I have time. I'm very sorry."

"Oh, that's all right, honey." Idabelle shrugged. "I wasn't going to let him kiss me, anyhow."

A customer came up and handed his bill to Idabelle. As she rang it up, Blind Jack laid his head on the counter and moaned.

Traffic rolled through town in the noon hour and people sat on benches, either eating lunch, reading the newspaper, or enthused in conversation. Nodding a greeting to a woman with a stroller, Marie crossed the lawn to the Commercial National Bank and went indoors. Overhead, wooden blades provided a draft and the main lights were off, so the interior was felt dark. Only a man in a blue pinstriped suit stood in line ahead of Marie. He carried a leather satchel and a copy of the morning *Pinckneyville Echo-Gazette*. The angle of his fedora gave Marie pause, as he resembled men she noticed in the "Wanted" posters on the wall just inside the door. Harry had written constantly that summer about crazed bootleggers. She watched the man for signs of criminal behavior while trying to imagine what she would do if he were to pull a revolver from his jacket. When he merely cashed a bond from the black satchel, Marie relaxed, completed her own transaction, and hurried outdoors again, the receipt tucked safely inside her purse. She had one more errand before returning home to prepare lunch for the children. On Main Street, she bought Milk of Magnesia and a pair of red peppermint sticks from Hooker's drugstore and a paper of pins for Maude at the five-and-dime. Then she hurried out Tyler Road past the livery stables and feedlots toward the outskirts of town where weeds grew tall and flies buzzed in the heat.

The afternoon train to Longview was preparing to depart when Marie walked past the rail depot. Black smoke cascaded downwind and she coughed from the foul odor of burning coal and hot grease. A steamwhistle shrieked and the telegraph operator from the cable office came out onto the platform and gave the engineer a wave and shouted something to him that Marie was unable to hear above the bell clanging. A quarter of a mile farther on, past the cotton mill, Marie veered off onto a footpath through the cemetery in a mossy grove of oaks and cottonwoods that led to the Tyler Road Bridge. Cissie had learned this shortcut from Lili Jessup early in the summer. Scattered about the shady field were wooden markers and carved headstones.

ELIZABETH
WIFE OF
ELDER W.H.ROBERTS
BORN
MAY 26, 1829
DIED
AUG. 30, 1900

She cannot come to me
but I shall go to her

FATHER
J.C. JONES
AUG.10,1847
NOV.1,1926

Christ is my hope

A shirtless Negro labored with a shovel in the heat and did not notice her crossing. Marie counted here and there names and dates of the deceased, many of whom were children when the Lord called. Boy-Allen himself rested in the shade of the southeast corner where birds chattered in an old cottonwood above. There were roses and daisies on his grave, and a toy automobile beside the headstone.

Nobody had forgotten him, even if justice had not yet tracked down his killer. Aunt Hattie would say he wasn't lonely in his everlasting sleep. Every time she used that expression, Marie wondered if she was actually speaking of little David, lying in the earth alone at the Lakewood cemetery. How long would he await his family whose plots were long since bought and paid for? Sometimes Marie felt more guilty over where her first born lay in the earth than about the dreadful circumstance that put him there. More dark thoughts. Walking among these headstones now, she noticed, too, those poor souls who had vacated this world in 1918, the year of the Flu. All that long summer and fall in Farrington, horsedrawn hearses and black carriages had paraded up and down Calvary Hill, Christian men and women in solemn mourning (her mother held the same black parasol at each burial), gravediggers at work day after day, family lots crowded by the Flu, grieving survivors seeking to interpret God's will in all their sorrow. Marie had lost Cousin Floyd, her aunt Rebecca, Grandpa Gustav, and her little cousin Ruthie on the sweetest blue morning of that summer. At the hour of her death, Ruthie failed to recognize her own mother and passed away humming a song Marie used to sing at bedtime. When the pandemic ended abruptly in the autumn of Armistice, few in Farrington had escaped the tragedy of loss during that long sad season.

A canopy of pecan trees, hickory, and sweetgum arched over the old plank bridge to Shantytown, shading the humid summer afternoon. This was where Maude had warned Marie not to go, the deep flowing water, a dividing line between white and black. But whose decision was this to make, hers or Maude's? All her life, somebody was telling Marie what to do, where to go, how to feel. Having Harry sell the house on Cedar Street and send her and the children down here to Texas ignited a change in Marie's heart. She was tired of being a milquetoast, sick of being treated like a child. If she wanted to take a job in Jimmy Delahaye's office, then that's just what she would do, and if flirting with her boss made the day go by and gave her heart flutters, then so much the better, Harry be damned. And today? She was going to Shantytown. She intended to cross this bridge and break every rule in Bellemont, even if it drew a nasty response from Maude or those gossips on College Street who spoke behind Marie's back when she passed, or her fellow Christians singing praise on Sundays to a Lord whose loving desires they ignored in daily living. Right this minute, Marie was going to walk across the bridge and do for once what she wanted to do because it was her choice and her life now, and everyone else better get used it.

Halfway across the river, Marie stopped to watch the muddy current flow by underneath her feet, cold and silent. She shuddered as that awful thought of submerging crossed her mind, and hurried on where she heard cardinals and bluejays tittering in the woods amid fragrant ivory blossoms from southern magnolias. At the far embankment, the road cut a flat and dusty scar through the pinewoods into Shantytown. By storm season, the water rose here, flooding the bottom floor of the houses nearest the river, carrying off everything not packed up and hidden from the high current. Sewage escaped from toppled outhouses, chickens and rabbits were swept away, disease threatened. Today, the sun glared down and baked the road where Negro children ran about barefoot and played at games familiar to Cissie and Henry. Dogs lolled under porch stoops, bluebottle flies spun circles over rusting tin cans and decrepit barrels and darted away from the lashing tail of a scrawny milk cow tied to a post beside a pig sty. The houses, mostly one-story Creole architecture with low shingled roofs and propped-up foundations under shaded galleries against the eventuality of flood, extended side by side down the long section of road out to the pinewoods and back under the pecan trees. There was no town center, just houses and weeds and dust.

Yet Shantytown was as alive as downtown Bellemont in the noon hour. Everywhere, people went about their business, working indoors and outdoors, scrubbing and digging and hauling, or eating and drinking and talking with one another, few paying Marie much notice as she passed by. Only an old dark woman on her hands and knees in the furrows of a small vegetable garden did so much as look up, offering a smile which Marie gladly returned, then giving her directions to a particular address, as Marie hadn't seen any house numbers so far.

"That ain't but a little farther on, child. Pretty basket of verbena and snapdragons on the porchfront."

"Thank you very kindly."

"My pleasure, honey."

"It's a pleasant day, isn't it?"

"Why, yes, honey, it is."

A flatbed truck carrying empty chicken cages sat in the middle of the road, steam rising from beneath its rusty hood. Three black men huddled around, while another had slid on his back under the engine. A young woman wearing a red scarf about her head spoke anxiously to one of the men and her eyes looked as if she had been crying recently. The address Marie sought was just past the stalled truck, surrounded by a low wire fence and stalks of sunflowers. The siding was gray and splintery, lacking paint or stain, weather worn and old. The porch overhang slumped visibly in the middle and the bottom step was split and broken to the left. The basket of verbena hung just off-center from the steps and a coffee-brown girl, barely younger than Rachel, sat beneath it, a bemused expression on her pretty face. She wore a faded rose frock and a little blue bow in her hair.

"He ain't here," the girl said to Marie, as she stopped in front of the house. She wore a wary expression.

"Mr. Reeves?"

"Been gone with Eva and Caroline since before I woke up. First to Longview, now maybe sortin' about at the dump again. I don't know."

"Well, I have something for him," said Marie, opening her handbag. She felt timid now, and a little flustered. Perhaps she ought not to have come. Maude wouldn't have approved of this walking trip to Shantytown, yet Marie did just as she pleased these days and if Maude was sore about that, well, so be it.

She asked the girl, "Could I leave it with you?"

"What is it?"

Marie smiled, trying to be polite and friendly. "Well, he's been bringing toys and lampshades and assorted discards for a play-circus my daughter's been building and I thought I'd like to pay him for some of it. I'm sure much of what he's found had value in trade somewhere and he deserves some compensation for his generosity." She drew a pair of bills from her pocketbook.

The girl brightened. "Why, you must be Cissie's mama."

Marie nodded. "Yes, I am."

The girl stood, offering a smile of her own. "I'm Lucy Hudson. Julius, he's my brother-in-law. Honey, come sit here out of the sun. I don't bite."

"Thank you," Marie replied, unlatching the wire gate and walking in. Perhaps she had been right in coming, after all.

Lucy backed up onto the porch and brought a wooden chair from the corner for Marie to sit on. Then she dragged another over for herself. "Go on, honey, sit yourself down. I been hearing a lot about you, seems like all summer long. Ain't nothing but 'Mrs. Hennesey this and Mrs. Hennesey that,' and those kids of hers and that little circus."

Marie laughed. "He's been wonderfully helpful. The children just adore him."

From inside the house, an infant's voice cried out briefly, and stopped. Lucy turned an ear to listen for a few moments, then lent her attention back to Marie. "Ain't hardly nothing Julius won't do for folks he likes. That's how he's always been. Sister says Julius always been more generous than most."

"He has a good heart."

"Yes, ma'am."

"Here," said Marie, handing the two dollar bills to Lucy. "I'm sure we owe him twice that."

"Oh, honey, he won't have you paying him for something he done free of charge."

Lucy tried to give the money back, but Marie shook her head and snapped her handbag shut. "He's the nicest person I've met since we've come here. I know that money won't buy kindness nor is it a fair reward, either, but I'd appreciate you giving it to him as a thank you on behalf of the children and myself."

"Well, isn't that sweet of you?" replied Lucy. "Tell the truth, he ain't used to receiving blessings like that from certain folks 'round here, if you understand my meaning."

"I suppose I do," Marie admitted, peeking indoors where a Negro child no more than three or four years old toddled across the floor toward the screen door, blanket in hand. "We've only lived here a few months, but I must say it does trouble me and I've been ashamed of what I've seen and heard, now and then. We're taught in the Bible to love all our neighbors. I've always believed in God's simplest truths. It's what we've learned in church since childhood."

Lucy smiled, touching Marie on the arm. "Honey, they got the same Bible down here. They just read it different, is all."

She studied Marie with eyes darkened by sorrow until Marie looked away, the most peculiar feeling in her heart. The child was at the screen door now, whimpering softly. A young boy's voice called out from farther inside the house and Marie heard running footsteps and then a door bang closed out back. Lucy got up and went to the screen and opened it and scooped the child into her arms. She looked back at Marie. "Do you care to step inside? Baby here needs to go to sleep and I got a child named Willie who won't stop causing commotion. I could get you a glass of lemonade if you like?"

"That'd be nice," Marie replied, getting to her feet. "I can't stay long, of course. My own children are waiting for lunch."

Lucy smiled. "You come here down Tyler Road past the old cemetery, did you?"

"Why, yes. What makes you ask?"

"I find that so strange."

"Oh? How come?"

Lucy giggled. "Our cemetery's about a mile from here, and I never set foot in it."

"Pardon?" She was confused.

The girl gave a mock shudder. "Most colored folks is afraid of ghosts. You ask Julius if you don't think it's so."

Marie smiled. "That's silly."

Lucy laughed. "Yes, ma'am."

Suppressing her own giggles, Marie followed the black girl into the front room where the air was dark and cool and smelled of fried catfish and butter oil. The wooden floor underfoot was covered in part by an old brown hook rug. There were four windows, each of which had a cotton quilt draped over the glass. An old pump organ like Marie's grandmother used to play, sat in one corner beside a burgundy sofa near to the kitchen entry.

"Sit yourself down, honey," Lucy told Marie, "I'll be back directly."

Feeling relaxed now and pleased with herself for coming here, Marie sat on the sofa and counted a number of small clay vases holding an assortment of summer wildflowers and studied a row of old photographs atop the fire mantel. Lucy came out of the kitchen with a glass of lemonade and sat down beside her. Marie took the lemonade thankfully and had a sip. It had been a fairly long walk from Delahaye's to Shantytown and she was parched from the heat.

"Sister Angela's gone away to Knoxville, so Julius and me been left to ourselves with five little ones to worry after. When he goes off to do his business, I've got no patience for all this trouble."

Marie said, "I'm fortunate to have Maude home to watch Cissie and Henry when I'm at work. Up north, it was just me when Harry traveled, though Cousin Emeline liked to babysit from time to time when her own husband was out of town. The children can be a trial."

The black girl nodded. "Ain't that a case."

"Maybe you could find someone to come help during the day."

"Naw, I don't mean like that. We come from Tennessee seven years ago, down here to be with my Aunt Ida and I hated it then and I hate it now. I didn't want to come. Sister made me do it 'cause Julius had it in his mind he wanted to go some place different after the War. So we came here and I just never cared for it."

"I don't understand."

Lucy got up and went into the back of the house. Marie heard her open a dresser and take something out. When she came, she was holding a flat box, which she gave to Marie. "Go on, open it."

Even in the hazy light of the front room, Marie recognized the medals placed there. She had seen both on display in the Farrington courthouse each Independence Day since 1919: the Distinguished

Service Cross and the French Croix de Guerre.

"Julius was a hero in the World War."

Marie smiled. "I know. Rachel told us. You must be very proud."

"He got shot up bad saving some boys, so they give him these rewards and told him he was a good soldier, even though back in Knoxville he was still just another colored fellow. Ain't that something?"

"Yes, it is." Marie sipped her lemonade and stared at Julius's medals from the Great War, shining honors for valor and courage. She hadn't any idea he had been wounded. Cousin Rory had lost a limb and the use of his left eye. Maggie Rutherford's brother had been blown to bits his first morning at the Argonne. Both Tommy Layton and Milton Metcalf had been gassed. Each of those who had come back from France had lost vitality and eagerness.

"Julius told Sister that the Army didn't want no colored boys carrying guns in the War, but they was so afraid of losing the war that they made the colored boys throw away those shovels and commence to training just like the white soldiers. Hardly any colored boys knew nothing about no Kaiser or where France was or nothing. They just went where they was ordered to go and did what they was told like any other good Americans. Julius said to Sister, 'Colored soldier love his country maybe more than the white 'cause he spilled more of his blood there. When this War come, all he wants is the chance to show Uncle Sam that he's a man, just like any other.'"

Marie felt embarrassed. She had never heard of such a thing. It was utterly disgraceful. Why hadn't Harry told her? Or Uncle Henry? Did they think she wouldn't understand?

Lucy said, "Over there, they worked harder'n anyone proving what Julius said, especially when the white soldiers started going on about how the coloreds got tails like monkeys and won't do nothing but drink liquor and rape white women. See, Julius come from Tennessee so he got sent into the army with the 92nd Division that had lots of Southern boys, white and colored, and the coloreds even had some of their own officers and that didn't make none of them white boys happy so they wouldn't salute or show respect for the uniform if it had a colored man in it. Then the shooting started up and soldiers were dying and it didn't make much matter what color was giving orders and there was a place where so many boys got themselves killed that Julius wanted to give up and come home like everybody else, but they had an awful battle one night and so many boys being blowed up that he crawled in the mud across the wires and hauled a lot of colored boys back with him in spite of his getting shot in three places, and then he went back into the gas and killed fourteen Germans that tried to shoot him and when he was done and crawled back to his own side again, everybody called him a hero and sent him home, after all."

"Good gracious! I don't know how I could've tolerated that."

Lucy shrugged. "He was sick in the hospital all winter and part of the next spring and only Sister was allowed to visit him. I knitted him a shirt and Papa bought him a new pair of boots and Mama scribbled his name in the family Bible and prayed he'd come back to us like he left. Then they had a big parade in Knoxville for the soldiers that fought for America over there, and Julius was still sick but he put his uniform on with them medals you're holding and got out of bed to be in it when he couldn't walk more than across the room yet. Well, he ought to've stayed right where he was in bed, 'cause the Army didn't allow no colored soldiers to march in that parade. You hear me, honey? He seen plenty of colored soldiers killing and getting killed for their country that wouldn't let a one of them march in that damned parade. It broke his poor heart. That's why we left Knoxville and come down here."

"I'm so sorry." Marie felt truly ashamed. She detested deliberate humiliations of any sort. If she believed most people here felt that way about their colored neighbors, she didn't know how long she and the children could remain here. Why hadn't Harry warned her? Did he hope she wouldn't notice?

"Ain't nothing you done to be sorry for, honey," said Lucy, taking the box of medals off Marie's lap and folding it shut. "That's just how it is."

"Well, I believe he's very courageous." She drank the last of her lemonade.

The back door flew open, and two small boys barefoot in dusty overalls and carrying old croquet mallets burst in, one chasing after the other, both crying and yelling simultaneously, "Lucy, Lucy! He hit me! He hit me!"

Marie recognized Willie Reeves from that day Cissie brought Mr. Slopey back from the river. The other boy she didn't know at all.

Lucy Hudson put the box of medals on the organ and got up. As Willie and his playmate reached the front room, bawling loudly, Lucy hollered, "First one of you two wants a whipping, come on in!"

Marie stood, too, setting her empty glass on the floor. "I better go along. I'm sure Henry's just as anxious as these two."

The boys had stopped cold, tears welling up, both staring at Marie as if she were a ghost. Lucy ignored them for the moment, saying to Marie, "I appreciate you coming down here today, bringing what you did. He'll be thankful."

"You're very welcome, dear."

The truck was still there in the middle of the road, but the hood was closed and one of the men was behind the wheel working over the starter. The woman in the red scarf had gotten herself surrounded by a pack of scrawny hounds, but didn't appear to mind. The sun burned down hotter than ever.

On the dirt road back to Bellemont, Marie thought about what she might say to Julius when next she saw him. His generosity and kindness toward her children pleased Marie, lent her strength and optimism in Harry's long absence. If in this small town a ray of divine light shone so brightly in one man, Marie wondered, why could it not in others?

She crossed over the cold river and wandered up the narrow road through the pinewoods, listening to the birds chattering in the trees. She felt safe here during the day, perhaps because she was reminded of the thick forest behind the farm at home. An automobile rattled by as she stepped back into the long grass and waved to the driver. Insects flew slantwise on the heated air ahead of her as she walked.

The road came out into sunlight just south of Watson Avenue. Another block and she saw Cissie atop Mr. Slopey, with Henry and Abel Kritt and Lili Jessup trailing just behind. Lili held her kitten and

Abel led a small terrier on a leash. When Marie called out, Cissie urged the old swayback forward and another mutt came running out from the bushes nearby and Henry and Lili ran, too.

"I thought you were going to wait for me to come home," Marie said, pausing in the shade. "Aren't you hungry?"

"Grandma told us to go on a picnic today," said Henry, showing his mother the small wicker basket.

"There's lots of people over there now, Momma," Cissie said. "All her club ladies and that man from the airfield, Mr. Beeswax."

"My momma's there, too," Lili added. "I guess it's a party for someone."

"Maybe Mr. Beeswax has a birthday," Henry suggested, taking a thick carrot out of the basket and breaking it in half. He gave the other half to Abel who wiped off his dusty eyeglasses, and fed a small chunk of it to the dog.

"Maybe," said Marie, curious now herself. Maude hadn't mentioned a word earlier that morning. "Well, I'll just go see for myself. You be careful where you have your picnic. Keep away from the road, and if you go to the river — "

"Stay out of the water," Cissie interrupted. "We know, Momma. We'll be good. I promise."

"All right, then. I have to go back to work after lunch, but I'll be home before supper."

"Bye-bye, Momma!"

When the children were safely off the main road and heading toward the river, Marie continued up the street to Maude's house. Two automobiles were parked out front, a green Nash and a tan Chevrolet. As Marie arrived at the gate to the backyard, "Benny Beeswax" from the Rickenbacker Aerodrome came out and climbed into the green Nash and motored off. Marie went into the yard, quickly took her morning linen off the line, and carried it indoors by way of the kitchen porch. The house was filled with voices. Two of Maude's club ladies, Beatrice and Emily, were just walking out of the kitchen as Marie came in, Emily saying, "When I was a little girl, I remember a lightning storm just like that. I was scared to death. Why, I thought I'd be struck dead for sure."

Marie set the basket on a stool beside the pantry just as Trudy and Leila Neal, whom Marie had met one afternoon downtown at Butler's Dry Goods, came in from the bedroom hallway, Trudy saying with a distinct frown, "Heavens, no, she'd only seen the boy since Easter and really hadn't made her mind up about anything. That's just idle gossip and you ought not to repeat a word of it."

When Trudy looked up and saw Marie standing beside the sink, she managed a weak smile. "Hello, honey."

Marie nodded a greeting, and asked, "Where's Maude?"

Her voice plaintive and low, Trudy replied, "Oh, she's still in with Rachel, the poor dear. They've given her two Asafetida tablets and sent for Doctor Bird."

Worried now, Marie asked, "Is she ill? Why, I saw her just this morning and she seemed fine. Did she catch something?"

Trudy's face went ashen. "Oh my goodness, honey, haven't you heard? Why, there's been a terrible accident. Oh, it's just awful. Two aeroplanes collided last night in a storm cloud over Lake Pontchartrain. Dearie, CW's been killed."

SEPTEMBER

WASHING OFF A SET of tableware in the sink, Marie looked out the kitchen window to a gloomy late-afternoon sky. Gray clouds roiled on the horizon. A gusty wind blew in the cottonwood grove across the road, perhaps some wayward thunderstorm, she thought, emerging from late summer heat. As she scrubbed the silver clean, cold tap water numbed her hands.

In the dry sunless sitting room, Rachel sat at the piano playing a few brief bars of an old Appalachian hymn. Woefully dispirited since CW's fatal airplane accident above Lake Pontchartrain, the past few weeks she had taken to spending her lunchtime at home with Maude, eating little meat sandwiches cut into triangles and rolling pie crusts for supper.

Bursting with energy, Maude roamed from room to room as she attended to the housekeeping while engaging in a conversation about epileptics and the peculiar fits they throw. From the unlit pantry, she called out, "Now, mind you, infirmity of any sort teaches us the Lord's humility, but when that poor dear girl fell off Edgar Foote's delivery wagon and nearly swallowed her own pigtails, well, it's clear to me how some of us have obviously misunderstood God's intentions in that regard."

Marie rinsed off a handful of forks under the sink faucet. Her hands ached from the cold. She felt tired and wished she could nap for an hour. She heard her daughter's voice carrying across the gusty wind from outdoors where Cissie and Lili and Henry were playing toad-in-the-hole inside the Jessup's smelly old chickencoop. Dust swirled in the empty street. Marie hoped the instructions she had given them regarding soiled school clothing had not been entirely ignored. Twice this week, Maude had administered arnica to Henry's wounds: once on a skinned left knee after he'd tripped over a milk can, and again on his right elbow where he had bumped into a wooden post. The fall school term had started and neither child was happy about it. Already Cissie had brought home a notice from the school principal after cracking a boy named Jerome Winning on the jaw for tugging at her pigtails. Her teacher, Mrs. Jarisch, wrote to Marie praising Cissie's fine reading skills and penmanship while expressing concern for her daily deportment. Henry had begun well enough himself, but then last week, little Abel Kritt and his mother left town. A truck had come in the middle of the night and taken them away with everything they owned, no explanations, and no good-byes except to Henry, who accepted guardianship of Abel's favorite turtle, and to Mary Snell, a close friend of Mrs. Kritt's, who shared with the neighbors Mrs. Kritt's troubling suggestion that children ought to be kept away from the river until iniquity was overcome. Most people assumed she was referring to the unsolved murder of poor Boy-Allen, but rumor suggested there was something more, a shameful hush about those hours little Abel had gone missing on the Fourth of July. Marie worried now whenever the children went into the woods and was glad school had begun.

Rachel's fingers danced once more up the piano scale, tinkling across the upper octaves, then quit altogether. She rose from the piano bench and came into the kitchen hallway where she addressed both Maude and Marie in a doleful voice. "Joanna says Thelma Waller's taken up Science because of Peggy's sickness. She's convinced that right thoughts will cure her daughter and that Mary Baker Eddy's inspired scripture is the key to her own salvation."

Setting a can of condensed milk on the breadboard, Maude snorted. "Beatrice shares Thelma's party line and she says that woman calls her house physician more often than Hooker's drugstore. Why, I doubt there's a soul in this county with a medicine closet fuller than Thelma Waller's, and I know for a fact she drinks lemon and salt from time to time to dispense with her periods and that she purchased a bottle of White Pine syrup just last week to ward off a silly little cold. Christian Science, indeed. Ha!"

Marie closed off the tap and took a towel to dry off her hands. The pink frock she wore was speckled with soapy water above the waist apron and she dabbed it clean. Her back still to Maude, she remarked, "Cissie tells me Peggy's quite a little darling, her awful affliction notwithstanding. I imagine she's awfully brave, too."

"Well, of course she is," agreed Maude, tying on a yellow check-ered apron. "I certainly didn't mean to suggest that any of this is her fault. She's only a child, after all."

Rachel came into the kitchen and fetched a ginger cookie from the Mason jar on the counter top under the cabinets. Enlivened by dispute, she perked up, her tone louder, closer to her usual self. "Oh, for heaven sakes, Mother, she's thirteen years old! Why, Thelma told Joanna that Peggy collects photographs of matinée idols now and pastes them onto the wall above her bed. Apparently she's got an awful crush on Gilbert Roland."

"My cousin Emeline collects teapots and Japanese dolls with paint-ed lashes," Marie added, having a ginger cookie of her own. She hadn't eaten a bite of lunch herself and her stomach felt pained and empty. "I envy her passion for them, although sometimes it does seem a little foolish."

"Oh, I think it's wonderful to be passionate," said Rachel. "I wish I were. Being in the doldrums is so tiresome I can hardly stand it. It's absolutely hateful."

Maude fetched a bottle of milk from the ice-box, then took down a glass from the cupboard and filled it for Marie. She reminded Rachel, "A cheerful heart is a good medicine. You know, dear, I seem to recall your own foolish enthusiasms for a particularly horrid Italian movie fellow who had both you and Francie Powell loafing about Hooker's drugstore in the evening reading *Photoplay* magazines and shaming yourselves with that sodajerker whose language would make a monkey blush."

"Good grief, Mother! Clarence did not have a foul mouth! Why, I doubt he uttered a cussword his entire life!" Rachel turned to Marie.

"He was the sweetest boy you'd ever like to meet. Francie hoped to marry Clarence when she graduated school, but a Bertha shell killed him in France six days before Armistice. I helped her arrange a pretty bouquet of orange poppies for his grave."

"That was nice of you. I'm sure she appreciated it. Kindness rarely goes unnoticed."

Maude handed the glass of milk to Marie, and poured one for Rachel. "Yet you weren't nearly so distraught as when that horrible Italian was poisoned."

Rachel burst into laughter. "Spaghetti Valentino was not poisoned, Mother! He died from peritonitis. That rumor was a vicious lie perpetrated by his enemies who were sick with envy from seeing how many millions of people were heartbroken at his passing. Why, I'm still carrying a torch for him." She smiled at Marie. "In fact, I'm sure most women agree he was the most adorable man ever born."

"I never shed one tear," said Maude, putting the bottle of milk back into the ice-box.

"I remember Harry and I watched the funeral on *Metrotone News* at the Gem in Farrington," Marie said, after finishing her ginger cookie. "I'd never seen so many mourners in my life. It was quite a spectacle." Harry thought the entire thing was a shameful waste of money, but Marie secretly envied all those girls who had fallen in love with a fellow they'd never even kissed.

Sipping from her milk, Rachel asked Marie, "Did you know Valentino's casket was draped in a cloth of gold?"

Marie shook her head. "Were you actually there at the funeral?"

"No, she was not," Maude interjected. "Although poor Rachel was so overwrought with grief, she did try to buy a train ticket to New York City. Of course, I refused to let her out of the house until all that nonsense was over with. You can't imagine the fuss she put up. She threw seven kinds of cat fits, and said things that were entirely uncalled for."

"Mother has absolutely no sense of drama," said Rachel, putting the glass of milk down and walking to the back door. When she opened it, a dank draft filled the kitchen, fluttering through the lace curtains above the window. According to the *Bellemont Oracle*, Monday last had been the hottest day of the year. Both humans and animals had suffered heat prostration: nine people had been admitted to the hospital by their doctors and a truckhorse harnessed to an old coal dray dropped dead in the Fourth Street alleyway downtown. After a record stretch of unearthly heat, everyone looked forward to a change in weather. As Rachel stepped out onto the back porch to look at the cloudy sky, Marie heard her remark, "I believe we may actually see some rain today."

— 2 —

Marie sat on her bed staring out past the pretty chinaberry tree to the washing on the laundry line she needed to bring indoors soon. Six months ago in Farrington, she had her own home with a back-yard veranda that looked out onto a garden of flower beds and fruit trees and vegetables where clouds of lightning bugs sparkled in the lavender dusk and feral cats stole by instinct through crape myrtle and clumps of deadly nightshade. Once each week, Cousin Emeline came by for tea and cookies and to exchange mail-order catalogues and idle gossip. She helped prune the rose bushes and urged Marie to regis-ter herself by maiden name in the telephone book. When Harry put the house up for sale after Easter, dear Emeline knelt beside Marie in the sunlit parlor filling stacks of packing boxes until each was tied shut and it was time to go. An hour before traintime in May, Marie crept through the cool of the morning garden with a studio photo-graph of Harry and the children and herself and buried it in a cigar box beneath the gnarled apple tree in the back corner of the yard. Afterward, propelled by steam locomotive through that vast windy emptiness of Missouri and Oklahoma in the middle of the night, Marie dreamt of seedtime and bloom on the Farrington plains, her bare fingers thrust into damp black loam, sweet fragrance of drip-ping honeysuckle rising on a faint breeze, a million crickets and glow-ing fireflies swarming a long humid summer twilight and her mother's persistent voice echoing across the starry dark, calling her only daughter home to supper.

There were days now when Marie felt lost and forgotten. Though she dearly loved Harry and trusted his reasoning for packing her off with the children to this distant place, the strangeness of lighted stores downtown whose proprietors she did not recognize on the sidewalks out front worried her lonely heart. Why had he sent her away? How much longer would they need to stay in this place? Would he ever love her as he once did? *"Oh, darling, you told me the story of your sorrow in such a plaintive voice, it seemed to be the voice of wounded love. I shall try so hard to never make such a break again. Oh, my sweetheart, I love you and you love me, and I will try so hard to be your good boy."* How had her life become so difficult? Maude, Rachel, CW, Delahaye, Julius Reeves, Boy-Allen, spinning like a carousel in her head. Why had things taken this course? In the big show window of Kelly's department store, a Majestic set broadcast unfamiliar voices from unfamiliar places performing radio-plays she could hardly make sense of. On Sunday mornings, she stood in a crowded pew next to Maude and Rachel as the Baptist congregation sang hymns whose verses she didn't know. One evening at the community hall, she overheard a woman from the other end of town refer to her as a "Yankee" in the same accusatory tone she had just been using to discuss the foul mystery of Boy-Allen's murder. In each typewritten letter from the city, Harry praised her courage, wrote how proud he was to have such a fine wife whose Christian sacrifice and selflessness lent encouragement both to himself and their children. Marie felt neither brave nor selfless, not in a very long while. Moreover, that sort of pride was a nuisance she could gladly do without if only Emeline would come to tea once a week or her mother would send Cousin Frenchy to fetch her for Sunday dinner in Uncle Harlow's old Stanley Steamer. If the children continued to smile at breakfast each morning, she would attempt to bear up and study patience when her heart spoke sadly, but remembrances often kindle on a sudden breeze and each letter she received unfailingly deepened her longing for home.

Farrington, Illinois
September 1st, 1929

Dearest Marie,

This summer past without you in our midst has been the saddest I have ever known. It's been lonesomer than thunder. Roy and Uncle Boyd both agree that you must come back to us tomorrow or no later than the day after. Do you see how dearly you are missed? Victor bought a secondhand Ford last Tuesday and promises to teach you how to drive if you hurry back soon, as Uncle Charlie has already told him to get rid of it. Auntie Emma and Lottie and Sam and Uncle Merrill came to breakfast this morning. They each send their love.

Yesterday the baby was sick and needed to see Dr. Mahoney who was very nice. I didn't mind going to him at all. Later in the afternoon I went for a walk with Luther in the pinewoods behind Esther York's peacock farm. We followed a narrow path beside the creekbed that led us so far into the thicket I thought we were lost. Did Effie ever tell you the story of how Great-aunt Sara was eaten by wolves near here? Mother says every word of it is true, so help her God. Well, dear cousin, just as I thought I'd need to send that old hound dog back for Roy to save my life, a miracle happened. I found God's sunlight up ahead shining through the pine trees upon a meadow of songbirds and Indian grass where long ago three silly little girls once dreamed they built a fairy throne from a rotting old stump. Do you recall our meadow in the beautiful moonlight? We were wild as cats ourselves with no fear of the dark. Roy keeps a coal oil lamp beside his bed when he sleeps, but I have no need of it. Our precious Violet was scared of wind and lightning and nothing else. In bed, spider-bitten, she swore that when the Lord came for her, she'd not hide. At the last she said to me, "Divine light shineth brightest by night." To this day I believe we ought to have set aside a corner of that pretty meadow for Violet and laid a tiara of snapdragons upon her marker each anniversary. Cor unum, via una. Our secret motto. Do you remember? One heart, one way. If only I could listen to dear Violet play mother's organ once again, perhaps I would not sleep as fitfully as I do.

Now Aunt Hattie has insisted I pass on to you all the latest Farrington gossip, so I will. Dear cousin, Mrs. Craswell died two weeks ago Saturday. She was about the sweetest old lady I ever knew and I was always very fond of her. What enjoyable visits I had in her home. I don't imagine she had very much besides her Crown Darby and that old walnut chifforobe, but whatever it is I hope her son William gets it because he has grown up to be a fine man. I am glad that he was able to be with her when she went. Her sister Margery doesn't need another penny, anyhow, and she is the most disagreeable woman in this county. Have you written Edith of late? Everett is working for the Bendix Co. so they both have a salary now and are on a week's vacation with pay in Mishawaka. I'm going downtown this afternoon to get some sherbet glasses for Edith. We don't want to spend a lot of money, but we ought to give her something for all the wonderful embroidery she did for Grandma Sayers. Don't you think so? Last Sunday after morning services, Mother had Ida Hawley over for dinner and I went out with Agnes in the afternoon. We went to a "sing" at the auditorium but there was such a crowd that we only stayed a short time, then we went for a ride. Agnes seems to be a very nice woman and I enjoy her. We had a good talk about youth nowadays. Agnes doesn't like the fact that her daughters are going with boys whose names they don't even know, nor the hours they keep. This disagreement is a fair one in my book. When we were girls there were no automobiles so we went to the square dance in a horse and buggy and found our husbands from the boys we knew at school. It was a fine arrangement. We saw the good and the bad in each other and knew what to make of it. When we married there were fewer surprises. How does a girl in Chicago know she is going with a gentleman and not a thief? I am grateful to have been born on a farm.

Well, dear cousin, I must bathe and dress the baby and get to Ruth's in time for lunch. Lloyd is coming out for supper tonight. What would he do without his friends? Read the Bible and water the chickens, says Auntie Emma, which I believe is heaven for her. Do you suppose we'll ever have picnics and fun again on holidays?

Please give my love to the children. We miss you all so very much.

Your loving cousin,

Emeline

— 3 —

After folding the last batch of laundry into a basket and carrying it indoors, Marie crossed the dusty yard to the Jessup's chickencoop. She had noticed on her last trip out of the house that Cissie's chirping voice had been lost in the banging of Maude's old storm-shutters shaken loose by the rising wind. Great gray clouds continued to darken the sky horizon and prickled the hairs on the back of her neck. If rainshowers were coming, she preferred the children play indoors. She called into the chickencoop and heard no answer. She leaned down to peek underneath, catching her hair on a bent nail. As she tugged loose, the Jessup's back screen door slammed and Lili's gray kitten, who had been sitting beside the porch, scrambled under the house. Concerned, Marie called again for Cissie and Henry. Where were they? A side window of the Jessup's house raised up and Mildred stuck her head out wrapped in curlpapers. A pale yellow lightbulb glowed from the ceiling behind her face. She held a cigarette in one hand. Mildred shouted to Marie, "Lost something?"

Marie stood and nodded as the wind gusted in the tall dry grass of the Jessup's yard. Walking over, she replied, "My children. I thought they were playing with Lili in the chickencoop, but they seem to be missing since coming home from school."

"Don't go nowhere, honey."

Mildred disappeared indoors and Marie heard her call to her brother Fritz who had barely set foot outside of the house since arriving four months ago. A doctor named Mulligan stopped by for an hour on Tuesday and Rachel claimed he had looked mad as the devil upon departing. Marie listened to Mildred and her brother shouting back and forth until Mildred stuck her head back out the bathroom window. She told Marie, "They ain't here. Fritz says Lili told him they were all going down to the drugstore to buy candy." She flicked redhot ash off her cigarette in the wind. Maude believed no woman in Bellemont smoked more than Mildred Jessup. "My brother's been swallowing dope pills all week. He ain't well."

"I'm sorry. Is there anything I can do?"

Her face drawn with fatigue, Mildred shrugged. "He come over here from Tallahachee just so's I could take care of him. He gets mean as hell when he's sick and his own doctor don't want to see him no more. Won't go to the hospital neither 'cause they won't serve him liquor in bed. Last winter we lost my sister Harriet to a cancer in her ovaries. None of us even knew she was sick until I got a telegraph from her friend Sophie telling me to come quick to Abilene. When I got there, I says, 'Honeypie, how come you never called for me?' And she says, 'Why Millie, when we were little you told me I was such a bother.' And that was the truth, too, because when we were girls, I did say she was a bother when she wouldn't stop following me around, trying on my prettiest clothes whenever I wasn't looking, but after the Lord took her home with Him, my heart just broke to think of poor little Harriet lying in bed with all that pain and not one of her own flesh and blood beside her to hold her hand." Mildred Jessup exhaled a lungful of cigarette smoke. "I believe it don't matter what's been said in the past. When you're in desperate need, family ought to take you in. That's why God grows us together, don't you agree?"

Marie nodded, sympathetic to Mildred's plight. "I expect that's so. It's nice to live away from home now and again, but strangers won't bring us soup in the dark."

Mildred leaned far enough out into the air to smell the dampness on the wind, then told Marie, "Honey, if you see my little girl, you tell her to get her fanny home. Supper's at six."

— **4** —

Rain fell two blocks from downtown, dappling the summer dust under the pecan trees. A humid odor ripe with soiled leaves scented the air where Marie hurried along on an errand for Maude who required some soda mint tablets, a fresh tube of dental cream, and a headache bromo. Wet branches swayed overhead. Sparrows flew in and out of the cloudy wood. An elderly nurse stood on the gallery of Mr. Gray's house, wrapped in a patchwork quilt, watching for lightning. In the narrow alley next door, a middle-aged Negro man in stained cotton overalls struggled atop a ladder with a hammer and a broken storm-shutter; by the next block, the sound of his banging was lost on the wind. A trio of passenger automobiles rattled past with windshields speckled by raindrops and left muddy tracks in the street. The last car, a black Model A Ford, had its motor lamps lit. When Marie had passed through here to work in the morning sunshine, she had seen two yellow dogs rolling in the dust and a small Negro boy with a fishing pole scooping worms back into a tin can he had just dropped by the side of the road. Down at the end of the block, a red-haired girl in braids, perhaps Cissie's age, skipped rope on the wooden sidewalk for the mailman while singing a child's nonsense rhyme. *"Acka-backa soda cracka, acka-backa boo! If your daddy chews tobacca, he's a dirty Jew!"* Now these tree-shrouded neighborhoods were silent except for a pattering of rain in the summer leaves. Miles of dense clouds blackened above the prairie and a warm damp wind gusted and Marie wondered why she had left the house without bringing Rachel's rose-handled umbrella along.

The ceiling lamps were lit indoors at Hooker's drugstore downtown as Marie peeked in through the plate-glass from beneath the sidewalk awning. Two teenage girls she didn't know sat on stools at the soda counter sipping cherry phosphates from Coca-Cola glasses. Maude's club friend Trudy stood fourth in line at the pharmacist window in front of a man named Mowry who worked in the textile building next to Delahaye's. Behind him were the buck-toothed Mitchell sisters, both of whom were older than Maude and suffered chronic rheumatism and recurring attacks of St. Anthony's Fire which kept them housebound most of the time. Though she didn't see the children, Marie went inside anyhow to ask the druggist if they had come in that afternoon. A little bell rang above the door as she stepped through. The pharmacist looked up with a smile. Marie edged over to the soda fountain, hoping to attract the attention of the druggist when he came out of the storage room. She felt increasingly antsy about her children and wanted to get back outdoors. The building was stuffy and warm, smelling of medication and rosewater perfume. Marie smiled at the two girls drinking cherry phosphates and they smiled back before continuing a conversation about a high school boy named Jimbo who had just gotten a job cleaning motorcars at a Dodge Agency in Texarkana. A burly man in a tan fedora emerged from behind an aisle near the magazine rack and went to talk with Mowry by the prescription counter. Leora Mitchell fetched a handkerchief from her purse and blew her nose. Her sister Amelia patted her on the back and whispered something in her ear. The bell over the door rang and a pretty Negro girl in a blue cotton dress came inside. Outdoors, a light rain swirled about on the wind. Store lights were visible clear across the town square and more than half of the automobiles downtown now rumbled by with headlamps lit. The Negro girl went to the soda fountain near the candy display and stood behind one of the stools, but did not sit. Neither of the two girls at the counter looked her way and Marie noticed the Negro girl paid them no mind, staring down at the penny candy in the glasscase, instead. By the pharmacy, Trudy paid for a brown bottle of Nux & Iron tablets with change from her small silvernet bag, thanked the young man behind the cash register, and stepped aside for Mowry and the other man beside him.

Tucking the bottle of tablets into her purse, Trudy saw Marie. With a frown, she said, "Beatrice feels we're in for a terrible storm tonight, dear. Worse than that awful evening Boy-Allen was murdered. She's gathered up all her cats and put them in the cellar with a candle and a big plate of tunafish. Has Maude remembered to take her morning laundry off the line?"

Marie smiled. "Yes, ma'am. We did it together when I came home for lunch. Do you really think there'll be a storm? I'm searching for the children. Mildred Jessup says they may have come downtown to buy candy this afternoon, but I'm afraid now they might've gone to play at the river. You haven't seen them, by any chance, have you? The look of the sky worries me."

"Oh, there'll be an awful storm! Beatrice says so. Why, she's been calling all over town this afternoon to let us know there'll be no Mah Jongg this evening."

The druggist came out of the back, wiping his hands with a white cloth towel. He glanced at the Negro girl by the candy display, then gave Marie a smile and stopped at the counter in front of Trudy who remarked, "Albert, your mother is a dirty cheat."

The druggist laughed. "Oh, she is, is she?"

"I should hope to tell you! She hasn't dealt me a fair hand since Decoration Day, and Beatrice has worn down nine pencils just this summer recording your mother's winning tricks. I've always maintained that it is immoral to be selfish with good fortune."

"Maybe y'all ought to find another game to play. Nobody ever beats Momma at whist."

"Well, that's no surprise at all when her dishonesty is taken into account. May I have my tablets with juice in the morning, Albert?"

The druggist shook his head. "Only mutton tea, warm milk, or lime-water."

Trudy turned to Marie with a frown. "It's positively mystifying why the Lord keeps me here when I'm not permitted to enjoy even the least of life's pleasures."

"That does seem cruel," agreed Marie. If she couldn't work in her garden, what would she do? *Simple joys are the best*, Granny Chamberlain always said. *Without them, our time here on earth would remain a fearsome puzzle and gut-mean.*

Albert laughed. "My guess is you've been scaring the bejeezus out of Him for a while now and He won't be calling you home any time soon. He knows there's no telling what you and your club ladies'll do to the Kingdom once y'all get there."

Trudy folded her purse under her arm. "Thank you for the compliment, Albert. I'll remember to save a seat for you in the pew on Sunday." Before departing, she reached over and laid a hand on Marie's wrist. "Dear, please remind Maude to wrap her wicker in wet canvas before dark. Beatrice truly believes there'll be a horrible storm tonight."

The downstairs of Delahaye's restaurant was hectic with roaring oilworkers and stiff-collared businessmen seated in a thick smoky haze of burning cigars and amber lamplight. Ignoring rude catcalls from a corner table, Marie crossed quickly to the cash register at the end of the bar where Idabelle sat tabulating dinner bills. Noise from the busy billiard room upstairs racketed in the rear stairwell. The back door was propped open to the lot behind the building and a swirling draft forced rain into the narrow entry hall. She peeked up the staircase to Jimmy Delahaye's office where she heard him on the telephone. They had gone to the movies twice now and had a fair time. Not alone, of course. Once Idabelle had come along, and another night Lucius brought a young lady from Longview whose voice was hoarse as a man's. Delahaye had been a prefect gentleman in not calling attention to himself and Marie as they sat in the theater. Then he had tried to kiss her again on the walk home that second night and she had turned her head to thwart him, why exactly she didn't know. She had wanted to apologize to Jimmy Delahaye and have him try again, but did not and so he had escorted her the rest of the way home in silence, leaving Marie feeling desolate and humiliated. Perhaps he was simply too handsome and she couldn't trust herself, any longer. How she behaved that night in his parlor worried her half to death. Never in her life had she been so careless. If Maude knew she had gone there, the children might still have a warm bed in her house, but Marie herself would likely be sleeping out back with the chickens. Whatever had come over her needed more attention. She was, after all, married to a man Marie believed she still loved. But then yesterday Delahaye invited her to another picture show on Saturday night, and she had accepted. Why? No good could come from any of this. Wasn't that so? What her heart required these days had become a mystery to her, and raising her thoughts to heaven provided little relief. Yet as she went about her business during the day, whether in haste or calm, she was curiously aware of the faintest change coming over her heart.

Counting a handful of dollar bills into the register, Idabelle remarked, "I declare, honey, you must be some kind of glutton for punishment."

"Pardon?" Marie frowned. "What do you mean by that?"

At the far end of the bar, Lucius Beauchamp wiped off the mahogany countertop with a cotton cloth. Idabelle called over to him above the din of voices. "LUCIUS, HONEY, LOOK WHO'S BACK!"

Lucius saw Marie and waved.

She waved back to the bartender, then asked Idabelle, "Why do you say that?" She never had any idea what was being said about her and half the time she didn't follow the jokes told in her presence, either.

Upstairs, a billiard ball hit the floor and rolled across the room. Raucous laughter erupted into the stairwell next to Delahaye's office. Marie glanced up the stairs and thought about Jimmy. She wanted to go up and see him for a minute or two, but she felt silly and scared. Out front of the restaurant, a motor horn blared as a truck narrowly avoiding crashing into a Ford on the wet pavement. Rain was falling harder now and Marie grew nervous imagining her children at play in the thick woods near the river.

"I just never seen anyone come back to work once she was done for the day," said Idabelle, shutting the cash register. "If I didn't know better, I might think you were sweet on Jimmy, after all."

Lucius walked along behind the bar toward Idabelle and Marie, wiping off the counter with the washcloth as he approached. A group of men from the cotton mill wearing black slicker coats came in from outdoors, rainwater dripping from their hats.

"That's the most ridiculous thing I've ever heard," Marie replied, blushing. "You know I can't imagine being married to any man but Harry." Then, in case those words might be relayed to Jimmy, she added, "Although I do admit that Mr. Delahaye is a fine dancer and an engaging storyteller. I'm sure any girl would find him quite good company on a date." Any girl with the nerve for romance, Marie thought, still ashamed of her cowardice. Maybe she'd go upstairs, after all.

"Not this one, honeypie," Idabelle cackled. "He's a drinker and a flirt."

"Name me a fellow in Texas over the age of twelve who ain't," said Lucius, wiping the counter clean near the cash register. He scratched his beard. "Old Jimmy ain't nothing special in that regard."

"He does flirt quite a lot," agreed Marie, "but what man doesn't? I still think he's awfully sweet, especially for a boss." She adored Jimmy Delahaye's flirtations. Harry flirted, but not with her any longer. Some mornings she wore perfume and he didn't even notice. Where had his heart gone? Too far from her, she worried.

"I won't date a man with roving eyes," Idabelle said. "I believe it's impolite and disrespectful. If he wants to go with me, he ought to have better manners than that."

"That's just it, sweetheart," Lucius told Idabelle. "He don't want to go with you. It's Marie here he's stuck on." He turned to Marie. "Ain't that right?"

She blushed. "I doubt that's true. We've only gone to the picture show twice, and certainly not as anything but friends. Besides, you ought to know I've been terribly busy. I doubt I'd have the time for romance, even if I weren't married, which I am, don't forget. In fact, I expect Harry to come down here by train next month." What balderdash! She doubted Harry would ever come down here unless one of the children got hurt or became seriously ill. But Marie knew it was important that she begin to deflect attention away from herself and Delahaye. This was all so difficult. What was she going to do?

"Don't wait too long to go again, honey," Idabelle advised. "Jimmy's got itchy feet."

A homely fellow in a blue business suit came up to the cash register and handed his ticket to Idabelle with a handful of coins. Marie got a whiff of bay rum and bootleg whiskey and avoided his drooping eyes, gazing instead out through the rear hallway to the grassy backyard where Julius Reeves had just come into the yard through the back gate carrying a shovel. He wore a long brown coat and a floppy cotton hat and his boots were covered in mud, his sooty face half-hidden by the sagging rim of the hat. He walked through the windy rain toward the side of the building where he called up to someone on the second floor. Another round of laughter from the billiard room echoed into the empty stairwell as the cash register rang closed and the homely man walked off.

"Jimmy didn't really call you back to work, did he?" Idabelle asked Marie, sitting back onto her stool. "Because if he did, why, I'd just have to go upstairs and give that man a piece of my mind. It's not right to expect you to come down here all hours of the day when you've got kiddies at home."

Hoping to change the topic of conversation away from her perplexing situation with Jimmy Delahaye, Marie asked, "Have you seen my children since school let out? I've been looking all over for them. Mildred Jessup thinks they might've walked downtown to buy candy."

Idabelle shook her head as Lucius slipped behind her, heading into the back hallway. He went to a storage closet under the stairwell and took out a mop and a bucket. Idabelle said to Marie, "I'm not concerned. When Rachel and I were little, we'd sneak out after bedtime and run all over downtown. One Halloween, we captured a raccoon in an old canvas sack and dropped him down mean old Widow Miller's coal chute. When he chewed himself free, Widow Miller thought he was a burglar come to steal her wedding ring, so she took a shot at him on the stairs with her father's old Confederate revolver and popped a hole in the basement furnace which started a fire and nearly burned up her whole house. Three firewagons had to be called. Of course, that was long before Boy-Allen. I'm not sure I'd have the nerve to go out after dark these days."

Lucius came back behind the bar with a bucket and a wet mop. "Looks like Jimmy's got poor old Julius digging a hole to China."

Marie saw Julius laboring with the shovel in the muddy grass a few feet from the plank fence. Idabelle left the cash register for a look, too.

Marie asked, "Why does he need to do that now? It's raining."

Lucius told her, "Sewer line's broke and there ain't nobody but a out-of-work nigger that's gonna dig a hole in the ground with a thunderstorm coming."

Idabelle stood alone in the drafty hall watching. Rain fell harder now, blown slantways on the wind. Julius paused briefly to pull his collar tight on the neck, and jammed the shovel back down into the wet earth. Marie shuddered. Why persuade someone to manual labor in a driving rain? She had never heard of such a thing. It seemed a mean and thoughtless imposition, regardless of the needful circumstance. Upstairs in the billiard room, Jimmy Delahaye shouted a crude obscenity and a roar of laughter ensued in the hollow staircase. Maybe Marie wouldn't go up, after all. No, she was much too busy. Besides, she needed to get the children home.

Strolling back to the register, Idabelle remarked, "I'd take a dime for every hole in the ground old Hardy Hooper's gonna be digging at Huntsville come wintertime."

"He'll be lucky if he ain't occupying a hole of his own," said Lucius, filling the bucket with water from a tap below the counter. He smelled strongly of corn liquor.

"Who's Hardy Hooper?" asked Marie.

"A sweet-talking colored fellow from Longview," Idabelle replied, ringing up a bill left at the register, "who come home last week and shot his wife in the head when he found out she didn't have his supper waiting for him."

"He claimed it wasn't the first time she ain't done it, neither," Lucius added. "Says he was justified 'cause of a contract with her daddy when Hardy married her that said Sallie couldn't never be late with supper or mending rents in his clothes. I guess Hardy didn't have no complaints with that second part 'cause he kept his shoes on the whole time they stood him up before Judge Bass."

Disturbed by the worsening rain, Marie asked Idabelle if anybody had an umbrella she might borrow when she went back outdoors again to look for the children. "I'm afraid they may have gone to the river."

"Now, that ain't too smart," said Lucius, mopping the floor behind the counter where he had spilled a pot of coffee an hour earlier. "Kids oughta know better'n to fool around out there in this weather. Storm comes, that river'll rise quicker'n a snake in a henhouse. They can be wadin' in the sand one moment, then suddenly find themselves floatin' down to the Gulf of Mexico."

"Lucius!" Idabelle scowled. "For goodness sakes, don't scare her!"

Marie felt herself go cold with fear. "I had no idea it was that dangerous. Mildred didn't say a word about floods."

Idabelle turned to Marie. "Honey, nobody's died in the river 'round here in years except Boy-Allen and he didn't fall in on his own. Those kids of yours are plenty smart enough to keep their feet out of the water when it begins to rise. Lili knows better anyhow. She'll see they don't get themselves in trouble. I'm sure they're playing somewhere in town with their friends. There's no sense in worrying. Go home. I'm sure they'll be back soon enough." She rang shut the cash register. "Wait here a moment."

Idabelle went down to the end of the bar and leaned into the coatroom where she grabbed her own umbrella off a hook. Outdoors, the rain had slowed again to a steady drizzle. Looking through the rear hallway to the backyard, Marie watched Julius laboring with the shovel, knee-deep in mud and grass, his clothing soaked, his stern face coal-dark in the rainy gloom. As another group of wet oilworkers entered the restaurant by the front door, Idabelle handed her umbrella over to Marie.

"Lucius'll take me home in his Ford," she smiled, slipping an arm about the bartender's waist. "Keep your kiddies indoors tonight, honey. Momma thinks there's a big storm coming."

— 5 —

Marie peeked out through the sitting room curtains at the cloudy gray sky, waiting anxiously for the children to come home for supper. Where on earth were they? She hoped Cissie hadn't taken them off on some silly adventure. When Marie was a girl, she and Violet and Emeline would get rowboats and go behind the paddle cruisers by the big wheels because they enjoyed the excitement of getting tossed by the waves. It never dawned on them what a terrible risk they were taking, but looking back Marie saw how absurdly dangerous it really was. She hoped her daughter had better sense.

Rain sprinkled in the street and the wind gusted off and on, shaking damp leaves from the cottonwoods. Indoors, a warm odor of toasted cheese filled the house and Maude had the lights on in the kitchen. Idle on the sofa after cleaning out her bedroom closet, Rachel put down Maude's thumbworn copy of *The Man Nobody Knows,* and sighed. "I have to tell you, dear, sometimes CW could be mean as a crab, although thinking back on it now I don't believe that was ever his truest intention. More often than not, he acted his cruelest when he was simply done in by work. You see, he always had quite a bit on his mind, flying concerns and so forth, that gave him fits and worry, and I can't say I was any great up-lifter, either. I honestly don't recall a single visit where I didn't pester him to take me here or there, or put on some silly show of affection to impress Mother who never felt any genuine fondness for him, anyhow."

"Don't remember that about CW," Marie advised, letting the curtain fall closed. She walked over to the sofa and sat down next to Rachel whose eyes still watered when she spoke of her lost aviator. "It's foolish to pierce your heart with misgivings over past errors. Honest to goodness, we trouble our lives so thoroughly by guilt and suspicions of failure, I often wonder what we think we're supposed to be doing. You've been more than adequate to the worst, dear, and I believe you'll make good from all of this if only you'll refuse the bitterness. CW loved you very much. You mustn't forget that."

"I suppose you're right."

"Just don't take on so about these supposed faults," Marie suggested, remembering something Aunt Hattie used to say. "Without windows, I'm sure we'd all look a fright."

Rachel got up and went over to the piano and lightly fingered the keys, tinkling a short scale as the wind gusted against the storm-shutters. She told Marie, "Mother's decided I ought to bundle myself out of doors and devote more time each evening to Baptist youth activities. She believes it'd give me more pep and dispense with what she calls my more vulgar impulses. Of course, Mother can no more refrain from criticizing me than she could quit breathing. It's so tiresome."

"You know, I've always found church fellowship to be inspiring. We weren't meant to walk alone. Belonging to something larger than ourselves offers the hope of the divine. These trials we endure throughout our lives would be fairly intolerable without the mercy of another's hand to hold. Really, as I grow older I'm convinced it's companionship, more than faith, that ties us to heaven."

Dishes clanked in the kitchen as Maude finished sorting her collection of sweet jellies in the pantry and began preparing for supper. Rain drummed on the rooftop. The gray sky seemed darker yet. Looking across the sitting room to the window, Marie noticed a flurry of windblown leaves shower the damp street outside. She was concerned that Cissie and Henry hadn't worn their raincoats out to play after school. She ought to have insisted. Had Boy-Allen's mother worried so for her own child's whereabouts the night he died? Or Mrs. Kritt that terrible afternoon of the Fourth? How can any mother care too much for her child?

Rachel went over to the radio and tuned to a performance of dance music, but kept the volume low. Then she reached into the walnut curio cabinet and drew something out which she brought back across the room to show Marie.

"Have you seen this?" She handed over a small ivory pendant carved in the shape of a figurine, perhaps three inches high.

Marie shook her head. "What is it?" She felt so badly for Rachel. That sweet boy she loved had gone and left her alone. Where would she ever find her true smile again?

"Mother of the Lamb," said Rachel, directing Marie's attention to the bowed head of the Madonna whose arms were folded as if cradling an infant. "CW wore it wherever he flew. When the wreck of his airplane was pulled from the waters of Lake Pontchartrain, the coroner collected it together with the rest of his belongings. CW's mother gave it to me on the morning of his funeral."

"How kind of her."

"Do you think so? I've been terribly afraid she's held a grudge against me in her heart for causing CW to fly away from here that awful evening. Of course, she's got every right in the world to despise me, but I'm not sure I could bear it if I thought she really did."

Returning the solemn icon to Rachel, Marie said, "Tell me, dear: would you live your life any differently if somehow you knew the hour of your passing beforehand?"

Rachel frowned. "Pardon?"

"Well, do you think we have a purpose that keeps us alert to the grim and tender, while preparing our hearts for the world to come?"

Rachel went to the window and drew back the curtain and glanced out on the rain-dampened street. She told Marie, "Since I was little, I've had peculiar suspicions of being swallowed up whole by such a dreadful sadness that sometimes I doubt I've ever been able to believe in the ordinary joy other people feel, and it's terrified me for so long that each morning I've risen from bed expecting to be borne away with grief over some sudden calamity. And then CW was killed, and cross my heart and body, dear, I realized I've lived all my life before in perfect peace."

— 6 —

Dressed in a black slicker, Marie raised Idabelle's umbrella under the veranda and watched a pair of motorcars pass by. She had waited for the children quite a while now and had finally surrendered to panic. While fitting her out in Maude's raincoat and galoshes, Rachel gave Marie directions through the woods to the river where she reluctantly guessed the children had gone after school. Maude telephoned the fire department. As the car lamps disappeared, Marie walked down the steps and crossed the street into the cottonwood grove. For the past hour, storm clouds had grown darker and rain drizzled through the treetops, sprinkling pools of muddy water where Marie trod ghostlike in the soggy earth. Fog swirled up from the afternoon bog like steam in the humid thicket and the slow rain fell soundless under the wind. She found a narrow path in the dense pine thicket and followed it for a while. Thunder rumbled off somewhere to the northeast and the wind rose and rain fell harder. Her shoes sank in grassy mud as she tramped forward, branches whipped about raking her face and arms. Brambles obscured the woods ahead. She stumbled across a fallen pine log and nearly fell. Treetops shook wildly overhead and her umbrella caught in a clump of low branches and tore apart when she pulled it free. Stepping into a narrow clearing without benefit of cover, Marie was soaked in a black downpour barely filtered through the ruined leaves above. Disoriented by this sudden deluge, she stumbled sideways into the thicket of mud and wet leaves that smelled of black rot, her eyes clouded with rain, shoes soaked and muddy, clothing damp and sticky. She shouted Cissie's name, then Henry's and Lili's, calling frantically for the children until a deafening thunderclap shook the muddy earth and the storm surged in the rainy dark treetops and she cowered in the underbrush, listening to the wind roar.

A drifting gust tore at the dripping cottonwood. Marie called to the children, listened, and called again. Rain streamed down from the trees, soaking the earth and leaves. Her clothes were drenched, her face and hands scratched from ragged discarded branches. Another electric flash of lightning lit the black cloudstrewn sky overhead. Harry would have been furious with her for allowing the children to wander off by themselves with a storm imminent, for failing to organize a proper search, for chasing off into the woods alone. He would have given her a lecture about carelessness and not spoken to her for a week — except to mention that cruel afternoon at Lake Calhoun. Again and again and again. Well, good gracious, where had *he* been that day? Did he not think *her* heart broke, too, with every thought of that tragedy? Who walked a longer road with guilt as a companion than she, forever bound to the horrid sight of her first-born child disappearing beneath the surface of that troubled water? Scolding her year after year was fine and fair. Perhaps she deserved it, but then why wasn't *he* here now to watch over the children who were every bit his responsibility as hers, were they not? What was wrong with *him*?

Rain streamed off her head, flooding her eyes and ears, soaking her dress beneath the raincoat. Under a damp pine tree she wiped her eyes and pushed away strands of wet hair that lay across her face. Frantic now and deafened by a thunderous wind, she trampled a narrow path into the thicket, fending off dipping branches as she hurried her fearful course to the river. She lost a shoe and grabbed it up muddy from the leafy bog and replaced it onto her foot. Boy-Allen had been murdered in these woods during the torrential downpour that bitter evening in May, and Marie heard there were Negroes from Shantytown piloting flat-bottomed skiffs on cloudy nights under the cypress gloom who maintained that poor Boy-Allen still huddled on a brush pile high atop the leafy riverbank clearly visible from deeper water in the smoky haze of hand-held kerosene lamps, his sad eyes phosphorescent like the foamy current, his little slicker and rubber boots perpetually mud-caked and bloody. Did his killer still haunt these woods?

When the rumble of an enormous thunderclap faded, Marie could hear the river rushing by the shore, dragging flotsam along down-stream, floating logs and the mud-splashed underpinnings of old fish-ing shacks torn to splinters in the rising storm. She worked her way past a blackberry bramble atop the riverbank and shouted for her children and searched the muddy sandbar in the gloom and called their names again and again across the steady gray rain while hiding her face from the storm that blew harder still. All she heard was the swollen river flowing past beneath her and the damp wind roaring through the soggy cypress leaves above. Somewhere down below she caught a glimpse of swirling water pitch-black with rotting leaves of lilies and broken saplings and mud. Keeping close to the bluff, she discovered an old fisherman's trail that led upriver through the dark bramble. A narrow footpath dipped below the bluff into a damp patch of blackberries and water reeds where she could smell the river and hear the steady hiss of heavy rainfall on the swift stream and see the ugly storm clouds above, roiling greenish-black with a rutted under-belly like hazy cobblestone. A false step toward the sandbar sank one foot into the muck and nearly threw her off-balance. She felt the spray of the rushing current on her face as she staggered free. Leaves flut-tered about on the wind and a child's anxious voice shrieked across the dark gray twilight. She looked up the embankment and saw a dog emerging from the bramble, soaked and frantic, Lili Jessup's collie. An instant later, it disappeared again. Marie struggled forward through the flattened reeds, scrambling toward higher ground, away from the sandbar and the rising water. She heard the collie barking somewhere off in the woods.

Rain fell harder. She sloshed upwards through the mud toward a shelter of pine trees that hung solemnly over the embankment. Across the river, somebody had lit a fire within a garbage can surrounded by human forms in the windy dark. More detritus released by the storm upstream drifted silently past. Reaching the largest pine, she cowered briefly beneath its sheltering boughs. In the thunder's lull, Marie thought she heard a child's cry again, not too far off. She stared hard toward the river and heard a wailing voice once more and knew she was near enough to respond, so she shouted back into the fierce downpour and heard a plaintive yell for help that sounded very much like her own daughter.

Cissie came out of a blackberry thicket above the river like a wild-eyed spook, dragging her little brother by the hand, both drenched in mud. Seeing her mother, she slumped and began to wail. Henry did, too, and Marie rushed to embrace them as a thunderous wind howled across the pinewoods, flailing millions of rain-sodden leaves and cracked saplings onto the river. Marie hugged and kissed them both and held them close and heard herself whimpering during a wind lull and whispered a prayer of abject humility for another prayer already answered.

For a short period, she cuddled with her children beneath a ragged cottonwood, grateful to the Lord for this rescue. Cissie was sobbing quietly while Henry pressed himself to Marie's bosom, both refusing to budge from her care. Rain hissed loudly on the water, dripping, too, from Marie's hair, which clung like damp brown seaweed to her narrow face. Cold and repentant, Cissie explained how she and Henry had wound up drenched and muddy in the river. "It was all Mr. Slopey's fault, Momma! He fell in the water and got stuck and couldn't get out! Then Biscuit started barking at him and he got scared and Lili went to get a rope and it began raining so hard I couldn't see, and then Henry tried to save Mr. Slopey all by himself and he went in the river and that's how he got stuck, too! And I had to swim with all my clothes on just to get him out! Oh, Momma, I never been so scared in my life!"

"Where's Lili now?"

"I don't know, Momma," Cissie moaned. "I called for her to come back to help us, but I guess she didn't hear me."

"I saw Lili's collie in the woods a few minutes before I found you,"

Marie told Cissie. "Do you suppose Lili was going to Shantytown for help?"

Cissie sobbed. "I don't know."

Still shivering, Henry spoke up for the first time, "I saw Mr. Slopey get drowned, Momma. I yelled at him to swim, but he didn't know how."

Cissie added, "Soon as he got himself unstuck from the mud, the river swept him away. We tried to grab his rope, but I couldn't! It was awful."

"My goodness."

"I'm scared, Momma," Henry whined.

"So am I, honey."

"Can we go home?"

Thoroughly spent from fright and relief, Marie hugged her son tightly to her breast. "Of course, we can, sweetie. Yes, yes, yes."

— 7 —

At the end of town, Maude stood under the eaves on her front porch, looking out toward the low black clouds approaching from the northeast. Lightning flashed here and there. Horses and cattle cornered in wide pastures fled to distant fencelines. A stiff wind swept across ten thousand acres of oak trees and summer grass, and brought more rain as a greater storm drew near. Next door at the Jessup's, storm-shutters banged loudly and Lili's chickens squawked in a dozen wire cages. Behind the open kitchen door, Rachel was shouting to somebody in the backyard when Marie followed her children up the muddy street to the house. A flurry of leaves swirled past the picket fence. Cissie called to Maude, "Grandma! Grandma!"

Rachel hurried out onto the back porch. Marie slowed her pace as both children sloshed off toward the house. Her legs were still trembling. She needed to lie down.

"Where in heaven's name have you been?" Maude cried after one look at the children, both dripping muddy water from their clothing.

"For goodness sakes, we've been calling all over town! You scared us half to death!"

"We were scared, too!" Cissie wailed. "Henry fell in the river and I tried to save him and almost drowned myself and then we got lost in the woods until Momma came and found us!"

"Good heavens!"

Rachel came to the back gate. "Oh, you poor dears!"

Maude waited on the porch as Marie came up to the house. Remaining under the porch eaves, she asked her daughter-in-law, "Honey, are you all right?"

"I suppose so," replied Marie, exhausted by the hike through the woods from the river. Rainwater dripped from her hair and Idabelle's umbrella had been blown to tatters. She felt like a wreck, but relieved, too, unburdened by their rescue. "It was quite an ordeal. I'm just grateful we're home."

A strong gust out of the cottonwoods across the street blew rain into the yard. Rachel was staring at the black thunderclouds rolling still closer to town. Her hair curled about her face as she turned back to Maude. "I tell you, it'll be a tornado, Mother, believe me. We'll have to hide in the potato cellar."

Marie's heart went cold. "Tornado?"

"Nonsense!" Maude snorted. "There hasn't been a tornado through here in eighty years. You can ask Beatrice."

Hearing the children's voices in the road, Mildred Jessup raised the window on her bedroom and shouted for her daughter, "Lili, you come home this instant! Supper's on the table!"

Marie hurried over to the Jessup's gate. "She's not here, Mrs. Jessup. The children had an accident at the river and Cissie says Lili went to Shantytown for help."

The window curtains parted and Mildred Jessup leaned out, horror on her face. "What sort of accident?"

Wind swept across the road, fanning leaves into both yards. Speaking above the damp gust, Marie replied, "I'm sure Lili's just fine! Apparently, that old swayback fell into the river and got washed away!"

"Good Lord!" Rachel cried, coming over. "Are you sure?"

Maude walked to the end of the veranda. "Haven't I told you that river's no place for children? Ever since Jimmy McGuire drowned I've stayed away."

"Mother, that was forty years ago. You just can't swim, is all. That's why you don't go to the river."

Rain began to fall harder again as the wind rose in the cotton-woods. Cissie passed through Maude's gate and crossed the yard to the Jessup's where she went to explain Lili's absence to Mildred. Henry stood in the rain with his hands held palms up, allowing some of the mud to wash off.

Lightning flashed in the northeast from the belly of the black thunderheads. The sky seemed darker. Wind blew hard in the street. Shaking her head, Maude left the porch for indoors, letting the screen door slam shut behind her.

Rachel told Marie, "Don't listen to Mother. She wouldn't recognize a tornado if one flew up her skirt. Believe you me, it's coming."

Thunder rumbled across the prairie. Henry went to sit on the porchsteps and watch the rain-gray sky for lightning. Marie looked quickly back toward the horizon where the huge greenish clouds had drifted closer to earth. She felt a prickling up the back of her neck.

"CW flew next to a tornado in Oklahoma once," Rachel said, with an eye on the approaching stormclouds. "His air route took him so close he could see roof shingles from Guthrie spinning in the funnel cloud. He told me it nearly pulled the wings off his airplane when he was still half a mile away. Can you imagine that? Only a fool wouldn't take cover if he knew one was coming." She glanced back at the porch. "Why, I swear sometimes Mother's become dippy in her old age."

Monstrous black clouds filled the sky horizon, lit by electric flashes of lightning. Raindrops blew about on the wind. Next door, Mildred Jessup was yelling at her brother as Cissie hurried back across the yard toward the kitchen. The chickencoop was alive with squawking hens.

"I need to go change clothes," Marie announced. "I'm soaking wet. So are the children."

"Of course you should," Rachel agreed. "I have to let the horses out to pasture before the storm arrives. Just don't dawdle. I've been telling Mother for more than an hour now that we ought to wait in the potato cellar until the storm passes. For the children's sake, at the very least."

"I'll make the suggestion myself," said Marie, and walked off to the front gate, her knees shaking from fear and fatigue. The rain softened again, but wind crackled in the pecan trees down the street and the town looked dark.

Indoors, kerosene lamps provided the sole illumination. All the electric power in Bellemont had gone down an hour earlier and amber shadows from the glass table lamps lent a gloomy cast to the interior of the small house. Cissie was already in the bedroom undressing when Marie came in.

"Honey, where's your brother?"

Cissie shrugged and pulled off her socks.

Marie frowned. She had seen Henry go indoors while she was still speaking with Rachel. He knew she wanted him out of the rain. If Harry were here, her son would not be so difficult.

"May I take a bath, Momma?" Cissie asked, as she stripped off the last of her wet clothing. "I'm awfully cold."

Marie peeked out the window to the backyard where the china-berry tree shook wildly in the wind. Thousands of dirty leaves blew slantways and rain pelted the roof of the house. Out of the corner of her eye, she saw Henry disappear into the chickencoop.

"Can I, Momma?" Cissie stood beside the bed wrapped in a cotton towel. She rubbed her sockless feet on the rug. "I feel dirty as a monkey."

A light rain blew against the windowglass. Dressed in only a lavender tea gown and one of her husband's old brown fedoras, Mildred Jessup was out in the backyard now, dragging an old canvas tarpaulin out from under her house. Rachel came around to the front and entered by the veranda. The door slammed shut in the draft and Marie heard Rachel open the windows in the parlor.

"Not now," she said to her daughter. She felt fear grow once again in her stomach. "Just put on something dry until later. You can have a bath before you go to bed."

"Momma!"

"Don't argue with me!"

After quickly changing into a dry khaki dress of her own, Marie left the bedroom to go bring Henry indoors. In the kitchen, Maude busied herself peeling red potatoes for a pot of vegetable stew simmering on the stove. A draft fluttered in the open window curtains above the sink. As Marie hurried by, Maude remarked, "We'll eat in half an hour."

From the living room hallway, Rachel called out, "For Godsakes, Mother, this house may be flying over Arkansas by then! Would you please put out that stove and take your shawl! We need to go to the cellar right now!"

Lightning flashed across the ugly green sky. Moments later, a rolling thunderclap shook the Haviland china in Maude's oak sideboard. Rachel cursed at her mother as Marie went out the back door into the wind. Most of the sky was blackened with thunderclouds, miles of summer grass bent low by rain. From the kitchen porch, one might have thought the world was shrinking: fields and pinewoods, old framehouses along the street, drawn into the widening dark and eradicated. Mildred Jessup leaned at the fence between yards. The canvas she sought to cover Lili's rabbit hutch with was torn and useless. Worry over her daughter showed on Mildred's face. Her brother Fritz had come out of the house and stood at the top of the stairs, dressed in a fine gray Sunday suit. His hair was combed nicely and slicked back with oil. A grim expression crossed his lips, though his eyes were keen in the dim gray light as he coughed violently and spoke to Mildred in a husky voice beneath the wind. Rachel raised the bedroom window behind the chinaberry tree, and Marie rushed down from the kitchen porch into the muddy yard directly to the chickencoop where she had last seen Henry. His little voice issued from within. Opening the screen door, she found him by the cages, feeding and watering the screeching chickens. A violent gust of wind shook the small structure and chilled her skin.

After slinging grain into one of the cages, Henry looked up and saw his mother. "Grandma forgot to feed 'em, Momma. They were hungry."

"I know, dear." Marie realized her lips were trembling.

"They're scared, too!"

"We have to go back indoors, honey. It's too dangerous to stay out here. There's a bad storm coming."

"But I'm not done yet!"

Another loud crack of thunder rattled the plank walls of the old chickencoop, startling Henry so that he dropped the pail of grain onto the dirt floor. Looking outdoors, Marie saw streams of water blowing wildly across the yard. Mildred had left the fence to send her brother back up the steps of the Jessup's porch where he stood now with his arms raised under the driving rain. Inside the chickencoop, Henry was on his hands and knees in the dirt scooping the grain he had spilled back into the tin pail. The chickens squawked. Lightning lit the sky overhead. Marie ran to her son and grabbed his arm and heaved him to his feet. "We have to go, honey."

"Momma, no!"

"Yes!"

She pried his fingers off the bucket, flinging it back into the dirt. A huge wind gust nearly toppled the chickencoop. The old door fell off its hinges. Rain blew inside. Henry struggled to pick up the grain pail and finish his chores.

"LEMME GO, MOMMA! LEMME GO!"

Then Marie heard Rachel's voice above the wind, screaming her name from the house. She swept Henry up into her arms and peeked out and saw Maude and Rachel and Cissie descending the back stair-case, carrying bundles. The chinaberry tree twisted and shook, raking the side of the house. Across the yard, millions of leaves and bro-ken twigs littered the black sky. Debris from College Street flew past the house. Both Mildred and her brother were gone from the Jessup's yard and the torn canvas tarpaulin blown to heaven. Rachel grabbed Marie's wrist and shouted directly into her face. "FOLLOW ME!"

Carrying her bunny rabbit Lulu-Belle, Cissie hurried by with Maude a few feet away. Rachel took Henry by the hand and led him off from the chickencoop around to the back of the house by the water pump and out to where the potato cellar lay half-hidden in the scrub grass and weeds. Although Marie knew the pasture fence was close by, she couldn't see it. Dirt stung her eyes. Rachel hurried to the cellar and flung the doors open. Both Henry and Cissie were screaming like birds, "GRANDMA! GRANDMA!"

Maude had fallen into the weeds, her hands shielding the wind-blown dirt from her face.

"MAUDE!" Marie went to help her up while Rachel urged the children down into the cellar. A thunderous roar rose on the prairie and the wind blew so hard Marie was certain her clothes were about to be torn from her body. Maude collapsed again into the weeds.

"MOTHER!" Rachel rushed over. She shouted to Marie above the wind, "GO DOWN INTO THE CELLAR WITH THE CHILDREN! I'LL HELP MOTHER!"

Mildred Jessup and Fritz arrived like ghosts out of the windy dark, wrapped in tattered brown cotton blankets. Mildred's face was streaked with muddy tears, her hair blown wild by the storm. Fritz wore a faint smile that offered no indication of fear. Neither spoke as they hurried toward the cellar entrance and disappeared beneath the damp earth. Rachel had Maude back on her feet now and guided her toward the potato cellar. At the top of the stairs, Marie took Maude's hand. From somewhere below, she heard Cissie screaming for her to hurry. Nearly blinded by blowing grass and leaves, Marie led Maude down into the cellar, then went to her children as Rachel let the doors slam shut overhead, exiling them into darkness.

An odor of dirt-soaked potatoes and fermenting fruit and mildew pervaded the dank cellar eight feet underground. Rachel bolted the doors, then lit a smoky lamp. Rain dripped through the cellar doors, which banged relentlessly in the roaring wind. Dust soft as mist from the plank ceiling filled the damp air of the small dirt enclosure. Maude sneezed aloud. Mildred and her brother scuttled to the rear of the cellar. Cissie held hands with Henry, whispering comfort in his ear. Marie huddled beside her children as a noise like thousands of stampeding horses grew louder. Rachel lit a second lamp and placed it on the dirt floor at her feet. The bright flame flickered in a damp draft from above.

"It's a cyclone, Momma, isn't it?" Cissie blurted out. "Like the one that took Dorothy to Oz!"

"Shhh!"

"But it is, isn't it?"

"I don't know, honey." She had never seen a tornado. Auntie Florence had one pass right over top of her at Gorham in '25 and barely survived. It was all she ever spoke of any more.

The cellar doors rattled violently from the wind gusts. Mildred Jessup moaned aloud back in her dark dusty corner. Her brother had his gaze fixed upon Rachel's burning lamp. He muffled a bad cough. Maude watched the cellar doors.

Hugging her bunny, Cissie murmured, "Should we say a prayer, Momma?"

"Of course."

"Will you do it for us, Momma? I'm too scared."

"All right." Unremitting belief in petition was something Marie had never forsaken, having committed dozens of supplications from the Book of Common Prayer to memory for a variety of needs since girlhood. Linking hands with her frightened children, she recited, "O God, merciful and compassionate, who are ever ready to hear the prayers of those who put their trust in thee; Graciously hearken to us who call upon thee, and grant us thy help in this our need; through Jesus Christ our Lord. Amen."

"Amen," Cissie repeated.

Henry sneezed in the shadows.

The rattling of the cellar doors persisted as Rachel murmured something to Maude who quickly shushed her. Mildred Jessup sobbed quietly in her black corner, but her brother Fritz spoke out from the dark in a grim voice, saying, "Once in Ohio, I saw a vision of Christ in a rainstorm where a trestle had collapsed. The river that ran underneath was filled with bodies from a passenger train that went over in the dark. I was up on the bluffs with a couple of fellows waving lanterns where we saw coal still burning red-hot underwater and we thought the engine had sank, and those few that hadn't already drowned were begging us to climb down and rescue them, though there wasn't any good way off the bluffs with the trestle gone. That's when I saw Him standing on the far shore looking like His picture in the Bible except He was naked as a jaybird and held a candle that burned bright as day when the sky was raining pitchforks. I watched the Lord jump into that cold river and swim back and forth from the wreck to the shore until sixteen lucky people were saved from drowning and nobody else called for help and His work was done and He swam off downriver alone."

The cellar doors wrenched hard at the bolt and hinges and the sodden floor beneath Marie's feet began to tremble like the world was about to end. Fritz coughed in the dark.

From the shadows, Maude raised her voice: *"Then the Lord answered Job out of the whirlwind, and said, 'Who is this that darkeneth counsel by words without knowledge?'"*

Rachel said, "Mother, you promised."

"I did nothing of the sort."

Rachel grabbed the lamp and thrust it into her mother's face. "Do not start quoting the Bible in this cellar!"

Marie shouted at her, "Rachel, please!"

Clearing his throat, Fritz spoke above the wind. "Jesus swam in the cold river that night like an ordinary man. Not once did He walk upon the water like He done at Galilee. He saved sixteen people's lives. That was His miracle. I saw a vision of Christ naked on the shore and He wasn't at all wondrous to look at, only what He did that night in the river. He saved sixteen human lives by Himself and swam away without asking for recompense, and I was blessed to witness, which is God's own truth."

The ground trembled as if a burly steam locomotive were crossing the pasture just a few yards away while the roaring of the wind rose to a high keening that suddenly drew close upon the old potato cellar.

"MOMMA!" Cissie shrieked. "MOMMA!"

The bunny wriggled out of her arms.

Then the cellar doors flew apart with a loud bang and both of Rachel's lanterns went out and the cellar became black and Mildred Jessup screamed and the noise from the wind was so great Marie had to pinch Cissie's arm to gain her attention and force Henry down between them both as the potato cellar filled with dust and debris and

Marie fought to breathe and thought she could not and believed that she and her children were about to perish right there underground. A deafening roar thundered from outside, screech of metal and wood reluctantly dividing in violent ascension. One of the cellar doors disappeared, drawn up into the sky with the cold lantern from the bottom of the stairs. Marie covered her ears. Rachel screamed and screamed as Maude's newly knit shawl was lost to the voracious wind and Mildred Jessup was struck in the head by an empty Mason jar and knocked unconscious while her brother Fritz crawled on his knees to the bottom of the cellar stairs for a look into the heart of the storm and Marie shut her eyes to the whirling dust and pressed herself against her children and repeated her fearful prayer over and over and over again … until at last the earth quit trembling and rain fell once more into the open cellar and the whirlwind roared off across the pasture like a great locomotive hurtling farther and farther away.

Dust and leaves littered the cellar floor. Thunder rumbled in the distance. Marie felt her children squirm beneath her. Rain fell steadily on the cellar steps. Still terrified, Marie whispered a brief prayer of thankfulness for her life and that of her children and looked about the cellar and saw Rachel and Maude huddled over Mildred Jessup. Rachel held her neighbor's injured head while Maude wrapped the wound with a garment cloth torn from the bundle she had brought out of the house before the storm arrived. Fritz stood to one side watching, his face nearly black with filth from the cascading wind. Another thunderous rumble crossed the yard from somewhere in the distance. The rainfall lightened.

"Is it gone, Momma?" Cissie asking, speaking for the first time since the storm passed overhead.

"I think so." Her hands shook. "Thank goodness." It was plainly a miracle they hadn't been lifted right out of the cellar.

"I was scared, Momma. Really, really scared."

"Me, too." She stroked Henry's hair and peered into his tiny eyes, which seemed empty in the dusty darkness. "Are you all right, honey?"

Her son nodded.

Rachel re-lit the other kerosene lamp as Fritz went back up the cellar stairs to the pasture. Marie craned her neck for a look of her own. She could hear wind blowing across the damp grass. It carried a smell of rain and dirt. The sky was black with clouds. Cissie stood and helped Henry to his feet, then looked about for her bunny rabbit. She found Lulu-Belle huddling in a corner of the cellar and went to fetch her. Marie also rose, seeing to it that Maude did not stumble in the dark, guiding her to the cellar stairs, letting her safely locate the bottom step.

Fritz's voice drifted across the rainy wind from out in the pasture above. Maude proceeded up the stairs. Mildred Jessup moaned with pain as Rachel brought her upright. A light gust of wind sprayed rain deep into the cellar.

"Can we go out, too, Momma?" Cissie asked at the bottom of the steps as she cradled the rabbit. Henry hid behind her, still trembling slightly. The wind fluttered through Maude's dress where she stood at the top of the cellar stairs.

"I suppose so," Marie replied, glancing back at Rachel who was guiding Mildred toward the stairs. She was still too frightened to think clearly. What should they do now?

Maude walked away from the broken cellar doors and disappeared from sight.

"Is it safe?" Cissie asked, only halfway up from the bottom. Henry climbed past her to the next step, his timid focus drawn to the black raindrawn sky overhead. Somewhere up above, Maude uttered a cry.

"Go on, honey." Marie urged her daughter up the cellar stairs. "It'll be all right."

Behind her, Rachel brought Mildred Jessup to the bottom of the steps. The children hurried up out of the cellar into the dark rainy wind. They were already running off toward the back of the house when Marie stepped clear of the cellar. Damp wind blew in her face. She hardly paid notice to the soft rain persisting. Somewhere just past the rear corner of the house, Cissie shouted, "Momma! Momma! Come look!"

The damp pasture of grass and oak trees behind College Street was black under the stormclouds and windblown rain. Marie hurried after her daughter's voice and came around the back corner of the house where the children waited and saw the wreckage of the chickencoop and the horse stalls, heaps of shattered boards and wire and little else to recognize in the rainy gloom, and beyond that where Fritz stood quietly in the mud, only a section of wooden fence and part of the back staircase where Mildred Jessup's house had sat just a quarter of an hour ago. All the rest was gone.

The kitchen door to Maude's house swung shut with a bang. Back at the potato cellar, Mildred shouted across the damp wind for her brother. Marie watched Fritz. He did not turn to answer, nor did he move at all even as Henry slowly approached to stand by the last pickets of the broken fence.

Cissie came over to Marie, asking, "Momma, what happened to Lili's house? Where did it go?"

"I don't know, honey. I think the wind took it away."

Marie looked at Maude's house and saw that all the windows on the Jessup's side had been blown out by the storm and the rough siding damaged by flying debris. Along the foundation only the small chinaberry tree survived of all Maude's flowerbeds and rose hedges. The side gate was also gone and the laundry lines, and Rachel's fresh vegetable garden had been ripped apart. Darting suddenly away from her mother, Cissie rushed through the torn rose hedge toward the road.

"Honey!"

"I have to see about my circus, Momma!" Cissie called back, as she disappeared around toward the front of the house.

Mildred entered the yard with Rachel beside her carrying the burning kerosene lamp. Stepping past the remains of the chickencoop, she gasped aloud, "Oh my Lord!"

Rain tossed about on the soft wind as Fritz stared wordlessly into the thick pile of wreckage that was left of his sister's home. A deep cough rattled his body. Rachel muttered a phrase Marie could not hear. A violet streak of lightning flared across the black clouds to the east. Mildred Jessup fell down in the dirt and began wailing.

— 8 —

Quiet passed over the town when the strong winds died half an hour later. Rain fell intermittently. Voices of the frightened and injured echoed out of the sidestreets. Neighbors wandered about together dazed and curious as night blackened the town and heaven was obscured by drifting stormclouds.

After getting Henry changed at last into dry clothes, Marie swept broken glass from her bedroom into a pile by the door. With Cissie holding a lamp beside the window, she had managed to locate most of the shards of glass and wind debris scattered onto the beds and across the rugs. The frame itself was fractured and needed repairing by a carpenter. Until then, a simple drape of bedsheets and pins would have to do for privacy and comfort. Since she and the children were safe and well, Marie had no complaints. In the kitchen, Maude boiled more water for treatment of Mildred Jessup's head wound after cleaning up cups and plates and utensils exposed to the storm when the ferocious wind flung open the back door. Rachel ignited kerosene lamps in each room of the house, then kept Mildred company in the parlor after attempting unsuccessfully to telephone downtown for the doctor. Lili had still not returned home.

"I'll walk!" Mildred insisted, as Marie entered the shadowy room with Cissie. She struggled to rise from the sofa where she had been resting. "I'll find my daughter without them if I have to. What if she's been hurt?" Then another spell of vertigo struck, and she was compelled to lie back again.

"See?" Rachel observed, adjusting the bandage on Mildred's forehead. Blood had soaked through the cotton swath requiring its replacement twice already. "Honey, you can't go anywhere. Soon as I can, I'll go downtown myself and find out where she is. You just lie still and rest."

"My poor little girl."

"I'm sure Lili's just fine," said Rachel, dabbing off a streak of dried blood. "She's a very clever child. She'd know where to find shelter. I'm not worried in the least."

Mildred moaned.

A damp draft swept into the room as Cissie opened the front door and went out onto the dark veranda. She shouted for Henry, then reached back to close the door behind her. Marie found it peculiar that Cissie seemed so unconcerned about Lili's absence. Had they been fighting earlier? She pulled aside the curtains to look out the window beside the piano. There were men in denim overall suits walking up the road, carrying burning kerosene lanterns. An enormous broken tree limb blocked the motor route to town, but the pack of men ignored it and detoured toward the rainy woods. When they were gone under the cottonwoods, Marie saw little Henry wander out into the dark empty street behind them. She knew she would be frantic if he or Cissie hadn't come home after the tornado struck. What would she have done? She hadn't any idea except to run out looking for them.

"I never seen it storm like that before," Mildred remarked, as Rachel pressed a piece of ice wrapped in cotton cloth to the head wound. "Dear God, the wind took my house away and didn't leave nothing behind. What'll Howard say when he comes down from Tulsa?"

"Do you expect him soon?" Marie asked, moving to the piano seat. Mildred rarely mentioned Howard who seemed more rumor than husband. Then again, Harry was gone, too, so who was she to judge the state of Mildred's marriage?

Mildred shrugged. "Maybe next week. Of course I'll have to wire him now about the tornado. He'll have a fit. We never bought a dollar of insurance. Howard always called it a cheat thought up by Jews."

"Oh dear, what will you do?" Marie couldn't imagine being destitute. How would they survive? Thank goodness Harry had a head for business, no matter what the market.

"I haven't any idea," Mildred replied, sagging on the couch. "Howard owns all the money."

"Well, I think we're very fortunate to be alive," Rachel suggested, squeezing cold water from a damp cloth. "Why, just seven years ago, Austin suffered the same tornado twice within an hour and the newspapers said more than a dozen people were killed. Idabelle's cousin Ray lost his wife Margaret and his home and his filling station and his two Chevrolet automobiles, and had to return to San Antonio to live with his mother."

"Imagine that," said Maude, leaning in from the hallway. She picked up a dustpan and poured its contents into a tin ashcan.

"He was quite humiliated, Mother!" Rachel snapped back at her. "When Ray went back to San Antonio, he was forty-four years old. I don't believe he's ever remarried."

"To his mother's enduring shame, no doubt."

"I didn't say that."

Shaking her head as she picked up the ashcan, Maude sighed. "When your children are small, they step on your toes. When they grow up, they step on your heart."

"Mother, please!"

"Rachel, not now!" Marie spoke up, hoping for a little peace between them tonight. "We've had enough of that." When would their bickering ever end?

Maude went back into the lamplit kitchen. Marie heard the screen door open and soon felt a cool draft sweep into the house as a stiff breeze rattled the shutters outdoors. The sound gave her a shiver. Did tornadoes really return? She worried about that, too.

"Oh, where's my darling Lili?" Mildred cried, shifting to rise once again from the couch. Rachel held her down. "I have to go find her."

"I'll take Cissie and go downtown to look for her myself," Marie offered, stealing another peek through the window. "Rachel can stay here with you." She saw Henry sitting on the fallen tree limb, calling to Cissie across the road. She felt like going out now. For some reason, being in the house made her jittery.

"Oh, honey, would you really do that?" Mildred asked, brushing her hair back. "I'd be terribly grateful."

"Certainly." She smiled at Mildred and touched her hand. "I'd be happy to."

"If she's been hurt, I don't know that I could forgive myself."

"It wouldn't be your fault," Rachel said, dunking the washcloth in ice water again. "After all, we didn't invite that tornado here, did we? At CW's funeral, the priest from Evangeline reminded us that fortune and tragedy follow the same sun across God's blue sky, and that blessed by one likewise binds us to the other. Sometimes we want our lives so justright, we forget that we're not yet in heaven. He said misfortune only gilds the reward to come."

Mildred whimpered softly as Rachel mopped her brow.

Marie went outdoors.

Down the street she saw lanterns under the pecan trees by Weaver Street. The night air felt muggy in spite of the breeze. On the side of the house, she found her daughter's makeshift circus ripped to pieces under the fig tree, her tents and carousels and midway booths torn apart, all the miniature painted toy figures flung about in the grass, the tiny colorful flags gone. Once Cissie saw the damage, she swore to everyone in the household that her play circus would be rebuilt, more gloriously than ever. Both she and Henry were across the road now near the cottonwood thicket. Marie called to them and Cissie waved back. Marie went out through the front gate and called again and her children came running out of the damp shadows.

"Momma, the wind knocked that tree right over," Cissie told her. "We could see the roots where it used to grow."

"I seen a million worms," Henry added, scratching his ear. "Can I go get a jar to put 'em in?"

Marie shook her head. "I promised Mrs. Jessup we'd try to find Lili for her."

"I'll bet she went to Shantytown, Momma," said Cissie, waving in that general direction, still sounding curiously indifferent.

"Well, then, that's where we'll go."

"It's a long walk, Momma," Henry said, an eye on the fallen tree trunk. "What if the cyclone comes back?"

"I think it's gone away, honey. I'm sure we'll be fine."

Rain sprinkled on the road. There were voices echoing farther down the block, urgent shouts rising and falling with the warm breeze. She began to wonder what the tornado had done to the rest of Bellemont. Had more people been injured? With the wires blown down and the telephones out of order, there had been no word from Maude's club ladies. What about Idabelle and Lucius and Jimmy Delahaye? She was afraid for Jimmy and prayed he was well.

Marie told Cissie, "Go get your raincoat, honey, so we can walk downtown. Henry, I want you to stay here and look after your grandmother."

"I want to go, too," he whined, kicking at the mud by the gatepost.

"Auntie Rachel needs you to stay here, honey. Grandma's still scared from the storm and she'll feel better knowing you're nearby, all right?" Marie turned to Cissie, feeling a sudden chill on her face. "Bring our umbrellas, too, will you? I'm sure we'll see more rain."

While the children went indoors, Marie went down the sidewalk as far as the Jessup's front fence to study again the utter destruction wrought by the tornado. Most of the white pickets were missing and the corner post by Maude's house had been uprooted. Mildred Jessup's house was hardly more than a pile of wet broken lumber. Marie found it difficult to imagine this junk as the home it had been earlier that evening. Where were the pretty window shutters and drapes and flower boxes and porch balustrades and raingutters? Indeed, where had Mildred Jessup's interior furnishings and possessions gone? Her appliances and furniture and dinnerware and framed pictures and knitted quilts? Her clothes and jewelry and dearest mementos? And Lili's possessions? Had all that poor child owned in her young life been blown far away into the sky, too? In the breeze off the dark meadow, Marie noticed, too, a smell from what was left of the Jessup's house that was more than damp wood and earth. Drifting across the evening air was an unimaginable mixture of toilet powders, perfume, laundry soap, cooking spices, tobacco, furniture oils, dried flowers, liquor, cedar chests, kerosene and dust conspiring, perhaps, to inform strangers passing by that once this ugly pile of shattered planks had been a home of people.

Mildred's brother Fritz strolled out of the darkness behind the wreckage of his sister's house toward the sidewalk where Marie stood. His suit was rumpled, disturbed by the wind, his hair wet under the drizzling rain. He stopped back of the broken fence in the mud beside Rachel's ruined vegetable garden, urgency of fatigue in his eyes. With a cold voice, he asked Marie, "Do you believe God loves His children?"

He coughed harshly, and wiped rainwater from his brow.

Warily, she answered, "I believe it's faith that cures our doubts."

"My sister called me here to be healed," Fritz said, knotting his hands together as if in prayer. "I've been sick longer than I can remember. I haven't earned a wage in years. I was branded a coward in France and had no dispute with that judgment. My sins are legion and I offer no excuse. Millie would save me, but she believes the Lord extends grace only to those who are most willing to receive it."

"We learn that in church," Marie replied, feeling the drizzling rain on her shoulders. "Christ teaches that many are called, but few are chosen."

"The keys to the Kingdom," Fritz said, as a rasping cough shook his chest. His eyes watered and his posture faltered briefly.

Realizing how ill he was, Marie suggested he ought to go indoors. "Mildred's on the couch now in the front room with Rachel."

Fritz shook his head. "The Lord offers mercy in exchange for obedience, but it's the Lord's bargain, not ours, and His promise to keep, or not to keep, according to His will, which we can only know through faith. Is that evidence enough for supplication?"

"We trust in His goodness," Marie explained, as Cissie came out onto Maude's veranda, "because of Christ's sacrifice on Golgotha. We accept His plan for our lives with patience and gratitude, knowing in His care we'll enjoy life everlasting."

She watched her daughter open the umbrella as she descended the steps to the front walk. By the tattered rose hedge, Cissie called out, "Momma, let's hurry before it starts raining again!"

Backing away from the broken fence, Fritz told Marie, "From the bottom of that cellar where we hid from the whirlwind, I swear to you I saw the face of the Savior on those black clouds that stole Millie's house away. His message has been made manifest, and I believe the bitter storm of His righteousness has not yet passed."

— **9** —

All the streets and alleyways and plank sidewalks leading to downtown were strewn with house debris and leaves and splintered branches dispersed by the tornado. Mr. Gray's darkened gallery was filthy with refuse and Dora Bennett's summer roses were buried under fallen roof shingles. Echoing out of the alleyways at Elm and Jackson Streets were the mournful cries of those who had been unlucky enough to feel the wrath of the tornado. Marie and Cissie saw groups of people with shovels, pickaxes, crowbars and kerosene lanterns, neighbors gathered to sift through the wreckage of homes ripped apart and blown to pieces. At the site of what was once a tall roominghouse on Rector Street, they stood on a debris-covered sidewalk, watching firemen search through the wreckage for a man named Gundersen and his two daughters who hadn't been seen anywhere since the tornado passed over the block. Tenants and neighbors believed both had taken shelter in the basement, a cement pit upon which most of the old roominghouse lay now. A group of small boys Henry's age stood beside a white ambulance where two attendants and a doctor prepared a stretcher. A light rain had begun to fall again. Marie and Cissie huddled under the umbrella at the back of the crowd. Both homes immediately adjacent to the roominghouse were damaged, their owners commiserating with each other. Behind them, a pack of dogs ran in the muddy street, the first animals Marie had seen since the storm hit. She wondered if the horses Rachel had freed to pasture before the tornado were safe. Not a feather was left from Maude's chickencoop, nor had Marie seen Lili's little gray kitten since the terrible whirlwind.

Downtown Bellemont was littered with hundreds of fractured tree limbs and shards of carpentry and broken glass from the shattered houses carried off by the tornado. Crowds of adults from all across town gathered in the square to share anecdotes of the thunderstorm. Marie watched a police car and a firetruck from Henderson roll past uptown. She supposed news of the awful tornado had gotten out across the county by now. Hooker's drugstore was lit inside with candles as the pharmacy doled out supplies to aid the injured. More men gathered at the Standard Oil filling station and across the street in the parking lot of the Ford Agency. A faint breeze blew off the prairie from the south and rain fell intermittently. Nobody appeared to pay it much notice.

"May I go buy a peppermint stick, Momma?" Cissie asked, brushing the hair out of her eyes. The breeze fluttered under her raincoat. She seemed dazed somehow, indifferent to the disaster. Perhaps Marie had made a mistake bringing her downtown.

She told her pretty daughter, "Oh, I think they're much too busy to sell candy, dear. You mustn't bother them." Marie looked into Hooker's drugstore, packed with people almost to the door. Wasn't anybody worried about the tornado coming back?

"I won't be a bother, Momma. I'll wait my turn."

"I don't know, honey." She wanted to go to the restaurant and see if Jimmy Delahaye was there, if he was all right.

A flatbed Ford truck emerged from the alleyway next to the National Bank building, loaded with oilworkers carrying shovels. Its headlamps threw long shadows on the townsquare, illuminating more people in the darkened streets.

Cissie tugged on Marie's coat sleeve. "Momma? May I go? Maybe somebody's seen Lili come back from Shantytown. I could ask everybody who comes in while I'm waiting. Please, Momma?"

"All right, but don't go anywhere else. I have to go over to the restaurant for a few minutes. I'll be right back."

"I promise."

Cissie drew a nickel from the pocket of her raincoat and dashed through the crowd to Hooker's drugstore while Marie went on down the sidewalk. Indoors at Delahaye's, the restaurant was empty. Only a pair of kerosene lamps burned in the main room. Upstairs was dark, too, but Marie heard a water faucet running in the kitchen and Lucius Beauchamp singing "Goodnight Ladies" in the billiard room.

She called out, "Hello?"

Outside, a pair of police cars from Longview drove by slowly, loaded with uniformed officers. Cigarette smoke wafted from the open windows. A group at the sidewalk in front of the mercantile building next door waved in greeting. One of the officers stuck his head out, shouting at somebody familiar.

Marie walked down to the end of the bar and looked up the dark staircase to Delahaye's office and the billiard room. She tried calling out again, "Hello!"

All the lights were extinguished and the doors shut for the night. She wondered where Jimmy Delahaye had been when the tornado struck. The hallway door to the backyard was open, bringing a rainy draft into the building. Marie called out once more. "Hello there!"

She walked out the door onto the back porch and studied the muddy yard where Julius Reeves had been digging in the dirt. There was a slit trench and a large piece of canvas lying nearby crumpled up in the wet grass. Rain fell more steadily now and the breeze felt cool on her skin. Rubbing her neck, Marie heard loud voices somewhere beyond the back fence, men shouting to each other across the dark for help in tearing loose a section of collapsed roof from a wind-damaged shack behind the mercantile building. A woman's voice followed as a distant echo from farther away, plaintive, worried, then dispersed by a gust in the thick pecan trees behind Delahaye's lot. Marie also noticed a strong odor of smoke on the breeze, a house fire, perhaps, ignited during the whirlwind.

"Why, honey, I heard y'all were wiped out by the tornado!"

Idabelle stood in the doorframe behind Marie. The glowing kerosene lantern she held cast a grotesque shadow in the narrow hallway. She was smiling.

Startled at first, Marie accepted a warm embrace from Idabelle. "We survived. It was very frightening, though. How are you, dear? Are you all right?"

"Al Clooney's been running all over town tonight telling folks how Maude Hennesey's house blew away."

The breeze stiffened, fanning rain across the small porch. Marie drew close toward Idabelle who retreated into the dark hallway. She told Idabelle, "I imagine he saw Mildred Jessup's home. It appears the tornado passed right through it. She lost everything she owned. It was quite a shock."

"Were y'all hurt at all?"

Marie shook her head. "Mildred has a bump on the head and the children were scared to death, of course, but we're fine, thank goodness."

"Well, when I heard Al, I didn't know what to think. Ansel Elliot lost a leg when his porch fell on him and George Stevens' mother had a heart attack. Doc Edmunds tried to save her, but she died not an hour ago."

"Oh my goodness."

The wet breeze gusted, sending Marie further indoors. Feeling the jitters again, she listened briefly to those men shouting behind the mercantile building, then told Idabelle what had happened in the woods earlier in the evening and along the flooding river with herself and the children. She said, "Mildred's worried that Lili hasn't come home yet. The children think she might've gone to Shantytown, but that was before the storm."

"Nobody's been across the river yet," Idabelle told her. "Lucius says a sixty-foot cedar tree fell on the bridge at Tyler Road. The busline to Henderson is closed, too, on account of some cottonwoods that came down on Watson Street. The tornado took the roof right off Mowry's feedstore, but Lucius says it didn't touch a thing inside. I find that so strange."

Marie looked around. "Where's Jimmy?" She had a terrific urge to see that he was all right. She worried that something horrible might have happened and she'd never see him again.

Idabelle shrugged. "He come in about a half hour before the tornado with a pair of fellows from the mill. They went upstairs to his office and called somebody on the telephone. When they come back down again, I guess they went out through here 'cause Lucius said one of them left the door open and got water on the floor that he had to mop up after."

Somebody waving a flashlight walked past the back fence. Marie heard rain drizzling in the muddy yard.

Lucius Beauchamp's thick voice issued from the upper staircase. "There's no going to Shantytown tonight!"

The stairs creaked under his weight. Idabelle craned her neck to see up the steps. "Is that you, honeypie?"

Lucius remarked, "Coloreds got their own trouble without folks from over here sticking their noses in. I say, leave 'em be."

He came down the stairs with a stack of mail-order catalogues under one arm. His overalls and suspenders were damp and his workboots muddy. When he reached the bottom, Marie told him, "I'm trying to find Lili. She hasn't come home yet and Mildred's worried to death about her. Cissie believes she may have gone over to Shantytown." Marie explained again about her harrowing adventure with the children at the swollen river. It sounded worse in the telling.

Lucius remarked, "You ought to ask Julius if he seen her at all."

"Is he still here?"

Idabelle shook her head. "Jimmy told him to go along home early when it got too muddy to dig that hole out there."

"Jimmy had no cause to keep him as long as he did," Lucius said, putting the stack of catalogues on the floor. Marie smelled gin on his breath. "Poor fellow's got two little girls sick from the mumps and a boy with whooping cough. He ought to've been home with them tonight. If Jimmy'd kept him here another hour, he might've been on the bridge when that old cedar fell over. Louie says it about cracked the damn bridge in half and killed a colored fellow named Cooty who tried to run underneath it."

"How awful! Well, I don't know what I should do now," Marie remarked, feeling a slight chill from the drafty hall. "I'd feel terrible having to go back home without any news for Mildred."

A siren wailed somewhere across town, adding to the commotion outdoors. More shouts echoed from behind the mercantile building. A truck engine roared. Marie felt a breeze rise in the drizzling dark.

"Lucius, honey, maybe you ought to go with her," Idabelle suggested, "see if you can't get across somehow."

"I don't see how. Louie says it's all blocked up from that cedar."

Marie said, "Maybe we could call a message across to see if Lili's over there, perhaps find out if she's safe. I'm sure poor Mildred would be happy just knowing that, even if Lili couldn't return until the bridge opens again."

In the amber glow from Idabelle's lantern, Marie noticed how ruddy Lucius' face appeared this evening. His hair was damp and filthy, too, smelling of wet earth. He looked tired, or drunk. And he seemed disturbed, too. But then again, who wasn't tonight?

Idabelle said, "That poor little girl must be frightened out of her wits. Why, I'll bet she's just as worried about her momma as Mildred is about her, don't you think, honey?"

"Yes," Marie agreed, "I'm sure she's just as scared as the rest of us."

Lucius shook his head. "I tell you, there just ain't no way across tonight. Mark my words. Louie said some colored fellows already tried pulling that tree off the bridge with a handwinch and one of them fell in the river and would've drowned for fair if the others hadn't been there to save him."

"But we can ask if anyone's seen Lili, can't we?" asked Marie, trying to sound hopeful. "They'll tell us, don't you agree? I'm sure someone will."

Lucius shrugged. "Can't go out Tyler Road. Tornado went right through there, tore everything up between the depot and the cotton mill. We'd have to angle over to Clevis and Sattley, then go Weaver Street to Finley Road and take the old path along the bluff to the bridge that way. I ain't sure it's safe, but I s'pose we could try."

Idabelle smiled. "There, then! It's settled! You'll take Marie there yourself and help her find out if anyone's seen Lili."

Lucius frowned. "Well, I ain't staying out there all night. If there's a dispute with any of the coloreds, we're coming back."

"All right," Marie agreed. "That's fair enough. It's certainly better than doing nothing."

Lucius picked up the mail-order catalogues. "I'll be in front of Hawley's barber shop in five minutes." Then he walked past Marie and Idabelle and out into the rainy dark of the backyard.

After Lucius had gone, Marie followed Idabelle back to the dining room where they watched another ambulance roll by. She noticed people outdoors now she hadn't seen on the streets of Bellemont all summer, men and women, boys and girls, drinking soda pop and eating sandwiches and showing off odd souvenirs of tornado damage picked up all over town. Apparently the drizzling rain mattered not at all, nor the horrific destruction here and there. Perhaps those truly wounded like Mildred Jessup were hiding away somewhere in the dark attended to by friends or family, while those blessed to have escaped the tornado uninjured felt free to celebrate. Were it not for the electric power lines having been blown down by the wind, closing Bellemont's restaurants and cafés and meeting halls, Marie imagined downtown might resemble Mardi Gras. She wished she could telephone to Harry this evening and tell him everything that had happened and ask him to come down by train tomorrow. She also wanted to pack up the children and go home to Illinois, now more than ever.

"You be careful, honey," Idabelle advised. "This is not a night to be waltzing about."

"Do you believe there's danger still?" What a silly question! Were it not for Lili and Mildred, Marie would be under a warm blanket with her children this very moment.

Idabelle furrowed her brow. "Only a fool ignores clear signs of warning. Myself, I intend to go home and have a warm bath before bed."

Then she gave Marie a hug for luck and let her out the front door.

Marie found Cissie on the crowded sidewalk by the Bijou picture house whose unlit marquee advertised John Barrymore and Camilla Horn in *Eternal Love*. A rambunctious group of high school youths surrounded the closed box office, trading loud bawdy jokes and passing a silver hipflask back and forth, gaiety evident on their faces. The boys had oil-slicked hair and two of them by the theater door smoked cigarettes. All the girls wore short dresses and had their hair bobbed and their faces painted like those silly flappers Marie saw in Rachel's *Vogue* magazines. Both sexes exchanged boldly flirtatious gestures and teased each other with rude expressions. Stirring a peppermint stick in a bottle of Coca-Cola, Cissie seemed eager to hear everything being said around her. She was clearly too sophisticated now to be satisfied with dolls and penny candy. Shortly, there would be boys of her own in white shirtsleeves and fancy collars calling at twilight, honeysweet perfume on her pink vanity, secrets she'd no longer share with her dear old mother.

As Marie crossed the street, Cissie stood and brushed off her skirt. She slipped a paper straw into the bottle of Coca-Cola beside her peppermint stick and took a long sip while a damp breeze blew in her hair. Clouds drifted restlessly overhead and Marie imagined she heard thunder rumbling somewhere not so far off. More automobiles passed in the street. Cissie went back to the box office and spoke briefly to one of the boys standing there. Something she said made him laugh and he dug into one of his trouser pockets and came out with a coin, which he handed over to her. Then Cissie dodged away through the sidewalk crowd to greet Marie.

She cried, "Momma, look what I just won!"

A truck horn roared behind them both in the street, hurrying pedestrians from its path.

"My goodness! How did you do that?" Marie asked, brushing a wisp of hair off her daughter's face. They needed to find out about Lili and get back home.

"Those boys bet me I couldn't spell 'hippopotamus,' but I did, Momma, so they gave me a nickel to buy another peppermint stick!"

"Do you need another one?" asked Marie, nodding at Cissie's Coca-Cola bottle.

"Not tonight, but tomorrow I will. Aren't you proud of me for winning the bet? I told you, Momma, I'm the best speller in the world!"

"How could they ever have doubted you?"

"Oh, those boys didn't know me at all," Cissie explained, walking up the wet sidewalk with her mother. She sipped again from the Coca-Cola bottle. A damp gust rustled through the willow trees by the bandshell. "Do you suppose I'll have lots of parties when I'm older?"

"Of course," Marie replied, as she watched another Ford automobile filled with young men rattle past. "I'm sure you'll be the most popular of them all."

"Oh, I hope so."

A group of men in mud-soiled khaki work overalls and flat caps smoked cigars by the red striped pole of Hawley's barbershop. Lucius was not around so Marie looked about for him, searching the downtown crowds and up the sidewalk. Next to the barbershop was a dark narrow alleyway leading to Fifth Street where she heard more men's voices speaking in the drizzling shadow. Burning ash glowed from lit cigarettes. Debris from the tornado cluttered the passage. One of the men held a dim flashlight. A damp gust of wind swept through the alleyway stirring up a cloud of dust. Several men coughed after a round of cursing. Cissie gave a tug on Marie's arm. "Momma?"

"Yes, dear?"

Cissie directed her mother's attention across the street. "Look, it's Auntie Rachel."

Rachel was on the far sidewalk with her raincoat and umbrella, consternation on her brow. She was searching for somebody in the crowd. Marie thought she appeared frightened, too, or worried. Was Mildred injured more badly than imagined? Marie tried calling to Rachel across the street, but a delivery truck rumbled by and she couldn't see Rachel and when the truck had passed Rachel was already off at the far end of the square walking into the darkness toward Ritter's department store. Lucius still hadn't arrived at the barbershop. Perhaps Marie had misunderstood him. What should she do if he didn't show up? She was afraid to go look for Lili by herself.

"Momma?" Cissie tugged her sleeve. "Shouldn't we tell Auntie Rachel we're here?"

Somewhere far across town another siren shrieked. Marie took Cissie by the hand and led her down the sidewalk past Hooker's drugstore and Bennett's Shoes and the Clothing House and Commercial National Bank and the Lone Star Café. They hurried across the street to Delahaye's where Marie knocked at the door and called for Idabelle and knocked again. A crowd of men in derby hats and long coats stood in front of the Temple Theater at the end of the block talking to Bellemont's chief of police and a pair of officers from Longview. She watched Rachel speak briefly with one of the men there.

"Maybe Auntie Rachel's looking for us, Momma," Cissie said, trying to peek through Delahaye's plate-glass window. The dining room was pitch-black, all of Idabelle's kerosene lanterns extinguished.

Marie looked back up the sidewalk toward the barbershop for Lucius. He still wasn't there, so she said to Cissie, "Would you like to run and ask her if she needs us?"

"May I?"

"Please."

Marie waited in front of Delahaye's while her daughter hurried down the sidewalk to the Temple Theater. It was late now, but strangers and young people were still arriving, flushed with nervous merriment and curiosity. Looking up at the night sky, Marie actually saw stars peeking through rifts of black clouds. The wind had faded to a soft breeze. Maybe the worst of the storm had passed, after all.

At Strebel's Hardware next door to the Temple Theater, Cissie grabbed Rachel by the wrist, giving her a start. She squealed with delight and Rachel laughed aloud and pinched Cissie's ear, and Cissie pointed back up the sidewalk to Marie out in front of Delahaye's. Rachel gave a wave, inviting Marie to come join them, which she did.

"Mildred became absolutely hysterical," Rachel told Marie, once she'd squeezed by the pack of men at the theater entrance, "insisting y'all were lost and that Mother should call out the Texas Rangers to organize a search. I finally had to bring her a hot toddy with a pinch of sleeping powder."

"I'm sure she'll feel much happier when we find Lili," Marie replied, as a window opened on the second story of the hardware store above. "Lucius said he'll help us. We're waiting for him."

"Where is he? We can't wait out here all night."

"I don't know. He said he'd be right along."

A man called down to the chief of police, inquiring about tornado damage to the cotton mill. Marie heard phonograph music playing indoors. Told that no damage to the mill had been reported, the man thanked the police and closed his window again to the street.

"I suppose you've asked all over," Rachel inquired.

"Well, I've spoken with Lucius and Idabelle. It's very worrisome, though I'm sure she's safe."

"Shouldn't we go to Shantytown, Momma?" Cissie asked. "Maybe she's visiting with Eva and Caroline."

"Aren't you afraid to go back to the river?" Rachel asked, sounding somewhat surprised. "I thought y'all nearly drowned."

"Oh, we can't cross," Marie told her, too afraid to try, anyhow. The very thought of cold swirling water in the darkness was terrifying. "Lucius says a tree's fallen on the Tyler Road bridge and somebody was killed."

"Well, I have no burning desire to be mutilated," Rachel admitted. "If it's that dangerous, perhaps we shouldn't go at all."

"I thought perhaps we'd just shout across the bridge to ask if anybody's seen her."

"Now, that's a fine idea," Rachel agreed. "If Lili's there, we can have her stay put until morning. Mildred'll be happy just to know she's all right."

"Won't it be awfully dark?" Cissie asked, a damp breeze tossing a shock of hair across her eyes. "I don't want to get scared again."

"Oh, I guess we'll be safe," Rachel said, as a green Hudson sedan rattled by, exhaust rising like steam in the dark. "I told Mother I'd be back in an hour or so. I think we should go now. We don't need Lucius. I know the way, but we'll have to hurry."

"Are you sure?"

"Of course."

Rachel led them across town past the millinery and Caldwell's furniture store, Doyle's Cigars and the old Masonic Hall, then down a narrow alleyway beyond the old blacksmith shop and livery stables whose desolate structures still stank of soot and dung. Away from downtown now, the night air was quiet except for the damp breeze in the cottonwoods whose wet leaves were strewn everywhere they walked. Peeking through a slatted fence into the backyards of the shabby gray framehouses on Weaver Street, Marie saw amber kerosene lamps glowing behind drawn roller shades. Cissie kicked at clumps of muddy grass in her path. Rachel's attention jumped about as they walked to the far end of the empty alleyway where it intersected Panola Street near the pinewoods. Tobacco smoke from somewhere nearby drifted on the breeze. Cissie scampered ahead, diverting to a warren of hackberry bushes, squatting down for a peek. "Momma, I think I saw a rabbit!"

"Be careful, dear."

"I will."

The wild grass lining the road smelled sweet in the rain-dampened air. Marie heard birds rustling high in the cottonwoods nearby, no doubt disturbed by the ferocious storm. Rachel stopped to pluck a pale lily from an overgrown patch of wildflowers. Marie thought her behavior in those harrowing minutes before the tornado struck was quite heroic, the way she had gathered everyone together and insisted they all go down into the potato cellar, how she had lighted lanterns and guided Maude to a safe place and been so assured in her manner. Marie felt certain that grace had entered Rachel's heart in that late hour of turmoil and she had proven herself worthy and courageous. She told her that CW would've been very proud of her.

"He gave me a lily on the night he died," Rachel replied, with half a smile. "He knew I was angry with him, yet insisted I take it as a token of his constant affections. I threw it out my bedroom window the moment I heard his automobile drive off and thought nothing of it until the funeral when I saw his casket draped with garlands of the most beautiful Resurrection lilies."

"Oh dear." Marie felt like crying herself at the very thought. She couldn't imagine losing Harry like that, regardless of the sourness that had passed between them these last few years. What makes the heart grow so cold in trying times? Why can't love be more persistent?

Across the breezy dark, Rachel's soft voice trembled. "At the services, CW's mother assured me that love and sorrow are faithful sisters in the heart. She believes we persuade ourselves they are not because we choose to deny that true joy is a gift from God. She says that life is a fair bargain we honor by loving another."

Marie watched Cissie hunting about the wet hackberry bush for her phantom rabbit. Children, she thought, must have a miraculous capacity to quiet the most appalling circumstances in their desire for normalcy. She told Rachel, "My dear old Granny Chamberlain always maintained that grief is itself another medicine."

"Oh, I'm sure that's the truth," Rachel said, raising the wild lily to her lips. "But I still hate it like poison."

Cissie had risen from the hackberry bush, resigned to failure in her brief rabbit hunt. She marched forward down the mud-soaked lane. The damp breeze fluttered through a dense grove of sycamore trees and Marie felt rain sprinkling on her cold skin once again.

Shame-faced in her gloom, Rachel asked, "Do you believe Mother would have ever tolerated CW as family?"

"Because he was Catholic?"

"Of course."

"Isn't a daughter's happiness worth more than opinions of faith?" Once when Marie was a girl, a retriever she owned had died of rabies. Asking her mother if they'd see him again in heaven, she was told very matter-of-factly that dogs most certainly do not go to heaven and that the very idea was silly. Grown up with children of her own, Marie realized what a terrible thing that was to say to a child, whether a Biblical truth or not.

Rachel shrugged. "Mother told me once that God despises ingratitude. For each penny we drop into the collection plate, one sin is forgiven. She says only pride keeps us wealthy Sunday mornings."

Marie remarked, "In Hosea, the Lord says He desires mercy and not sacrifice. If we deny love to one another, how can any of us hope to share His lasting reward, whether here on earth or in heaven to come?"

Perhaps fifty yards ahead, Cissie stopped by the bend of the road. There were at least half a dozen fresh automobile tire tracks in the mud sloshed through the intersection of Panola Street and Finley Road that led toward the river. Cissie darted back and forth across the narrow motor route like a wood sprite. Wet leaves fluttered to earth here and there. A dog barked loudly in the direction of town. The way to the river now was shrouded in darkness. Walking close to Rachel, Marie watched Cissie prance ahead, her little raincoat barely visible through the oily black drizzle. Back toward town, an automobile horn honked loudly twice, then went silent. A faint calling voice in the same direction echoed across the night. Soon, a pair of motor lamps lit the woods. A black Ford sedan drove out of the dark. Cissie stepped back off the road as it clattered past. Rachel and Marie ducked down into the grass as well when the Ford drew near to them. The driver sped by without slowing. Marie saw two men in the back seat huddled over somebody in a thick blanket between them.

"That was Doctor Wharton behind the wheel," Rachel said, watching the black Ford's taillights disappear into the drizzling gloom toward town.

Cissie shouted from the dark for Marie to come quick. Her voice sounded urgent. Farther down the road, another figure emerged from the rainy woods, a youth in tan overalls and a brown floppy hat. He was jogging through the mud, a wet grin on his face. When he came upon Marie, he slowed to a walk, caught his breath, and proudly announced, "We got us the nigger that killed Boy-Allen!"

"Pardon me?"

The boy reeked of corn liquor and sweat. Mud caked his overalls. Rainwater dripped off his grimy face. "Roy and Frankie catched him by the bridge trying to drown a little girl. They're gonna string him up!" The boy giggled with glee. "I just know'd a nigger done it!"

The boy whooped aloud and ran off up the rainy road toward town, yelling wildly into the night. When Cissie called out again, Marie left Rachel by the grass and went ahead down the road. Rachel shouted something nasty back at the grimy youth. Vaguely frightened now, Marie saw other figures in the dense woods, drifting like shades under the dripping cottonwoods and pine trees, and a glow of lights across the dark, flickering dimly through the drizzling rain.

"Momma!"

"I'm coming, honey."

Farther on, Marie saw automobiles parked on the edge of the road, still a quarter mile away from the bridge, while beside the trunk of a ragged pecan tree, Cissie watched small groups of faceless men in ordinary hats and garments soiled by the storm entering the black woods through the thick wet grass. Their voices echoed across the dark, ranting and indistinguishable. Several of them carried rifles or shotguns. Others led hound dogs on long leashes. When the breeze changed, Marie smelled burning firewood in the air. She looked back for Rachel and discovered to her surprise that Finley Road was empty in both directions. She stopped walking and called Rachel's name, but got no answer. She waited and listened, and heard only another automobile in the distance and a faint barking of hound dogs. Rain hissed in the woods. Marie shouted again for Rachel, but she was gone.

Quietly, Cissie crouched beside the pecan tree, one arm on the damp trunk, legs lost in the tall grass. As her mother approached from the road, Cissie asked, "Where's Auntie Rachel? Did she go home? Aren't we going to find Lili?"

"I don't know, honey. Maybe," Marie replied, worry growing in her heart. "I think we should get you to bed. It's awfully late. I'm sure we'll see Lili in the morning."

"Who are all those men, Momma?"

The burning kerosene lanterns carried by the men glowed like huge fireflies through the pines. Down the road, an automobile engine started up and its headlamps came on. Marie took Cissie by the hand and led her away from the pecan tree, a dozen yards deeper into the woods. As the automobile drove by slowly, Marie saw it was a police car. It didn't occur to her to call out for help, nor had she any urge to chase the automobile up the road. A peculiar disquietude infiltrated her heart that told her to take her daughter away that instant and forget she had seen men with lanterns and guns and dogs in the middle of the night. She felt herself shivering. A pale murmur of cool rain in the leaves increased. What did she intend to do? Wasn't it awfully late now? Why weren't they leaving? But she wondered, too, if the little girl the boy yelled about was Lili Jessup herself.

"Aren't we going home, Momma?"

"Yes, honey. Soon."

Another automobile came down Finley Road toward the river, this one rolling slowly, not more than ten miles an hour. The boy Marie and Rachel had encountered hung his head out the back window, shouting obscenities. The driver slapped the side of the car as he maneuvered down the road. Frightened, Marie took Cissie by the hand again and led her farther into the pine woods, parallel to the yellow lanterns, which seemed more luminous now, collecting together a hundred yards or so from the road, near enough for Marie to smell kerosene smoke on the damp air and to hear a man's hysterical protests above yelping hound dogs and the cruelest human imprecations.

Cissie broke free and ran.

Marie shouted for her daughter to stop, but Cissie rushed ahead anyhow through a soaked tangle of sycamore branches and disappeared into the lightless thicket. A man's scream echoed across the darkness of soggy earth and trees and the hounds began barking furiously. A shotgun boomed. Marie saw Cissie burst out of the wet underbrush a dozen yards ahead, not away from the lanterns, but toward them. Bewildered by her daughter's behavior, Marie tried to follow. She stumbled across a gutted log and past the dead trunk of a storm-beaten cottonwood, while her daughter snuck between thick clumps of trees and flickering kerosene shadows toward the shabby group of men whose hounds yelped and yelped at some frightened soul trapped and outnumbered in a damp pine grove ahead. As she drew near, the loud voices became uglier and she saw torches burning and smelled the woodsmoke and kerosene and expected D.C. Stephenson's hoods and robes, but saw instead only dark grimy faces whose particular features were hidden in shadow. In front of them, a shirtless Negro had been tied by wire to a tall pine. Another man was flogging him with a riding whip. When Marie angled past the rear of the grove farther to her left and fought through a wild hedge of hackberries, she saw that the man being beaten was Julius Reeves and that his tormentor was her handsome boss, Jimmy Delahaye.

This scene was so shocking, she thought at first it had to be a terrible mistake. Delahaye must have discovered Julius already bound to that tree and was trying to free him somehow. Nobody she had allowed to kiss her could be so reckless and cruel. Her head swam. She crept closer, just outside the flickering lantern glow, still seeking Cissie in the black underbrush. Fear made her sick to her stomach because she knew her daughter was somewhere nearby, witnessing something unfathomably hideous.

Thirty feet away now, Marie could hear Delahaye's voice above the drizzling rain as he spoke to Julius. Was this the darling fellow in whose office she had sat so many mornings, admiring the strength of his jaw, the man in whose parlor she had nearly made love? Could it be so? He was shouting now, "Do you hear me, boy? I will cut your nigger hide to shreds if you don't tell me how come you killed Boy-Allen and that little girl."

The black man mumbled something and Marie watched in horror as Jimmy Delahaye lashed him across the chest with the whip. Julius raised his head and spat back at him. Delahaye swore aloud and a burly fellow called J.G. Schofield who operated the Texaco filling station south of town stepped forward and punched Julius in the face. Blood and saliva sprayed from his lacerated nostrils. Delahaye fumbled in his coat pocket and drew out a handkerchief, wadded it up, and jammed it past the black man's teeth deep into his mouth.

Marie felt paralyzed with fear and horror. She could neither run nor quit watching. She was crying, too. Where was Cissie?

"Let's just string him up now, Jimmy," said a man named Hawkins who worked mornings at the feed store. He held a large thick coil of rope in his left hand. "We're getting wet out here and I got a hell of a mess in my yard to clean up."

"I want to know how come he done it," answered Delahaye. "That poor kid delivered my paper every morning and his momma deserves an answer." He curled his hand about the riding whip, drew it back, and lashed Julius again across his bare chest, drawing more blood. The Negro's cry was muffled by the handkerchief. Shouts of approval echoed from the large noisy group of men farther back in the pine grove. More faces became familiar, too, men Marie had passed on the sidewalks of downtown or met walking to church on Sundays, men with whom Rachel worked and Maude spoke to by telephone, whom Harry had likely known in school when he was young, whose children Cissie and Henry played with most afternoons when the sun was out: a handful of oilworkers, a pair of Dodge agency and Equitable Life Insurance salesmen, a carpenter, a plumber, a young clerk from Lowe's Department Store, a bus driver, a crowd of pig-farmers and several well-to-do businessmen who had greeted Marie all summer long with Christian civility and pleasant smiles. She was terrified and heartbroken altogether. What had come over Jimmy Delahaye? How could he be so mean? She looked into the woods for her sweet daughter. Good gracious, was she really seeing this?

"Do you hear me, boy?" Delahaye yelled in Julius' face. "I want to know how come you killed Boy-Allen and that little girl."

He kicked the black man hard in the groin with toe of his boot, drawing a stiff grunt. As Julius slumped in pain, Delahaye lashed his shoulders with the whip. "You hear me?"

The black man groaned.

"He ain't gonna tell us, Jimmy," Hawkins argued, wiping rainwater from his brow. The coil of rope in his left hand unraveled. "Come on now. I say we string the sonofabitch up and go home."

His opinion was echoed from the mob. "YOU HEARD HIM, JIMMY! STRING THE NIGGER UP!"

Marie felt herself go faint. What should she do?

Delahaye shouted back, "Not 'til he tells me why he did it!"

"It don't matter why," Hawkins persisted, "only that he done it and he's gonna hang."

A tall gaunt man named Carson who sold Bibles and vacuum cleaners farm to farm on the long empty roads of East Texas slipped out of the pack with a burning torch that reeked of kerosene. He approached Julius, staring him in the eye. Loud enough for every man there to hear, he announced: "THEN THE ANGEL TOOK THE CENSER AND FILLED IT WITH FIRE FROM THE ALTAR AND THREW IT ON THE EARTH."

He tossed the torch between the black man's feet. Somebody behind Hawkins laughed. Then a ghastly howl erupted from Julius's throat as his trousers ignited in flame.

"You sonofabitch!" Delahaye cried, shoving the traveling salesman backward, knocking him over into the mud. "Goddamnit!"

A dozen yards or so to Marie's right, Cissie burst from her hiding place in the rainsoaked bramble toward the pine tree, screaming, "Help him, Momma! Help him!"

Marie rushed forward into the drizzling light and ran to her daughter, grabbing her before she reached the mob, many of whom were cheering. She snatched Cissie up and held her tightly to her breast, while Delahaye kicked mud and wet pine needles onto the flames. Julius expelled the handkerchief from his mouth along with blood and mucus. He retched violently and vomited as Delahaye kicked more dirt onto the smoldering trousers.

When the fire was put out, Delahaye yelled into Julius' face. "You see that, boy? These fellows don't have much patience for donkey-ass niggers tonight! Now, you tell me why you did what you did and we'll get this over with."

The skin on both his legs burned away with his trousers below the knees, Julius moaned in agony.

Marie released Cissie and rushed to the tree and began clawing furiously at the wire that bound Julius's neck. He wouldn't die. She would set him free herself, everyone else be damned. A strong hand grabbed her arm and jerked her backward.

"Stop that, honey!" Delahaye held her by the wrist, his grip tight and painful.

"Let go of me!" She tried to twist loose, but he was strong as iron.

Cissie screamed, "MOMMA!"

Marie squirmed in Delahaye's grasp. She felt frantic now, crazy with fear and anger. She struck out at him, hitting him the chest and shoulder, clawing at his face. She kicked him in the shins."Let me go! Let me go!"

He freed her with a shove away from the tree, and she lost her balance and fell into the mud. Cissie ran to help her up, sobbing violently.

Jimmy Delahaye stared at Marie who held her sobbing daughter close in her arms in the crowded pine grove. Delahaye's face was filthy with sweat and mud, his blue serge suit soaked from the drizzling rain. Whatever had made her think he was grand and handsome? How could this be the man who had asked her to dance at the Pavilion on the Fourth of July, that wonderful fellow who had kissed her under the cottonwood tree and nearly made her swoon? This dreadful person?

He look Marie straight in the eye, and told her plainly, "Sweetheart, this ain't your concern. I suggest you take that little girl and get along home." His voice was ugly and cruel. She hardly recognized him as the sweet Jimmy Delahaye who flirted with her every morning in his upstairs office at the restaurant. Now she was ashamed she had ever taken that job, ashamed she had almost given herself to him. Where was Harry?

She fought back tears. "How could you do this? I don't understand. Who says he had anything to do with hurting Boy-Allen, or anyone else? You don't know, do you? No, you don't! None of you know!"

"Honey, there's no nigger in Texas that decided his own future more than this one here," Delahaye answered, wrapping the whip over his fist again. "When morning comes, won't nobody around here be grieving for this sonofabitch."

Julius' eyes were filmy and cold, his head hung low, blood dripping from his nose and mouth; a bitter odor wafted from his direction. Schofield spat tobacco juice into the mud. Hawkins stood near Delahaye, curling the rope in his hand. Two dozen men behind him watched in silence.

Cissie shook with sobs and Marie hugged her daughter tightly. Her heart contracted and she felt frightened half out of her wits, yet still, with her lips quivering, she spoke her mind out loud: "Mr. Delahaye, my husband told me there were men here in Bellemont whose cowardice proved that faith in God has nothing to do with sitting in a church pew on Sundays. We're taught since childhood that it is a sin to judge without mercy. If the least among us can't expect justice and decency from his fellow man, how dare any of us ask forgiveness of the Lord?"

Then she wept unashamed.

The hound dogs began barking and somebody shouted to Jimmy Delahaye from the back of the rainy pine grove where a group of noisy men were retreating from a disturbance in the surrounding woods. Looking up, Marie saw a Negro woman holding an infant emerge from a stand of dark cottonwoods fifty yards away. After a few moments, she was joined by another Negro woman and four elderly Negro men carrying lanterns across the cold evening rain.

Shaking his head, Hawkins said to Delahaye, "What did I tell you?"

J.G. Schofield drew a pistol from his coat.

Dozens more black faces came out of the darkness, old and young, male and female, dressed as if they had walked straight from the supper table to this muddy clearing in the woods. Each appeared soaking wet.

"What the hell?" Delahaye said, refusing to budge from his spot near the pine tree. In no time at all, the woods all about filled with Negroes, not one of whom had yet uttered a word. "Where'd they all come from?"

"Shantytown," said Hawkins, wrapping the rope up under his arm.

"No, sir." Schofield shook his head. "The bridge is out."

"By God," said the traveling salesman, "they forded the river."

"It's a goddamn flood tonight," spoke another man behind Hawkins. "What the hell'd they want to do that for?"

"Likely to set this nigger free," suggested the traveling salesman, "like Moses down in Egypt."

Delahaye frowned. "Well, this ain't Egypt and he ain't going nowhere. He killed Boy-Allen and that little girl and we're gonna hang him and that's all there is to it. To hell with the niggers. They can watch if they like." He shouted into the drizzle, "Y'ALL HEAR THAT? WE GOT US SOME BUSINESS WITH THIS FELLOW HERE THAT AIN'T GOT NOTHING TO DO WITH NONE OF YOU! IT'S AN EYE FOR AN EYE NOW, AND A TOOTH FOR A TOOTH, JUST LIKE YOUR BIBLE SAYS!"

Not one black voice offered protest. Instead, Marie saw nearly a hundred faces staring toward Delahaye from the woods, mostly expressionless and mute: Negro women in wet scarves and long cotton skirts, some rocking children in their arms, a crowd of Negro men and youths whose work overalls were smeared with mud, dozens of Negro girls huddling together, faces golden in the damp kerosene light. The cool drizzling rain dripped evenly from the pine trees. Cissie sobbed quietly at her mother's side.

A light hand touched Marie's shoulder. She turned to see Rachel standing behind her in the shadows. Marie blinked tears away. "Where did you go?" Her voice trembled. She felt lost and defeated.

"Shhh." Rachel put a finger to her lips and shook her head. Marie noticed that her umbrella was gone and her hair was soaked and that Rachel's dress was filthier than her own.

In the pine grove, Jimmy Delahaye spoke briefly to Hawkins who unraveled the rope. Schofield kept the revolver in plain view of the silent Negroes. The larger group of white men with lanterns shrank back away from the woods closer to the middle of the grove, muttering insults to older blacks nearby. Several hound dogs whined to be free of their leashes.

Delahaye approached Julius again. Raising his voice to an ugly tone, he said, "Boy, there's a world of difference between a man and a child, and I don't know why you did what you did to Boy-Allen, or why the hell you did it again to that little girl, but my daddy once told me there's a devil hiding in every nigger and if you don't watch 'em close they're always gonna sneak around getting themselves into trouble 'cause doing right by other folks ain't in a nigger's heart." Delahaye stepped closer to Julius, whose brown eyes flickered unconsciously. "Are you listening, boy? I know you're no hero like they say you are. A nigger with medals? Why, that just doesn't make sense to me."

The Negroes from Shantytown stood like ragged ghosts in the drizzling rain, watching quietly in soiled clothing, some weeping, some not. They seemed to Marie more numerous than the trees. Mystified, she whispered to Rachel, "Why aren't they doing anything?"

"There's nothing they can do."

"Then why did they come across the river?"

Rachel shook her head. "I'm not sure."

Marie had never seen so many colored people in her life. If they hadn't come to rescue Julius, what were they here for? How could they just stand there and do nothing?

Cissie murmured into her ear, something Marie would never forget, "It's true, Momma, what the Scarecrow says. Cruel people are always cowards."

A breeze came up, shaking the dark pine branches overhead. Water dripped off the brim of Schofield's hat. He waved the revolver at a group of sullen Negro youths off to his left. Somebody's dog began barking until his owner stifled him with a kick to the ribs.

"Tommy?" said Delahaye, still staring Julius in the eye.

Hawkins nodded and came forward with the rope and slung it over a thick sturdy branch ten or twelve feet above Julius' head. He pulled a length of it down and began knotting a hangman's noose. Marie hid Cissie in the wet folds of her raincoat, readying them both to depart if the worst should occur. Such venality was incomprehensible to her and she felt desperately nauseous. Blood dripped from Julius' nose. His eyes were shut now, his breathing hoarse and shallow.

Jimmy Delahaye leaned down over him. "We both know you did it, boy, and we know that God don't forgive niggers that sneak around murdering children, so you're gonna burn in hell tonight, you sonofabitch, and nobody's gonna care you're gone."

Julius groaned.

His sister-in-law Lucy Hudson appeared in the dark at the rear of the pine grove, her pretty face stony and cold. *Honey, they got the same Bible down here. They just read it different, is all.* Marie was horrified to see her. How did she expect to watch Julius die so dreadfully? Hawkins finished the noose and slipped it over Julius' head. Schofield walked up to Delahaye and murmured to him under the wind. A pack of men who had been standing with Hawkins came up, too. One of them took out a pair of cutters and snipped apart the wire that bound Julius to the trunk of the pine tree. Hawkins caught him as he slumped forward. The others helped prop him up. Schofield watched Hawkins tighten the noose. Horrified, Marie grabbed her daughter again when Jimmy Delahaye told the men, "Go ahead, string him up!"

As these men raised Julius to the taut rope, a woman's angry voice shouted from the woods. "DON'T YOU DARE!"

Marie looked behind her into the damp black thicket where she heard tramping in the wet leaves. She noticed Rachel smiling. Vague shadowy figures were approaching from the direction of town, speaking urgently among themselves. Within a few moments they came out of the woods single file, four women under raincoats and umbrellas, Maude Hennesey with her club ladies: Emily Haskins, Beatrice Stebbins and Trudy Crouch. Through the drizzling amber glow of the kerosene lanterns, Maude marched with the other ladies up to the crowd of men in the pine grove.

Jimmy Delahaye let the riding whip drop to his side. J.G. Schofield held his revolver at rest, while Hawkins and the men propping up Julius Reeves stood still beneath the dripping pine. None spoke.

Furious, Maude shouted at Delahaye, "My goodness, are you men deranged? Never in my life have I endured such a shock as when my daughter walked into the kitchen not twenty minutes ago to tell me what you fellows were intending to do to this poor man! Is it your desire to humiliate the entire community?"

Delahaye shot back, "He killed a little girl tonight! We got the right to do something about that!"

"Piffle! Why, I've just been assured by Lyman Wharton that Lili Jessup is not the least bit deceased! In fact, I believe she's with Mildred this very moment on her way to the hospital in Longview to have a cast put on her leg. Lyman says he expects her to do quite well, considering."

"Somebody's been telling fibs tonight," Trudy remarked, adjusting her umbrella.

"Rotten lies," said Beatrice.

Emily Haskins asked, "Just how did you intend explaining this to those of us too busy cleaning up after the tornado to come out here and pretend lynching is codified in the law?"

"This nigger killed Boy-Allen!" Hawkins shouted back, jerking the rope around Julius' neck. "And Roy Cooper seen him with that little girl by the bridge just after the twister, didn't you, Roy?"

A damp bulging man in a rainsoaked hat responded from the mob, "Yessir!"

"So if he ain't done it," Hawkins argued, "who did? And if he did do it, why, you're damned right he oughta be lynched! Why the hell not?"

"You ladies oughta go on home to your card games and peppermint drops," said Delahaye, "and let us finish up what we come out here to do."

Marie noticed the Negroes in the dark pinewoods hadn't moved an inch since the club ladies arrived, nor had any of them uttered a sound. Cold seeped into the rainy darkness.

Maude was livid as she spoke to Delahaye. "Since my late husband Jonas brought me here from Waxahachie forty-two years ago, I have refused to be ashamed of any Christian man or woman for the clumsy deceits practiced in this town." She stared at Julius bound painfully beside the damp pine tree, then glanced over at Marie. "I've tried to convince my daughter-in-law that we've inherited this profanity from a different time and that we have too much temper here to dismiss our own wretched inclinations. Too much temper?" She shook her head. "Well, I'm no less a hypocrite than anyone else in Bellemont for having believed that intolerance is no more sinful than drinking whiskey on Sundays. Even the arrangement of property encourages us to contemplate our superiority. Now only an eccentric crosses the river by design. Truth is, intolerance has stolen our good senses and desecrated our virtue, and not one of us has been immune. We've allowed our dignity to jump the track with small appreciation of the peril and now some of us have come out here in the rain to prove to our colored neighbors just how despicable this petty vindictiveness has become. Well, I will not stand here and see this disgrace continue. Turn him loose this instant."

"The hell I will!" Delahaye shouted. "No silly old widows club's gonna tell me I can't string this nigger up like he deserves! Tommy?"

Immediately, Hawkins pulled the rope at Julius' neck, jerking the black man to his full height.

Emily Haskins spoke in a level voice. "Mr. Delahaye, this silly old widow is entirely prepared to go home and tear up your lease on the building she owns if you choose to inflict further injury upon that poor man."

Delahaye frowned. "You can't do that."

"She mostly certainly can!" said Trudy. "Just as I can, and will, tear up your lease, Mr. Schofield, for the city lot which your silly little grocery store and filling station occupies."

"Turn him loose, Mr. Hawkins," Beatrice ordered, stepping forward, too. "Or by tomorrow morning, neither you nor your friends will have employment at the feed merchant, because there won't be a feed merchant on my property to employ you." She redirected her attention across the crowd to a group of men standing silently by with flashlights in hand. "Nor will you, Mr. DeCamp, have a bank to operate, nor you, Mr. Haines, an insurance office. Not in this town, not so long as I'm alive."

"You're all crazy," said Delahaye. "We'll get us a lawyer, Willy Lickliter from Austin who'll — "

"Do exactly as Judge Dakin tells him to do," Maude interrupted, "which will be to ignore the case and stay home. I tell you, times change slowly and we have always lived on intimate terms with our heritage, perhaps too often with pride than reluctance, but maladies of judgment have proven that no one here has been cut out for sanctification and neither is the Kingdom of Heaven built upon contradictions of race." She swept the men in the pine clearing with her fury. "Do you hear me? Our consciences are already sewn with violations of Christian duty, and we've sinned as if it were a natural process that would bring us closer to God. Fact is, we've rarely worried about consequences, and silence is a discipline we've practiced too well. Now it is finished. Mr. Delahaye, as sure as the day is long, we are prepared to evict every tenant and employee here tonight from our buildings and properties unless you turn this man loose right now. Is that clear? If he is not set free this instant, you may just as well go home tonight and pack your bags because come tomorrow morning there'll be no place for you in Bellemont."

"For the sake of truth and common decency," Emily Haskins added.

"And it don't matter to you ladies that this nigger murdered a child?" Delahaye added.

Holding her umbrella firmly overhead, Maude walked up close to the pine tree where Julius was held by rope and hand. She looked Jimmy Delahaye straight in the eye. "It was our very own Lucius Beauchamp who killed Boy-Allen and broke Lili Jessup's leg this evening trying to drown her in the river at Tyler Crossing. He confessed to his crimes in Rufus Palmer's office at the City Jail just half an hour ago, including a very terrible obscenity he inflicted upon poor Abel Kritt in the woods last July. He also admitted it was Julius here who drove him off during the storm and saved Lili's life."

"Lucius?"

"He's apparently a very troubled soul," said Maude, while a damp gusty breeze swept through the grove. "Perhaps you ought to pay him a visit."

Tossing the riding whip into the mud, Delahaye turned away from the club ladies. Hawkins let the rope go slack in his hands. Schofield hid the pistol in his coat. Delahaye walked off alone into the thick dark woods without uttering another word.

Soon enough, the kerosene lanterns went cold and most of those men Marie knew from the morning sidewalks of Bellemont slipped past the gathered Negroes and went quietly home. Rain hissed steadily in the pine grove. Standing with Rachel and Maude, Marie no longer felt the chill. Cissie pressed her small fingers tightly into her mother's hand within the folds of the damp raincoat as Lucy Hudson came unattended through the crowd of those who remained and freed her brother-in-law from the rope under the dripping pine tree and held him in her arms and washed the blood from his face and cried for a very long while.

Bellemont, Texas
September 14, 1929

Dear Auntie Eff,

It is an age since I've written to you. I've tried so often to find time, but could never do it. I hope you and all the rest of the family are well. I have felt very anxious not being able to hear from you for so long. I would use a portion of the day that I usually spend in your society remembering you and praying that we might soon again bake pies together in Mother's kitchen. The children and I are quite well and have seen more of the world than I ever expected. The more I see, the more I feel that "there is no place like home." Auntie dear, I love you and I do so long to see you. It seems strange that one who loves home as I do should be obliged to travel around as I am doing. Although I've had a fine time over here, it isn't like being home with you and Mother. I feel sort of like an outsider and I miss having someone I can depend upon. Do you ever feel that way? I will be so glad when we come back and get into a house of our own again. Harry believes that I ought to have another garden. This is surely going to be the longest week I've spent in a long time.

I got a letter from Florence Francis Haviland yesterday thanking me for the divinity fudge that I made for her. It was the nuttiest letter I ever got. Apparently she is quite gone on Minister Talmadge. Last week she bought some eggs for him when she was over town which she insisted on delivering herself. She brought along her big rooster named Teddy whom she admires very much and wanted to show off with her new Ford. When she left him unattended outside the pantry to visit with Minister Talmadge in his parlor, somehow Teddy flew up the laundry chute and onto Constance Talmadge's lap in the upstairs bath. Hearing his daughter's cry of surprise gave Minister Talmadge such a start, he spilled the fresh eggs onto his new carpet! Thank goodness I don't have to live with Florence or she would drive me crazy.

Oh dear Auntie Eff, Louie's letter has just come and it seems as if my heart would break. I have hoped all the time that my darling uncle would get well and that I should see him again in this world. Often I found myself saying, "The Lord bless thee and bring thee back in safety again." He was always such a dear compassionate uncle, and I love him so. He was such a comfort to me that tearful summer at St. Paul. I shall not forget it as long as I live. But if he is going where "They shall no more say I am sick" and where our dear ones are, oh kiss him for me, give him my dearest love. There is so much of my treasure there.

Now Auntie, I must tell you of one thing that has been running in my mind, the first thing that I thought of upon awaking. There is a man I know named Mr. Gray who has been here about eleven years and has a big corn biz in Albuquerque. His health gave out several years ago, and being paralyzed, he goes around in a wheeled chair. He lives in the third house from ours and I go down every so often when the sun shines and talk with him. He has been so much alone that he enjoys my visits very much. He reads newspapers instead of the Bible and declares that this old world of ours is losing its struggle with politics and sin. Once Mr. Gray was a carpenter who built houses for strangers. He had a fine reputation and earned a fair living. Then his wife was stolen by influenza and he took up drinking and one morning fell off a ladder and broke his neck. Because he couldn't work any longer to pay off his debts, the bank offered his home and property at auction to a family of Presbyterians and he took a room at a boardinghouse for invalids. On the floor above his own lived a Serbian Jewess whose husband had been killed fighting the Austrian cavalry. She had been crippled by an ice wagon after the War and her religious habits and poor speech left her to herself. Often Mr. Gray heard her singing alone in her room after dark, strange and beautiful melodies. One Sunday during evening services a fire broke out in the kitchen and the boardinghouse burned to the ground. As she was not a Christian woman, her name had not been included on the Sunday attendance roll and none bothered to recall that she sat by herself upstairs. Therefore, she perished in the fire. Nor did anyone come to mourn for her. There was no House of Israel in that town, nobody to speak for her faith. The Baptist minister who had attended to the boardinghouse performed a brief service over her casket bitter with pious lamentations that condemned as profane her chosen repudiation of Christ. She was buried in a potter's field with an unmarked plot. The next winter, a rising flood swept her earthly remains into the river, after which she was forgotten by all but those who recalled her lovely voice at night. Mr. Gray told me that our infirmities in this life proceed from the false witness we bear against each other and the burden of righteousness that shame provides. I did not dispute his opinion. Reverence for truth is no riddle to ponder. It is plain as the nose on our face. Intolerance binds us to the grave.

Auntie, I speak the truth of my heart when I say that while I look forward to the future, I do not look for a life of ease and pleasure as much as I look for a life of good works, little kindnesses done. I will try to live down the bad and bring up the good. If God's grace allows, we will enjoy ourselves to the limit and our sweet fortune will be His glory. Oh Auntie Eff, it is so nice to dream these dreams, when we know they will all be realized some day.

And now darling I can't wait until Sunday to see you, so I am going to fix this letter and send it to you. There are the children to be washed, dressed and combed. Cissie has written you a letter and I will send a few lines with it. I hope to start Henry to school with her at Brookfield next week. Auntie, I love you, my sympathies and prayers are with you all the time. I just want to reach out and give you a hugging. If I could only be with you all tonight, but God has not seen fit to make it possible.

God bless and keep you all in the hollow of His hand.

Your adoring niece,

Marie

— 10 —

The house in Bellemont had many windows and many rooms visited with mild breezes which once bore the scent of summer roses in bloom. Days of joy and sorrow. God's sunlight came and went in the wake of murmured prayers, and the simulacrum of grace collected in dusty mementos. Tears were wept, then forgotten. Tending to gravity's portion and silence ceased. Sparrows darted once more under the shadowed eaves. Meals were cooked and disposed of. Housework had no end. Society persisted. From all across town, ladies visited for tea and ginger cookies, while the radiant laughter of children in and out of doors lent humor and purpose to each tomorrow.

Marie stood by her bedstead in the mid-afternoon shade of the chinaberry tree, emptying clothes from the bottom drawer of the oak dresser into a small open suitcase in front of her on the mattress. Three larger tan suitcases and an old steamer trunk sat nearby on the wooden floor. The room felt hollow. She had written to Harry and told him with utter certainty that she and the children were returning home to Farrington. It was not his decision, but hers. Since he was still in the city, pursuing his own fortune (whatever he thought that might be), whether he approved or not, she didn't care. They were leaving Bellemont. Emeline had already prepared a room upstairs in her home downtown where Marie and the children could live until Harry put them back into a house of their own once again. No longer would Marie live under someone else's heel and order. She still loved her husband, but this summer past had led her to see how necessary it was that she find her own way in this world. How could anyone disagree? And if they did? Her face was already turned.

Peeking now and then through the curtain lace, she watched Cissie play cripple with Lili Jessup's crutches in the backyard as Henry ran with the collie toward the grassy oak pasture. Both had been cautioned not to go too far today. Rachel promised to join them at the train depot before departure at six. Until then she had an appointment downtown to have her hair curled and shingled for an old-fashioned fancy dress ball later that evening in Kilgore. "Of course, if I hate it," she told Marie at the door as she left, "I'll probably blow my brains out." Maude had been laboring the past hour with corn meal and a rolling pin and sugar sweets that smelled of cinnamon and vanilla. Now Marie heard her rummaging through the empty tonic bottles and jelly glasses and white stone-china jars atop the pantry cupboard shelves. Earlier in the morning, Maude had allowed Cissie to choose from a selection of old attic clothing to take back with her to Illinois: two black wool dresses, three basket skirts, a white chambray bonnet, a taffeta petticoat, and a pretty black basque with white collar and cuffs. Though all were much too big to wear now, Cissie had insisted that one day when she was married and lived in a fancy house she would need such wonderful clothing to receive her many visitors. Maude also gave her granddaughter a tiny bottle of Orange Flower perfume and a Spanish comb Jonas Hennesey had brought back from the Gulf of Mexico one summer long ago. From another corner of the attic, little Henry appropriated a brown necktie and one of his grandfather's buggy whips and a corncob pipe and a strip of old crowbait. He was sure it was Christmas come early. Marie packed her son's gifts together into the steamer trunk with a cigar box full of bird feathers and pine needles he had collected in the woods by the river.

"Beatrice had another dizzy spell this morning," Maude told Marie from the hallway, stuffing a cotton-filled comforter into the wall linen closet. "Trudy believes the poor dear is still suffering the effects of smoking Edgar's old medicated cigarettes."

While Marie carefully sorted out Cissie's clothes, Maude shut the hall closet and entered the bedroom carrying a laundry basket full of bleached hemstitched bed sheets and pillowcases. She remarked, "To each his own, I used to say, though I couldn't abide that terrible smell on Jonas, and told him so. He claimed that smoking warded off mosquitoes. That may well be, I told him, but we've none in-doors and if he didn't stop the habit, he'd find his next bride at the County Home." She put the linen on the bed. "When he was alive, Edgar Stebbins was more stubborn than a mule. Now Beatrice has adopted his vice to preserve the virtue of his memory. I find it quite mysterious how often age steals our loved ones and our good senses all together."

Glad to be finishing this final chore, Marie placed a pair of Cissie's chambray dresses and a corset waist into the last empty suit-case. She had taken the laundry off the line an hour ago. Packing occupied nearly two full days. Cissie and Henry took the surviving remnants of their circus over to Shantytown to give to little Eva and Caroline and a colored girl Cissie's age named Mae Hudson who cried when she spun the toy carousel. Though both children had thrown fits at having to leave Farrington last spring, now neither wanted to go back. Cissie cried for the better part of an hour in Lili Jessup's arms, her dearest friend forever, while Henry crawled into a corner of the bedroom closet and refused to come out until Rachel promised to mail him one of her roosters named Will Rogers.

Sitting up, Marie told Maude, "My mother's always supposed that our longing for loved ones is a premonition of sorts. If ever somebody in the Pendergast family goes on a trip or becomes ill, she brings fresh flowers to Grandma's marker in the cemetery and sings louder than the choir at Sunday services. Nor will she abide any discussion of recuperation or reunion until it's become fact. She's always insisted that only heaven heals a broken heart. Of course, Harry thinks we're all hopelessly maudlin in Farrington. Although I can't say he's entirely wrong, I do believe we are surprised by jubilance from time to time."

She watched Maude peek through the bedroom window, out past the chinaberry tree toward the cloudless blue horizon. A girl's voice echoed across the empty yard, Lili Jessup calling after her old collie. A tall carpenter named Klingelhofer had come from Henderson to rebuild the Jessup's house. He promised Lili she would sleep in her own bed by Thanksgiving.

Fetching a whiskbroom from the pantry, Maude turned the empty drawer upside down and swept the dust out of it. Then she said, "When Harry was still in knee breeches, Jonas had a plowhorse die of the heaves out in the hayfields and didn't know it until evening when the wind lent a bitter taste to supper. Jonas rode out with a hired man to load the carcass onto the wagon and he brought Harry along to teach him a lesson about mortality. Harry yelled and stamped and swore he wouldn't go, but Jonas refused to quarrel so he put Harry on the buckboard and drove him out there. Well, I didn't get half the dishes washed before I heard a clatter out on the back porch and came to find Harry shivering outside the door, dingy and soiled, his face white as milk and all tied up in knots. Jonas said that when they began loading the carcass onto the wagon, the hired man had a heart failure and dropped dead in his tracks which scared Harry so that he took off like a jackrabbit and ran all the way home in the dark by himself." Maude laughed. "The poor dear hid in here for two days. It was a hard pull just persuading him to come out to eat."

Marie smiled as she shuffled Cissie's dresses to a better fit within the suitcase. "He's never told me that story."

Did she really know her husband? To hear Harry tell it, he had never been afraid of anything, but she'd always known better. Fear guides our judgment and no one's heart is exempt.

Helping Marie fold some of Henry's trousers, Maude said, "Oh, my son is much too proud to admit suffering that fear. I used to tell him, 'Honey, there's a rare day with no threats in it.' When he was a boy, he didn't understand my meaning. Now I believe he does. We each share our humanity in the Lord and none of us are lacking in weakness."

Marie tried to imagine Harry huddled under his bedcovers, terrified by pictures of dark mortality. She wondered what portion of that fear still dwelled in his soul, if somehow it carried responsibility for his selling of the house on Cedar Street or the puzzling solitudes her husband had chosen lately to pursue, those tiresome and endless struggles between the two of them. Was he really to blame for all their misfortune? Could healing begin somehow with her? For a few moments, Marie quit folding clothes and sat on the bed next to the window frame where light through the pretty chinaberry tree diffused in ragged shadow. The afternoon felt quiet and restful.

Eventually, she said to Maude, "I love Harry for more than his virtues. If it were his nature to be only half as strong, I would still love him as much. My children adore their father, and so do I, because goodness and decency, I believe, have always resided in his heart. I don't deny that Harry's absence has been awfully painful for us, and there are certainly times I wish he wouldn't work another day if that meant he'd be home with us for supper each evening, but in all these years I've made no sacrifices unwillingly, and I would marry your son again tomorrow if only the morning train would wait." Was that the truth, after all? Would she really do this all again? Yes, perhaps so.

Maude smiled as she put three pairs of Henry's overalls and a gray cotton wash suit into the last suitcase. Outdoors, Lili Jessup shouted for the other children from a summer hammock that swayed in a light wind between two laundry poles. Marie repacked the children's clothing into the small suitcase, and fastened the latches shut. When next they were opened, she would be back in Illinois. How curious it was to travel so far and see so much and end up where she had started last spring.

Rising to her feet after replacing the bottom drawer into the oak chest, Maude said to Marie, "Well, dear, Jonas was no different. My husband had a good head for business and offered few alibis for his failures. His family predicted he'd end up a wastrel when he quit the farm, yet we wanted for little in hard times and considered ourselves better off than most. Some might hiss and growl and get the heartburn over high grocery bills and sugar ants in the coat closet. Not Jonas. He saw no use in reprimands whose purpose was to criticize and shame imperfection. On our wedding night I promised that if he carved an oak cradle for me, I would give him a son — a bargain we both kept. When Jonas built this house, Rachel rewarded our joy together. Now I've come to believe the Lord has blessed our days with obstacles to teach forbearance and humility. The morning my husband was laid to rest, I picked a basketful of bluebonnets in the meadow to bind into a wreath for his grave. *The sun also ariseth, and the sun goeth down, and hasteth to his place where he arose."*

With a deep sigh, Maude picked up her laundry basket. "You see, honey, I am reminded daily how this small truth is shared equally by the sinner and the saint. If I have regrets, it is that we gave more worry to poverty than dissolution. My dear, I slept in the same bed with that man for twenty-nine years. After he was gone I could not stand the dark, so I kept an oil lamp burning on the nightstand and another outside my door. Jonas would think me a superstitious old woman, but a widow has fears. I've never been any hand to cry or walk the floor, yet often enough I've trembled awake at night knowing I will never see my husband again in this life, never smell the odor of his clothing after he's worn it, never again hear him breathing beside me. I am alone now with my night dreams and my private thoughts and it is a trial."

Maude retreated to the door threshold where she stopped and looked back to Marie, her eyes softened at last. She said, "Sometimes the simplest life can own the most imponderable riddles, but, honey, I would tell you this: hold close to that which you find most dear to you. It is precious beyond all words."

— **11** —

Now the late summer meadows were windy, and tired old leaves blew across wild grass cropped by horses and cattle. Sunset was coming soon and the afternoon sky was white to the west. The faint odor of livery stables chased on a cool draft that gave Marie's skin gooseflesh. She was long past the fenceline on the footpath her children had run toward the oak cluttered horizon. By traintime, both would be exhausted and Henry would likely sleep clear through Missouri. With each lull in the gusts, Marie heard a tune tinkling on the piano from the house far behind her. Time was, when season upon season, she had learned the meaning of devotion through the trying solitudes of marriage. Now another summer had come and gone, and the mint bed she had planted before Easter provided for somebody else's tea and jelly. *It is human to seek togetherness,* her mother had once said of living on this earth, *but if a woman keeps her children bathed and her husband fed, little wrong can be thought of her.*

Marie watched her children frolic in the grassy meadow where a great blue sky surrounded the whole world. Soon they would be traveling home again and one day she would have another lovely sun garden whose golden zinnias and fine rutabaga would summon favorable notices from all about. Persistence, she would tell her children, reveals the lasting spirit of our convictions. As wind through the summer grass blows, so, too, must we keep our faith in love, true forever.

THE AUTHOR GRATEFULLY ACKNOWLEDGES THOSE WHO SHARED THIS FARAWAY SUMMER FROM THE LONG, LONG AGO.

MICHELE BACON, SANDY BACON, MARIANNE DOUGHERTY, WYLENE DUNBAR, KAREN FORD, IDA GARRETT, BONNIE HICKS, NICOLE KEENE, ERIN KIELTY-SCHULZ, SHELLY LOWENKOPF, KIM MEES, GARDNER MEIN, STU MILLER, ERIC REYNOLDS, PHILIP SPITZER, JANE ST. CLAIR, GEETS & STU VINCENT, BARBARA ZITWER.

AND, OF COURSE, GARY GROTH, WHO BELIEVED THIS WAS A STORY WORTH OFFERING.

LASTLY, NICOLE MARIE STARCZAK, FOR HER MANY SUMMERS STILL TO COME.